Mrs Shackleton

KT-405-066

CONTINENTAL DRIFTS

In *Continental Drifts* Nicholas Fraser takes an entirely fresh look at Europe as it approaches the end of the century. There are chapters on the French mind, the Eurocrats, the rebuilding of Berlin, the ruins of Bosnia, the invention of Ireland – and visits to Warsaw, Ypres, St Petersburg and Grantham. Part reportorial, part chronological, it is always informal and fully aware of the central role of irony in Europe's character. New frontiers, popular nationalism and a voyage through the Wild East – all are here in Nicholas Fraser's vibrantly entertaining journey.

NICHOLAS FRASER

Nicholas Fraser was born in London and educated at Oxford. He has worked for most major newspapers in London and New York, as well as being a prize-winning commissioning editor for Channel 4 and the BBC.

Nicholas Fraser
June 1998.

Nicholas Fraser

CONTINENTAL DRIFTS

Travels in the New Europe

VINTAGE

Published by Vintage 1998

2 4 6 8 10 9 7 5 3 1

Copyright © Nicholas Fraser, 1997

The right of Nicholas Fraser to be identified as the author of this work has been asserted by him in accordance with the Copyright, Designs and Patents Act, 1988

This book is sold subject to the condition that it shall not by way of trade or otherwise, be lent, resold, hired out, or otherwise circulated without the publisher's prior consent in any form of binding or cover other than that in which it is published and without a similar condition including this condition being imposed on the subsequent purchaser

First published in Great Britain by
Martin Secker & Warburg Limited in 1997

Vintage
Random House, 20 Vauxhall Bridge Road,
London SW1V 2SA

Random House Australia (Pty) Limited
20 Alfred Street, Milsons Point, Sydney
New South Wales 2061, Australia

Random House New Zealand Limited
18 Poland Road, Glenfield,
Auckland 10, New Zealand

Random House South Africa (Pty) Limited
Endulini, 5A Jubilee Road, Parktown 2193,
South Africa

Random House UK Limited Reg. No. 954009

A CIP catalogue record for this book
is available from the British Library

ISBN 0749 38610 X

Papers used by Random House UK Ltd are natural, recyclable products made from wood grown in sustainable forests. The manufacturing processes conform to the environmental regulations of the country of origin

Printed and bound in Great Britain by
Mackays of Chatham PLC, Chatham, Kent

For my mother,
for Joanne
and of course Isabelle

Contents

Acknowledgements

My special thanks go to Lewis Lapham, editor of *Harper's Magazine* in New York, who cajoled me into finding a way of conveying what I thought of contemporary Europe; and to Ann Gollin and Ben Metcalf.

A special debt is owed to my patient and tolerant employer, the BBC; and to Paul Hamann, Mark Thompson and Michael Jackson.

I have had many memorable conversations about Europe in odd places with Michael Jones, Jacques Rupnik and Norman Stone.

Many people bore with my ignorance and naïveté, and gave me illumination – too many to list. I received special help in Brussels from Kathleen de Béthune, Nigel Gardner, Elisabeth Guigou, Nora de Herdt and Phillip Whitehead; in Austria from Sebastian Cody, Udi Eichler, Elke Mühlleitner, Johannes Reichmayr and Stefan Schinkovits; in Italy and TV Land from Asa Briggs, Matteo Maggiore, Gaetano Stucchi, John Tusa and Marta Wöhrle; in France from Armelle, Celal, my uncle Etienne Dennis, my sister Anne de Fayet, Jean-Michel Gaillard, Jean Labib, Christopher and Pascale Mallaby, Claude Posternak and Antoine Rufenacht; in Britain from Roger Alton of the *Guardian*, Don and Hilary Boyd, Williams Cole, Jadzia Denselow, Sir Norman Foster, Rosie Gapper, Bobbie and Alex Glasbey, for their encouragement, Jo and Dee Lustig, Elisabeth Martin, Kate Roberts and my sister Elisabeth Rutherford; in Poland from Ella Kasprzycka, Antoni Libera, Antonia Lloyd Jones, Maria Polachowska and Tadeusz

Szyma; in Bosnia from Yasmina Alibegović, Janine di Giovanni, Vera Kordić, Sonja Pastuović, Ariane Quentier, Senad Saoić, Tony Smith; in Ireland from Darragh Byrne, Seamus Deane, Colin MacCabe, Muiris MacConghail, Kevin Pakenham, John Ranelagh and Rod Stoneman; in Germany from Cosima Dannoritzer, Christoph Jorg, Hagen Lamdsdorff, Daniel and Nina Libeskind, Bärbel Mauch, Ulrich Meier, Rosa von Praunheim and Jürgen Seidler; in St Petersburg from Jane Balfour, Teresa Cherfas, Lloyd Donaldson, Viv Groskop, Viktor Kossakovsky, Helena Reyszentul and Viola Stephan.

Gill Coleridge gave me much and needed inspiration. So did my editor Geoffrey Mulligan. My family stuck by me through absences and distraction, and gave me love. This book is dedicated to them.

Nicholas Fraser,
London, December 1996

In the Waiting Room

I sat in a huge waiting room,
and it was called Europe . . .

Erich Kästner (1926)

Building bridges in Stockholm, designing airports in Madrid, dreaming up a Millennium Tower in London as high as the Empire State Building while he flew his twin-engined jet from city to city throughout Europe, the British architect Sir Norman Foster embarked in April 1996 on what he described as his most ticklish assignment – the design and construction of a new German eagle for the Reichstag he had restored in Berlin in time for the end of the century. Methodically, he looked at the iconography of eagles in European tradition – how they were depicted hovering or in flight or (more rarely) sedentary. Then he plotted the heraldic expression of the eagle as it flew through history. There was a white, anaemic-looking Polish eagle, a black, double-headed Habsburg one, a Romanoff one, now largely confined to vodka bottles, and many representatives of the bald-headed American species, perched on crags or soaring over canyons when they weren't – the moment was brief, like the American Empire itself – immobilized in bronze or concrete. But the most interesting and problematic bird was the German one. It looked to the right and it was cast in a variety of durable metals. At its most extreme the bird expressed not heraldic nicety but the unadorned spirit of power itself. Many of the best eagles, as the British architect discovered, were expressions of the most poisonous aspects of Germanness – they were beautiful as well as terrifying, and they were associated with the death of nations. They were some of the worst things about the vanishing century. But the diligent architect also examined the tamer, post-war birds made for the Republic of which the capital was boring Bonn, and he discovered that he didn't like them – when they weren't shrunk to the dimensions of fish skeletons they were like large hens or turkeys, and they appeared to squat in the air like a dodo mysteriously given powers of levitation. 'No doubt the best social or aesthetic criteria had gone into their making,' he explained. 'But the result was, shall we say, unexciting.'

I first talked to Sir Norman when he was still struggling with the problem. 'I want a new eagle, a friendly eagle, a born-again eagle,' the architect said. It should be easy to create a bird that was neither imperialist nor triumphal and yet carried its own weight of unassuming dignity, but it wasn't. His first idea had been to remove the bird from above the speakers' dais, placing it instead at the spot where the deputies walked in and out of the chamber. But should the eagle be looking West or East? Where was the Republic going? He decided that the moment required an eagle that faced both ways, depending on the side from which you looked at it. This was fine in principle, except that early efforts were too like the Austrian emblem. Finally, he hit on the idea of making the image from a fine-meshed bronze – it looked like gold leaf, giving his bird a Cecil B. de Mille aspect – which meant that it could be very large, up to eight metres across, and the image would seem solid from each side without being overpowering.

Sir Norman presented his bird to a committee of German members of the Bundestag, who in their turn advised their party leaders – everyone who was anyone in Germany wanted to know how the eagle was going to be. This was, if not the largest, certainly the most delicate individual project he had undertaken. He drummed his fingers on the table as he described the bird. Neat and self-possessed, a master-builder whose projects displayed no glimmer of uncertainty, and whose aesthetics were founded on lack of ambiguity, Sir Norman appeared nonetheless to be perplexed. The image he created would, if it was accepted, decorate stationery, stamps, even parliamentary doorknobs. It would become the way in which not just eighty million Germans but the rest of the world thought of the new country – 'I've never undertaken a project like this,' he said. 'I really do respect Germans – but still, even after winning all the competitions, I can't quite be sure how it was that they selected a British architect for this task. I'm keeping my fingers crossed.'

Like Sir Norman, perhaps, I started this book in a bemused state of innocence, with the simple desire to know what was going on in Europe. Then I was mugged by a blunt object carrying the weight of history, and introduced to something altogether more complicated. I can date my own awareness of this condition. It was a raw early winter morning in Brussels, and I stood outside a newsagent watching two stout women in *chadors* exercising outsize hounds over scrubby grass. To my side were racks of garish magazines. '*Ça gode dur!*' and '*Troussez la gueuse!*' headlines in red type declared to their *bruxellois* readers, or else they asked: '*Les princesses ont-elles le droit à l'amour?*' Waiting to see someone, I walked up and down the block, crossing and re-crossing a display of varicose-vein stockings, anticellulite packs, and Zimmer frames. I opened my French highbrow purchases of the day. '*Un Monde sans Cap*' declared the lead story of the monthly *Le Monde Diplomatique*, and it went on to detail 'a crisis of comprehensibility' threatening to put an end to the universe created during the Enlightenment. I folded the paper, flipping open its sister daily publication at the fashion pages. There I was told that the current *prêt à porter* collections reflected 'the mood of disenchantment' of the times. With the exception of Japanese designers, who were presumably immune to the European *Zeitgeist*, I learnt that the fashion world had succumbed to the 'ambient spleen' of the *fin de siècle*, and that current ideas, such as they were, consisted either of a return to the 'safe' Audrey Hepburn neo-classicism of the pre-revolutionary 1960s, or T-shirts attached to fashionable causes.

Recent efforts to displace its hegemony notwithstanding, French culture, I suppose, is a beacon to the rest of us, so I wasn't surprised to read a few months later about the projected Olympic performance of their swimming team. This consisted of a four-minute ballet set to John Williams' music from Steven Spielberg's *Schindler's List*. Wearing black or grey suits, the swimmers were to goose-step to the edge of the pool and, once in the water, re-enact the process whereby those arriving by train at Auschwitz-Birkenau were separated into two groups and marched off the ramp, either to the gas chambers or to the labour camp. After due public pressure, the act was reluctantly cancelled, but I wished I had been present at the rehearsal when the precise choreographical movements were discussed. Who was going to play the SS and their dogs? Would the swimmers switch positions for each performance, from victim to executioner? The French coach pointed out that French skaters had depicted human-rights issues such as torture in their gyrations. The message of her underwater routine was clear – racism must be combated. Meanwhile she appeared to be annoyed that the team would now have to come up at short notice with another act, probably not as good as the first one.

I could sympathize with the harried, perfectionist coach but the episode seemed to reflect the spirit of the time – not wholly heedless nor indeed amnesiac, but nonetheless floundering conceptually. I wondered what would ultimately happen to Europe. What shape would it take, after so many years of division? Could it ever mature into the technocratic dream of federalism? And what would happen to the 'oldness' of Europe – the patchwork inheritance of hatreds or rivalries which had engendered the real European past of the nation-state – if some form of federalism, however loose, ever came to pass? These were the questions that political scientists or members of the European political class had asked themselves for decades, and now finally, it seemed, they were being put to the test. But it was also evident that no one really believed they would be resolved, at least not according to the precise terms in which they had been posed. As an escape from such uncertainty, or merely because timetables had been constructed, Europeans were rushing to complete their grand projects on time, as if the activity of packaging the old century itself ensured that an end could be put to its evil consequences when the old numbers finally ran out.

Moods are what historians professionally abhor, and what journalists, schooled in shorter time-spans and hungry for the isolated event, mistrust; but there are times like ours when they became significant. This is an exchange from a 1913 drinks party, taken from *The Man Without Qualities*, by the Austrian novelist Robert Musil:

> 'So there you are,' the General muttered in relief. 'The Minister wants to know what an "ethos" is.'
> 'Why an ethos?'
> 'I don't know. What's an ethos?'
> 'An eternal truth,' Ulrich defined, 'that is neither eternal nor true, but valid for a time to serve as a standard for people to go by. It's a philosophical and sociological term, and not often used.'
> 'Ah, that'll be it,' sighed the General.

Nervously at first, but with increasing confidence, I began to look for the ethos. I accumulated dissonant, anxious adjectives, or expressions of uncertainty. In time they began to pile up faster than I could save them. As I wrote this paragraph, for instance, on February 3, 1996, I heard that Chancellor Helmut Kohl, in the course of a speech at Louvain University (Catholic universities in Belgium are where serious pronouncements about Europe are made), had declared the nation-state dead, quoting his dead friend François Mitterrand: 'Nationalism – that is war.' As a view of the vanishing century this was certainly more profound than the views of the French swimming coach. But what, I wondered, would be put in its place? Well, something must come, declared the Chancellor, though from his speech it seemed he wasn't certain what.

Perhaps it would be possible to describe end-of-the-century Europe not through blow-by-blow accounts of bureaucratic trivia, but by means of an examination, half-systematic in character, dependent on the spirit of place, of how its inhabitants thought about themselves. My amassing of adjectives told me that, mercifully, the language of crisis had disappeared with the Cold War; but it had been succeeded by the low-level buzz of *Angst*. One could be contemplating the state of the British national beef herd, the desirability of having the model Claudia Schiffer introduce designs for the euro, the relentless falling of the Danish sperm count, or the non-performance of the EU's predominantly Irish-staffed Audit Office in Luxembourg – one way or another, doubt was bound to enter the equation.

Nothing could really happen in Europe which was entirely isolated from the complicated past. Churchmen and economic forecasters saw such negativity as a malaise, and yet I came to regard it instead as a syndrome – at times it seemed as if the entire old world of Europe, or what was left of it, was approaching its uncertain future like a snake eating its tail. But I also noticed that the impending twin anniversary – the end both of a century and of a millennium – had itself created a degree of conceptual confusion among Europeans. What was there to celebrate, after all? Were we looking at endings or beginnings? To pose such questions was to risk irritation, or indifference. In my own country, the heir to the throne talked about 'the danger of apocalyptic pessimism and despair' counselling instead 'a spirit of renewal', but his old-world urgency was muffled by the response of sour derision, churlishly directed towards his own lack of qualifications as a moral prophet evident in the serio-comic circumstances of his much-scrutinized private life.

I began to suspect that the Millennium itself was too large, and too remote from contemporary preoccupations, to be capable of attracting real interest. More than a hundred years ago, the French historian Jules Michelet described the first Millennium, with a Voltairean wink towards his frock-coated secular readership, as a time when 'what we tended to call life was really death, and the end of the world might be the beginning of life, and the end of death'. Painted horrors were the stuff of Grand Opera in nineteenth-century Europe, and Michelet made fun of the monks waiting in their solitary beds for the devil to 'pull back the bedclothes, and say gaily "You're damned" '. There had been millenarian movements in the past European century, culminating in the *grande peur* of the early 1980s in which hundreds of thousands of German and Scandinavian Greens marched around dolmen-like missile sites, warning their complacent co-citizens that they were doomed to destruction by means of thermonuclear war. But these emotions were not, in the strictest sense, biblically rooted – few Europeans read the Book of Revelations, fewer still regarded it in the light of literal truth; and by 1995 the spirit of secular indifference had triumphed over primitive awe.

The same could not be said about the effect of the imminent end of the century, which, given the special circumstances of the past eighty-odd years in Europe, was bound to create an atmosphere of perplexity. 'What if the *fin de siècle* becomes the *fin du monde*?' asks one of Oscar Wilde's characters. This had indeed happened – the end of the world was evident in the many, primarily European atrocities of what Isaiah Berlin had called 'the most terrible century in Western history'. Although so negative a summary of our vanishing century couldn't be argued with, I felt that Berlin, too, had been cheated by the plot. For the European world did not end in sackcloth and ashes. Instead, after a long period in which the toys were removed from the bad children who had broken them, Europe had been restored, late in the century and without much forewarning, to its old geographical dimensions if not its privileged place in the world. But there was a problem here – not much had happened since the cutting of the barbed wire, and this was not what the crowds wanted. In the middle of the last decade of the century, everyone was waiting for something else to happen.

Not as a refuge, which was how many British people now viewed the past, but to gain some point of comparison, I became interested in the old *fin de siècle*. What had people expected from the new century? Had they, too, experienced the sense of anti-climax?

On the first day of January, 1900, the newspapers of the Top Power, the British Empire, conceded that a note of caution was due in relation to yesterday's German naval manoeuvres, overseen by the Kaiser himself, and the growing power of German industry. But they were also able to look back over the past century with an unrecoverable tone of high imperial nostalgia. 'The twentieth century has dawned upon us, and as we float past this great landmark on the shores of time, feelings of awe and wonder naturally creep over us,' declared *The Times*. In the *Spectator* public impatience with the idea of retrospection was noted:

We fancy that, beside the numerical temptation, there is a latent eagerness in the public mind to be done with a division of time of which they have grown weary and to commence a new one which may have more in it of the fulfilment of hope. They are somewhat ungrateful; for the last hundred years, if not greater than any which preceded them, have certainly secured for mankind more of the elements of happiness. There is more freedom, more happiness, more practical altruism than has ever before been visible in the history of the world.

These were the confident accents of classical Anglo-Saxon liberalism; and yet for some – they were statistically small minorities interested in the avant-garde, in literature, music or painting, or merely in the more intense examination, through scientific methods, of their environment or their individual lives – the fulfilment of hope took second place to the exploration of new possibilities.

The end of the nineteenth century has acquired a reputation for 'decadence'; and yet this is how Musil, looking back from the vantage-point of bankrupt 1920s Vienna, could recall the hopeful arrival of the new century:

> No one knew what was in the making; nobody could have said whether it was to be a new art, a new humanity, a new morality, or perhaps a reshuffling of society . . . There were those who loved the overman and those who loved the underman; there were health cults and sun cults and the cults of consumptive maidens; there was enthusiasm for the hero worshippers and for the believer in the Common Man; people were devout and sceptical, robust and morbid; they dreamed of old tree-lined avenues in palace parks, autumnal gardens, glassy ponds, hashish, disease and demonism, but also of prairies, immense horizons, forges and rolling mills, naked wrestlers, slave uprisings, early man and the smashing of society.

One could encounter contemporary versions of Musil's new culture on hoardings or in telephone kiosks – it wasn't necessary to browse through the Internet. But these observations also told me that epochs, if not dates, could easily be moved around. Musil's *fin de siècle* began earlier than the century, and it lasted until the assassination of Archduke Ferdinand in Sarajevo on Sunday June 28, 1914, which rang down the curtain on the world he loved, replacing it with the second coming of barbarism. This date remained the only important one, the moment when the nineteenth century was replaced by our own.

As the end of our century approached I noticed sharp movements in historical stocks – away from such blue chips as Nazism and the Soviet-inspired catastrophe, and towards the period before 1914 exemplified by the strange collapse of the Habsburg Empire. In Brussels, Kracow, Lubljana, a sneaking Habsburgism was evident – it spelt for Europeans a reversion to the tradition of genteel dynastic goings-on, and the illusion that order among squabbling nations could be sustained by sober-suited technocrats. Among serious historians like Eric Hobsbawm, however, reconsideration of the European past took the form of a recognition that the century, which had begun in 1914, had also ended earlier, with the pulling down of the Wall in 1989. Hobsbawm's 'short century' was dominated by two threats to liberal capitalism: National Socialism and Marxism-Leninism. Although the defeat of both these movements had enshrined liberalism as the late-century religion, forming a neat symmetry with its beginning, it was also apparent that many of the horrors associated with tooth-and-claw capitalism had not been conjured out of existence. In the meantime another mutation of market-derived culture had occurred – the tendency to destroy its own past by sawing off the branches on which it sat. The effect of this would ultimately be the end of memory, and the perpetual dominance of the present in a world in which all the old maps and charts had become suddenly obsolete, leaving mankind afloat on a strange, blank sea of oblivion.

One commemoration succeeded another as the century came to a close with the regularity of waltz beats; but it was easy to find oneself removed from the flow of retrospection. On June 28, 1992, President Mitterrand, who was dying of cancer, visited the besieged city of Sarajevo. He posed on the pitted airport runway while someone threw a flak jacket over his shoulders. Then he went away again. For the evening news his visit was described, not in terms of relevance to the present of the fateful event he had, perhaps misguidedly, meant to mark, but as a sign of his own remarkable historical erudition – a quality assumed to be nowadays in short supply.

No one in Europe, it seemed, could any more truly grasp the magnitude of suffering implied by the twentieth century. Were four or six million people killed at Auschwitz, or did no one die there, as a small collection of neo-Nazi sects continued to affirm? Were 187 million people really either killed, or allowed to die by other humans, during the twentieth century? Was Hitler's bunker really located under a patch of sand adjacent to Potsdamer Platz? These were reckonings the significance of which could not be understood, least of all by Europeans; and the failure to find a way of understanding was reflected in the number of cancelled, uncompleted or otherwise botched memorials of the time. The newspapers were filled with anxious evocations of the threat posed to European tradition by the new economies of the Pacific, but I became certain that it was the weight of a half-acknowledged past, and not the prospect of endless competition, that elicited so many instances of 'ambient spleen' in Europe. At the least some form of recognition of the true shape of the past was needed before Europeans were able to direct their attention to the new worlds threatening to engulf them.

The worst fantasy of a reporter is not to be proved wrong in his predictions (which are usually worthless) but to be out of date. I thought about this problem from time to time, but I took consolation from the example of the English commentator Henry Wickham Steed. In 1913 he published a book in which he described, in the studied, leisurely manner of the day, the results of several years as *The Times* correspondent in Vienna spent untangling Balkan crises for the benefit of Edwardian readers. Steed mistrusted the Jewishness of Vienna, disliking the prevailing taste in modern architecture or psychoanalysis; and, like the good Anglo-Saxon he was, abhorred what he considered to be the lightness of Austrian morals. He was a fan of the Austrian monarchy, half-believing in its pretensions to represent a multi-ethnic Europe, and he hoped it would mature into a British-style constitutional monarchy. Steed retained his belief in the future despite the irritation of a lawsuit brought by a minor Austrian official, alleging an insult to the Emperor in his book. However, the second edition of *The Habsburg Empire* was acquired by the London Library in the month when war broke out – when it was wholly out of date.

Travelling, talking to people, or making my own way through the European labyrinth, I wondered what Steed felt in August 1914 when his Europe was destroyed by Austria's precipitate actions. As it happened, I knew a bit about him, having located a piece of forgotten news footage from the 1938 Munich crisis in which, small and dapper, wearing a bow tie and a surprisingly un-English suit, he assailed the British government of Neville Chamberlain for its craven attitude to Hitler. Only five seconds of anger remained – the rest was snipped away by the censors. But I learnt, too, that he was born in modest circumstances, that he was astonishingly gifted both as a linguist and as a cryptographer; and that, having attained his lifelong ambition of becoming editor of *The Times*, he was brave enough to resign when he was placed under pressure by a new proprietor with whose views he disagreed, leaving an empty chair at the daily editorial meeting for the first time in the paper's history.

I could easily forgive Steed his Edwardian optimism, just as I learnt to ignore the glumness of many of the Europeans I interviewed. Instant history is an illusion fostered by the understandable desire to know what is going on, but the sort of knowledge it represents can never be more than provisional. In the end neither prophecy nor dogmatism become the reporter; and I just had to hope that the *fin de siècle*, like the whiskered Emperor and his officials, stayed in place long enough for the group photograph. After that, as Sir Norman remarked about his eagle, it became a matter of keeping one's fingers crossed.

Adventures in Euroland

Europe is a vacuum-packed phantasmagoria.

Jean Baudrillard

Somewhere in Brussels towards the end of 1994, I lost my British passport. It was one of the last of the old batch: dark blue, the size of a small book, made of stiff half-waterproof card with a lion and unicorn in extravagantly embossed gold, covered with the usual reassuring stuff about Her Britannic Majesty, and adorned with a disorderly configuration of Masonic-sounding letters and numerals of which 007 himself would have been proud; and I realized how sad I was to see it go. Of course I wanted to be a European, I reflected, fumbling in the rain, these days we all do. Still, there was something not entirely appetizing about a new, back-pocket-size pink passport with a floppy cover. Without knowing quite why, not for the first time I felt let down by the idea of Europe.

I experienced the same emotion two days later when I went to hear King Carlos of Spain in the medieval cloth market of Bruges. Outside were parked rows of brand-new BMWs. Inside it was hot and stuffy, and there were flags representing every kind of European geographical entity: Palatinates, Grand Duchies, Länder, Provinces, Regions, Cities, not to mention the usual over-familiar collection of nation-states. Each side of me and for many rows behind were commissioners, *chefs de cabinet*, second secretaries, *rapporteurs, stagiaires*, wives, mistresses, chauffeurs, pastry-cooks, electronic recorders, or humble court scribes like myself. His Highness was tanned and elegant, even better in the flesh than in ¡*Hola*! magazine, very much the perfect democrat and playboy monarch. After praising the work of a pre-Inquisition Spanish theologian who was named European Personality of the Year for his efforts to convert Islam peacefully, he said that Europe must consist of 'values', and that it must seek its own heart, and he appealed to intellectuals to take part in the enterprise lest it flag suddenly (we were at present between Presidents, one Belgian candidate having been vetoed by the British). 'We require solidarity and cohesion in the construction of Europe,' he concluded firmly. 'This is a delicate moment. In Europe, widening and deepening are two verbs that need conjugating together. And our own European identity will surely be based on the way we treat others.'

Shutting our notebooks, we rose gratefully to our feet for the anthem: Schiller's 'Ode To Joy' from Beethoven's 9th Symphony. Afterwards, amid the enthusiastic applause, I wondered if I had missed something. Had I perhaps wandered off during the kingly peroration, reflecting on the significance of the elegant purple stripe in Juan Carlos' British double-breasted worsted, or scrutinizing Queen Sophie's High Catholic smile for signs of emotion? Alas, no, the King's speech was as empty as the Queen's smile, which was why he was being applauded.

There were swan-filled canals in Bruges amid the weath-ered-brick belfries, and many ultra-Catholic renderings of happy martyrdoms; but the town, which made its living from Eurojamborees such as the King's, was also more prosaically decorated with small blue plastic flags bearing tasteful clusters of yellow stars. I walked around in the rainy dusk, and sat drinking gin with a friend who works in Brussels. You could be what is known as a Euro-sceptic these days, which in Britain meant that you hated or despised the European Union; and yet neither of us was quite prepared to lay claim to that title. Perhaps, I suggested, we were just experiencing the worrying, but not fatal, condition of Eurodespondency. My friend dished out money to the struggling countries of the old Eastern bloc, and he was concerned with the inefficiency and platitude which he encountered each day as well as with the reluctance of Europeans to confront the perilous world which had opened up on their doorstep. As an outsider, I had different feelings, both more diffident and, in some respects, deeper. I had been coming to Brussels for some years, but as a supplicant rather than an enquiring reporter. I was shocked by my own views; like many Europeans, I had expected more from this late-century Utopia. I certainly hadn't thought that I would find myself sitting over my Flemish gin by the fireplace, giving voice to the lowest expectations.

The swans were inky-black in the canals by the time we walked back to the station. It occurred to me with a twinge of envy that by British, even American standards, Flemish Belgium, like most of Northern Europe, was astonishingly, even embarrassingly rich. I paused in front of a vast pile of gold-wrapped chocolates, lit by spotlights and surmounted by a fake-Gothic arch dotted with dinky blue and yellow insignia, Euro-teddies and blue-rinsed smurfs; and I contemplated tipsily the phenomenon of boredom. Why was the New Europe so horrendously boring, I asked my companion? What had gone wrong with our own heartland of civilization that it had come, finally, to chocolate poisoning, recycled Schiller and little blue flags?

Living as he did in Brussels, with the attendant climate of professional optimism, my colleague shrugged eloquently. 'It is boring, but only if you're inside,' he said. 'From the outside, it looks better. We're just the last bourgeois; we just have the old guilts about our own success. But you have to remember, too, that all Utopias are boring. No one ever said that Europe was going to be exciting.'

I thought about what he had said while walking from functionary to functionary in the following days. Many years in gestation, this now ageing New Europe had altered its identity slowly, going from six countries, then to nine, then twelve; by the following year it would be fifteen, and, somewhere beyond the Millennium, between twenty and twenty-five. At its birth, amid post-war rubble, the new Utopia was called the European Coal and Steel Community, and then, following the 1957 Treaty of Rome, it acquired the more grandiose name of the European Community. In 1993, in the wake of the 1992 Treaty of Maastricht, it became, finally, the European Union. However, the name changes reflected not so much altered functions as increased pretensions. Beneath the concrete skin, 'Europe', as I was beginning to understand, was still pretty much the same creature. Self-evidently imperfect the Union might be, but it still shone each day with clerkly busyness, recomposing itself as an ideal bureaucratic creation, as if the European élite had at some point been shipped *en masse* to a large, blank hangar whence, after listening to Schiller and consuming chocolate spiked with the untruth drug, they returned federalized, blessed with optimism. I wondered whether there was some place in each Brussels building to which one could repair each day for remedial indoctrination, reading a special edition of the early works of H. G. Wells and ingesting a large blue and yellow pill.

I had suppressed such views in the past, but after my encounter with the King I resolved to do so no longer. Getting around Brussels, I sensed a distillation of bad things previously encountered in other, half-forgotten lives. To be sure, I had seen grander and bigger bureaucracies, such as the American-Imperial one, or bigger and shoddier ones, in *ancien régime* Socialism, and yet something here – perhaps the utter absence of style – was quite distinctive. I emerged with the whiff of rubber in my nostrils from the Métro stop on Place Schuman, and walked around the five-sided, starfish-shaped Berlaymont building, built on stilts, scene of so many forgotten bureaucratic triumphs and setbacks, now being gutted of asbestos. Next I paused in the cold, on top of a low hill, on a roundabout. The cityscape of Brussels was dense and confused, pleasantly ugly in a familiar North European way; but here it had been catastrophically shuffled into order. I walked past rain-slicked caramel marble, dumped inelegantly on several levels of a slope, and the buildings in which the Council of Ministers and the various permanent committees representing the member states had their seats. At the bottom of the hill, crossing roads and car parks, I reached a set of buildings like expensive shopping malls, and a vast open site festooned with yellow cranes. Here stood the as yet unfinished Parliament, built to house the 518 MEPs (and their staffs) when they were not sitting in plenary session in a similar slab some 250 miles away. Again and again, walking between arcades of reflecting glass that wouldn't have been out of place in Ceaușescu's Bucharest, I concluded that among the worst-looking cities in Europe were those left unscarred by World War Two, and later modernized at great expense. Perhaps Europe, its conservationist reputation to the contrary, was as bad at adding to things as it had been successful at distributing rubble in every direction. First you made a hash of modernity; and then, at great cost, you tried to make amends, making things worse – I was sure that the EU had sponsored many well-attended colloquies on the subject of serial abuse in architecture.

I opened my notebook in each office, but found as a matter of course that I had shut it within five minutes. Apart from the odd, hopeless reprobate, kept on out of compassion, or to show the world that the odd patch of dissidence could be tolerated, these shirt-sleeved, slim and tanned officials looked much the same, speaking in the same tongue. They were high-tech plumbers, manipulating institutional organigrams as if these were prefabricated luxury bathrooms ready for the houses of the well-to-do. French academicians had long complained, perhaps with justice, of the horrors perpetrated on the French language; but I felt that it was time that they became aware of the tin ear Desperanto that passed for English in *bruxellois* circles. I began to accumulate a glossary of sorts. 'Home', or better still '*maison*', was the noun used in counterpoint to brutalist architecture in order to disguise the essentially disparate nature of Europe. The verb '*faire*' or '*construire*' occurred frequently (it dated from the 1930s League of Nations, I discovered; but French collaborationist intellectuals had used it, too, in the context of the wartime Franco-German effort). Also current was the more recent Pierre Cardin-sounding noun '*espace*' – as if the cluttered reality of Europe was an empty space in which new styles of thought or architecture could stand alone. In clubby, *Médoc*-swilling days, before there were quite so many languages and meetings, the word '*communautaire*' had been popular, meaning, in the equivalent English argot, 'a good egg', but I noticed that this had disappeared, and that there was ominously nothing ('federast' carried the wrong connotations) to take its place. The unappealing 1980s word 'cohesion' was used, referring to the current need (or obligation) to take awkward countries or people in tow, usually by paying them off; but it came gracelessly hitched to its ugly younger 1990s sister 'subsidiarity'. This appeared to describe the boundary between what the Union could legitimately do under the new Maastricht Treaty and what should instead be left to whatever remained by now of the old nation-states. Like all boundaries, however, particularly those in Brussels, the perceptual reach of 'subsidiarity' shifted continually, depending on the light or the time of day. But I also noted new and unwholesome 1990s coinages such as 'hard core' and 'variable geometry'. These were not highbrow items of pornography or optional degree courses at fashionably eclectic universities; instead they served to describe a situation, imminent in most officials' minds, where some countries would want to do things which others didn't want to do. Principal among these things, of course, was the Single Currency, which might or might not happen (for two years afterwards, while I was writing this book, its prospective existence was in doubt), but if it did would perhaps be beyond the reach or inclination of a majority of countries. When I asked a young, shiny-eyed official how it would be possible to run a parliamentary or administrative system under such circumstances, he put his head between his hands. 'I don't know,' he said, smiling. 'I really haven't a clue.'

Naïvely, perhaps because I wasn't, like many outsiders, wholly familiar with the traditions of the élite French bureaucratese in which all Euro-directives were formulated, or the Papal-encyclical style of sweeping statement, I had taken seriously the buzz or clatter of pronouncements that regularly issued forth from Brussels. I had thus failed to see what was already there, set unattractively in concrete, specifically the enormous gap between the high-sounding pronouncements and the mundane accomplishments forced through by the most traditional of political methods. There was at present no 'kind of a United States of Europe' – the phrase was Churchill's, from 1946 – nor, most probably, would there ever be one. Much of the power of the Union was still vested in nation-states, and they retained a veto over all important matters. Although many of these nation-states were currently in various states of deep disrepair, it occurred to me that they wouldn't conveniently disappear, leaving the field to the federalists – indeed it was possible that in their decline, or dotage, they would prove to be a greater brake on the progress of the Union than they had been when they were stronger, and therefore more in a position to understand 'Europe', or feel grateful for the advantages it conferred.

I steeped myself in the theory of 'Europe'. In 1951, the first declaration of the Coal and Steel Community bathetically described its purposes in this way:

> Resolved to bring instead of centuries-old rivalries a fusion of their essential interests, to create through the introduction of an economic community the first gatherings of a community larger and deeper between peoples . . . and to lay the foundations for institutions capable of directing a destiny henceforth to be shared . . . [they] have decided to create a European Community of coal and steel . . .

Privately, the French Foreign Minister Robert Schuman was more candid. 'We can't think of abolishing frontiers,' he wrote in his memoirs. 'In other times they disappeared as a consequence of violent conquest or fruitful dynastic marriages. These days, it will be enough to devalue their importance.' But Schuman and the over-iconized 'founding fathers' of Europe either didn't know exactly what they wanted – hardly to be considered a lapse in those rubble-strewn days – or, like Jean Monnet, Europe's first fixer, wanted it both ways. They engineered a so-called 'supra-national authority' – one that tended to preserve the identity of its members, all the while augmenting their own power – and, when the benign coerciveness implied by collective economic policy had taken effect, they hoped for a federal organization in which nation-states would ultimately cease to figure. Meanwhile (another disaster, though one for which they once again could not be blamed) they incarcerated their new creation within the conventional wisdom of their day, which demanded that power over such slippery things as money and markets should be lodged firmly at the centre, in the hands of kindly, impartial guardians. 'The pragmatic style which we had chosen,' wrote Monnet, 'would therefore lead to a federation with legitimate popular authority, but this federation would merely be the crown of an already existing economic and political reality.'

Exactly how Europeans would consent to do without their old homelands was left conveniently vague, as federalists more and more laid emphasis on the non-political, purely administrative aspects of their mission. Meanwhile, long before Mrs Thatcher and her handbag, opponents of the federal project began to make their voices heard. 'One cannot delegate sovereignty,' wrote the anthropologist and ex-*résistant* Jacques Soustelle as early as 1955. 'Nor responsibility.' Removing France from the Council of Ministers in 1965, thus creating the famous 'empty chair', de Gaulle raged at Brussels *aéropage* – the windbaggery of a technocratic Europe 'removed from nationhood and responsibility'. He did come back to the table, but so, enshrined first in French then in British policy, did his objections to Brussels; and the result, in the 1970s, was a long period disdainfully referred to by Community chroniclers as an era of drift, in which decisions were taken either in unanimity, or not at all. It was to avoid another such era that officials were busy with their plumbing diagrams.

I had struggled through these and other tomes recounting the glories of Brussels with a mounting sense of misgiving. One could look at such official accounts of Utopia in a positive light, like the Whig history I had learnt as a child, finding progress interspersed with occasional obstructiveness (the British played the part of lesser peoples now, Celts or Indians); but it was also possible to find in the real history of the EU a recurrent manic-depressive pattern. Of course there were spurts of bureaucratic activity in each decade, but they were succeeded by listlessness; rhetoric aside, which piled up remorselessly like the notorious lakes of officially sponsored excess, it was hard to say whether advances had been made. At present Brussels appeared to be poised between acceptance of stasis and another hectic bout of activity, and I experienced the strange phenomenon of bureaucrats worrying, as they would with a kindly and patient therapist, about their own power as well as their weakness.

They were shocked by the hostility which was now felt towards them, following the near-catastrophes of Maastricht, in which not just the Danes and the British, but also the French, had almost rejected the treaty. Democracy, or 'transparency', was now in vogue; and apologies were accordingly in order. Outsiders, I was told, had traditionally underestimated the enormous discretionary powers vested in the Brussels bureaucracy, and the ability of the bureaucracy to secure consent by depicting the new European institutions as somehow above or beyond politics. The Brussels reflex, confronted with a difficult bureaucratic conundrum, was to make more rules. Speaking off the record, officials lamented this state of affairs. However, they also thought that a wholly 'transparent' system – one where it was apparent just how much poor legislation was forced onto the system by governments eager not to take the blame for it – was unworkable. No representative of a nation-state would want its electorate to know what really went on in Brussels.

I had put away my notebook by now, and in these conversations I asked the bureaucrats to consider the collapse of the European film industry. For many years, Directorate 10 of the Commission, which was in charge of the portentously named 'audiovisual policy', had struggled with the question of why Europeans watch American movies. From the outside, it might look as if the triumph of Hollywood was a fact of global life, like the vanishing rain-forests or the fate of salamanders, but, no, this was too simple. Various think-tanks had been summoned, staffed expensively with audiovisual worthies. They had come up with complicated proposals for rejuvenating European movies by spending billions of *écus* creating new European product, or trans-frontier multilingual information super-highways to carry them – when they were not advocating quotas. However, most of these proposals threatened not just the Gatt agreements but also the freedom of individual governments to support their own film industries in the way they wished without EU interference. In consequence, nothing much had been done. Europeans continued to desert art-houses for the works of Steven Spielberg, abandoning cute Catalonian glove-puppets for *The Simpsons*.

Nodding, my interlocutors shrugged in reply. 'It's a vicious circle,' said the young English official who had lectured me about plumbing systems. 'Lack of power creates the need for gestures.' I could agree with this – except that in the past the EU's remoteness had proved beneficial to its interests. Strangely, the characterlessness of the Commission ensured that it remained immune to criticism at a time when, in almost every European country, politicians had fallen into disrepute. Officials were supposed to cast off their political loyalties when they came to Brussels, but they did not. Well paid, never specially corrupt – the odd suicide took place, but it was rare – they nonetheless generated corruption on a grand scale, in particular in relation to agricultural policy, or to the various 'coherence schemes' by means of which money from richer states like Germany, France or Britain was passed to poorer ones in return for favours performed. One scandal that came to light in 1994 concerned the passing-off of over $70 million of foreign imported beef as Irish, so that it could be exported to Iraq while becoming eligible for the various subsidies granted to farmers as compensation for overproduction. Non-existent and redundant crops or animals were by now woven into the rich tapestry of European protectionism; even the Queen of England, still the richest woman in Europe, received subsidies for planting or not planting various items of greenery. And yet, eccentric British nationalists apart, it had never really occurred to anyone to blame the Union itself for such profligacy.

Half-French myself, I came to recognize many dead or

decaying aspects of France unhealthily bedded into the foundations of the Union. There were few Anglo-Saxon-style 'counter-cultural' organizations in Brussels prepared to harass bureaucrats; and the press reported goings-on in the flat, less than critical style of court or institutional chronicles. The cumbersome if dignified procedural style was a creation of the French bureaucratic consciousness, as was the localized passion for standardization. Other than ennui, the most important product of Brussels was uniformity. Whether you were there to discuss permissible banana curvatures or the number of hours animals might be carried in a closed truck before they were slaughtered, the European day was the same. You arrived early, after a flight, entering an airless room with translation boxes. Many people were there – too many for real business – and the morning was therefore spent in procedural wrangling. By midday, the British and French were at war – *bien entendu* – but stomachs were rumbling. At lunch a delicacy was consumed – the white truffle, perhaps. But the afternoon mood was no better, and the assembly began to fragment, North against South, Protestant against Catholic and, by the end, everyone else against the Danes and the British. At six o'clock, however, when dusk was turning the windows grey-violet, the bureaucrats moved in to negotiate a resolution. No one was happy with the outcome, but everyone was free to cast blame and take comfort in the memory of the white truffle.

I had briefly worked as a reporter at the UN, and I found in Brussels the same strange distillation of goodwill and cynicism:

'It's immense, you understand. 1600 doors, each with four

layers of paint so that the white is immaculate. I know, I often came here while they were doing it up – and each door has its own identifying frame. And then there are 1900 radiators, 23,000 cubic metres of linoleum, 212 kilometres of electric wiring, 1500 taps, 57 hydrants, 150 fire extinguishers. That's something, isn't it? It's gigantic, gigantic. How many W.C.s do you think we have?'

'I don't know.'

'Guess.'

'Five.'

'Six hundred and sixty-eight.'

This was from Albert Cohen's *Belle de Seigneur*, a French novel set amid the futility of the League of Nations, but little had changed. Wanting to find democracy in Brussels, I turned my attention from the Commission to the nearby Parliament. In the lobby, sitting among a group of multilingual computer-paper salesmen from Ghent, I nervously fingered the 1992 Treaty of Maastricht. It was a tough read, as if a railway timetable had been painstakingly drafted by a fuddled *Nouveau Romancier* and then, at the last minute, someone had decided they weren't sure the trains had wheels, or could move at all. Apparently, the legislators meant to say in the preamble that a federal state was on its unstoppable way; but this was vetoed by the British, and we now had yet another pious Schillerism about 'ever-growing unity'. Elsewhere, Escher-style, the document expressed logical contradictions in the shape of a monstrous geometric puzzle, in which not four, or even ten sides had to look the same, but at least a hundred. After struggling through the leaden clauses of Chapter 4, innocuously entitled 'Transitional Provisions', turning to the Protocols excluding Denmark and Britain it became clear that the game finally proved too difficult for its participants. What the Treaty said is that one could join the Union by agreeing, at a specified date, to have the same currency; but if one didn't want to meet the deadline, or couldn't, that was all right, too. Banally yet comfortingly, it appeared that everyone could in the end do what they wanted. This, I felt, was the new Brussels wisdom.

I walked through marbled halls, beneath still more flags and statues of well-known Luxembourgeois Christian Democrats. In a passage adjoining the immense canteen, stocked with more than half-decent subsidized Bordeaux, I encountered a row of coloured metal artworks depicting the national characteristics of member states. The Germans, I noted, were praised for their 'receptivity to ideas', the British for their 'love of tradition'. Belgium, mysteriously, got a pat on the back for being 'in the forefront of information'.

Deprived of real influence, lacking even the opportunity to initiate legislation, Parliament resembled an outsize game of Cluedo where there were lots of libraries but no crimes, and in which the guests were handsomely cosseted by squads of pleasant-faced, sharp-elbowed young Jeeveses known as *stagiaires*. Aside from the usual *Medusa* raft of flat-earthers, careerists and absenteeists, the present roster included Nana Mouskouri, the 1960s Greek *chanteuse*; Prince Otto of Habsburg; Dany ('*le rouge*') Cohn-Bendit, begetter as a student of the 1968 Paris riots; the Rev. Ian Paisley, hater of the Pope and brass-lunged hell-fire preacher; Jack Lang, the dapper, Thierry Mugler-attired post-modern aesthete, who as Minister of Culture put I. M. Pei's pyramid in front of the Louvre; Bernard Tapie, the ex-football club owner and capitalist, who as a bankrupt and convicted felon was forced to resign his seat, beginning a

m star; and, perhaps most remarkably, Sir
mith, the exotic Anglo-French billionaire,
cal interests had shifted from purely ecological
o an implacable opposition to the European
sed on the restoration of the old nation-state.

Formerly, it was the dog-eared British Tories who gave a
grudging, negative style, born of post-imperial disgruntlement, to parliamentary opposition. No such inhibitions
affected Sir James, who as a newcomer to Euroland had
cheekily taken to parking his limousine in the wrong spaces,
and publishing the aggrieved letters he received from
bemused officials. Bumptiously beady-eyed, rich enough to
play the *frondeur*, Sir James had turned his sense of dis-
comfiture into a personal art form.

Europe des Patries, as the '*Groupe Goldsmith*' were formally called, were moving into the corridor allocated to
them, and there was a beginning-of-term smell of fresh
stationery. Sir James's deputy, a sandy-haired, bespectacled
young French judge who had been pushed aside after his
inconvenient investigations into the Mitterrand family's
wealth, was unpacking documents from cardboard boxes.
He complained about the latest revelations about overspends on the Parliament buildings – they included various
Belgian property companies, and a duff contract allowing
overspends which had been sanctioned and signed by the
EU. After some delay, I was able to speak to Sir James on his
mobile telephone. 'The Brussels Parliament is an extraordinary place,' he told me. 'It's infinitely worse than you
could imagine. You don't debate here, you exist to serve the
interests of an executive. When you do speak, you're
allowed only three minutes, and it turns out that the vote
has been rigged anyhow. The atmosphere is that of the
Third Estate just before the French Revolution got going,

except that technocrats have taken the place of the monarchy.'

I repeated what my friend had said in Bruges. Why, if things were so awful here, did people want to join? Perhaps, whatever he felt, Europeans were sick of their old nation-states, which seemed increasingly ill-attuned to reality. Mrs Thatcher had gambled her career on defending the nation-state, and she had failed.

'There is no alternative to nation-states in Europe,' he said testily. 'You can't just abolish them when there's nothing to put in their place. Do you think French people don't want to be French? Do you really imagine that Germany will wither away, just like that?'

Thanks to a junk-food empire, and a number of successful corporate raids in the 1980s American stock market, Sir James had more than enough money to take on the EU, but I wondered how he would fare in his role as an anti-politician – it would be difficult to sustain the posture of opposition to the existence of an organization while working in it.

'I won't be there long,' the billionaire boomed between bridges and tunnels, somewhere in Europe. 'You wait – I'm a hooligan. I'll destroy the place, then I'll be off.'

I was off faster than Sir James, but it was significant that back in London, despite periodic rantings to acquaintances and my patient family, I declined to join the camp of Euro-phobes. For one thing, it occurred to me that governments everywhere were discredited in ways that no one quite understood, and that there was nothing unique about the non-performance of the EU. But I did worry about its apparent functionlessness. Elsewhere the problem was that organizations did either too much or too little, both annoying citizens by their petty intrusiveness and, when the moment for action came in relation to what were perceived as the really great problems, failing to do anything. In Brussels, this wasn't the case – mainly because the EU did, if not exactly nothing, very little. At present it appeared to be the equivalent of what A. J. P. Taylor, writing in the Fifties about the British Establishment, called The Thing – a harmless congregation of overpaid people who met to discuss abstruse matters of precedent, and allocate minor jobs to themselves – with the qualification that in Brussels one ate better. But this essentially cynical position irritated me, too. I felt that the real Europe deserved better, and that, like the League of Nations, the place would anyhow be destroyed if it failed to measure up to the expectations of minimal reality. Without feeling that the matter was in any way within my control, I didn't really want to see this happen.

So I decided to return to Brussels, and almost exactly a year later, in late 1995, I sat in the hemicycle under bright lights with 650-odd other Europeans. We had been summoned, as the Belgian chairperson patronizingly told us, 'to remind people what democracy is like' and so that the Parliament could test – or appear to have tested – public opinion in its search for reforms prior to the next Intergovernmental Conference of 1997. The speeches were timed to last five minutes by means of a large electronic clock, and a buzzer rang if anyone spoke for any longer. Judged by the strictest Periclean democratic standards, the gathering was something of a fraud, since the organizations represented were overwhelmingly associated with the EU; but the speeches were nonetheless revealing. It was evident that, like myself, people both expected a lot and felt certain that they would be disappointed. Applause was loudest for the most critical speeches, whether they proposed the introduction of Esperanto, the extension of conscientious objection to military service, the speedy adoption of homosexual marriage, or (in one inspired instance, coming from a bearded French speaker who looked like a nineteenth-century anarchist) the abolition of Parliament itself.

A vast stuffiness came over us. I noticed how speakers, hesitating over their notes, took fear in the enormous space, losing confidence before they finished. Intended as a means of bridging the gulf between the European political class and its subjects, the gathering had merely dramatized its existence.

'That was terrible,' said a blonde, pamphlet-laden teacher from the Belgian Council of Francophone Women, after giving a particularly acerbic speech eloquently describing the inanities of the EU's books and pamphlets for children. 'I was terrified. Still, I was as hard as I meant to be. Do you think they will listen?'

I couldn't easily answer her question. It seemed to depend on who 'they' were, or how distracted they proved to be. So far as I could judge from this second visit, the life of an MEP consisted of a ceaseless, occasionally heroic struggle against non-meaning. Connected by ramps and walkways, flagged by the kind of misleading signs the Home Guard erected to confuse German paratroopers, the corridors stretched everywhere and nowhere. Early, after the Moroccan cleaners had left, the buildings began to fill up. There were grey schoolroom metal boxes (these were used to ferry material to Strasbourg and back) outside each room, and polite messengers came by with fresh piles of documents, labelled pink, grey, yellow or purple according to language. From time to time, the proceedings of committees would begin, and there was a rush to the lifts, where, amid pinging bells, bonhomous MEPs nodded at each other across the language frontier.

The committee rooms were decorated in yellow and red, with green chairs. There were nine booths for translators, each of them functioning at all times. Depending on who was chairing, or what item was being discussed, the proceedings ranged from the fascinating to the terminally dull; but the participants, I had discovered, were interested in procedural meaning rather than literal significance. I heard a French geologist describe the 'fracturation zones' in the Mururoa coral. This appeared to be a more authoritative condemnation of French nuclear testing than any I had read – however, the journalists around me were more interested in whether the Commission would or would not decide whether such evidence was relevant under the terms of the Euratom treaty, thus allowing them to censure the culprits. In the end, the Commission concluded that it was not; and France emerged unscathed. I witnessed the same procedural jockeying at a committee session at which (yet again) television quotas were discussed. Although there were the usual denunciations of predatory American behaviour ('It goes back to the Marshall Plan – they never wanted us to have our culture,' one French Communist speaker cried) the content of the speeches was wholly unimportant. People were not interested in re-discussing quotas. They wanted to know who would be the *rapporteur* of the parliamentary committee presenting the draft to the plenary session. If the draft was over-ruled, which was likely to happen, Parliament could invoke a new procedure of co-decision, thus forcing the Commission to establish a new committee attended jointly by governmental representatives and members of parliament. Within that entity, by some mysterious process (and it would take years rather than months, I was assured by a lobbyist), the question of the quotas might ultimately be resolved. On the other hand, the question would be dropped if Parliament, voting to refer the question to co-decision, failed to secure an absolute majority in its favour. This was indeed what happened a year later.

Only deranged romantics could these days believe in the purity of action, but, like the crowd in the hemicycle the previous day, I began to feel overwhelmed. To function properly, an organism required some sort of sphere or arena of action, or at the very least an equivalent of the small urban space required by domestic animals for their well-being. Denied such a space, parliamentarians became first cranky, then fractious. Symptoms of fractiousness took different forms; but I noticed that the sense of possibility diminished markedly the longer people stayed in Brussels.

My friend the British Socialist MEP Phillip Whitehead was new to the place. Energetic, holding his documents rolled up like a grizzled Punch, he went excitedly from committee to committee, trading jokes and gossip in the lifts. Between plane trips to Bucharest and Helsinki he believed it was possible to bring the interests of his Derby constituents to Brussels and, by doing so, repair the effects of more than a decade of British indifference to Europe. 'It is moving here,' he said, as we ate *couscous* in a deserted restaurant. 'There will be a different Europe, and this will ultimately be a functioning Parliament, I'm sure of this. The real question is whether we will be able to fulfil the demands placed on us.'

I sensed such geniality among newcomers of all ages in Brussels, and I was grateful for its existence. However, Euro-truculence appeared to set in around the sixth year. I met a handsome Danish Lutheran pastor, who had written newspaper columns and given sermons on television. She was elected to oppose the Maastricht Treaty, but she had become disillusioned. Over the canteen steak and *béarnaise*, Madame Ulla Sanbaek, wearing a brown and grey New Age tunic and white woollen leggings, with a silver Celtic cross, explained how difficult it was to be a dissident in the prevailing ethos of optimism. Her views were heterodox in the sense that she opposed the encroachments of the European State, but also found that much of its legislation, in matters of the environment above all, was not strict enough. She was opposed to mass immigration on the grounds that it would destroy the kind of small rural community in which she conducted marriages, funerals and baptisms. Europe should be protected; but Europeans should pay the rest of the world in return for not taking their goods. She also believed there should be a tax on polluters. For these reasons she sat and voted with the Goldsmith Group.

'I won't stay here,' she said. 'Someone else can take up the banner. You have to pit yourself ceaselessly against the people who believe it can work – and that means you are obliged to cast yourself in a negative light, which is ultimately damaging. There's a pseudo-religious aspect to life here; always, people are involved in illusions. I like real religion; and I prefer to walk in the woods getting mushrooms.'

I said that I had found scepticism everywhere I went, a feature of Brussels which might or might not be considered healthy. She looked at me without smiling. 'That's what they say – but they are a privileged class apart, like the *nomenklatura* of the old Communist countries. No one finds it easy to admit failure. Here the failure is on such a scale that it's far easier to go on. And you *can* go on – even if the actions are entirely meaningless. The world is full of lives without meaning.'

Chastened by these other-worldly remarks, seeking urbanity, I called that evening on Elisabeth Guigou, who had been President Mitterrand's Minister for Europe, and who was still a strong supporter of the Union, sitting on various committees considering possible reforms. The last article of hers I had read placed her as a half-federalist, and a redoubtable enemy of those (most of all the British, whom she was able to out-debate with conspicuous ease) who wished to wind down the New Europe; but she was also a defender of trades-union rights against the depredations of what – the word sounded better than the Anglo-Saxon globalization – she referred to as *mondialisation*. Mme Guigou was slight and good-looking, soft-voiced, dressed in a dark blue suit with large gold buttons, the coat of which was thrown idly over the back of a chair. The Brussels light was fading into various shades of bronze and violet, lending an apocalyptic quality to her near-monologue, which lasted the best part of an hour.

She said that fifty years ago, at the end of the war, the idea of Europe had seemed simple; but that politicians had now lost their way. They were obsessed with the 'how' questions, with polls, with this week's or next week's news. The words *idiot* or *crétin* – directed principally, though not exclusively, at French politicians – recurred frequently in her speech. Many of the earliest goals of Europe – collaboration in relation to economic matters, for instance – had been achieved; but she worried, ultimately, about the non-existence of European public opinion. No one cared about Europe, and its policies, such as they were, only served to give focus to those of the xenophobic right for whom the notion of a 'Europe' packed with technocrats had become a substitute for such 1930s hate figures as '*la juiverie*' – a phantom international capitalism destroying jobs and countries in the name of some remote authority. Without politics, it seemed to her, there was only death – and there were no European politics worth speaking of, only committees and technocrats, bits of paper and flags.

I suggested that 'Europe' – the post-war creation – had never expressed any real politics. Its purpose had been to stand above the national scene. In any case, it had been easier for Europeans, confronted by the power blocs of the Cold War, to retreat from politics. Germany, the most important European country, had been denied its identity for forty-five years. But the notion of a void was insupportable to her. She shrugged, brushing aside my objections by waving her hands, as if to say that behind the pouring of so much concrete and the laying down of all that tasteful carpet, somewhere there must have been a governing political idea.

'Right now we'd be better off saying: "It's pretty bad," ' she concluded. 'It's worse now than it was five years ago at the time of the Maastricht Treaty because the crisis isn't overt. And you'll see – we'll manage never again to have an overt crisis. Instead we'll have the appearance of success, carefully stage-managed. The officials will do what they've always done in the past, behind the dais on which the leaders stand. They'll congratulate themselves on having achieved a consensus in relation to the emptiest things. Nobody will really know, until, in ten years' time, it will be clear that there is nothing here at all.'

This sounded as if she had lost hope. 'Almost,' she said, with what in Britain would have been called a stiff upper lip, but came across as a not unattractive *moue*. 'In France, everyone has lost hope. Lack of hope is contagious – but I hope to resist the plague for some time yet.'

I walked back through the corridors from which weary parliamentarians, clutching briefcases and mounds of coloured paper, emerged briskly. I had been to Strasbourg, where there was a Soyuz-like hemicycle stuffed with antiquated Eurasian technology and echoing with quaint bleepings or squawkings; and yet the vacancy of Brussels was deeper and more threatening. Through offices, I could see the violet dusk, and I heard doors slamming. It would be possible to spend many years in this place without achieving anything special, neither speaking much nor taking part in the ornamental goings-on. In 'Europe', mustiness was synonymous with the acceptance of failure. Everybody clamoured for renewal without knowing how it could be achieved. Although notions like cyberspace or virtual reality had only recently come into vogue, the New Europe had from its beginnings consisted of what the French sociologist Jean Baudrillard called a 'vacuum-packed phantasmagoria':

> Europe will take place neither in anyone's head, nor in their dreams, nor in anyone's natural inspiration (at least if the desire to act is real) but rather in the sleep-walker's space in which politicians increasingly move, in dossiers, speeches, programmes, budgetary or fiscal projects – and in the artificially manufactured public opinion of universal suffrage cunningly manipulated by professionals ... As things are going, Europe is a computer model mocking us amidst the desert of our dreams of a genuine political community ...

In the end, I balked at this post-modern assessment, attractive as it seemed in its finality, and I craved for the confidence (I knew the idea was archaic as soon as it occurred to me) with which real nations were formed by means of words that meant something.

I also felt that so much pessimism, like the over-stuffed optimism of Brussels, wasn't wholly convincing. Much of the bad or artificial side of 'Europe' – its half-lies, the way in which it never amounted to anything coherent – was the consequence of the actions of Europeans themselves, determined to hold onto their old, separate identities; but it was also clear that the continent was being re-formed at a speed beyond anyone's expectations. Somewhere, surely, there were real Europes which had no need of the quote-marks implied by reflexive irony. Some of these Europes would be good, some bad – but none of them, I imagined, would be boring.

Meanwhile the uncertainty was bracing, even exhilarating. I left the Parliament building, heading up the hill past Volvo- and Mercedes-filled car parks to the asbestos-poisoned vacant emblem of the Berlaymont building. I resolved to look for Europe first in Brussels itself, and Belgium.

Brussels: Die, Belgium!

*Belgium is a country invented
by the British to annoy the French.*

Charles de Gaulle

Every day I was in Brussels, it rained some of the time. I
went by Métro one grey afternoon to Mini-Europe, a rendering of the Union in its current configuration to the scale
of a largish miniature golf course. Aside from one elderly
Japanese tourist, thoughtfully equipped with a waterproof
pork-pie hat, I had the exhibits to myself. The Acropolis
had been kicked, perhaps by irate football fans from the
nearby Heysel stadium – this was where supporters of Liv-
erpool F.C. had killed or maimed thirty-nine Italians in
1985, one of the worst episodes of European football – and
someone appeared to have sat on the Colosseum. Aside
from these incidental details, however, it was the odd scale
of things that caught my attention. Some sites – those representing countries which had joined earliest, like
Luxembourg, depicted by a model suspension bridge –
were, relatively speaking, large. Those allocated to late
joiners such as Finland, in which one could see bedraggled
groups of six-inch-high reindeer, were very small indeed.
No geographical criteria appeared to have governed the
assembly, which made the old nineteenth-century countries
of Europe seem as jumbled and formless as Belgium itself.

But the exhibit, if one chose to ignore aesthetic and carto-
graphic criteria, was far from lacking in charm or interest,
and I went away with a very precise sense of how Europe
would look if it was reconstructed as Belgium.

Later that afternoon, I followed teachers and their rich-
kid charges from the international schools of Brussels
around the Surrealist rooms of the subterranean Museum
of Modern Art. They paused briefly between the trams and
plumpish moonlit nudes of Delvaux, leading their charges
down the ramp to the Magrittes. I watched a French-
speaking teacher summon her class to the famous *Domaine
d'Arnheim*, a canvas representing two white eggs in a nest in
front of a bluish range of mountains, one central peak of
which had been painted in the shape of an eagle. 'What is
important to you about this painting?' the teacher asked.
The six-year-old children mentioned the eggs, or the eagle.
'Good,' said the teacher. 'That's good.' Then she explained
to her charges about the concepts of scale and size. By
making small things large, and vice versa, Magritte was
really asking the question: what was bigness? The class
hesitated at this point, confused by her use of abstraction,
so she tried again. Were eggs big? Was a mountain really
much bigger than an egg? When the children laughed, she
asked them if Belgium was big. How big was Belgium,
really? They raised their hands diffidently, and let them fall.

I began to share their uncertainty. Belgian paintings were
either very large or very small. Upstairs, in the charmingly
named Gallery of Older Art, I paused before *The School
Inspection* (1878), where Jan Verhas had painted a group of
fifty-odd girls *en crocodile* in their straw boaters and nice
dresses on a canvas of the sort of size which Meissonier
had used to capture Napoleon's retreat from Moscow. One
could admire the fetishistic interest in bootees (this was

before the appalling revelations of a Charleroi paedophile ring in 1996 in which two-eight-year old girls died after being kept in a cellar for six months), the profusion of cinches and sashes from the local lace industry, above all the *petit bourgeois* post-Dodgson cuteness of pink, round faces and rakish hats. Alternatively, one could take pleasure in the cheated perspective which gave to the small, enclosed Walloon town in which the scene was set the dimension of Buenos Aires or Chicago. Like Magritte, it seemed as if the painter was engaged in a form of national bet-hedging, or special pleading. Looked at from one angle the country was painfully small, a matter of water, grey skies, vistas blocked either by failing light or by more buildings. On the other hand, with luck, or artistic sleight of hand, which were the tricks to which talented Belgians were obliged to resort, it could seem spacious indeed, a gamble against perceptual odds spectacularly brought off.

Brussels seemed made for voyeurs. On first arrival I not so briefly glimpsed someone undressing from the vantage point of a flyover. The apartment I was staying in was as long and dark as a Métro station, filled with old sofas and even older lamps, with a view of more mysterious spaces across the rain-slicked road, each of them shrouded with lace curtains and hidden by aspidistra. It was never light before nine o'clock, but I woke eagerly, Tintin-style, walking out each day into the city in search of Belgian mysteries, and I was never disappointed. I liked the provincialism of Brussels, and its balance of intense privacy and crudely aggressive public spaces; I liked its darkness. Since the mid-nineteenth century, when Haussmann began to rip apart Paris in the name of modernity, Brussels had subsisted in uneasy emulation of its greater francophone sister. Its river, the Senne, was, according to Baudelaire, 'so dark that it is incapable of reflecting a single ray of the brightest light', but in a series of grandiose and inept building projects, it was covered up and turned into linked canals which bequeathed a fetid aura to the city centre. An insane mid-century building fever gripped the greedy city-father entrepreneurs (it was repeated a century later, with equally catastrophic results, when NATO and the EC came to town) which culminated in the construction of what the literary critic and cartoonist Benoît Peeters called Brüsel: a foggy, fractured metropolis consisting of old and yet beautiful broken neighbourhoods placed side by side with hideous, nervously executed experiments in the gratuitous piling-up of masonry. According to Peeters, Brüsel was a manifestation of the same spirit which led Belgium to acquire a colonial empire eighty-one times its size, in the Congo. Both actions were an externalization of the deep Belgian sense of insecurity; both, characteristically, ended in deflation and fantasy.

Each time I revisited the EU, I found that I longed to immerse myself in the dark shabbiness of Belgium. One winter's early dusk, I came to what *bruxellois* call 'the Palace' – not the one occupied by the Royal Family, nor any seat of the EU, but the law courts destined by the city fathers to be 'the greatest monument, if not the only one, of the twentieth century'. The architect, Joseph Poelaert, had designed only a column and a portion of a church when he received the commission as a consequence of his Masonic connections. The Palace became his life's work, and he altered its plans while construction was taking place, working by night, disdaining all efforts to limit his budget, disappearing on several occasions and yet returning, in the nick of time, to undo the more prosaic additions effected by his successors. In the approved style of the nineteenth-century artist, Poelaert died before completing his work, and yet he left behind an enigmatic structure which excited the imagination of Orson Welles, who wished to use the building as a location for his film of Kafka's *The Trial*, and Adolf Hitler, who instructed Albert Speer, after the invasion of Belgium in 1940, to have replica plans and sketches made so that elements could be incorporated into his new Berlin. In the accurately named *Salle des Pas Perdus* lawyers dressed in Daumier black with white collars assembled with their clients at large mahogany tables lit by green-shaded lights. The roof of the vast space was fogged-looking, and there were funerary configurations of marble on the walls. Wishing to commemorate the rule of law, the building had ended by freezing and immuring it; like much of Belgian architecture, indeed like Belgian history itself, it was an experiment in cryogenics.

One scandal followed another in Belgium, as I learnt, and there were so many that the pretext or indeed details – kickbacks in the purchase of helicopters, the suspected murder of a Walloon socialist by a colleague, at one time Minister of the Interior – came to seem unimportant. In Europe the existence of some sort of government, no matter how corrupt or inept, was taken for granted, but nowhere outside Italy was the expectation of graft so widespread. It was necessary to remember that the aura of respectability surrounding Belgium was relatively recent, and that its pervasive sense of normality was delusory, itself a means of dampening down the hatreds that periodically threatened to pull the country apart. Slowly, however, the old devices of graft were ceasing to fulfil their functions as they, too, were taken over by those who no longer cared whether the country existed or not; and the country was settling into its separate pieces. Only Brussels, which was in many respects a foreign city, existed to remind people that something had once been there which held them together.

After some difficulties, I found the ill-frequented and dusty *Musée de la Dynastie* situated in a remote wing of the Royal Palace. There I was escorted by an elderly and devout guide through rooms filled with cases containing relics: Queen Astrid's mouldering wedding gown, King Albert's climbing gear, the commemorative wooden plaque taken from Eton College, marking Leopold III's brief and unsuccessful scholarly career. My guide pointed with pride at the simple family tree, descending to the present with only the odd interruption; and the numerous photographs of tall royalty standing next to pygmies. He was particularly concerned that I should appreciate the exhibits relating to the rule of King Baudouin, who had ascended to the throne in 1951, living a saintly Catholic life with Queen Fabiola until his death in 1973, when hundreds of thousands of his subjects queued to say farewell to him. For Catholic (or loyalist) Belgians the example of Baudouin, my guide explained, now related to an exemplary time when less was questioned, and the future seemed secure. Tongue-tied, hair *en brosse*, eternally youthful in his awful uniforms and yet possessing an undeniable Boy Scout dignity, he remained a touching figure, at once hilariously innocent and detached from reality, and wholly appropriate for the country over which he presided with some success.

I had imagined, examining these cases, that the Belgian Royal Family might prove to be, in their dullness, a model for their wayward British counterparts; but that evening I was put right by the daughter of an official who drew up the annual civil list on behalf of the Government. The Royal Family had striven to see the country right; but, as with other dynasties, there were scandals. Elizabeth, famous for her charity work, had affairs with a series of violinists and flute-players; Albert I, it is now thought, was murdered in the Alps. Leopold III did kill Astrid as a consequence of his poor driving, but his wartime behaviour once taken prisoner by the Germans also left much to be desired. When he abdicated in 1951, after holding a referendum in which he secured only the narrowest majority, he stripped the palace of its furniture rather than leave it for Baudouin. As for Baudouin, he was a member of Opus Dei, the secret Catholic organization. His childlessness, deemed by propagandists to be an aspect of his saintliness, was the consequence of Queen Fabiola's refusal to countenance any form of artificial insemination. The most bizarre episode in Belgian or indeed European modern constitutional history arose, this friend reminded me, when the King, confronted in 1990 by a law legalizing abortion, which he could not reconcile with his conscience, abdicated rather than sign it, only to be reinstated by Parliament the following day once the law had been passed.

I asked whether the monarchy didn't fulfil some sort of role in holding the country together, but she put me right. 'They're nonentities who stay here only because of money,' she said. 'They don't really live here. The day will come when nobody wants to be King – it won't seem worth it any more.'

I began to see the texture of Belgium, rainy solidity and *frites* notwithstanding, as a series of elaborate fictions. In Tervuren, a Delvaux tram's ride from the centre of Brussels, set in a small brickwork and glass pavilion amid woods, I found dioramas, stuffed apes and birds, tribal tableaux of contentment. But this pastoral greenness commemorating Belgium's African ventures failed to recount the scale of plunder exercised by Leopold II, who operated the colonies as a private concession. *'Il faut à la Belgique une colonie,'* he told his finance minister. Riding his enormous tricycle around the palace grounds when he went to see his pregnant sixteen-year-old mistress Blanche Delacroix, the sixty-five-year-old autocrat refused to countenance reform, no matter how many progressive Englishmen risked their lives to denounce his works. Leopold's *fin de siècle* represented a new sprucing up of *Brüsel*, including boulevards, an Exhibition devoted to Progress, and a palace for himself; but the 'yellow' which Joseph Conrad's hero of 'Heart of Darkness', Marlow, noticed at the heart of Africa was emphatically Belgian in character. In the Congo, the slave trade continued. 'It is an extraordinary thing,' wrote Conrad to Roger Casement, after the latter had submitted a damning report to the Foreign Office, 'that the conscience of Europe which seventy years ago has put down the slave trade on humanitarian grounds tolerates the Congo State today. It is as if the moral clock has been put back. . . .'

Throughout the twentieth century the question of where the Belgian moral clock was located, or whether it even existed, continued to amuse snooty foreign observers. 'The cold statistician must not overlook the fact that the Belgian people possess the instinct of self-preservation unusually well-developed,' wrote John Maynard Keynes in 1919, confronted by what he considered to be excessive claims for compensation after World War One; and, perhaps unfairly, other than as cyclists or objects of party games, it was as survivors, or perpetrators, of obscure, unpunished crimes that Belgians existed in the European imagination. In the 1950s the British historian Richard Cobb celebrated the suburb of Ixelles, with its ponds, its shabby boulevards, its *merceries, pâtisseries, ressemelage, blanchisserie, cordonnerie, papeterie,* its *marchand de journaux,* the 'specific rich odour and colour' of chocolates and cheroots:

> The *Royaume de Belgique* itself is a quilted patchwork of immense historical variety, tied together as much by inter-marriage across the linguistic borders, by common cultural attitudes, by common reactions to others, and, above all, by common reactions to immediate neighbours ... [as by] a desire never to be taken in; a very basic common sense; a refusal to be unduly impressed, whether by uniform, titles, or literary reputations; a large reserve of scepticism ... an appetite always considerable and not easily satisfied; a mon-archy which is touchingly popular and middle-class.

I walked around Ixelles one Sunday morning, following Cobb's itinerary from boulevard to ponds. The smell of chocolate and cigars was still there in abundance, titillating the palate with the forbidden and familiar, although the streets had long ago been occupied by EU functionaries and their wives; so, too, judging by the appearance of many respectable bourgeois, who seemed to blink or stagger, was the habit of self-indulgence. Of the once popular monarchy, however, all that remained, as in the rest of Belgium, were headlines in the newsagents: hagiological re-renderings of the saintly Fabiola, minor misdeeds in Monaco of the King's daughters. As for the refusal to be impressed, that was evident in each chipped or drenched piece of brick-work, or in the flaked paint of each window shuttered against the soft, indifferent grey.

In the old days Belgian films tended to recount the mishaps of would-be cycling champions or honest Joe detectives, but by the 1990s it had at last become possible to convey by oblique means the wrenching apart of the country. *Man Bites Dog* recounted the adventures of a serial killer – the hero was played by a comedian famous for his depiction on television of the Belgian 'little man' – so happy to oblige the dumb and impecunious film crew following him around that he ended up by murdering people in order to help them out. Another depiction of misorientation was Jan Bucquoy's *La Vie Sexuelle des Belges*, an unembarrassed but cringe-making account of growing up left-wing and sexually frustrated in lower-middle-class Flemish Belgium. In between horrible camping holidays in sites adjacent to the vile North Sea, catastrophic relationships with good, motherly Catholic girls, epic bouts of masturbation and visits to outsize hookers, the loutish if amiable hero sat perusing *Le Soir* in bed, or, on special post-coital occasions when celebration was called for, *The Favourite Fairy-tales of Queen Fabiola*.

I asked Bucquoy about '*belgitude*', as I had heard it called. Did the country exist? Was there really such a place as Belgium outside his own fables? 'Oh yes,' he said. He believed passionately in Belgium. Like many other small countries, it had frequently been invaded and now it had been broken in two. But there were things which became progressively more interesting the closer they came to destruction – the much-abused Belgian common culture was one of them. In the past, people had tended to think of Belgianness as something between Frenchness and Anglo-Saxon culture – now it was more interesting.

'Belgium is a way of asking: what is real?' Bucquoy said. 'If you think of Belgium now it is as the equivalent of the famous Magritte picture of a pipe, but with the inscription "*Ceci n'est pas un pays*" over the map of Belgium.'

Large and genial, like his movie hero, Bucquoy wanted his trilogy to encompass the entire contemporary cultural life of Belgium, and he proposed to play himself in the third episode ('when I look old enough') set in the 1980s. I wanted to know how seriously he took the Royal Family. He said that he had been a Trotskyist at university, but that the Royal Family now seemed to be a magic glue, keeping what remained of the kingdom in one piece.

'Being Belgian is about jousting with ridicule,' he said. 'You stand somewhere on a ladder, between concrete and the distant blue sky; and you show your arse.'

I drove out of Brussels through industrial waste, and small red-brick towns under a full sky. Like the good Catholics they still professed to be, living in a dark northern land, Belgians set great store by museums or monuments. At Dixmuide, standing near the sea in a flat landscape as horribly desolate as the Thames marshes of East England in which Pip encountered the convict Magwitch, was a large black plinth covered with names and the inscription AVV VVK: *Alles Voor Vlaanderen, Vlaanderen Voor Kristus* (All For Flanders, Flanders For Christ). Here, each August, some 50,000 Flemish Belgians assembled to commemorate the 1914 battle of the Yser, when King Albert I ordered the bungs pulled out of the dykes, halting the German advance with great loss of life. Traditionally, the banners displayed each August were Catholic and pacifist, held up by busty Virgin-worshipping teenagers in peasant costumes; but in recent years a rancorous tone had crept into the speeches as the gathering became a centre frequented by neo-Fascist groups from all over Europe. Good King Albert, it was now suggested, wasn't the hero of confected Belgian national legend, but a man who betrayed his Flemish subjects by sending them out to die commanded by officers who couldn't understand them against a foe with whom, linguistically and culturally, they had far more in common.

I confess that I knew little about Flemish nationalism, except that I had seen *Daenst*, an intriguing biopic about a Catholic priest who left the church in 1900 and became head of the first Flemish-speaking political party in Belgium. Poignantly old-fashioned in style, recalling the 'clog epics' favoured by British regional television companies in the 1960s and after, the film – financed in part by the EU – depicted Daenst as an exemplary if stubborn man who stood for the usual package of workers' rights of that time, but for whom linguistic subordination was the *via crucis*. Daenst spoke French haltingly, and he couldn't stand on equal footing with the French-speaking bosses. It was a matter of outrage for him that the girls working in Flemish textile factories were not able to communicate with the factory inspectors who asked them about their work conditions. But when he went to Brussels, the hoity-toity frenchified style of the Belgian court rendered him, literally, speechless, so that he could only rage like a dog.

I drove past nondescript factories and shopping malls until I reached Antwerp, where I parked the car, and ate mussels and fries under a plastic awning flapping in the wind. Nowadays, the Flemish part of Belgium was richer than French-speaking Wallonia; and the latter-day Daensts had what they wanted: a snug homeland in which Flemish was spoken, a bilingual Brussels in which even parking tickets were in two languages, Flemish education, Flemish television, Flemish road signs, Flemish local and regional assemblies. But these measures had given Belgium a large level of public indebtedness without significantly quieting Flemish resentment; indeed they had merely encouraged separatists to ask for more, causing demands to arise that no further subsidies should be given to the now ailing South, and that the country should therefore cease to share provisions of welfare and pensions. As many people had pointed out, this would in effect mean that Belgium had become two separate countries.

In a dog-fouled back street of the port of Antwerp, behind the municipal bus station, next door to some elderly prostitutes catering by the hour for visiting seamen, I found the offices of *Vlaams Blok*, the Flemish Nationalist Party. Undiscreetly racist, calling for the repatriation of all foreign workers, though significantly not the rich Jewish diamond-cutting and -dealing community, the party had on various occasions displayed an attachment to the memory of the Third Reich, on the dubious but no doubt historically correct grounds that Adolf Hitler abetted the cause of the Flemish language. In the 1994 local elections the *Vlaams Blok* were the largest single party, polling up to 46 per cent in some districts.

Yellow-black flags with a lion rampant were inscribed, pithily, *Belgie Baarst!* (Die, Belgium!) and a pervasive smell of knackwurst and stale beer hung over the committee rooms. I wanted to talk about Belgian history. Why, I wondered, did they wish to get rid of Belgium? Why bother to destroy something when you already had most of what you wanted? But Filip Dewinter, who was secretary of the local party, brushed aside my interest.

'This is old stuff, you know,' he said. 'Belgium is already finished. By now Belgium is not an interesting subject; it could vanish tomorrow, by means of legislation, and everyone who now lives in the country would still be here. You know who the only real Belgians are? The Royal Family, and they're Austrians, anyhow, they were put here by the Great Powers. As a geopolitical entity, Belgium belongs in the European Museum. We say – let it die.'

Fortyish, groomed in a 1950s style, dressed like a Tintin

character in a natty shiny blue suit, fingering his small steel-rimmed glasses and speaking more than passable Berlitz English, Dewinter had learnt not to fall into the easy traps set by visitors. He talked about Europe and the Flemish tradition, and how much easier it was to be a small nation at a time when frontiers had been rendered meaningless. When I suggested that this was all very well, but that sending foreign workers home wasn't compatible with the supranational, liberal character of the Europe in relation to which he claimed membership, he shrugged affably and smiled. 'The Flemish people believe in the integrity of their own culture, and they want to preserve its character,' he said. 'They also are Europeans. There is no contradiction.'

From rainy Antwerp I drove southwards, crossing and re-crossing the linguistic divide as I went from province to province. Everywhere there were signs, but the inscriptions were in one language, and I often lost my way. I intuited that Ghent was presumably the same as Gand, but what was Kootrijk? Courtrai perhaps? And was Mons really the same place as Bergen? Leave us alone, is what these signs untactfully and decisively said; don't come near us. I knew that smallness was sentimentally associated in the late twentieth century with the existence of a sense of community or a spirit of democracy, but in Belgium the lack of real distance meant that you could live side by side with your fellow-men while continuing either to hate their guts or wishing, more or less heartily, to have nothing whatsoever to do with them. Many people believed that the progressive federalization of Europe, or the diminishment of nationality (they were often considered to be the same thing), would lead to the Belgification of Europe. I found myself hoping that this would not be the case.

Around the ugly town of Ieper – Ypres, as it was known

when hundreds of thousands were killed there during the Great War – I drove from cemetery to cemetery, and the soft countryside disappeared entirely into low, insignificant hills or dead flatness. The German and French stones were simple affairs – names, dates, the pretext or occasion of death – but the British ones, laid out around elaborate architectural creations, garden huts or memorial arches, evoked a network of cultural loyalties, to King or Empire, or old geographical loyalties, to counties and portions of extinct colonies, all the more poignant because they lost their meaning many years ago.

It was still raining, but I began to to look at the books kept in each cemetery, bearing the names of those buried there. My own family got off relatively lightly – a British great-uncle blinded at the Somme, aged nineteen, my French grandfather wounded at Verdun, several hundred kilometres to the east – but I noticed many dead bearing my own name, from Australian and Canadian as well as Scottish regiments. Apparently, it had been possible at the end of the war to walk across these fields and date the progress of the attacks by the remains – Australian cap badges, British or Canadian gas masks and so on – that lay heaped by the skulls. In the trenches themselves, the practices of national cultures were observable – the German ones were deep, methodically built, implying the wish to stay there, the French ones temporary and efficient, smelling of cooking, while the British ones were the least well-constructed, 'amateur, vague, ad hoc and temporary', in the words of the American literary critic Paul Fussell. Pausing at the horribly misnamed Sanctuary Wood, with its rusting relics assembled to form the inevitable museum of death promoting a café, I noticed I was being followed at snail's pace by a cortège of black-clad motor-cyclists; but when they stopped and dismounted, taking off their helmets and goggles, they introduced themselves not as Hell's Angels but as God-fearing, bourgeois members of the Motor-cycle Club of Brabant.

We went slowly in convoy through the rain. Somewhere in these dull fields, I recalled, Adolf Hitler was gassed in 1918, blinded for three weeks. Near here, too, a British platoon came across a man lodged up to his knees in mud. They couldn't pull him out, and they went away for help; two days later, when they found him again, he was up to his neck in mud, and had gone mad.

Ypres was one of the places where the old European ideas of grandeur and nationality foundered, and where the idea of any moral worth inherent in a nation-state expired. 'I came to hate this place,' a British soldier, J. W. Naylor, wrote. 'I was always dreaming of these awful names: Zonnebeke, Zillebeke, Hill 60, which filled us with terror before we got there, so horrible were their associations. Going to Passchendaele once more was the last straw ... I would think: "What is the point of going on? What do I care who wins this bloody war?"'

We said goodbye to each other at the gates of Tyne Cot, a British cemetery where 50,000 bodies had been collected from nearby fields and painstakingly reassembled, and in the design of which King George V had become interested, paying special attention to the siting of the cross next to a barn which had been used as a bunker and then a dressing station. Bedraggled and shining in their black leather, the motor-cyclists carefully wiped their moustaches with handkerchiefs, and prepared to drive home. 'It won't happen again in Belgium,' one of them said, shaking my hand. 'We can be sure it won't happen again.'

I could see that he might be right. No one could complain

that only five kilometres away trucks passed and re-passed over the frontier. No one could possibly wish for a replay of the emotions which had led to such carnage. But it struck me, too, that, notwithstanding many assertions to the contrary, people had not yet found a substitute for the national public or civic culture which, though it had made possible such appalling and misguided sacrifices, remained the only way that people could find a way of living side by side without killing each other.

I supposed that for a believer in federalism (and there were not so many of them) the problem was not an important one; they would tend to suppose that something else could inevitably take the place of the old national cultures. But in Belgium, where the decomposition or death of the old national order was most advanced, no such transfer of emotions had occurred. No one, it appeared to me, knew what a stateless and nationless Europe would be like. Later, as I waited for the plane, I wondered, not wholly as an idle exercise, what would be the very worst thing the European Union could do to Europe. Well, whatever it was, there would be no early-morning coercion, no gulag to which recalcitrants were sent. Instead we Europeans would probably wake up in a very large rainproof shopping mall, full of separate areas designated Germany, France, Britain, Finland, Flanders, Denmark, each of them selling whatever remained of national habits or institutions, good or bad. We might or might not have our special currency, of course, or our magnetized swipe passes; and yet compared to the hordes outside, we'd think ourselves fortunate. At regular intervals the 'Ode To Joy' would be piped to us. Some days, peering out at the chaos on earth, we might ask ourselves whether we were really happy; and then decide yes, we were. Whatever we had lost – it was forgotten by now, like a child's bad dream – hadn't been worth keeping.

However, I could only half accept such a future, and back in London, which seemed diminished after my discoveries, I re-examined the matter of contemporary scale. The rest of the world was in one way or another growing larger; but not so Europe, which had decided either to stay the size it was or to shrink itself. And yet how small did one have to be, I wondered, to be considered a small (and therefore fortunate) country? Perhaps Denmark and Portugal fitted the bill, and Finland, too. Malta, Latvia and Estonia, among the next group of entrants, would so be considered. But was Ireland small? And what about Scotland? I was able to consider such questions when, a few months later, I went by train to Luxembourg, arriving on a Friday afternoon when the banks were shutting and the last Eurocrats were leaving their posts. It was sunny but cold, and I walked to the main square, which was filled with Luxembourgeois escorting Tekels or Great Danes. Skirting the diminutive battlements, the hotel-sized palace, the adjacent miniaturized, mansard-roofed, yellowish Parliament building and the downsized *Palais de Justice*, I was back where I had begun within ten minutes. I tried to buy a bond as a souvenir, but I was told either that the bank was shutting (the dialect, *Letzburgesch*, was apparently an amalgamation of French and German, but it came over as grumpiness) or that none were for sale. Standing before a tripe and sausage shop, I wondered what to do with the rest of the day. Then I saw a small fox terrier escorted by a baldish, pink-faced middle-aged man dressed fashionably in Loden green and carrying a polished leather briefcase bulging with documents, deeds or banknotes. We smiled at each other nervously, and it seemed to me that he raised his hand in recognition.

In the earliest Tintin books, the boy journalist, driven by idealism or the curiosity of his creator, Georges Remi, rushed around the world in search of stolen artefacts or lost causes; but towards the end of his career, after Remi's dubious acquiescence during the German occupation, and his flirtation with Buddhism, he came home to Moulinsart, an ugly fake-Renaissance pile somewhere in the Belgian countryside. By the time he had become rich and famous, Remi was bored with his sexless, royalist, Catholic uncynical hero-journalist. A late adventure book, *The Castafiore Emerald*, recounted Tintin's quest in his own back yard for a diva's lost trinkets. They turned out to be made of paste, insured beyond their worth, and to have been stolen not by the pariah gypsies living on the fringe of the Belgian village, as had been suspected, but by magpies. The book, I recalled, came as close to the evocation of adult ennui as any children's author might do without losing readers, but it was also wonderfully full of ensemble players in the European style: pompous butlers, drunks, mad inventors of three-dimensional television, hangers-on carrying odd packages around the woods.

However, *Tintin and the Alph-Art*, Remi's last, unfinished work, was a distinctly darker matter. Here Tintin was kidnapped by the usual collection of foreigners, but, instead of being detained, he was packed up Christo-style and turned into an art-work. The boy detective – the narrative left the question open – appeared to finish his days on the oatmeal-coloured walls of a Luxembourg bank. But perhaps Hergé (Remi's *nom-de-plume*) was being unnecessarily gloomy, and Tintin would have made a career in Europe, like so many ambitious Belgians and Luxembourgeois, becoming an MEP, an untaxed official in Directorate one hundred and seventeen and a half, or (like Willy Claes, civilized concert pianist, forced to resign because of the corrupt friends he kept) the head of NATO. I could certainly envisage a middle-aged Tintin selling obscure financial instruments. Above all, I could see him selling the Grand Duchy of Luxembourg.

Without borders, without taxes to speak of, without work if you discounted the 220-odd banks and the satellite uplink stations, with a reigning, scandal-free Grand Duke whose name no one could quite remember, a disenfranchised population of foreigners (laws had been passed stopping foreigners from voting in local elections, which they were allowed to do in the rest of Europe), a vigorous local cuisine based on pig's neck and offal, and the highest standard of living in Europe, Luxembourg was the prototype nationless state. If Croatia, Scotland or the Isle of Man were to become statelets, this was how they would end up.

I reflected that one wouldn't be able to sell Britain or France much longer; and there was little or no Italy left to sell. Luxembourg, however, was a different matter – packed up, shipped and reassembled, in original or replica, exhibited under glass or plastic, left to weather in any climate, the Grand Duchy was the perfect gift for a successful magnate, reformed criminal, formerly charismatic strongman or Messiah. The country appeared not to be anything much, but as a kingdom of convenience it turned out to have everything. Nothing was even more than less. Embroidered on dynastic lace or bathrobes, punched out on computer paper, embossed on pigskin restaurant menus or hand-painted on the sides of stretched black Mercedes limos, that could be the motto of the New Europe. It didn't seem to require translation into Latin.

Vienna: the Sense of *Déjà Vu*

*I dreamed that I had died for my country,
and right away a coffin-lid opener was there,
holding out his hand for a tip.*

Karl Kraus

In Vienna during the early summer of 1995, I sat in the Café Griensteidl, behind the Hofburg, flanked by quiet opera-loving couples in expensive English tweeds. I looked at the gate out of which Franz Josef drove by horse-drawn carriage, even after the automobile was invented, and idly wondered whether I should go to the Museum of the Austrian Undertaker to see the special exhibit of mortuary ceremonial through the ages. I supposed I had come to Vienna looking for signs of recrudescent Nazism, primed for a siege of journalistic outrage, but two days scrutinizing the evasions of right-wing politicians made the emotion seem superfluous. At my café table behind the old imperial palace, looking at the exquisitely modern Looshaus, which the ageing Emperor hated so much that he caused the palace shutters to be kept permanently closed, it occurred to me that, although we were all ostensibly concerned with the past, history was mysteriously losing its value. Why be interested in the fate of the Weimar Republic when you might have bought Hermann Göring's yacht in 1945 and watched its cash value multiply at a rate higher than that of a Van Gogh sunflower? Why go to the Museum of the Austrian Undertaker when Vienna itself was the cemetery of the twentieth century?

So much of what was beautiful, horrible or merely silly in our times originated here, and most of it was thrown away: Esperanto, pan-Germanism, Zionism, dental technology, consensual sado-masochism, symbolic logic, political anti-Semitism, atonal music, gutter journalism, Freudian and Reichian psychoanalysis, subsidized public housing, affirmative action, ethnic cleansing, lederhosen, plastic antler buttons and fibreglass ski equipment. Vienna showed me, not that the past could be brought back, or made use of, but that it piled up gratuitously, horror upon horror, losing its significance. The only lessons available in Vienna were those conventionally associated with death, or whipped cream.

Still, from the perspective of our vanishing century the Austrian past seemed ready for re-annexation, in particular the endlessly replicated serial void implied by such local products as baroque or the waltz. Heartlessness and insouciance were thought to be as characteristic of the Viennese – they were noted with disapproval by sober-minded Anglo-Saxon commentators – as they are now of Bombay or Beverly Hills people. Looking at such relics of Empire as the eagles still to be found sculpted over favoured shops selling hair tonic or riding equipment, or the beautiful dark green and ochre in which Habsburg palaces, churches and police stations were decorated, I felt that many of our own makeshift arrangements might as easily slide away. No one by 1913 knew why the Empire was sinking, or cared excessively about the fate of civilization; no one cared much now. The pre-Great-War Viennese press offered up its daily version of events with a chilly and gruesome precision worthy of Rupert Murdoch; just as now, conspicuous works of genius were considered irrelevant beside such absorbing occurrences as the last words of a handsome serial killer, the testimony of a surviving member of a family of street vendors who jumped in unison from a window ledge, or the diminishing wheat content of the Standard Imperial Army Loaf.

Diving each day through the intact wreckage of this European Atlantis, I felt able to reclaim the Habsburg disaster for the present. The pompous buildings erected on the chestnut-tree-shaded Ring in a variety of mega-Ruritanian styles – Parliament was rendered in French-style neo-classical bombast, City Hall in contrasting Gothic, copied from Britain – were meant to celebrate the triumph of a new Monarchy of Law, but they seemed contemporary in their over-anxious sense of ornament, like the corporate head-quarters of insolvent banks. Passing from Catholic autocracy to mass democracy, the Empire buckled and cracked in what sociologists, examining the Shah of Iran's oil-based empire of kitsch, would later call 'a crisis of modernization'. Instead of maturing into liberal consti-tutionalism, Austria-Hungary fell prey to fundamentalist nationalist demagogy. Most of the fifteen-odd national groups – among them Germans, Czechs, Hungarians, Ruthenians, Slovenes and, by 1908, Bosnians and Croats – hated each other; but all of them feared and resented what the Viennese economist Joseph Schumpeter later called the 'creative gale' of liberal capitalism. In particular they came to hate those whom they held responsible for their impover-ishment and deracination and who were the only real 'people of the Empire' unconditionally loyal to the Crown: cosmopolitan urban liberal Jews.

One reason for the world's lack of preparedness for the

Habsburg collapse was that no one could remember a time when the dynasty was taken entirely seriously. Soldierly, plodding Franz Josef spoke nineteen languages and wouldn't use the telephone; but when he wasn't climbing the Alps, dressed in knee-breeches and in quest of fowl, he was at his papers every morning at six o'clock. He was serious – over-serious perhaps, spending less time than he should have done with the Empress Sisi, who was murdered by an Italian anarchist while boarding a boat in Geneva, with the plump actresses in whose lakeside villas he did or didn't enjoy carnal relations – the evidence is contradictory – or with his syphilitic, liberal heir Rudolf, who killed himself and his own mistress in the imperial hunting lodge at Mayerling. But, alas, the Emperor was a man who believed fatally in the solitary exercise of duty. During his sixty-eight-year reign he strove first to ignore the forces of democracy and ethnicity, then to accommodate them, and, towards the end, to become resigned to catastrophe. 'If the Monarchy must die,' he said, with appropriate *fin de siècle* gloom, 'then it must at least die with honour.' But, unlike his subjects, the Emperor did in a muddled and remote way take seriously the *mélange* of conflicting cultures entrusted to him by history. When a minister bemoaned the imminent arrival of Galician Jews in the capital in 1914, Franz Josef offered to accommodate them in the grounds of his summer residence at Schönbrunn.

Ponderous and repetitious, the Austrian nineteenth century was filled with the noise of expensive furniture mysteriously cracking apart. Logically, the end should have been apparent in 1867, when the dynasty was booted out of Germany by the Prussian Army, but the Emperor's increasingly fictional power was redistributed between Hungary and the rest of the Empire. Although the Empire was now called Austria-Hungary, the Austrian part became known as Cisleithania after the Leitha, a muddy stream trickling along the border. Equally mysterious designations applied to the Emperor's vanishing authority. Where Hungary was concerned, his edicts were known as K. (*königlich*), and where his wishes were exclusively Austrian they were K.K. (*kaiserlich-königlich*); but where the two were involved together, in relation to regiments, or even torte and hair lotion, an *und* was inserted, making K. *und* K.

On a small scale, with due nineteenth-century pedantry and insanely fulsome constitutional legalisms – endless dull tomes were written on the subject of the 'Austrian idea', and the creation of hemicycle-shaped banquettes, along with irony and café chairs, became a growth industry – the Empire was supposed to become the equivalent, with a Habsburg at its head, of the European Union: a multi-national state neutrally administered by kindly bureaucrats. After a less than productive morning spent trying to focus on the gentian-blue eyes and ski-instructor physique of the right-wing politician Jorg Haider, listening to his disavowals of the Nazi past and his expressions of admiration for Mrs Thatcher, whose favourite shade of blue he had taken for his office curtains, I walked through marbled corridors until I stood in the old chamber to which representatives were supposed to come from the farthest provinces of Empire. Here I experienced once again the shock of recognition: I might have been inspecting a lost prototype of Brussels or Strasbourg. The dome of the Parliament chamber was patterned with luscious art deco flowers, in the style of a Paris *brasserie*. Above one line of benches stood off-the-peg togaed Romans, in machine-cut marble; from above the other glared the bewhiskered visage of the Emperor, in his habitual military fancy dress, flanked by busty sphinxes. In this room the noble ideal of Austrian democracy rapidly withered and died, and with it the conviction that the European future belonged to a new world order of rational and progressive liberalism. Deputies banged their desk tops and threw inkpots at each other over the issue of Czech or Slovene linguistic rights or abused their parliamentary privilege by offering bounty for anyone prepared to kill rich Jewish businessmen. Adolf Hitler was shocked in 1907 by the snoring and the rowdy behaviour, and it became his pretext for wishing to abolish representative democracy – acting in the name of free speech, or simple convenience, art-loving liberal bureaucrats governed instead by decree, appealing to the diminishing authority of the kindly imperial figure, of Reaganesque imperturbability, whose likeness was affixed to the wall above their desks.

You could be taken down the sewers in Vienna, in search of the spot where Carol Reed placed Orson Welles beneath a grille, or you could be ferried from meadow to meadow in search of the Trapp family, by means of a bus thoughtfully equipped with stereo. Only one tour wasn't on offer, and that consisted of the Viennese haunts of the century's most significant Austrian, Adolf Hitler. One afternoon, I went by U-bahn to remote bits of the city where behind ugly façades concierges stared suspiciously at me through net curtains. Two boys were kicking a football in the cobbled yard of Felberstrasse 22, and I walked past dados and chipped doors. I paused outside apartment number six, and a man with a large, reddish neck came down the stairs adjusting his shiny double-breasted suit, followed by a woman stuffed into a yellow dress with a slipping *décolletage*. '*Grüss Gott*,' the man said to me. Later, I alighted at the Heiligentor terminus on the edge of the city, walking past quadrangles of 1920s workers' housing and under railway bridges. It was dusk when I reached Meldemannstrasse, but I found the dark hulk of a building where Hitler lived for four years. Not a doss-house, exactly, or even a *mitteleuropa* boarding-house of the kind made familiar by Ernst Lubitsch, the Home for Single Men (it was opened by the Emperor himself, with much fanfare) was a place where the genteel near-poor could be accommodated bug-free so long as they behaved themselves. Crankily removed from fellow-humans, Hitler squabbled with the Jewish agent who did or didn't sell his awful paintings, and otherwise busied himself reading about Rosicrucianism and Guild Socialism when he wasn't annoying his fellow inmates with his accumulated half-expertise about Wagner or neo-classicism. Nowadays, a porter with beer breath and a wall eye told me, the home had come down in the world, and it was frequented by the Viennese poor. Sometimes Japanese film crews came by, and made its decrepit inmates pose outside the building. 'I would be able to sell many postcards,' he said. 'It's a shame they won't let me.'

Little Austria had been neutral since 1945, and the old Habsburg parade grounds had long ago been ploughed up to create suburban Alpine-style weekend retreats, with small, gnome-filled gardens. But walking through the Moorish arches of the Museum of Military History I found an array of military uniforms. They seemed made for cor-seted munchkins, in children's party bumble-bee or magic-marker colours; and the hats were covered with forgotten inscriptions, studded with odd pistachio-coloured plumes, or garnished with the feathers of ducks or obscure Alpine fowls. The only prize ever won in modern times by the Imperial Army was at the 1900 Paris Exposition, and it was for the perfect uniform. No one in Austria took military affairs seriously, or was in the least surprised when the

Empire was soundly defeated; but it nonetheless came as a shock to see the imperial heir-apparent Franz Ferdinand's bloodstained uniform under glass, and the bathtub-shaped car (manufactured in Vienna, the ultimate non-getaway appliance) in which he was assassinated in Sarajevo by a Serb nationalist on June 28, 1914. A likeness of Franz Ferdinand gazed goofily down on this macabre tableau – he looked like Prince Philip when judging coaching trials.

You could delve anywhere in Austrian history and find the rottenness of our Europe. As early as 1895 the anti-Semitic Karl Lueger became the first European politician to adopt a platform of ethnic discrimination when he recommended, to the applause of his German and Catholic supporters, that city jobs should henceforth be allocated according not to talent but to racial origins. Dismayed, the Emperor refused to acknowledge Lueger's government, but he was forced to give in to democratic pressures. It became impossible for civilized people, particularly if they were Jewish, to participate in political culture. Instead, they interested themselves in the marvellously available cir-cumstances of *douceur*: making money, performing or sponsoring art, and, like the Herzls or the Wittgensteins, encouraging their children to become geniuses. In France, individuals broke noisily and self-consciously with their bourgeois past; in Austria, an entire class stood wholly outside the murderous frivolity of politics. Amid the stuffi-ness and hypocrisy of the dying Empire, there was a large, dangerous edge of creativity characterized by an ironic sense of defeat or impending disaster. Everybody knew the gates to the enchanted garden would be shut long before the Austrian élite declared war on Serbia, destroying them-selves and the rest of Europe in the most terrible way imaginable.

As everyone knew, the Austrians had a problem with their past – their Nazi past above all – but I was beginning to feel that the question was a larger one, encapsulating the European collapse and beyond that, perhaps, the limits of memory itself. The dusk was bluish, full of the clanking noises of trams, when I stood outside the Opera House on the night the Vienna bourgeoisie attended a sold-out concert dedicated to the memory of the Jewish musicians and singers who were purged in 1938, and later murdered. People *grüss-gotted* in polite whispers and kissed one another on the cheeks with laborious precision. Most of them were embarrassed, as people are when they attend the funeral of someone they never really knew; and I felt nervously party – again, the same lingering fear – to the pervasive air of bad faith. It was as if Margaret Thatcher, acting against her better judgement, had chosen to attend a commemorative function celebrating the heroic lives of martyred animal-rights activists or Irish republicans.

The Empire ended at the instigation of Woodrow Wilson in November 1918, with the creation of a diminished, ethnically cleansed Republic of 'German Austria', now sawn off from its subject lands. Everywhere tradesmen pulled down the imperial eagles from store-fronts while generals removed the cockades from their hats. 'The Vienna cafés are fuller than before,' noted the journalist and wit Alfred Polgar, who later emigrated to Brooklyn. 'They were always the centre of Viennese life. Now they are the centre of the Viennese death agony. In times like these, the perspiration of one's fellow-men is a nerve-strengthening fluid, and when two or more tremble together, they give off a calming sound.'

Most Viennese writers came from or knew rich families which had lost everything; a new edge of desperation came into their work. 'The real end of the world,' Karl Kraus wrote in 1922, 'is the destruction of the spirit; after that there remains only the insignificant attempts to see whether after such a destruction the world can go on.' Kraus, whose work was said to be nearly impossible to translate and who was almost forgotten outside Germany, represented a tradition that was by now almost dead. 'A journalist is someone with no opinions and the ability to express them,' he wrote. Author and publisher, for almost forty years, of *Die Fackel* ('The Torch'), described by him as an 'anti-paper', in which he reviewed the contemporary scene, Kraus freely exercised the journalistic prerogative of malice, but he did so with comprehensive, unforgiving intelligence. Like most Jewish intellectuals of his generation, Kraus experienced a periodic sense of love, tempered by exasperation, for his half-finished, moribund homeland; but he had seen through the wretched pasteboard popular cult of the Habsburg monarchy. He now feared the impending Germanization of Central Europe, but, like most Viennese in the ruins of the inter-war period, he sensed his café-bound impotence very clearly.

Like Mahler or Stefan Zweig, Kraus, who converted to Catholicism but then abandoned the church, was attacked as a 'self-hating' or 'anti-Semitic' Jew, and the label stuck to him. He did attack Theodore Herzl's Zionism for what he saw as its social divisiveness, but many of his polemics, such as the one entitled 'Rabbits with Jewish accents' aimed at Felix Salten, the author of *Bambi*, were motivated by his rigorous concern for truth rather than commercial fakery. Like Zweig, too, Kraus felt equally ill-at-ease in the fusty hierarchy of Habsburg Catholicism and the narrow, pleasure-denying, *shtetl* culture of traditional Jewishness. He was aware of the corrosive effect of his work on the fabric around him; and his intense sensitivity to the nuances of lies and self-delusion caused him to become, in Elias Canetti's words, 'a kind of scourge of God for guilt-ridden Mankind'. Rapidly, his oratorical performances in the *Musikverein* began to draw capacity crowds. Kraus's most successful recital, *The Guided Tour To Hell*, took as its point of departure an advertisement he had found in the *Basel News*, offering a tour of the French-German battlefields, with a privileged view of the Thiaumont Ossuary, where the recently dead were being reburied, and a luncheon ('gratuities and wine included') at the best hotel in Verdun. Kraus immersed himself in the junk of his time; he wrote an eight-hour play about the Great War entitled *The Last Days of Mankind*, composed of moronic newspaper items and by now bizarrely anachronistic communiqués of the Imperial General Staff. He was the first journalist to see that it was pointless to talk nobly about serving truth when the machine of 'public opinion' – a set of collusive arrangements between press magnates and advertisers, abetted by an indifferent or impotent State for whose representatives public morality had ceased to be important – existed to service the appetite for spectacle. Standing outside politics, he blamed the catastrophe of Austria on the fecklessness and ignorance of its educated class, among whom he included his fellow-journalists and, more reluctantly, himself. 'I have nothing to say about Hitler,' he wrote just before his death in 1936, before devoting sixty-odd pages to the crass prose style and murderous views of the pro-Hitler press. Two years later, the Anschluss destroyed Austria for a second time.

Half-abandoned, a meteorite fallen from space, the city was enormous and full of green spaces, threatening in its emptiness. On the U-bahn, watching old people carrying string bags full of provisions, I wondered where all that apocalypse had gone. In an apartment on Linke Wien, once a grand avenue built to provide the Emperor with a fitting approach to the Imperial City, I watched Czech workers scrape away cream and purple layers of paint, exposing domed plasterwork in a series of magniloquently vulgar parquet-floored salons to which a separate marbled *porte-cochère* gave handsome access via a Hollywood-Lubitsch wrought-iron stairway. The first owner had been a Jewish textile magnate from Brno, who went bust in the 1920s crash. Later, the rooms were turned into a dance school, where you could learn waltzes, tangos and polkas. I fingered a set of ballroom tickets, found behind the wainscoting; they came wrapped in a National Socialist flyer.

In truncated Austria, it became fashionable, among dispossessed Jewish intellectuals in particular, to mourn the possibilities of the lost European Atlantis, in particular the idea of multinationality. Abetted by the carefully marketed schmaltz of Hollywood *émigrés*, who milked the shakos and waltzes for all they were worth, the Habsburg cult began to thrive. The past was poignantly given operatic dimensions in a wonderful Galician ballroom scene, full of Magyars insulting each other and everyone else while war broke out, in Joseph Roth's act of retrospective patriotism, *The Radetsky March*. But the irresistible, distinctly European notion of pre-apocalypse *douceur* found its ultimate expression in Robert Musil's vast, uncompleted novel, *The Man Without Qualities*, written between the wars, but set in 1913.

Musil died penniless in Zurich in 1943 while returning to his room-sized manuscript after a bout of callisthenics. His novel exhaustively described the never-never land of Kakania, 'that state since vanished which no one understood'. Kakania resembled contemporary Berlin or New York in everything except the proliferation of gold braid outside luxury hotels, and the persistence with which Musil's characters touchingly struggled against the enveloping doom even while they strove unsuccessfully to bring meaning to their own lives. The Parallel Committee consisted of a group of aristocratic, middle-class and intellectual worthies, soldiers, visiting German capitalists and society hostesses given the task of devising a celebration of the Emperor's seventieth jubilee in 1918. A scientist turned philosopher, Musil prematurely understood the baroque epistemological fantasies inherent in the notion of 'virtual reality'. Trapped in the Kakanian equivalent of cyberspace, his characters were pilgrims in a country without progress. Was the future going to be Nietzschean, managerial-technocratic or New Age Utopian-mystical? Were the nihilistic passions of intransigent minorities to be deplored or, with clumsy magnanimity, given accommodation, even when it was clear that they would destroy the shape of the world? These discussions were doomed to inconsequence; we all knew that the Emperor died before his jubilee could be celebrated.

The daffiness of *The Man Without Qualities* rendered an otherwise awesomely self-conscious work of High Culture wholly addictive. 'She had only one fault,' it was said about a woman character, who from listening to the diagnosis of sex therapists had come to think of herself as a nymphomaniac: 'she could become inordinately aroused at the sight of a man.' The *Zeitgeist* washed pitilessly over everyone, sparing neither moral scruple nor nicety of expression. In Kakania piles of bedside reading materialized and disappeared – they were tasted and put to one side, like the food at Louis XIV's Versailles, or late-night TV shows – and wisdom was conveyed to the masses in foreshortened, mutilated form, just as the camisoles of Diotima, the beautiful and overweight muse of the Committee, were snipped, resewn and handed on to her diminutive Jewish maid Rachel.

Death had stalked the century everywhere in Europe, and yet only Austria looked and felt wholly moribund. Going through patches of sunlight and tunnels under the cracked side walls behind the façades of old tenements, I took the U-bahn away from the Danube to the Hüttelsdorf terminus on the edge of the Vienna woods. There I sat in a small house full of bright paintings, and listened to Elfriede Jelinek, who wrote clever, minor-key end-of-the-world novels whose characters were sociopathic students, victim piano teachers or dumb and murderous *glühwein*-cheeked ski instructors. Tall and blonde, dressed in punkish clothes, Ms Jelinek had gone out of her way to annoy genteel Austria, posing for a German magazine in black leather, tied to a bed. I wanted to know how it was possible for individuals to write, or even live, in such circumstances. What did the death of a culture feel like?

'Ghosts are our only means of survival – it's all a matter of what we do with our ghosts,' she said. 'As a people we have a negative identity, based on no longer really being what we were, or on the lies we continually tell about ourselves. Our greatest lie is that of High Culture. The real Austria had a predominantly Jewish culture, and it was popular, a mixture of schmaltz and intelligence; we killed it. The High Culture lie – music, of course, but you get the countryside thrown in, too – has become very profitable to us. It's the way we keep the tourists coming in. But it's why we look to the world like a glossy corpse.'

I said that I was perplexed by the fitful or self-contradictory acts of remembrance towards the Nazi past. For instance, I had just visited an exhibition of anti-Semitic artefacts at the Rathaus – Hanging Jew watch-fobs and yarmulkaed money-lenders executed in Meissen porcelain – and yet I was perplexed to see that swastikas were painstakingly removed from imported American kits of model aircraft. The Austrian prosecution of neo-Nazis amounted to petty harassment: one could be jailed for sporting the swastika, or, in the case of an overweight neo-Nazi who had appeared in a film I had produced, immoderately criticizing the activities of the 'anti-Nazi' lobby, with its righteous pamphlets and self-conscious zeal. I hadn't much enjoyed meeting Jorg Haider, but I found his elevation to bogeyman confusing if not actually dishonest. He wasn't the only person whose father and mother had been Nazis – and many Austrians, I imagined, agreed with him when he praised Hitler for reducing unemployment. Meanwhile, most gestures of reparation from even so-called 'correct' politicians were too late and consisted of too little. Why had the Austrian Parliament in 1995, finally, offered only £20 million to the survivors of *Kristallnacht*? Why had it taken all this time for Austrian politicians to acknowledge that the country was a participant as well as a war victim?

'More lies, more delusions, more shit,' she said briskly. 'The neo-Nazis aren't in themselves important. They're like cranky fundamentalist religious sects, and they do sometimes try to kill people. However, they represent the hidden reality of Austria – and that is what we all of us fear. After all we supplied the *verlederhosung* – the lederhosenization – of National Socialism. We were all of us Nazis, really. The homo-erotic side of Nazism comes from Austria, and the association with the Catholic Church. So we repress what we think we still might love – self-

repression is a national industry. Our fear is of what we are
– deep kitsch, deep Nazism, deepest Austria.'

You can get round Austria quickly, and I drove clockwise
from Vienna, first east and southwards, to the Hungarian
border, and then to the west, into the old German provinces
of the Empire. Between long, dark tunnels and distant
snowy Alps, I saw Trapp-like meadows, and, as I passed
roadside *Gasthäuser* or small houses, brazen pink or red
flowers lodged picturesquely on dark-wood window-ledges
from which leant twinkly-eyed peasants dressed in dark
blue, wearing caps or checked kerchiefs. At the German
frontier at last, I stopped in the gabled *platz* of Braunau
on the Inn, and I walked a few hundred yards to Hitler's
birthplace, a comfortable, three-storey bourgeois building,
exactly the sort of homely, dignified place in which you
would expect to find the family of a minor imperial official.
The Hitler apartment had tactfully been turned into a
children's library, and I could glimpse the side of Big Bird's
head through the window, amid stacks of neatly piled books
and primary-coloured building blocks. Today was April 30,
1995, the fiftieth anniversary of Hitler's death in his Berlin
bunker, attended by Eva Braun and his faithful dog, after a
last vegetarian meal. In this so-quiet Austrian street there
stood a lump of stone to mark the site, piously dedicated to
the victims of Fascism, scrubbed free of furtive graffiti
and the stains of hastily dumped impromptu bouquets.

I drove back to the Danube, following the route taken by
Hitler's troops when he returned in 1938, driving through
village after village, each of them spotless, hung with red-
and-white flags ready for May Day, eerily empty in the
sunlight. Finally, I parked the car by the river in Linz. This
was where Hitler, like Ludwig Wittgenstein, attended the
Realschule from 1900 to 1902 (Hitler's grades were poor,

unlike Wittgenstein's, and he lied about them), learning about disgruntled German nationalism from a militant schoolmaster. The *Führer* loved Linz as an ideal Great German place as much as he detested cosmopolitan Jew-dominated Vienna, and in his bunker he kept a scale model of the city, showing astonished visitors the renovations he had in mind when the war was finished. From time to time a debate arose over whether some sort of public acknow-ledgement of Hitler's Austrianness should be made; but the answer, sustained by the expressed fear that such a site might become a cult object or a sacred place of pilgrimage, was always no. I walked around the city, which was green and leafy, boring in a distinctively German way. On the *platz* teenagers took part in a skateboarding contest spon-sored by the makers of ski lifts, and as I celebrated the moment of Hitler's death by eating a *Linzertorte* – brown but chocolate-free, unlike its superior Vienna counterparts – I tried to imagine how the members of the Parallel Com-mittee, given the assignment, would have tackled the problem of commemoration. Well, they would have talked to the usual charlatan anthropologists, performance artists, bouffant-haired game-show hosts and corporate astrolog-ists; and I imagine – times were more liberal then, remember – they would dutifully have consulted a few of the more respectable skinheads, trucked in from sewing ski clothing in their progressive prisons. But I felt certain that these worthies would fastidiously have come to no readily formulated conclusions.

For we wanted memory in Europe, but not its evil or painful consequences. Knowing and not knowing, which was the Austrian style of correctness, had become our ideal state, reflected in the absurd but pervasive conception of 'heritage', affixed to any site tasteful enough to accommo-

date paying visitors. 'In Western Europe you have
cathedrals,' a Polish friend once said to me lugubriously;
'here we only have concentration camps.' But, as he would
be the first to acknowledge, the Shoah business was now
thriving; and battlefield tours of Sarajevo and its environs,
gratuities included, were sure to be advertised soon. You
could catch oblivion fever as well as cold amid the rain-
lashed Marne valley battlefields of 1914 while shaking
hands with Pluto; and now a disco bunker in Berlin was
on the cards, and, on the territory of the old, unlamented
German Democratic Republic, an instructional park dedicated to the horrors of Communism complete with dogs,
barbed wire and police fiches.

Walking by the Danube, where Hitler wanted to erect an
opera house seating 35,000, an art gallery and a 300-foot
bell tower dedicated to German Culture, as well as a mauso-
leum for his parents, I came across lighted stores and
enormous tents. Outside, children bought and hugged huge
fair-haired dolls, or were twirled upside down screaming in
machines from Stuttgart; inside, while I ate *bauernwurst* and
frankfurters, Ferdy and His Outlaws, an all-male oompah
band wearing lederhosen, high heels, D-cup bras and blond
wigs plaited with red braid, sang very loud songs in which
the words *Prosit* and *Gemütlichkeit* occurred with great
regularity. With each chorus, people banged their mugs on
the table, swaying happily. A stout waitress came by and
asked if I wanted a torte. I looked at the quaking chocolate
alps and the streaming glacier cakes. No, I said, perhaps
later; and I walked out into the night, which was still full of
noise and light, heavy with the smell of burning meat.

Standing by the glass-black Danube, I finally located the
source of the fear which had pursued me in Austria. It came
not from the Biblical realization that everything would be

ultimately forgotten but from the acknowledgement that death, in particular the death of those with whom one shares nothing, doesn't matter. I recalled that Karl Kraus described Austria as 'the experimental ground of European destruction', and in this, as in so many other things, he was surely correct. But now I was certain that the real Austrian mistake – it was a common one, easily made – was merely to have insisted so unequivocally, so very tactlessly and unhypocritically, on the right to forget.

None of this, I imagined, was exactly what Austrians, who retained a high opinion of their national inheritance, specially wanted to hear, but it did occur to me that they could take consolation from the notion that, as historical memory was replaced by the organized sentimentalism of Heritage Culture, much of Europe was beginning to seem distinctly Austrian. Meanwhile, I resolved to think of tortes and the Danube as each waltz bar jogged us closer to oblivion.

Bologna: in the Loop

Orthodoxy is unconsciousness.

1984, George Orwell

In Bologna I was introduced to a distinguished, silver-haired ex-correspondent of RAI, the Italian State broadcaster. He had been hurriedly appointed to a post in Moscow in the early 1960s as part of a last-minute effort to fill the hitherto neglected Socialist quota. Later he had hosted experimental game shows sponsored by non-existent makers of imaginary products, and had forced teachers from remote Sicilian villages to try out their pedagogic style on the rush-hour crowds in Rome. But at some point in the 1980s, shortly after the failure of his experimental drama, a remake of Virgil's *Aeneid*, set in the remote Sardinia of Mussolini's 1930s Italy and featuring the island's breed of black-faced sheep, his career had appeared to falter. He was side-lined, receiving the obscure but bureaucratically important post of acting as liaison between RAI and the political parties. Although he had lost his faith in the present dispensation, Vittorio still believed in the power for good or evil of television. I can't remember exactly when it was – over the *funghi porcini* or *porchetto* – that he started talking about theology. Television, he maintained, had been once been Catholic in character, but now its inspiration was essentially Protestant. Not just for

Italians, but for all Europeans, indeed for the entire world, it had ceased to represent the totality of things, becoming instead a vehicle for the expression of an aggregate of small, insignificant actions, like buying or selling things. Its death, he suggested, would shortly follow, just as the Enlightenment had followed the Counter-Reformation, and paintings of small dogs or *pulchinelli* had come after Michelangelo. Nowadays, he said with a touch of bitterness, there was nothing real about television, just as there was nothing significant about Italian political life – it was all fakery.

I asked Vittorio what he thought about Silvio Berlusconi, Europe's first politician to be wholly created by television. He had been Prime Minister until six months ago, and was now engaged in a series of obscure manoeuvres which would enable him both to keep his holdings and to run again as head of the new party, *Forza Italia*, which he had created. I pointed out that Berlusconi's campaign had been notorious for its espousal of Catholic family values – he had even signed up a television prelate to give tone to his utterances.

'There you are,' Vittorio said, ignoring my observation. 'Berlusconi is a sign of the new non-reality. The question is: did we create him? I feel he has been with me all my life. Sometimes, watching him on television, I feel I am him. I feel I dreamed him into existence.'

I didn't share Vittorio's highly developed terror of Berlusconi, but at some point in the 1990s I did begin to experience a certain queasiness in relation not merely to the power of television, but to its reality quotient, too. My first day back at the BBC, a bright, cold day in April, when the clocks were striking thirteen, I went to the canteen. Someone I hadn't seen for twenty years was eating what appeared to be a well-preserved helping of pork and crackling with apple sauce while reading the *Guardian*. He greeted me without apparent surprise, as if I'd never been away.

I walked down green and brown corridors, and they were reassuringly full of memories; so was the strange institutional smell. Turning a corner – they came at the end of long stretches of straight passageway, and they were like doglegs on the old arterial roads – I could have been in the world inhabited by the tweedy, neurotic BBC man played by Dirk Bogarde in John Schlesinger's 1960s movie *Darling*, shafted without afterthought by bitch goddess Julie Christie.

'For most people there are only two places in the world,' says a character in Don DeLillo's *White Noise*, a novel which describes the problematic relationship between Americans and whatever appears on their TV screens each night: 'Where they live and their TV set.' In American television this second place was easily identifiable, coming as it did within the interstices of advertisements for products and containing entertainment; but in Europe television had been fussed over since its inception by élites who dreaded its misuse, and were determined that it shouldn't ever exceed some sort of permitted limit of unseriousness. By the 1990s, however, what had been perceived as the exceptional nature of television had progressively vanished – it had come to seem like any other place. True, efforts were being made to protect it, as they had been made in relation to rapeseed or orange groves. But I felt that television was winning the battle, and not its high-minded guardians. There was more television each year, even if it wasn't 'European' in the sense that had been understood. Certainly, albeit in ways that no one yet quite understood, European television was changing the character of Europe itself.

I recalled that Orwell had worked during the war in the Indian Service, and that he used the BBC as a model for *1984*, but I was nonetheless surprised to be walking straight into a cosier version of the cubicle of the Ministry of Truth occupied by Winston Smith, with its telescreen, its speak-write orifice, and the gratings or tubes (they were updated as e-mail, but no one made use of the facility) through which messages could be sent or received. Not just the newspeak, but the BBC dissident culture, too, I noticed, was neo-Orwellian, consisting of whispers, paranoiacally heightened, about the 'vaporization' of much-loved colleagues, or the ejection of cherished projects down the 'memory hole'.

Although he fretted ceaselessly, claiming to have discovered that none of his broadcasts ever reached their Indian destination, Orwell did much good work, which gave him pleasure, and he retained some sense of the need for the wartime BBC – a fact which went some way towards explaining why *1984*, despite the fall of totalitarianism throughout the world, remained so powerful and interesting a fable of the perversion of information. 'Re cynicism, you'd be cynical yourself if you were in this job,' remarked Orwell to his friend Rayner Heppenstall in 1943, shortly after he had committed an on-air gaffe, and a Church of England clergyman had been allocated to him as a censor, sitting beside him to press the button if he erred once again. 'At present I am just an orange that has been trodden on by a very dirty boot.'

When I arrived in 1994 the BBC had just spent six years in the quest of what its enemies (of whom there were many) called a more up-to-date version of Orwell's boot. One chilly morning, we were ordered into a training session where we watched a video telling us how to deal with our staff. Done as cheerful parody, the film purported to show the worst traits of British management by means of a series of teeth-grating sketches. After a few minutes, I realized that every one of the actors was a stalwart of BBC comedy shows; and I recalled that the company which had made the film, and thus the director and the scriptwriter, had also come from the BBC. What they had ended by depicting, perhaps affectionately, but with deadly accuracy, were the foibles of the Corporation itself.

A week later I was sent to a leadership training course held in a St Trinian's-style former girls' school somewhere in the Home Counties, where I spent two days contemplating such matters as Corporate Strategy and Niche Marketing before settling down to the Definition of Leadership. The corporate models, displayed by means of complicated diagrams rendered on acetate, were American, pre-1968 in their inspiration, predominantly drawn from discredited branches of the behavioural sciences; they bore scant resemblance to my own experience. As a journalist, I was what one earnest leisure-suited course instructor called 'one of nature's puncturers'; now I was being asked, Winston Smith-style, along with my restless or confused peers, to become a 'builder'. Perversely, to put off the awesome task of mental prosthetics, I wondered first about the conspicuous absence of leadership in the contemporary world, and then about the need for an institution so old and widely respected as the BBC to submit itself to so protracted a process of self-reconstruction.

Like Vittorio, I was forced at last to think about broadcasting. What was the point of television? What did it do to those who (like myself) watched it a great deal? Was it a drug or a means of illumination? The American journalist Edward R. Murrow warned solemnly as long ago as 1962 of the failure of television. If the medium ceased to fulfil its educational or journalistic function, Murrow said, in a famous speech given to a group of advertisers, which effectively ended his television career, it would become 'nothing but a box full of wires'. The same point was made in a 1990 lecture at Oxford by Saul Bellow, only in more disgruntled and apocalyptic tones:

> Nothing can be done. Television has proved that millions of people passionately love lust and violence. I am concerned here with the contribution TV makes to our distractions. It is the principal source of the noise peculiar to our time – an illuminated noise that claims our attention not in order to concentrate it, but to disperse it. Watching the tube we are induced to focus on nothing in particular . . . And perhaps what we look for is distraction – distraction in the form of a phantom or an approximate reality.

At the end of the film *Quiz Show*, a character remarked, apropos the 1950s Congressional investigations of fraud: 'If we don't get television, television will get us.' Not just in New York, but in London, too, fashionable audiences applauded these lines. Although I didn't agree with the Bellow analysis in its entirety I did come to feel that television was perceptibly ageing, with the century. The old promises of technology were increasingly directed outside television itself – to the Utopian Internet, for instance – or restricted to narrower questions involving 'choice', such as the number of channels, or the means – pay per view, online archives, and so on – by which such choices could be brought to customers. Meanwhile private interests had come to dominate the international scene, dwarfing the BBC and rendering plausible the eventuality of huge Big-

Brother-like baronies whose remote owners were effort-lessly capable of dominating our imaginations.

Ten years ago, one might confidently have contrasted the varieties of public, or semi-public, television in Europe with the commercial model originating in America; but the balance between public and private had been destroyed. Now the European broadcasters, if not actually threatened with extinction, were defensive, seemingly lost, lacking in *raison d'être*. If they competed against their new commercial rivals, they seemed to become like them; if they failed to compete, they lost their privileged position as recipients of public money or trust. In France, Germany, Italy, even in Finland, old-style 'pubcasters', as the magazine *Variety* called them, had panicked, shedding their customs and sometimes even their clothes in the pursuit of ratings.

Executives from European stations came by busload to visit the BBC as if it were a secular shrine, and they mar-velled at the shabby, characterless buildings as if some portion of British history – something from the heroic days of World War Two, or the costume series they bought and laughed at – had been cunningly or mysteriously preserved. But I noticed that their own presentations, which were full of charts and graphs, stressed the indistinguishability of their product from those of their commercial rivals. I asked the head of one of the French public stations how he could justify so little apparently serious or informational material in prime time, and he replied that it was inevitable; that was how the advertisers now wanted things. 'We would much rather not take advertisements, like the BBC,' he said in excellent English. 'Still, we are different from our commer-cial rivals. We've kept some elements of taste. We do show less *cul* – less ass.'

The trouble was that there was no real way of knowing

what television did or didn't do – and any conclusions to the effect that it had or hadn't been better, were invariably affected by such extraneous factors as the age, or grumpiness, of the observer. However, some qualitative change had taken place in the scope or influence of television. This came from the growing capability of television to invent our own lives, and, having done so, take them over. The most perceptive views of this 'phantom reality' came from Italy, also the European country where television was, by common consent, most appalling. One of the characters in Nanni Moretti's film *Dear Diary*, an essay examining the debauched state of contemporary Italian culture, was a professor who, in whatever ravishing site he found himself, had only one unbudgeable priority: to find out what had happened to the characters in his favourite soap, *The Bold and the Beautiful*. The professor's addiction had gone so far that he now disliked nature, running down hills and jumping onto departing ferries in order to get back to TV. 'Gods!' he cried out: 'Goddesses! Children watch television to daydream, as they did in the old days, listening to fables. Television is wonderful!'

In Bologna, there were arcades everywhere, and the streets were a reddish-ochre colour festooned with half-ripped posters advertising past political rallies, or hauntingly faded rust-coloured blinds, ripped in places, hanging adrift. I walked each morning past shops selling bags and shoes, skin mags or soft-porn videos, and, in the covered markets, carefully stacked small mountains of *porcini, radicchio, grana* cheese, pears and apples. Crossing the piazza, which was pleasantly used-looking, I turned under the statue of Neptune, flanked by sphinx-like overweight nymphs, climbing the high stairs around a shaded courtyard. There, in a small cubicle, as a juror of the prestigious

Prix Italia, harassed intermittently by kindly red-suited teenage attendants whenever I tried to escape, I sat before a large television screen for ten days.

The first day started well with a three-hour film recounting the struggles of two young black basketball players in Chicago. *Hoop Dreams* had taken five years to make; but it had earned fame and money for its makers, being shown in cinemas as well as on television. After the showing of a Belgian film about prostitution on the Cuba beach front, the proceedings faltered. However, it required the showing of a Greek modern-day version of the passion, featuring a cut-price look-alike of Melina Mercouri playing a Mary Magdalen with unshaven armpits, before I realized exactly what we were in for.

In the following days, like demented Phileas Foggs, we were rotated in a bizarre global centrifuge through Finnish monasteries, Irish cemeteries, Russian unmarked graves, German war rubble, Belgian old people's homes, severely handicapped, winsome French girls, Danish fertility clinics full of pink, unexciting couples, and vast, featureless, Mexican rubbish tips. We were entertained by Croatian violinists, Slovakian hot-air ballooners, Cameroon footballers, and offered, as objects of sympathy, Macedonian teenage gypsies and small emaciated Haitian boys. I felt I now knew that small boys ate food from the rubbish dumps of the rich; and I was aware that hookers leant through car windows in the course of their negotiations. Craving air and Bologna I began to note varieties of badness: *pseudo-verité* films that scrutinized their subjects as if they were cut-price watches in air terminals or piles of half-frozen sushi; vacuous, opportunistic 'histories' accompanied by portentous wind music; ethnic sentimentalism of the chummy, mateish sort practised by the bureaucracies of *ancien régime* socialism. Several years ago, every dolphin, Andy Warhol-style, had his minute of honking stardom; then it was the turn of transvestites, and AIDS victims; and after that Plains Indians. Now, particularly among wealthy Europeans, socio-sexual tourism was in vogue.

Back in my hotel room, I noticed the pervasive ornateness of Italian television, and its disconnectedness. As Vittorio had explained, it had come to resemble a series of less than relevant details in a baroque ceiling – fluffy clouds, a hand raised in exclamation, dogs playing around billowing white Papal robes while they waited for their food. Everywhere, I found parody versions of families entertaining each other. The teen stars resembled the motherly, not quite blonde, game-show hosts, and they bore some remote familial resemblance to the grey-haired newscasters gesticulating over pictures of Camorra killings, or reports of somnambulism in Calabrian schools. I saw a lot of the Pope, who was being entertained by frisky, straw-skirted tribal dancers in Africa. I also saw Berlusconi frequently, on his own channels in particular, at football matches or through car windows. Yet it was the colours that perplexed me most: pistachios, mulberry pinks, halo-yellow hairdos, fleecy whites and cerulean blues. I remembered that a friend of mine, coming from the old Eastern bloc, found her eyes hurting in Milan – test after test was required to convince her that in Italy things *were* brighter.

Each day I walked through the rust-redness of Bologna. Once upon a time the city had served as a model of what a Communist government could do; now it was cited proudly as an instance of what good could come of Italian chaos. It had the air not of a small provincial centre, but of a confident city state. 'Basso, Bye Bye,' a message said on the side of the buses – which turned out to mean that one could now buy panties which eliminated the low-slung *culo*. Climbing a great number of stairs of a medieval tower situated at the end of Via Rizzoli I reached a dizzy look-out, from which could be seen, growing outwards into the green plain, red roofs, hangars, campanile towers, factories. There was nothing special about these individual pieces, and yet they fitted together. One evening I passed a large crowd of people waiting for a night-club to open. They were wearing white stiletto heels, striped matelot tunics, distressed boots or jackets, and their hair was gelled, or cut into elaborate topiary shapes. They looked wonderful. Italians had invented popular culture; and I wondered why so little of its inventive spirit was available on television.

I could distinguish Berlusconi's representatives from the RAI men only by the superior quality of suit, a top-of-the-range model in the formers' case, cut with a double breast, and worn with a brighter spangled tie. None of them particularly wanted to talk to me about their boss. In between lengthy colloquies, I learnt that RAI had been the creation of Mussolini's Fascist state, but it was allowed to survive after the war, so long as it adapted itself to democracy. In the early years, there was a spirit of optimism; many bold initiatives were taken, including the creation of the *Prix Italia*. For thirty-five years, RAI exercised its monopoly under the tutelage of the Vatican and the political parties. If its identity was determined largely by patronage its tone was overwhelmingly moral and pedagogical, and such banal accomplishments as news reporting took second place to the preservation of morals in a time of mass internal emigration and changing mores. In 1957, when advertising was introduced, the Vatican insisted that the spots should not be spread throughout the evening, but grouped in one half-hour, transmitted at peak time, before the evening news. *Carosello* became the most popular show on television. The film-maker Pier Paolo Pasolini understood exactly what was going on:

> The Vatican never understood what it should or should not have censored. For example, it should have censored *Carosello* because it is here that the new type of Italian life explodes on our screens with absolute clarity . . . On the other hand the purely religious broadcasts are so tedious and so repressive in spirit that the Vatican would have done well to censor the lot.

Attempts were made to reform RAI; but they ended in a tightening of the political noose. Often, good or even great films were made, by such directors as Roberto Rossellini or the Taviani brothers; but there were fewer of them as '*lottizzazione*' – the parcelling-out of jobs as political favours – spread through the organization.

When the monopoly finally ended in 1979, predominantly local private stations which had been created at RAI's insistence – the idea was that they would be too weak to compete – went bust rapidly. Many of them were bought up by a Milanese supermarket operator, real-estate developer, publisher and football fan, Silvio Berlusconi. He had worked as a crooner on a cruise ship, and he had a degree in marketing. Now he wanted to own an Italian network. Because he was forbidden to do this by law he began to ship tapes by motor-cycle courier, supplying the same programmes to each local station with instructions on how, and when, to present them. This gave viewers the illusion that his channel was a national one.

Berlusconi started with Channel Five, but he next acquired *Italia 1* and *Retequattro*. It was impossible for him to broadcast either sport or news because RAI controlled the transmitters – instead he showed foreign soaps. He began to distinguish the channels by colours. Red stood for Channel Five, which was packed with family fare, mostly imported cartoons, talk shows, variety acts; blue was prominent on *Italia 1*, the colour for young people; and pink ('the colour of all women') characterized *Retequattro*. Simple as it may seem, the Berlusconi formula was disastrous for his competitors. Within three years of the creation of these makeshift networks, Berlusconi had drawn level with RAI. He had also transformed Fininvest, the holding company of his various operations, into the third largest commercial group in Italy (it was the largest private company) and, with Kirsch, Bertelsmann and the Murdoch interests, one of the most significant media concentrations in Europe, borrowing trillions of lire in order to do so.

I watched a series of tapes made by Berlusconi's own employees. The political commercials were, to anyone exposed to North American professionalism in such matters, strikingly dated. They presented their quiet-voiced boss as a Mr Clean circa 1960, well-suited and a little dull, against choirs and swelling music. More revealing were the revivalist tones in which Berlusconi's marketing experts coached new political activists (most of Berlusconi's supporters owed their livelihoods to him, either directly or as a consequence of emulation) by contrasting the psychometric profiles of the various candidates. It turned out that enthusiasm and novelty were the qualities most admired in Berlusconi, and his supporters were not unnaturally encouraged to replicate them. *Forza Italia* ('Go Italy'), Berlusconi's political movement, was based on the idea of a football supporters' club, with flags and other rewards for financial expressions of activism. Berlusconi's policies were not merely tested, but in many instances formulated by means of the polling organizations which he also owned, and which did work for his television stations, supermarkets and publishing houses. It would have been possible by the mid-1990s for an Italian to live in a Berlusconi home, shop in his supermarkets, read his papers, buy his books and watch his television, while belonging to his football club or his political party.

How had he been able to accumulate so much power? In between hits of espresso the suited luminaries of Italian TV to whom I spoke explained that people wanted a 'safe' resolution to the grotesque outburst of scandals of the 1990s; what they got – and it lasted as long as a medium-size television run – was the illusion of safety. Secure within the loop he owned, protected from rude interruptions of reality, Berlusconi was as much a creation of his own marketing instincts as his channels had been – and this accounted for his maladroit behaviour when confronted by what remained of the 'real' public world of Italian politics. He tried, unsuccessfully, to sack the board of RAI; and he was rebuffed in his attempts to privatize one of RAI's three channels. However, Fininvest did survive an equally maladroit effort to destroy the Berlusconi hold on Italian media, and in a typical Italian way, therefore, conflict had ended in stalemate and compromise – with a deepening of the contempt in which Italians held their politicians, and their national institutions.

Prizes were handed out in the gilt surroundings of the *Teatro Municipale* after a *con brio* performance of an obscure bassoon concerto executed by a soloist with a Gorgon head of hair and beard. The Berlusconi-appointed President of RAI was the wife of a businessman who owned a cable franchise in Lombardy. She was handsome in a horse-faced way, dressed from head to toe in lurid Versace pinks; and her handshake was a steel trap. I sat next to Vittorio during her speech, which was very long, containing words like pluralism, market, competitiveness, new technology, deregulation. 'Well, she has a good memory, though her little girl voice is a bit much,' Vittorio whispered loudly to me. At the end, amid the applause, which was perfunctory, he turned to me. 'It never really ends,' he said sadly. 'All Italians, and Berlusconi most of all, have no sense whatever of what is decent or merely appropriate. In the *haute bour-geoisie*, when the children leave home, it's usual for the wife to open a shop – selling flowers maybe, or clothes. Letizia was lucky – instead of a shop, she got RAI.'

Next day I went to a narrow, cypress-lined street filled with the kind of shuttered, anonymous villas frequented by currency smugglers or quack psychologists. Dressed in an elegant aquamarine Prince of Wales jacket, the Professor of Semiology and best-selling novelist Umberto Eco was on his knees rummaging through piles of books. He had just opened a conference in Milan dedicated to the theme of Information Utopia, and he was about to travel for a month, promoting his new novel about a man lost in the sixteenth century on the international dateline.

In the old days, Eco explained, he had written about the concept of hyper-reality, or the parallel existence, inside and outside the media, of complementary versions of the world. But he had failed to anticipate how the world could start to live through television itself. The problem now was that we didn't know what the President of the Republic thought: we were only aware of what television said or implied that he might be thinking. Berlusconi had by now become a part of the reality which he described. In a sense he had become more important than the Italian State itself.

But it was also possible to exaggerate the importance of Berlusconi – if there was no such person, a similar, perhaps even more grotesque phenomenon would have arisen.

Eco slithered happily from one category to another in a most un-Anglo-Saxon way. It was easy to interview him, harder to grasp the implications of what he was saying. I remembered how ambivalent he had been about the claims of technology twenty years previously, when he wasn't a best-selling novelist, and I wondered what he thought of the Internet Utopia.

'I browse,' he said. 'The problem – it's the essence of the end of the century – is that there's too much of everything. In the end, the abundance of information, just like the excess of food, or sleep, or love, leads to boredom if not paralysis. A man in America has put photographs of his colon on the Internet – just imagine it! How do you know something will be useful any more? How do you acquire information about information?'

He looked at book after book. Most of them were dense semiological treatises. Smiling, he lifted a small pile towards me.

'I bought a bag in Paris,' he said. 'It carried four or five books, and you could stow it under an aircraft seat. Then I went back to the shop, and it wasn't there any more. As a bag, it was too good for the price – they stopped making it. Well, that has been the fate of television. It was possible to make wonderful things for television, but people had no economic reason to go on making them.'

I asked him whether he despaired of television. 'Not entirely,' he said, shrugging. It was clear that he was keen to pack his bags.

At Bologna airport the planes were late because of an air traffic controllers' strike. Instead of attending to the complaints, the Mastroianniesque officials took their rowdy charges to the aircraft, leaving them waiting while the engines turned. It was raining hard in Milan, and huge trucks pushed their way around the cramped road system. When I came to the studios I glimpsed barbed wire on top of perimeter fences, and a huge half-completed tower. After that the plate glass closed behind me.

I saw quiz shows, variety shows, family shows, news shows. In one small studio, where a stoutish, *décolletée*, faded blonde hostess was earnestly plumping a mattress of what appeared to be a spare bed, the young executive paused, conferring with our translator. 'Teleshopping,' the translator said. 'Much of our time is taken up with this. It takes longer than the shows.' Parliament, I learned, had passed a regulation punishing Berlusconi by forbidding the sponsorship of programmes. However, the Fininvest lawyers had established that it was all right for hosts to plug products on air, so long as their messages followed both the credits and the advertisements at the end of each show. Hence the spare bed.

We paused in front of the turquoise and yellow set of *La Ruota della Fortuna* (*The Wheel Of Fortune*), in which no less than three shows were recorded each day with the same audience. Another studio was divided into two – having sat through 'Do you know the one about?' (a rip-off the oldie *Candid Camera*) the audience could move seats for 'Joking Apart' (amateur comedy where one voted on whether the acts were funny or not). In another studio a platinum-haired teen star dressed in knee-length silver foil and wearing turquoise contact lenses was singing a torch song accompanied by a crowd of teenagers wearing pressed jeans and freshly laundered T-shirts. The effect was cold and eerie, as if the Moonies had annexed Sorrento.

Standing in the rain, I watched the teenage chorus file by.
They were talking eagerly about the show. Twenty or thirty
years ago, they might have attended Christian Democrat or
Communist rallies, or thought of placing bombs in railway
stations. I had been told that Berlusconi had destroyed the
old Italy of ideologies and parties, replacing it with his
brand of plebiscitary television politics. I had been
informed, too, that this was the real Fascism of the future.
But I was astonished at how little of Berlusconi's presence
there was in the building – no statue, no photograph, not
even a marble plaque. His blandness was of a piece with the
affectless, repetitious world of his programmes. Like sand
on the Italian beach towel, he had come and gone; and in
this respect, Berlusconi was like television itself.

I watched television differently after my encounter with
the Berlusconi empire – like a pathologist, or a tree doctor, I
was looking for the tell-tale signs of degradation. Along with
the rest of the world, I had been late in understanding the
new outlines of the post-Cold War world, and I could now
see in Berlusconi, like Rupert Murdoch, or American giants
such as Time Warner, a prototype, not necessarily of
political power – his attempts had been too gross, finally,
too incompetent – but of imaginative annexation. And I
could also imagine how in the Orwell style indifference
might characterize the acceptance of the new regime, so
that we wouldn't care to know what had happened to us.

A month later, I made my way through a turnstile surrounded by private security guards dressed in leopard-spot
camouflage battle dress, entering a *dacha* in the snowy
woods on the edge of St Petersburg. Inside there were
marble fireplaces, samovars, nineteenth-century land-
scapes. This was the headquarters of the Russkoye Video
Corporation, a 'state media company' formed out of the

wreckage of the old propaganda *apparat*. I wanted to see how the 'new' Russian capitalism functioned but what I found instead was an infant Berlusconi system. Like Fininvest, the company imported foreign television programmes. To begin with, it had given them free of charge to local stations, arranging for foreign advertisers to pay the American distributors, taking its fees by dubbing and shipping the tapes. Now that the company was richer, Russkoye Video could afford to buy Russian rights to the programmes. The company had its own TV station, it sold advertising – and it hoped to be able to send programmes anywhere in Russia. From being a mildly disreputable organization, used reluctantly by foreigners, 'RV' had come to occupy a privileged position, policing the market in imported videos, and insuring its own clients, mostly Americans, against piracy.

Nikita Matveyev, its amiable, bushy-moustached CEO for foreign affairs, was dressed in a Harris tweed jacket, with a blue button-down shirt and a rep tie. There was a diamond ring on his finger, and he spoke expansively, happily, circling his hands over a sheet of white paper.

'*Baywatch*,' he said. 'Russians love *Baywatch*. What is it about these life-savers in Santa Monica with large bosoms? The colder it is in Russia, the more miserable people are, the more they watch *Baywatch*.'

I asked him if he could buy local stations. 'Of course you can buy stations,' he said. 'If you have the money, you can buy anything. But it's less complicated not to buy them. It's better to send the programmes and sell the advertising. All they have to do is put the programme in the machine and turn it on.'

I asked him if he knew about Berlusconi. Was there a chance of creating that sort of concentration in Russia?

Who would be prepared to stop the equivalent of Berlusconi accumulating power?

'Nobody thinks about having that sort of power,' he said. 'At present they're more interested in money. But in Russia the State can decide anything. You don't need a case against a person, as you appear to require in Italy; you don't need magistrates. All you need is a car crash.'

I said that it would be a shame if Russian broadcasting, having existed so long as a state monopoly, was turned into a private one.

'One thing at a time,' he said affably. 'More *Baywatch*, please.'

Back at home at the BBC I found myself assailed by the past. I was in an antique brass-fitted rusty cream liner, sailing through the over-charted waters of British national culture. In 1995 the historian Asa Briggs completed the fifth volume of his vast and authoritative history of broadcasting in Britain, taking the persistent reader to 1974. Broadcasting, it emerged from this painstaking account, was half quiet administration and half adroit diplomacy, both activities being needed to keep the politicians and pressure groups at bay. And yet a hidden story began to emerge over thousands of pages – the inexorable dragging of the mandarinate of civil servants who ran the old BBC closer and closer to such vulgar notions as 'the market'. Nonetheless, I felt that the account was incomplete – what it didn't, or couldn't, show was the change in character of broadcasting itself, so that television, far from passively recording whatever was placed in front of it, had begun to alter or dissolve whatever it depicted. I couldn't date the emergence of television as agent; but I knew that what I had observed in Italy and Russia took place in a different world to the one governed by the old certainties.

In 1924, Lord Reith, the Calvinist founder of the BBC, set down his conception of 'the public' as part of its efforts to define what broadcasting should henceforth mean. Reith's views reflected those of his day – for him the public was the Great and the Good, with special emphasis placed on the sabbatarian character of Britain, and the Royal Family, whom Reith, by the importunate broadcasting of so many tedious minor weddings and flower-show openings, made into the divinely ordained and anointed idols of his new electronic realm. Reith was a monstrous man in many respects, a bully, a bigot and a hypocrite; and his personal views unattractively mixed toadyism with Presbyterian flummery – the historian A. J. P. Taylor complained that under his influence broadcasting was a dictatorship – but he spared the BBC both the abuses of totalitarianism and, for a long time, the depredations of market capitalism. But it was significant, too, that Reith hated and feared the power of the new medium which he sought to control – much of his credibility as a censor arose from the fact that he was willing to control a monster which members of the British Establishment of the day didn't deign to touch.

By the 1990s, however, Reith's high-mindedness as well as his old-fashioned powers of censorship were no longer in demand; both had been dissolved in the flood. In the old days exiles howled coyote-style at the BBC's Stalinist centralism, but nowadays their anger was directed at what they considered to be the absurd management practices legitimated by the pursuit of commercialism. I crossed London one evening, and sat talking to John Tusa in a psychedelically decorated office at the Barbican Centre, where, as director of the complex, he was trying to reorganize a concert schedule.

Tusa's father emigrated to Britain from post-war

Czechoslovakia. Unusually, Tusa *fils* rose in the BBC to become a journalist of consequence as well as a bureaucrat. He was head of the World Service radio at the time of the end of the Cold War; but he left after being passed over for the top job of director-general. Tusa now saw the dilemmas of broadcasters as part of a far wider problem, that of contemporary belief. Broadcasters were in his view bound to uphold the values that contributed to their privileged place – this was a very Reithian view – but they had signally failed to do so. The surrender had come about as a consequence of the end of the Cold War, which had downgraded the function of information while leading people to believe that the battles for freedom were over. He believed that society had lost the vocabulary for the definition of activities in any other than market terms. 'Well, that's not strictly true,' he said, avoiding the sweeping statement, as he had been taught to do. 'You *can* find economists prepared to offer a definition of public good. But such concepts only make sense if they are alive to people – and I don't think they are any more.'

Tusa had earnest, staring eyes, and sharp features arranged around an Expressionist sculptor's dream of bone structure; he spoke with a fluency that was astonishing. So much anglicization had ensured that he looked and dressed and sounded like *homo* BBC; but his *mitteleuropa* origins were apparent in a refusal to patronize as well as a reluctance to hide the certainty that he was right. Not unpleasantly I experienced a whiff of the old and celebrated BBC microphone authority.

I asked him how the BBC – or any other broadcaster – could differ in its attitudes from the rest of society. It was difficult to see how an island of conscience could be located in an archipelago of indifference. I could understand how he felt it should be possible for the BBC to defend itself against the enemies of barbarism; but not when people elsewhere were laying down their arms. In his austere way he did appear to be conceding that nothing about the times encouraged resistance.

'The BBC has evaded the obligation to define itself in terms of values,' he said. 'There's a logical contradiction at work in the present. At present BBC values can exist only if they can be reconciled with the market. But once you've analysed them in this way, you've effectively conceded the point. You've swallowed the values of the graph. It means that you dare not stand up and say: "Well, this is ours, this is here for other reasons." '

I thought of Orwell as I drove back through the London traffic. He would have been the first to warn that while things had got better, it had also become more difficult to resist the new evils. It was widely supposed that in *1984* people were conditioned to accept coerciveness; but the important thing about the book was that Orwell's characters chose their bondage. He would have said that we were handing power over our lives to people just as powerful as the old dictators, while mindlessly celebrating the values of 'freedom'. People felt they had no reason to resist – they wanted to be the things that destroyed them; but it would be too late by the time we all woke up.

Two important events occurred in British television during the 1990s. On the rock-bottom-budget cable channel Live TV, Kelvin MacKenzie, former editor of the *Sun*, inaugurated the News Bunny, a life-size puppet seated next to the dyslexic newsreader, grimacing or giving thumbs down to glum items while applauding occurrences that were likely to cheer up viewers. On November 12, 1995, the BBC broadcast a long interview with the Princess of Wales. Her giant-panda eye-shadow and mussed-up hair threw a pall of solemnity over the excessively rehearsed, frequently bathetic account of the coldness of her royal husband and the way she was let down by her lover, a not very intelligent, caddish Guards officer. I had a high temperature, and flu, and found it possible – briefly, before the prospect of so much sadness in the world was eclipsed by the intriguing revelation that she didn't think her husband was capable of being king – to take her seriously as she pleaded to be 'queen in our hearts'. Twenty-four million people hung on her words – the largest audience for a piece of BBC journalism – and I tried as I watched to translate the dilemma which John Tusa had expressed into the distorting-mirror world represented by the Princess and her sadness.

Television, I concluded as I watched the Princess and her eye-shadow, long ago engulfed the world it once pretended to mirror. It had exalted feelings over analysis, creating its own Utopian way of seeing things based on the illusion that everything was instantly comprehensible. On television everything was turned into simple, easily repeated plot-lines. Europeans had imagined that it was possible to create a 'cultural' form of television – but now the old rituals of state, church, even the vestiges of privacy or objectivity were being washed away, as Bellow had anticipated, in the cause of 'phantom reality'.

The Princess described how she liked to visit people in hospital, her sad eyes looming closer on the screen, and I could see millions in her face; but in my fever I knew that the currency was imperfectly franked even while I was addicted to its value. I took a large swig not of Victory Gin, but of Free World Vodka; and as I did so leaned forward, and like Winston Smith, watching Big Brother on his telescreen in the run-down circumstances of Victory Mansions, found my own flu-ridden face reflected in the image of the Princess. Quickly, I switched over to the News Bunny.

Paris: in the Abstract

Rien de nouveau.

Antoine Roquentin in *La Nausée*,
Jean-Paul Sartre (1938)

My acquaintance with abstract France began the day my French grandmother began to send me parcels of books at the posh English public school to which I had been sent. The parcels were poorly wrapped, covered with French stamps bearing the likeness of various bewigged grandees or minor provincial monuments; and I opened them avidly. Sometimes the books were untouched *Livres de Poche*, crisp and brightly coloured; other times she sent me her own NRF Gallimard copies, covered for re-reading by thick transparent paper, of the kind in which cakes were wrapped, tirelessly annotated in her spidery scrawl. I loved these books. I was happy to write the reader's reports which my grandmother demanded, and which she returned, corrected in red ink. She sent me Gide first – an odd choice, given his interest in boys, for a British single-sex school – then Camus, Sartre, Malraux, even Proust. I read them with hope and passion; this is how I came to believe in the power of the French word.

Which brings me to Bill. I can't remember which year I met him in Paris, but it must have been some time in the late 1970s. He hadn't yet sold his first script, indeed he had just abandoned a novel of six hundred pages, and he had been dumped not just by a studio, but by a girl-friend, too. That was why he was in Paris, and how I met him sitting with the tourists in the corniest of places, the *Café de Flore*, on the Boulevard St-Germain. Bill spoke no French whatsoever, but his knowledge of French literature, of the Left Bank in particular, and of its long-forgotten squabbles, was compendious. He had read an astonishing amount, mostly, as he explained, while working as a rent officer for New York City. He knew about existentialism because he had taken a degree, thanks to night classes, at the New School. About French people, however, he was relatively ignorant, and he was determined that I should redress this shortcoming.

'Show me some real intellectuals,' he said. 'I don't mind who they are, I don't mind if I have to pay for them. Just find me some real ones.'

It occurred to me that he wouldn't want to be told that, perhaps, French intellectuals weren't what he had been led to believe they were. Besides, I was curious myself. I had no idea what they would make of someone like Bill, or what he would think of them. But I found some intellectuals and booked a table at the *Brasserie Lipp*.

The Philliberts behaved properly. True, they didn't talk directly to Bill, or even to myself. They never asked questions. But they did give a full account of themselves – they told us what was the state of their particular world. It was like listening to the commentary of an old-fashioned dancing competition. Out they came, in a great rush, attached to concepts or *tendances*: psycho-linguistics, post-Marxism, meta-discursiveness, Michel, François, Louis-Ferdinand. A person could once have been something; now he or she (women figured very little here) was something else. Positions were adopted and abandoned; interests came and went. The dance went on. Bill drank astonishing quantities of wine. He slid steadily towards hostility through the meal. But he remained patient until Jean-Claude and Marguerite began to describe the altered sexual orientation of a couple they knew.

She had more than one degree in Mandarin Chinese, and would inherit a chateau in the vicinity of the Loire where Balzac had once written a minor *conte*. He was not from a good family, but nonetheless a *normalien*. They lived in some style somewhere nearby. As a consequence of her Lacanian analysis, it seemed as if she was contemplating an extensive programme of sexual self-revision. She had moved in with a woman friend – someone also *très bien*. But – here was the problem – it would be easier if he followed her. The question was whether he, too, could be induced to discover that he was homosexual.

'It can't be easy for him,' I said.

'Why not?' asked Jean-Claude.

'I don't see how it would be easy,' I said.

Marguerite added her own wisdom to the conversation. Her English was better than her husband's.

'She's always been, how do you say, clitoral . . .'

Jean-Claude raised his hands.

'Of course,' he said. 'He was attracted to her because of her *clitoralité*.'

That proved his point. He meant to say that sexual preferences, like anything else, could be shaped by words. His gesture expressed triumph. *Voilà!*

I looked at Bill, who had begun to laugh. He was very drunk, and his voice was deep and plummy, rumbling away, like that of Orson Welles.

'Clitoral,' he said. 'Clitoralness. The clitoral life – well, it's an idea to conjure with. I love it. Does the adjective qualify the noun, or is it governed by it? Does it apply to males as well as females? Could it apply to animals? Is it a state of mind? "And now to the Left Bank for the clitoral life . . ." You can't do better than that.'

He was still laughing as we stumbled along the Boulevard St-Germain to the river.

'Cocksuckers,' he boomed. 'Charlatans. The greatest buildings, the best food and the worst people. Maggots, all of them.'

We stood facing the Seine. It was an early summer evening, and cars drove past in the bluish light. Bill sniffed at the brackish river air in the style of Boudu looking to take a jump.

'You know *The Fall*?' Bill asked.

The Camus novella had been one of my grandmother's first and most valued presents – I had read it many times. The miserably smarmy hero, Jean-Baptiste Clamence, was a Left Bank lawyer, a proponent of good causes who came to distrust his altruistic impulses. He decided that he believed in nothing. Instead of keeping quiet about his loss of belief, he wished to impose it on the rest of the world. So he hung out in bars, in search of strangers, whom he attempted to convert to nihilism.

'You know the scene where he comes back from dinner. Where he's crossing the bridge in Paris, and he sees a woman by the parapet. Where he gets to the Left Bank, hears her scream, and doesn't turn back to get her. He delayed, and he was too late – he was thinking of something. He didn't do anything. That's the point of the book, right? Well, I've never been convinced by it. I want to know whether he could have jumped off after her.'

In the book the episode was supposed to have taken place on the Pont Royal, but we didn't have a copy of *The Fall*.

Starting at the Pont de la Concorde, we tried the nine-odd bridges to the end of the Ile de la Cité. The girl had to be standing near the parapet when she cried out; to jump after her, Jean-Baptiste had to be able to run either to the bank, or to the bridge. The quayside road, built since Camus' day, made it harder to go after suicides; and high parapets ruled out many of the bridges. Ultimately, we were in disagreement. I felt that, given the right bridge, a rescue might have taken place. Bill thought that such a feat, had it been attempted, would have impaled its perpetrator on a spike.

'I wonder if it matters,' I said finally. 'After all, he could be lying. It could never have happened at all. Or the girl might have jumped off, but in circumstances where he could never have saved her. He could simply be giving himself the pretext for guilt.'

We were standing outside Bill's hotel. He swayed towards me.

'You're right,' he said. 'The people here don't need excuses to feel guilty.'

He made a gesture of tipping a hat in the darkness.

'Farewell,' he said lugubriously. 'There has to be one place in the world like Paris, where you go to be let down.'

Many years reading the jokes in *Private Eye* hadn't entirely destroyed my respect for the French mind, but I was thinking of Bill the day I went to see Bernard-Henri Lévy. It was hot, and France were playing England at rugby for third place in the World Cup. I'd been given an address on the Boulevard St-Germain, between a shop selling large leather sofas and an outpost of the French Foreign Ministry. A butler dressed in a white jacket took me into a large sitting-room with high windows overlooking the street. I noticed an orientalist décor: foulards thrown over low couches, brass tables, spiked chairs, assemblages on coffee tables of scarabs and elephants. At one end of the room was a large Annunciation seemingly featuring a Virgin who convincingly resembled the actress Sarah Bernhardt. I sat down awkwardly, and waited. Outside, I could hear a phone being put down, and the butler returned, accompanied by a man who appeared to be his twin. It took me a while to understand that the butlers were from India, and spoke beautiful English. There had been some sort of a mistake, they explained; and they were very sorry. Perhaps I could come back later.

I crossed the Boulevard in the heat, taking the Rue des Saints-Pères until I reached the Rue de Grenelle. I could see my grandmother's old apartment on the corner, high above the street, and I remembered the irregular series of rooms, the various shades of grey and green in the upholstery, the strange whistling noise made by swallows. I also noticed that the door to the dark courtyard smelling of cats was now secured by a mechanism requiring you to dial a code.

The indifferent restaurant opposite was still there, so was the bar frequented by the smarty-boots students of the *Institut des Sciences Politiques* – *Sciences Po* as it was known – and their shrill-voiced *seizième* girl-friends. Elsewhere, things had changed. There were dress shops now instead of *cordonniers* or *papeteries* – magenta, scarlet and black shifts, or suits with short skirts, stood suspended above court pumps as if proclaiming the fashion status of levitation. I walked down to the Boulevard Raspail, oppressively shadowed by tall *Belle Epoque* buildings with brass doctors' plates inside each lobby, and I bought a collection of Camus' essays. Then I went to the *Café de Flore* where I sat and waited for BHL.

I'd read the latest instalment of BHL's oeuvre, *La Pureté Dangereuse* (*Dangerous Purity*), and it was much what I had expected: another *fin de siècle* lament, evoking fashionable doubts about the ability of democracy to survive the threats posed to its existence by the new 'fundamentalisms'. Now I opened the Camus at random, and came across 'Witness and Liberty', the speech he made before a packed audience of the left, when he broke with the Communists in 1948 after the *coups d'état* in Eastern Europe:

> To tell the truth, we French have somewhat fallen behind. Just about everywhere in the world, executioners have parked themselves in ministerial armchairs. All they have had to do is replace the blade with a rubber stamp. When death becomes a matter of statistics and administrative fiat, one has to come to the conclusion that the world is in a poor state. But if death becomes an abstraction, this is because life, too, is abstract. And the life of each individual can only be abstract from the moment that one decides that it should be subordinated to an ideology.

Seated at the café, I could smell the cigarette smoke in the Salle Pleyel, and I experienced the physical sensation of hatred. One didn't say such things in the company of intellectuals at the height of the Cold War – Camus made many enemies, among them Jean-Paul Sartre. An Algiers provincial, a poor boy rescued by the great French educational system, Camus was made to suffer for his courage. His own confidence, and the sense of his beautiful gifts, disappeared. 'A cynical or so-called realistic position makes it possible to be brutal or to despise people,' he wrote in his diary. 'That is why such qualities are so attractive to intellectuals.'

Camus withdrew from Paris after winning the Nobel Prize. He went to football matches, and set out to write a book about his lost life in Algeria before he fell among the Left Bank thieves. But Camus died in a car crash before finishing *The First Man*; and he went out of favour during the 1960s, a decade in which the claims of fanaticism were much prized. Now, by a process that would have made him smile, he was once more in fashion, fêted for his prescience by left and right alike. I wondered how he would have dealt with such slavish and indiscriminate praise.

France won at rugby, but it was a bad game, full of slipshod play. The butlers were waiting for me when I returned, and this time I was taken to a large *boiserie*-lined room with a view over the courtyard. BHL was wearing a summer version in linen of his famous black and white ensemble, with the habitual *décolletage*. He was talking on the phone to *Le Monde* about Salman Rushdie, whose release from the *fatwa* was said to be imminent. He couldn't do dinner because there was a piece to write about the lifting of the *fatwa* for *El País*. And now there was an Englishman here, and he had to go. But the phone kept ringing as we talked, first the copy desk of *Le Monde*, checking some aspect of his statement (the rumour, alas turned out to be false – BHL had underestimated the persistence of bigotry), then a member of the committee of support for Bosnia, to go through details of tomorrow's meeting with the President, and finally another dinner invitation, accepted with alacrity.

In France, Lévy was mildly resented for his raven-haired Malrauxesque looks, his beautiful actress wife, Arielle Dombasle, his talents and his considerable wealth, which came from a Jewish businessman father. He was considered by other intellectuals to be a pushy lightweight, whose achievements – a book of interviews about men and women with Françoise Giroud, collections of polemical essays, documentaries about Bosnia or the history of French intellectuals – lay in the realm of self-promotion. Nonetheless, it was Lévy, as as a member of the oddly titled *Nouveaux Philosophes*, who offered a critique of Soviet Communism during the 1970s – before it was fashionable in Paris to do so. For many French people, living far from the Left Bank, and watching television, Lévy was the real thing. The BHL profile was strong, easily recognized, *médiatique* – Lévy and Arielle had been targeted five times by the Belgian performance artist Noël Godin for *entartement* – custard pies thrown at celebrities.

I wanted to ask Lévy what particular qualities should cause the world these days to heed the views of a French intellectual. My point was a simple one – Marxism had created the need for a lay hieratic group capable of explaining its texts and punishing dissidence, and French intellectuals had been ideally placed to fulfil this role, due to the emphasis placed on exposition in French education, and the convenient proximity in Paris of small magazines, University lecture halls and café chairs. Now there were no ideologies capable of taking the place of Marxism, and people read fewer and fewer books.

Lévy appeared to be mildly shocked by what I had said. He explained that he did have an ideology, but it was a personal one. When I suggested that no one much liked Muslim fundamentalism, and wondered whether he hadn't become that ancient object of French reprobation, the Anglo-Saxon liberal, he threw his head back against the cushions of his sofa. 'Are you a journalist?' he asked. 'You don't look like one.'

I insisted that I was. It was on this basis that I had secured an interview with him.

'Well, I do have a system of thought that I have developed throughout my life, and that will come to an end only the

day I die. I'm definitely not one of those intellectuals who
have abandoned all efforts at cohesion.'

I suggested that the idea of a portmanteau global conscience was beginning to look dog-eared. I could see Camus
as a reporter, working in Bosnia; but it seemed that politicians throughout our soft Europe were deaf to such
appeals.

BHL shrugged. I had liked his film. Unlike his critics, I
appreciated the fact that he had been prepared to go to
Sarajevo, donning an elegant flak jacket. At least he had
been prepared to challenge politicians, in particular President Mitterrand. But I also thought the film was overstated
and excessively rhetorical.

'The cynicism of politicians bothers me less than it used
to,' he said. 'I no longer appeal to the conscience of states.
The real problem for me is the value placed by French
people on having any point of view, no matter what it is.
You know French people are always saying: "*Où sont les
polémistes d'antan?*" – where are the rows we used to have?'

Then the phone rang again. He gestured to me, indi-
cating that the audience was at an end. One of the butlers
smiled politely as he showed me to the door.

Next day I walked past the orderly hives of the bee-
keeping school in the *Jardin du Luxembourg*, skirting a multitude of pear and apple trees pinned back or fastened for
pedagogical display. Pausing at the children's puppet
theatre, where the same *Little Red Riding Hood* that I had
attended as a child was playing to packed houses, I entered,
abruptly and without warning, a piece of the old bourgeois
Paris out of Lartigue or Cartier-Bresson.

Poodles frisked aesthetically amid old men seated on dark
green chairs reading *L'Équipe*, and stern, yellow-eyed
women were still ritually appraising teenagers wearing pony

tails in the style of Brigitte Bardot. Around me, statues of ill-assorted worthies adorned the various tightly planned walks: Baudelaire, his cravat askew and his wide-eyed stare giving him the appearance of a coke sniffer; the busty Contesse de Ségur (née Rostropovich); minor bourgeois dramatist José Maria de Heredia, and, to one side, elegant Semitic features garlanded with birdshit, Pierre Mendès-France, the brave and civilized bourgeois socialist politician who during the 1950s got the French Army out of its fatal Indo-Chinese entanglement, and quixotically attempted – needless to say, it was a failure, on a par with BHL's efforts to get the *fatwa* lifted – to coerce the French into drinking milk rather than wine.

I felt suddenly important, as if I had walked into an expensive restaurant. By no means all of my bourgeois French family were rich or successful, but they shared a sense of social cohesion which was disappearing elsewhere in Europe. The notion that you were someone was considered to be a democratic right in France, not a privilege; it came free, legally tied to the definition of citizenship. French people did express their own sense of superiority to each other, but through the hierarchy of language. The educational system separated the talented from the less able, at the earliest age, and the consciousness of superiority was sculpted into each step climbed towards the various plinths of educational pre-eminence. I remembered my mother, my aunts or my grandmother grading children. They might say so-and-so had done well that year; but the real question was whether the child was intelligent or not. And no one bothered to conceal the existence of intelligence in France.

For the brightest children, membership of the various castes in France – the old *École Normale Supérieure*, the engineering *Polytechnique*, or the *École Nationale d'Adminis-tration* – conferred the ultimate privilege in France: the certainty that one was an important person. I had grown up revering these places and their acronyms – but experien-cing, too, a revulsion towards the claims of superior intelligence which their existence implied. For these were not egalitarian institutions – they existed by courtesy of the bourgeois world, to ensure its survival. By the crass standards of the world outside the garden, they granted unthinkable privileges.

My own doubts about the claims of French intelligence had nonetheless surfaced early, during the outbursts of the 1960s. Was violence really as *convenable* as French intellec-tuals made out? 'A revolutionary regime must dispose of a certain number of individuals which threaten it, and I can see no other means of accomplishing this than death. One can always get out of prison. The 1793 revolutionaries probably didn't kill enough people.' This was the middle-aged Maoist Sartre, addressing his groupies after the Cul-tural Revolution from the safety of the Left Bank. When Sartre died in 1980, he was a national hero; 100,000 people walked behind his coffin to the *Père Lachaise* cemetery. 'One doesn't imprison Voltaire,' de Gaulle remarked amiably, when Sartre's seditious broadsheet-selling activities were brought to his attention. This was all right as a remark – but it seemed unfair to Voltaire, who to his credit never thought killing people was a good idea.

I reached the edge of the gravel paths, where they com-bined to meet an elegant balustrade overlooking the small pond and, beyond it, the palace. A convent was sacked here during the Revolution, but the *sans-culottes* had had the good aesthetic sense to leave intact the statuary depicting the Kings and Queens of France. The garden, as my Gallimard guide informed me, was easily restored to its pre-revolutionary elegance. Brief and theatrical, revolutionary episodes in France endured as words. The babble of the mass media notwithstanding, words were still considered to be eternal; they alone could establish the claim to universality of French culture. I paused in the sunlight, looking around. There must be some connection between the finished, unalterable air of aesthetic perfection, the cult of words and the exercise of violence. Perhaps that was the real French contribution to civilization.

Outside the green and gold gates I crossed the sticky waste of Boulevard St-Michel. This was where, during the summer months of 1968, large barricades were created by the students of the Quartier Latin. I didn't go to Paris – I recalled reading a piece in the left-wing *New Statesman* casting doubt on the notion that this was anything new, and, rightly or wrongly, feeling reassured. In Prague, the rioting led to a Russian invasion, prefiguring the end of *ancien régime* Communism twenty-two years later; and in the United States radicals established that it would henceforth be impossible to fight an unpopular war lasting longer than the odd month. In Paris, however, the bourgeois right returned to power after a brief, unpleasant shock. The French students, practically speaking, accomplished nothing. Many of them ended up making television pro-grammes devoted to the mythology which they had created.

I walked up Rue Soufflot to the Panthéon. A Swedish student was with me when the gate opened; otherwise the dark, echoing space was entirely empty. Sleek, ineffably *de ses jours* in its original conception, that of a rationalist Lumières church cunningly mixing architectural styles, the building underwent ceaseless modification in the next century, according to the ideological orientation of the current regime. It became a shrine dedicated to the cult of great men during the Revolution, was reconsecrated under Napoleon, rededicated to secularism in 1830, adapted to dual sacred and profane use in 1852, and finally returned to exclusively secular use in 1885, just before the one hundredth anniversary of the Revolution. I looked at the Puvis de Chavannes rendering of Ste Geneviève saving the people of Paris from their Goth invaders; perched on postmodern-looking battlements, she was neatly dressed in fashionable oatmeal, and her studious air gave her the appearance of a young Simone de Beauvoir. Downstairs, I passed the tombs of Jaurès, Hugo, Schoelcher, Voltaire, and I paused at the gold hand suggestively passing a baton from Rousseau's tomb. Then I heard distant music beckoning me, and I walked over to a video exhibit in which, to the accompaniment of the 'Ode To Joy', President Mitterrand strolled through the crypt I had just left, looking to each side and carrying large pink roses.

I remembered the ceremony, which had taken place in 1981; indeed I had written about it. The Quartier Latin was cordoned off, while Mitterrand and his supporters walked 1968-style through the streets arm-in-arm to the strains of Daniel Barenboim conducting the *Orchestre de Paris*. But I also recalled an interview six months previously which I had viewed in the unappealing circumstances of a cheap Belgian hotel. There, Mitterrand, dying of prostate cancer after fourteen years in power, surrounded by the wreckage of French socialism manifested by endless corruption, still upholding a set of policies that might have been designed to punish his followers, had given an account – not always accurate, certainly not complete – of his youth as a right-wing student and fitful Vichy collaborationist.

Standing in the crypt, the scale of his betrayal was

suddenly apparent to me. I felt cold, and, with my shirt sticking to my skin, I looked again at the small man wandering among tombs to the strains of Beethoven. His brown suit was ill-fitting, his teeth misarranged around a smile. François Mitterrand was said by those who had met him to be irresistibly charming, to women in particular; but this was something I had never understood. I looked for signs of malice, ambition or duplicity – all I saw was the wolf from the children's theatre.

Now Mitterrand was dying slowly, and his successor, Jacques Chirac, had unremarkably taken power. On the face of it nothing could serve better to illustrate the unexpected institutional placidity which France, unusually in its history, and in strange emulation of its disliked Anglo-Saxon neighbour, had begun to exhibit. But the surveys of public opinion told a different story – that French people, habituated to their version of the good life, felt that it couldn't last. Time, it would seem, was running out for Frenchness, and a sub-millennial fear of the future stalked the land, reflected in the perceived decline of many cherished French cultural items – the *Gauloises brunes*, the *zinc* of the corner café, the *baccalauréat*, the *fonctionnaire*'s or *cadre*'s life job, culminating in *la retraite* in some corner of deep France packed with sunflowers and ennui. The emotion of *morosité* was deep-rooted, transcending the monthly indices of rising unemployment or the *attentats* in suburbs long ago abandoned by Frenchmen as well as by God; but it was the scapegoating that caught my eye. In the past the French had blamed groups of outsiders – Jews, Masons, Anglo-Saxons, Germans, Arabs – for their problems. To be sure, they hadn't abandoned this practice, but they appeared to be losing faith in the ability of their own distinct culture of intelligence to resolve their problems. A symptom of this, strange to anyone who had watched the astonishing success of this caste from across the Channel, measuring their performance in relation to that of their discredited English counterparts, was the disrepute into which the French élite had now fallen.

That summer, I took the new canary yellow and blue Eurostar. Going out, the French side of me was exhilarated by the swift increase of speed after the tunnel, and the way the train reached its astonishing top speed of 300 kph among the cornfields of Northern France; and, going back, I experienced my Englishness crawling among the back yards of suburban London. But things, I told myself, had not always been thus. As the train juddered yet again to a halt somewhere near Ashford I recalled the opening of *Parade's End*, Ford Madox Ford's eve-of-apocalypse novel set in 1913:

> The two young men – they were of the English public official class – sat in the perfectly appointed railway carriage. The leather straps to the windows were of virgin newness; the mirrors beneath the new luggage racks immaculate as if they had reflected very little . . . The compartment smelt faintly, hygienically of admirable varnish; the train ran as smoothly – Tietjens remembered thinking – as British gilt-edged securities.
>
> It travelled fast; yet had it swayed or jolted over the rail joints, except at the curve before Tonbridge or over the points at Ashford where these eccentricities are expected and allowed for, Macmaster, Tietjens felt certain, would have written to the company. Perhaps he would even have written to *The Times*.

People did still write to *The Times*; but Ford's tweedy Establishmentarians had long ago lost their nerve. In France, however, which was the epitome of sloppiness and *douceur* in Ford's day, a 'public official class', of relatively recent creation, appeared to be thriving. Such people still wrote in learned style, with properly formed sentences, about 'the Arts, diplomacy, inter-imperial trade'; and they complained within the pages of *Le Monde*, which they considered with some justice to be their own newspaper, about 'the French This or That'.

Until recently this class of people were popularly known to the hem-kissing press as 'technocrats'; but now they were called '*Énarques*', in spite or out of resentment, after the austere *École Nationale d'Administration*, situated in a dull building in the Left Bank down the hill from the Panthéon, from which they had graduated. There were *Énarques* everywhere – in the interminable meetings which character-ized the business of private industry as well as in the great number of obscurely titled *cabinets* composing the intimate workings of the French governmental system. The *Énarchie* had long ago left the sphere of merely advising, or carrying out policy; now no one could expect to get on at the most serious levels of French power unless they were a graduate. During the previous elections all three candidates – Bal-ladur, Chirac and Jospin – had attended the ENA; the present Prime Minister, Alain Juppé, was a graduate, so were the head of the *Banque de France* and the President of Elf. In press coverage of the disasters engineered by *Énar-ques*, I felt it was significant that the otherwise bland French press took care to report, parodying the high administrative style, in what position out of his class (there were women *Énarques*, but none of them had so far conspicuously failed) the perpetrator had graduated.

Jean-Michel Gaillard was my first *Énarque*, and I

encountered him seated across a table in a summer garden. His parents were Communist teachers near the Vaucluse, in Southern France, and he passed the right exams, glowingly. By his mid-forties, he had, in rapid succession, served at the Quai d'Orsay, the President's private cabinet, run a television station and the *Cour des Comptes*, the branch of the French bureaucracy which conducts annual investigations into the fiscal behaviour of the French State. Now he was writing a book about his old school to coincide with its fiftieth anniversary, which fell due in 1995. His perception was that the ENA, formed to engineer the recovery of France in emulation of the British civil service, was part victim of its own success, part victim of recent developments whereby the authority of the French State had been undermined by such phenomena as the global liberal economy, or the growth of power of Europe at the expense of nation-states. So the school, which had slavishly mirrored the State, must change or die. In some respects this was the dilemma confronting France.

I asked him about the French élite. Was it still as successful as it had been? 'Well, it depends on what you think it's for,' he said. 'You can only judge its efficacy if you accept its premises.' I wondered what these could be. In Britain, no one ever entertained the notion that an élite required any premises other than bricks and mortar. 'We were taught nothing,' one peer explained about his education at Eton. 'However, they taught us nothing damn well.' Needing money for school fees and crumbling country piles, lacking a supply of American heiresses, the British élite had latterly hocked itself to the neo-liberal *Zeitgeist* represented by the City of London.

Grand as Jean-Michel had become, he nonetheless

retained some pedagogical earnestness, carefully leavened with a bright student's irony.

'It's a mistake to think of any one élite,' he said. 'There are different schools and, within the schools, varying levels of eminence. You can find within the entire élite distinct classes of officials. It's like the *ancien régime*, where you had provincial nobility, who scraped a living, and, at the other extreme, magnates such as Mazarin or Foucault. But these *Grandes Écoles* are merely the culmination of the French system. They teach what French children learn at the age of ten: the systematization of reality. It's the essence of Cartesianism: everything has to contain three or four principles, everything must be reduced to the scope of a dossier. Once you've done that, you can do anything in France: run a bank, create a new country, make a feature film or launch a new perfume.'

In a recent enquiry concerning the loss of 70 billion francs (£10 billion) incurred through currency speculation at the *Crédit Lyonnais*, one of the culprits complained about his difficulty in co-operating with his successor, who was a *Polytechnicien*. 'He couldn't understand what I was saying,' the official said. 'He hadn't been to ENA.'

'It's true that you can't fail as an *Énarque*,' Jean-Michel said. 'The exams are so demanding physically that those who are going to crack up take the opportunity to do so. It's now quite fashionable in business to hire a mediocre *Énarque* – you can blame him for your own errors. But I do think, sadly, that the idea of an élite based on intelligence is anachronistic. Big businesses are now obliged to hire *Enarques* to get round the red tape of the system. I think that's a decline in status. The only true field of French bureaucratic endeavour lies in Europe. In conception, Brussels remains French; administration is our greatest export.'

He seemed to see the future in Europe as a formal garden watered by French administrative fiat, and I wondered whether that, too, wasn't a fantasy of yesterday. Jean-Michel smiled. 'Reorganizing a bureaucracy to take account of the arrival of more countries is the perfect task for the *Énarchie*,' he said. 'I could imagine setting a paper for students on the subject.'

As I listened to him speak, I looked in vain for a stiff wig, a quill pen, a set of bound vellum statutes. I couldn't rid myself of the idea that I had travelled deep into the French past, and that I was gazing out of louvred windows into a vast enclosed garden in which impeccably dressed labourers toiled happily – pruning improved varieties of pear trees, or working hard at administrative taxonomy. The French system was both Utopian and deeply anti-democratic. True, it represented a compromise between the Republic and its *ancien régime* past, in the sense that privilege was openly competed for; but that could be taken to mean merely that the old system had successfully modernized itself.

He laughed at my naïveté. 'No one ever said that the French system is democratic,' he said. 'France is conservative. That's what we are.'

During the next week I went uncomfortably through a heatwave from *Énarque* to *Énarque*. Most of them appeared to work as consultants for rich American companies whose fresh-faced, suited representatives sweated in the heat; and their offices, kitted out in pastels, with huge Pompidou-era sofas, were on the posh but dull Right Bank, usually facing the head offices of eminent couturiers. Dapper and agitated, resembling small birds whose blood circulated at faster than human speeds, they clearly had no interest in the questions I asked them, but they were indulgent, too. I realized that I was in the presence of a class, an ethos, above all a method. In the strictest, formal terms, judged by the political company they kept, one might place them ideologically on the left or the right; but this appeared to be of scant significance. What they said was identical, broken down into four points, taking no less and no more than six minutes.

I was listening to the committee members of a rich golf course suddenly threatened by mange on the green and rivals. They started with an expression of pessimism – international capitalism was out of hand. They went on to deplore the behaviour of the poor of the earth in seeking to be exploited, thus undercutting French labour costs. They mentioned the European Union, which had proved disappointing in some respects, but was redeemed in part by its reliance on French administrative method. And they ended by contrasting France's condition with that of other, less fortunate countries. The Germans had more money, of course, and the British (from some points of view, if one was disposed to be charitable) more democracy; only France had, deeded by history and the character of its inhabitants, the special qualities required for survival in the next century. So what were these qualities then? Well, they turned out to be those exemplified by French intelligence and French culture – a grasp of which their proponents had, *bien entendu*, amply displayed in their exposition of the last few minutes. But how could such qualities survive in a porous, internationalized world? Well, that was simple. Only the French State – guided by themselves, and their equally adept successors – could ensure their survival. A powerful State was necessary; there was no room for the messiness and inconsequentiality of Anglo-Saxon liberalism.

I had been to see the British Ambassador, who told me in the best English manner that *Énarques* were good with paper, but that their ideas shouldn't always be taken literally. Nonetheless, I persisted in my interrogation of *Énarques* – hadn't the twentieth century taught the errors of allowing so much power to be concentrated in so few hands? Wasn't there something deeply unattractive, as well as anachronistic, about such methods? Alain Minc – right-wing ENA, a *balladurien*, the begetter of many pamphlets warning of national decline as well as a National Plan, now the author of popular biography – sighed indulgently. 'France is potentially so full of disorder,' he said to me. 'It's not like England. You must understand how much we need such structures.'

Liking them for their intelligence, I was nonetheless wary of so much fluency. The *Énarque* Attali had been sacked by the European Bank of Reconstruction in London after a dispute over the cost of marble in the lobbies; and there were others who had apparently not excelled as investment consultants. But these failures were perceived to be insignificant. To be successful in France, it was necessary merely to demonstrate the presence of intelligence. Like the old literary or political studies, this new mystique of applied state power appeared to feed off itself, generating new definitions of problems without ever really examining them. Were there limits, I wondered, to the application of so much formal intelligence?

At Orly airport the air-conditioning had broken down. I sat waiting among grumpy executives and harassed air hostesses. Perversely, the unreconstructed odours coming through the over-sleek surfaces of French life pleased me. Notwithstanding its astonishing innovative success during my own lifetime, in some important respects France was still only half-capitalist. It accepted capitalist innovations, but grudgingly. Where the rest of the advanced world, willingly or not, had adopted the model of market capitalism, France had wholly declined to do so, hanging onto its state monopolies as vigorously as it opposed world free trade to protect French farmers, or strove, against the will of its partners and common sense, to protect the French language by means of absurd television quotas.

Translated into the vulgate, the élite distrust of liberal capitalism slotted neatly into a generalized dislike of 'Anglo-Saxonism'. Most French people knew little or nothing about America, outside the movies; and yet the idea of American chaos, conveniently extended to Britain, existed both as a system of mythology and as a warning of what could happen: unregulated finance markets, random crime, the obliteration of French culture by the new and violent forms of mass entertainment. One might suppose that, with economic convergence, European countries would come more and more to resemble each other; but the French declined to do so. Long after she had been unceremoniously ejected from power, French commentators continued to refer violently to Mrs Thatcher as an image of what must never, no matter what the circumstances – mobs in the streets, the collapse of the Bordeaux harvest – be attempted in France.

It was hot in the plane, and the women travellers dabbed nervously at their faces, folding and refolding linen *costumes*. Nostalgically, I remembered how in Old France the *toilette* could be combined with such rudimentary facilities as so-called Turkish stand-up toilets. Meanwhile I skimmed the newspapers. That day's *Le Monde* contained the latest instalment of the *Énarque* story – a statistical breakdown, *cabinet* by *cabinet*, of the governmental presence. There was, as usual, no gossip – a consequence of privacy laws which made it impossible to publish the simplest profile of a famous person. I recalled how Bernard-Henri Lévy had lamented the lost vigour of French intellectual life, and I could sympathize with him.

In Strasbourg EU flags drooped over hot canal-side terraces. Moved here by President Mitterrand, in a spirit of ostentatious Europeanism, the ENA occupied a large brick building, formerly a convent and then a prison. It was done up in light greys and greens, a contemporary version of the Panopticon, Jeremy Bentham's humane corrective institution. I wanted to talk to some students and, while I waited for them to finish their seminar, I looked at examination papers. In one test you were given four hours to prepare a '*note de synthèse*' for a Minister, based on a stack of official papers describing the regulatory contradictions of French telecommunications policy in relation to Europe. In the other you spent ten weeks working in a group to produce a critique of the way in which French policy was presented in Brussels. But I was relieved to meet the students, who turned out to be good-looking, sulky, bourgeois overachievers of a kind I was only too familiar with. After six months in Strasbourg, they were bored by what they called rigour. I asked what that meant. 'Rigour is how you appear to do something, not what you do,' said one bespectacled student. 'Administrative rigour is defined as the ability to forget things,' a young woman said. 'What they teach you here is that nothing is worth remembering.' Someone said: 'The definition of an *Énarque* is: "someone who will talk to you for an entire hour about something he knows nothing about." '

I wanted to know whether they were aware of such anti-bureaucratic classics as Noam Chomsky's essays, which explained how the 'value-free' policies of the American mandarinate had caused the heedless expansion of American power into south-east Asia. Was the study of bureaucratic reform on the ENA agenda? Did they consider the notion – it was written into the American Constitution, and had proved of surprising durability, appealing to the American left and right alike – of antibodies, or counter-cultures, which undermined bureaucracy? 'Method alone is important here, not thought,' a student explained, with the thin *Énarque* smile of irony. 'Method is what gives the French State its reason for existing. And besides, the incorporation of ideology would lay the school open to criticism.' I asked them whether they would rather serve the French State, or whether they wished ultimately to have careers as politicians. They were silent. 'There is so much ambition here that no one dares talk about the future,' one of them said. 'But it depends how we graduate in our class. Everything depends on how we are placed.' They laughed warily at each other.

I discovered a new image of French perfection that summer. This was the skin of a duck's neck from which the gunk and cartilage had been removed and replaced by sundry delicacies from the stomach and other unmentionable parts. Stuffed, the old skin was neither recognizable nor specially elegant, but the *charcutière's* skill gave it a rhomboid, asymmetrical appearance, like a botched piece of 1950s sculpture. During that summer candidates for the philosophy *baccalauréat*, including François Mitterrand's illegitimate daughter, Mazarine, answered one or another of the following questions: 'Can one compare the history of humanity to the life history of a man? Is there such a thing as a good prejudice? Is it possible to harbour a passion without nurturing an illusion? Can one be indifferent to the truth?'

Alone among European cultures, France had retained the notion of human perfectibility – and yet, taken as individuals, French people, as any casual visitor could ascertain, were persistently, unassuageably grumpy. This was a paradox that required explanation:

> The French have for long held the world record as drinkers of alcohol. The reason is not that they produce the best wines, for they have now added to their laurels the world record for the consumption of tranquillizers and sleeping pills. It is more plausible to suggest that theirs is a civilization which has esteemed artificiality as well as art; to trim a garden hedge into strange shapes, to wear clothes which make each individual even more unique, to speak in precious prose ... Their escape has not been into oblivion but into a condition which enables them to approach more nearly the ideal of a sociable being, able to cope with the hazards of existence.

As much as hedges, irony came cropped in the most unexpected forms; and yet I found myself reading this paragraph of Theodore Zeldin's over and over again, with bafflement. What could he possibly mean? What France was he talking about?

I drove through yellow fields of sunflowers, over sumptuous brown ridges and through deep hillside copses, coming back in time for the firework display of the 14th of July in which the entire population of the small town of Lectoure, packed on the terrace of the *Mairie*, or standing below the swimming-pool in the road, applauded beautifully coloured rockets. In the Department of Gers, which is in south-west France and part of the old pre-revolutionary province known as Gascony, the small towns on hills were packed with butchers, bakers, chemists; families camped, shopped, ate the local gastronomic products, fashioned mostly from ducks, lay in the intense heat by lakes or swimming-pools. I could see why the world persisted in taking seriously the French quest for happiness – but to me it seemed a falsehood of sorts nonetheless, like the idea of French diversity. 'So many differences result in lack of cohesion,' wrote the historian Fernand Braudel; but I felt that this, too, though it might have been true at the beginning of the century, was by now an illusion. In France the idea of happiness itself was co-opted and refashioned – the process went on generation after generation. Starting with a Marxist critique of consumer society, the radicals of my age had ended by constructing the most perfect system of social control. It was effective because it was moulded so precisely to the French obsession with method. Imposed rigidly and with few real possibilities of dissent, the ultimate product of France was Frenchness itself.

I met a 1968 generation left-winger, specializing in image-making and psephology, who had sold his shares in an advertising agency and bought an enormous manor house, settling down to grow vines and dabble in the local political scene. His house, his wife, his children, his slobbery pets and his swimming-pool – all seemed to come from the perfect French bourgeois movie. But Claude was a far more complicated man than he seemed at first sight. He wasn't experiencing a mid-life crisis – he had distanced himself from the power brokers of French socialism because they were corrupt, and because they had failed. From the fields behind his house, where he had planted new vines, covered by polythene sleeves, we could see yellow slopes and isolated farms. Claude explained that the farmers were, most of them, drowning in debt to the French nationalized *Crédit Agricole*. They were kept going only by payments from the French State, or through the EU's Common Agricultural Policy, which now rewarded them both for growing certain things – sunflowers, for instance – and for letting other fields lie fallow. Like everything else in France, the nature of peasant life was now determined by urban, administrative-capitalist fashion. Each year, the face of the countryside was altered: vines were ripped up, horses or cattle sent to the knacker's yard, and the duck population grew or shrank with precipitous speed. What one might have interpreted as taste, cunning or aesthetic good sense was a symptom of desperation allied to bureaucratic whim. As for the luxury produce of the area – the foie gras from ducks down whose throats kindly old ladies had pushed the notorious *gaveuse*, a funnel with a small pump for moist meal – the peasantry, having lost their knowledge of markets, were unable to sell it.

'I don't take money from the State,' Claude said. 'But I'm rich, and I don't have to.' Then he said: 'Well, people here are nice, they don't yet vote for the National Front in large numbers. But they might do if they get angry. If they feel let down they will get angry.' Everyone expressed a sense of anxiety in France. I asked him if he was really worried, and he shrugged amiably. 'What do you think?' he asked.

The bombings started in late summer – nails packed with explosive placed in public places, where they would maim a great many people, frightening tourists and causing the police to come on the streets. Then a young Muslim, Khaled Kelkal, was cornered by a unit of parachutist gendarmes and gunned down. A television crew was present, and they recorded the words 'finish him off', though these were thoughtfully removed for the evening news bulletins. But a surprise awaited Parisians returning from their holidays, in the form of a lengthy interview with Kelkal, conducted by a German sociologist a couple of years previously as part of a study into the mind of alienated youth and reprinted in *Le Monde*. The interview was heartbreaking both in the intensity of Kelkal's feeling of rejection, and in the literary skill – the text might have come from a short story of Camus – with which his feelings were expressed. For Kelkal maintained that he might have succeeded in France. What had stopped him was not necessarily lack of opportunity, but the obligation, coming with success, to conform, which he refused to do. 'I could have succeeded, but it wasn't going to happen,' he said. 'Integration just wasn't possible for me: to forget who I was, eat pork, I couldn't do that. They had never seen an Arab in their class – to be honest, you're the only Arab, they said – and when they got to know me, they said: "You're an exception." But they always talked more easily among themselves than to me.'

Kelkal had only recently been killed, but no one appeared to be certain whether the bombs were his work or not. Stopped and frisked beneath the glass arcade of the Gare St Lazare, I was pleased when we passed the vile, scarred suburbs, heading for green Normandy by the side of weedy, small rivers, high poplars and vast, spotted cows. I wanted to see Le Havre because I was sick of Parisian infallibility, and because my family had lived in the city when it was France's great Atlantic port. My grandfather managed the Le Havre Football Club, not wholly successfully, and lost the family money in the Great Crash. My mother often told me about the niceness of Le Havre, when there were regattas or tennis parties, and Jean-Paul Sartre taught at the local *lycée*, giving lectures on Balzac and taunting the bourgeoisie. But the town was destroyed in one British air raid in 1944; and Le Havre was turned over by successive Communist administrations to the planners, acquiring a reputation for brutalist-inspired ennui. To everyone's surprise, however, Antoine Rufenacht, a distant cousin – an *Énarque* – had just dislodged the Communists from the Hotel de Ville, standing as a liberal Gaullist. He wished to do something about the town ghettoes, where there had been rioting after some skinheads threw an Algerian into the harbour, killing him.

A stiff wind was blowing from the sea, over the distant oil refinery, and towards the *haute ville*, dotted with white, gabled villas. It rained briefly, and then it stopped; I became aware, as I passed block after block of low buildings arranged on a grid plan, of the weight of the modern past. If God had wished Stalin to be French, I reflected, this is what the Commune of Eurasia would have looked like. Walking further, however, I noticed varieties of concrete, how it could be put up in sheets or pebbledash, laid down in vast cracked squares, or turned into flagstone-shaped emptiness polished by the wind, and how, within a narrow range of colour, it was susceptible, almost like the miraculously changing Boudin sky itself, to wind and water. I marvelled at the vast Hotel de Ville, carrying a belfry with a retro alarm-clock face, and at the St Joseph church, the scaled-down-Chrysler-building tower of which was filled with lollipop-coloured lozenges of stained glass. The architect of the new city, Auguste Perrin, had built a number of eccentric masterpieces in Paris, but for poor provincial Le Havre, my guidebook informed me, this grandee had worked according to the dictum – so very French, so breath-taking in its assumptions of what constituted the true measure of civilization – that 'in matters of style there is no plural'. Still, I reflected, Le Havre had come good, after a fashion; perhaps it would have been better for everyone if Stalin had been French.

Antoine had erected a Dufyesque line of tricolours rippling and clinking in the stiff breeze outside the Hotel de Ville; but otherwise, his scope was somewhat limited. Out of a population of 200,000 there were over 3000 *fonctionnaires* on his payroll; and the British option of mass sackings, Thatcher-style, was not open to him. Meanwhile, the physical shape of the town was determined by the style in which, decade after decade, Communist bosses had increased the scope of their patronage by erecting public housing. As immigrants from Northern Africa arrived to take the most menial port jobs, they were housed together – which meant that this smallish city acquired ghettoes, grouped, like those of Paris, around the periphery. Painted in pinks or sky blues, accompanied by social centres and schools named after Stalinist lyric poets, the blocks were less tatty than they would have been in Britain; but the damage wrought was more spectacular – gashes in the surface, wrecked masonry, burnt apartments. Side by side with these estates were small, older houses, grouped in threes or fours – built by the municipality, too, as Antoine explained, but housing white French, who voted for the National Front.

Suddenly, the Parisian way of looking at things seemed particularily ill-attuned to the grey, precarious banality of *havrais* life, most of all with respect to the dirty secret of French racism. Members of the French élite still believed that the great crisis of the Republic lay in the reluctance of immigrants, once they acquired citizenship, to behave like French people, an attitude which caused real French people (not otherwise racist in their actions) to regard them as foreigners. Laicization was the answer: no Muslim schools, no *chadors* or odd cooking smells. I was struck by the pedagogic rigidity of this attitude; it seemed another instance of the French style of abstraction. Nor was I wholly convinced by the notion that French people wouldn't behave like racists if immigrants kept their side of the bargain. As for the idea – frequently proffered to me, even by North African intellectuals – that brown or black people could somehow rely in perpetuity on the formal rights enshrined in the Constitution, it seemed an instance of wishful thinking, contradicted by the abrogation of Jewish rights under the Pétainist regime of the last war, and the alacrity with which some French men and women had persecuted refugees who depended on them for their lives.

I took a svelte, heavily subsidized municipal bus to the periphery of the *haute ville*. Passing one block after another, many of them comprehensively vandalized, I went to the huge Auchan supermarket on the edge of the periphery. Four years ago, the supermarket had also been vandalized; but it had been kept open as a consequence of the North African community, whose leader, Fawzi Gharram, had opened a club for young unemployed blacks and Arabs, and proposed to the supermarket that they should be employed as guards. *Trait d'Union*, as Gharram's organization was called, financed in part by private sources, was the first of its kind; now it was famous throughout France.

In a breeze-block tunnel with windows, fitted out with a boxing ring, I was offered sugared mint tea. Gharram was born in Le Havre after the end of the colonial war, in 1962. However, his parents re-migrated to Algeria four years later, and he returned to France in 1982, though it took him four years to re-acquire French citizenship. He had the good looks of a film star, and an easy, open politician's manner which was rare among North Africans in France. 'The words are a real problem,' he said. 'I'm fed up with the use of the word "integration" – by intellectuals. It implies that the opposite – disintegration – is a real danger. I don't think people from North Africa need to do anything to become French. What you are really looking at is a hostility against the Moslem religion. French people don't like Islam – that's where their tolerance breaks down.'

Everywhere in France I sensed this terror of separateness, and therefore disorder. People dreaded the existence of ghettoes (misleadingly, they contrasted their own 'integrated' country with what they saw as the American, and even British, experience of ghettoization and *laisser-faire* separatism) yet they were afraid of taking any action that might antagonize white French people. I felt that the very idea of race, with its implications of unbridgeable difference, caused the French mind to seize up.

'You have to look at what is really going on,' Gharram said. 'First, it doesn't matter if you have Senegalese, Camerounais, Algerian or Tunisian tower blocks. We all live in Le Havre, after all; we just need work. Also, the idea of separation is ending in France, inexorably. Why? Well, because of intermarriage. You have many French boys marrying *maghrebines*, and vice versa. Still, I suppose we are lucky in Le Havre. This isn't Paris; the city is small enough for the problems to seem resolvable.'

Next day, I climbed the hill behind the city until I found the old bourgeois quarter. These gabled, fake-half-timbered red-brick villas were familiar to me from many photographs – christenings, courtship rituals, half-forgotten great-aunts in wheelchairs. Now I had come to see a M. Fouché-Saillenfest, ophthalmologist, author of dank erotic poems and latterly, to the surprise of *bien-pensant havrais* circles, representative of the National Front. Waiting in his so-bourgeois villa, amid bibelots of a traditional nature, I had no idea what to expect; and I was surprised to see the very image of a nineteenth-century savant – a courteous, bearded man wearing a pince-nez, with steel-grey eyes. M. Fouché-Saillenfest had been training to be a teacher – his family voted socialist – when he first heard Le Pen speak, and he was instantly converted. He started to speak about how he really liked blacks, but mercifully lost interest. Instead, once he knew of my *havrais* connections, he wanted to talk about literature. I found myself discussing humanism in literature. The fashionable view was that French writing had dried up because of its excessive, reductive Frenchness; it needed de-Frenching. France needed to find a fresh version of universalism, one that wasn't based on its own image. Of course he believed the opposite – that French culture would be finished unless it learnt to turn away from American global culture. He poured me glasses of Suze, the quintessentially French aperitif, sweet and sticky; and he leant over the balustrade as I left. 'Read Céline,' he shouted at me. 'Read Sartre, even if he's a bad writer and a bad man.'

The blue skies lasted while I was in Le Havre, and I sat down, in wind-raked café after café, to read *Nausea*, Sartre's first novel, written in 1936, when he was teaching at the Havre *lycée*. The adventures of the world-weary middle-aged failure, Antoine Roquentin in Bouville, were in places a bit *passé*; but I was surprised how much Sartre had respected the bourgeois milieu he had excoriated. There were good moments in an art gallery filled with flattering images of the dull and philistine bourgeois city fathers; and a poignant scene in which the Autodidact, who read all the

books from A to Z in the public library (destroyed in
the 1960s, I noticed in my guide book), was entrapped
by the bossy, large-breasted librarian, and humiliatingly
exposed as a paedophile. One famous episode, in which
Roquentin managed to overcome the ultimate Cartesian
trap of consciousness by thinking his way into the nature of
the soggy public park ('If one existed, one had to exist
utterly, up to and into the damp itself . . .'), acquired poign-
ancy as a consequence of a hideous social-realist statue,
entitled *Rural Idyll*, in front of which newly wed couples
and their doting families were posing in the early autumn
sun.

And yet it was the blunt savagery of Sartre's writing that
touched me. Even then, as an obscure provincial teacher,
he possessed a wholly strategic, thuggishly enunciated *arri-
viste*'s disregard for the received *politesse* of his day:

> I've known so many of them! The radical humanist is a
> friend of bureaucrats. The so-called left-wing humanist
> worries about the need to conserve 'human values'; he
> doesn't join political parties because he doesn't want to spoil
> his own notion of ideal humanity, but his sympathies go to
> suffering humanity; to the poor of the earth he dedicates his
> beautiful culture . . . he loves dogs, cats, all higher mammals.
> The Communist writer has loved mankind ever since the
> second five-year plan; he tortures mankind out of his own
> love . . .

Nowadays, a Sartre seeking a socially acceptable form of
nihilism would be obliged to attack not merely the various,
largely predictable French ideological positions, or the
excessively formal rules of progressive culture, but the idea
of Frenchness, too. But where, I wondered, were the baby

Sartres? Were they perhaps waiting to become *Énarques* by studying such topics as 'Does the State fulfil a role in relation to culture?' Were they evolving a fresh *toilette*, post-BHL-style, a *mélange* of Left Bank, Moscow and Glasgow? Or were they already looking for the right primary school capable of receiving a neatly packaged lethal dustbin bomb?

I was still thinking about Sartre stewing in his *lycée* when I came to the *Maison de la Culture*, designed in 1979 by Oscar Niemeyer, the architect who created Brasilia. Shaped like a bloated ship's funnel, whitewashed, it contained movie houses, cafés and galleries, each with an acreage of red seats; and it stood reproachfully before a nondescript section of canal at the other end of which stood a grim war memorial dedicated to the victims of the British raid. A bald, pink-headed man in yellow-rimmed spectacles was standing before it. He told me that his job under the preceding administration had been to create street theatre, and his last work had consisted of a forty-foot-high wooden puppet, embodying humanity, repressed under capitalism and then liberated, which he and his troupe had dragged around the rain-lashed streets assisted by crowds of children. Worried about my cousin's excessively conservative aesthetic predilections ('An opera house? He wants to build an opera house?'), he was nonetheless planning a new, less politicized exhibit, featuring an outsize rhinoceros.

He drove me to the dry docks, where the prestige liner *France* had once been fitted out, and I watched him clamber under green cranes inside an enormous gouged-out space lined with painted bricks. By now the sky was turning sullen, with the usual grey clouds. I wished him well, and hoped he would convince my cousin of the eligibility for municipal funds of the rhinoceros he wished to make. I turned away in order to catch the train to Paris – like Sartre, like every *havrais* – and as I did so he seemed unimaginably, sadly fragile. I swung round again to look at him, and the city I was leaving, and then I wondered: whatever would Europe do without the irritant of French culture? For that matter, whatever would I do without the idea of France?

London: Post-everything

It's no go the merrygoround, it's no go the rickshaw,
All we want is a limousine and a ticket for the peepshow.

Louis MacNeice

There were two eighteenth-century prints by William Hogarth hanging above my desk. They were best-selling images of early British Empire, crudely but vigorously executed in the polemical style still practised by the British press, and one of them depicted a group of skinny, priest-ridden Frenchmen at Calais eating frogs' legs and garlic spit-roasted on a sword under an inn sign that read 'Meagre Soup at the King's Clog'. There were no clogs or priests, indeed no intimations whatsoever of deprivation in the other print, which depicted free (and somewhat overweight) Englishmen contentedly feasting on 'Old England's Beef and Beer' while preparing to give the Frenchies another thrashing. I looked nostalgically at the images in the spring of 1995 when it was suggested by medical authorities that over ten people had died from British beef as a consequence of Bovine Spongiform Encephalopathy (BSE), or what was more popularly known as Mad Cow Disease; and I looked again, with a sense of loss akin to the tragic, as the entire world declined to consume this last symbol of British supremacy to a bellowing chorus of outrage on the part of our scoundrel politicians and our moronic nationalist press.

Trapped somewhere between anger and derision, I began to wonder what Hogarth could have found now as an illustration of Britishness. It struck me that societies on the make, like eighteenth-century Britain, could afford a few simple and durable symbols, but that in the state of post-decline, or however one cared to define the current British condition, no such leisurely attachments were available. Perhaps the British scene now required something more elaborate – not one or two images, but a device, like the philosopher Jeremy Bentham's Panopticon, by means of which a prison guard, juggling manically with mirrors or computer screens, could see everything at once, or if that seemed too up-to-date, a carousel of sorts where the same, or similar, images rotated faster and faster, detotemizing or retotemizing themselves at breakneck speed.

I tried to see Britain not as someone who lived there but as a foreigner might do – and one not overcome by Anglophilia. But I found it difficult to seize what was going on, and I came to think that in its perverseness, and through the depth of its contrasts, Britain remained the most difficult European nation to understand. The country was quite prosperous – but it wasn't specially happy. Odd as it might seem to the rest of the world, and despite our well-earned reputation for self-irony, we British remained serious people, particularly where the idea of our own decline was concerned. There were many things that we still needed to know, or so it seemed – that we abhorred paedophiles if they did not come as protected members of the old upper class, that we endured with the greatest reluctance the presence of the yellow and blue flag of the European Union over our buildings, that our wretched cricket team was incapable of connecting willow to leather, that our aggrieved sense of nationality could be brought once again to fervid life by the spectacle of the well-fed bulk of Helmut Kohl embracing our skinnier, insubstantial-looking Prime Minister on the steps of No. 10 Downing Street. But I felt that it was the spectacle of our Royal Family, at once despised for having come down in the world like the rest of us and remembered guiltily as objects of former veneration, that best set the bells and lights going on the old carousel. We wanted to know that our dear Queen read out the wrong speech in Poland, omitting all mention of the Holocaust, just as we required details of the funeral arrangements for the ninety-six-year-old Queen Mother, or that young Wills, second in line to the throne, and receiving an expensive Eton education, was hunkier than his balding, water-colourist, adulterous father. We also had to receive frequent reassurance to the effect that Charles's middle-aged, horsey-faced mistress – the one he met and loved before Di, and to whom he touchingly confessed, while being bugged, that he would like to be her tampon, but whom, according to polls conducted in Welsh supermarkets, we didn't want him to marry – had smoker's breath as well as bandy legs. Just for so long as it took to be reassured by the utter rancidness of national emotion, we needed to be utterly certain about these things. Then we could drag ourselves away, heartlessly but with a sense of duty fulfilled, to the carousel's next offering.

So much emotion gratuitously expressed ended by exhausting itself, and I began to wonder how Britons would preserve their sense of themselves. In Hogarth's time the sense of hostility towards the French was quite focused, corresponding to what the British élite of the day con-sidered to be the national interest – and it was, of course, fully reciprocated, except by such Anglophiles as Voltaire, for whom Britain was a libertarian paradise where a man could indeed feel equal to his King. But things were different now. 'Would you buy an onion string from this man?' the *Daily Mail* asked on the first day of Jacques Chirac's visit to Britain. Well, why not, was the answer – or so it seemed, for Francophobia rang no bells that week, and the coverage thenceforth became favourable. Would British tabloids not modify their editorial views, I wondered, if they ever depended on foreign sales for their profits? What was the connection between the warped reflex of patriotism and the business of covering newsprint with big black type? At the time of the beef war, the *Sun* delivered twenty suggestions to its fortunate readers. Number 10 was 'If you've got a record of the German anthem, play it backwards'; number 19: 'Near Germans, tell as many jokes as you can and laugh uproariously. Germans are famous for their lack of humour.' The trouble with such advice was not whether it was good or bad – judged by any rational criteria, such as the effect on exports or diplomacy, or the more generalized perception of whether we in Britain were crazy or not, it was certainly the latter – but that no one knew any more how seriously it should be taken. On the eve of the European cup semi-final against Germany (which Britain lost in a penalty shoot-out) the *Daily Mirror* ran a front-page picture of the footballer Paul Gascoigne wearing a tin hat. A poll of British schoolchildren revealed that 57 per cent of them thought of Germany as the most boring European country. But was this really how we British now saw the world?

I went one evening to see the National Lottery draw at the BBC because everyone I knew hated it so much, and because I wanted to find out what the fuss was about.

Beside me in line were two French girls attending language school, a hyperactive boy with a cellular phone, and a retired white-haired couple from Lancashire who were holding hands. While the French girls complained about the coldness of London, the boy made angry phone calls to BBC high-ups, pretending to represent a powerful Hong Kong gambling syndicate. As we shuffled forwards, I talked to the couple. They spent about ten pounds a week, but that was all they had won in the last year. To retain their sense of motivation, they kept charts of recurrent numbers (14 had performed best, followed by 22, although 1,2,3,4,5,6 were the ones most commonly selected by players) or they wandered around town, looking at street numbers, or at supermarket displays, for promising combinations. Like Dick Whittington, they had come to London because they thought it would bring them luck.

Polite foreigners, I told myself, inured to British snoot-iness in relation to their own demotic culture, were perhaps less than aware of the existence, often matching their efforts, of home-grown vulgarity; but it was surely present in the studio. We watched as a peroxide Home Counties blonde screamed at us through expensive bridgework that it was double rollover night, with a jackpot of over £33 million. Hurriedly, she introduced the astrologer called Mystic Meg, who gabbled at us through clouds of dry ice. She ushered forward the dour, suited representative of a delinquent boys' home, presenting him with an outsize cheque for £300,000. Then she brought forward Shirley Bassey, a singer popular since the 1960s, and who now gave a spirited rendering of 'Big Spender'. Time was short, we had almost come to the business of the evening, and a man in a suit approached commuters at Victoria Station, asking them to choose between two outsize brown envelopes each containing the name of a Lottery machine. The chosen envelope contained the name Lancelot – cunningly, the lottery operators, who had been criticized for excess profits, called their company Camelot, and the mystique of knightly acts pervaded their brochures – and there on the stage was a cheap-looking machine made of ungainly plastic pipes, filled with nondescript ping-pong-sized balls of different colours. Ms Bassey pressed a button; and in a matter of seconds, we had six new numbers. Like myself, the couple next to me had failed to choose even one of them – but they seemed happy enough to have witnessed the occasion.

I wondered about the British and their luck. Numbers were nowadays chased across the globe in a simulation of the old pre-scientific idea of perpetual motion, but in no country did so many permutations of the idea of chance exercise such a hold on the imagination as in Britain. Long ago, before Adam Smith invented the notion of a providential market justly rewarding the industrious, gambling was more or less the only licensed form of social mobility, allowed to aristocrats and their retainers alike; and yet lotteries, with their implied danger to solvency and morals, were always suspect, forbidden at the instigation of philanthropists in 1834. You could bet on horses, whippets, cocks, pit bull terriers, pigeons, hawks, prize fighters or wrestlers, you could play the football pools, stake your money on the movement of bowls or snooker balls; but outside the innocuous activity of bingo, or housey-housey, evolved to fill the afternoons of working-class housewives, money-making through the manipulation of numbers themselves was prudently restricted. In quest of such pleasures, an Englishman, if he could afford them, went to exclusive clubs where he could play roulette or *chemin de fer*, or to such upper-middle-class syndicates as Lloyds or the Baltic Exchange, and, of course, to capitalism's holy of holies, the Stock Exchange itself, the elaborate rules of which required a lifetime's study dressed in a top hat and holding small sheafs of obscurely marked pieces of paper.

Such prohibitions were loosened in the 1960s, with the growth of private casinos and betting shops, but they had now disappeared entirely. Started in 1994 by a government looking for the provision of 'fun' to offset its singular lack of popularity, and increase its revenues, the Lottery was now the indisputable national form of recreation, encouraging over half the population to buy tickets to the value of £100 million each week, creating 115 new millionaires who guessed six numbers correctly, and enriching various 'good causes' – they ranged from scholarships for people expressing 'moral qualities' to the refurbishing of the Royal Opera House and the construction of so-called millennial projects – to which over £1.25 billion had so far been given. Perhaps all of this might have brought a degree of good cheer in another country; but in 1990s Britain, significantly I felt, it had not. The tabloid press, when not filled with hard-luck stories – £10,000 LOTTERY TICKET SNATCHED, MOTHER OF THREE WHO KILLED HER CHILDREN WAS DEPRESSED OVER LOT-TERY – tended to recount, as elaborate cautionary tales, the appalling things which had happened to winners: bur-glaries, ostracism on the part of resentful neighbours, nervous breakdowns. Soon after 'lottery rat' Mark Gar-dener, described as a glazier, won £18 million, he was attacked by both wives, whom he had deserted, and his adoptive mother as well as his real mother. 'I have a vision of Mark finishing up with a Ferrari going into a brick wall,' the latter said, 'and I hope it's tomorrow.' A 'one-time best friend' who had allegedly saved his life now referred to his heroism as 'the worst thing I ever did'. The first winner, a Muslim, was so hounded by his co-religionists for infringing the Islamic gambling laws that he moved house and changed his name. He sued his wife to stop her taking any of the money, though the couple later said that they were getting on fine.

Uncertain of my own feelings, I began to poll various acquaintances on the subject of the Lottery. I had expected that isolated churchmen would object to the size of the prizes – while taking money to repair their damaged spires, as it was pointed out – but more surprising to me was the attitude of friends, in particular members of what in Britain were called 'the chattering classes'. Those who admitted to playing – one friend got five numbers right, instead of the six needed for millions, buying a new TV set and a ping-pong table – did so sheepishly, with the air of having let the side down; or, like myself, said weasel-style that they did it to please their children. Those who didn't indulge in the weekly flutter – a majority – sounded like the Methodist preacher John Wesley in full oratorical flood. I was reminded that the Lottery had all but destroyed the takings of charities, now forced to compete with it for private donations. I was told repeatedly (at odds of 14 million to one against the jackpot, mathematicians were adamant on this point) that playing the numbers game was a mark of idiocy, particularly if you compared it with older gambling pastimes, such as the football pools, or the horses, each of which required the cultivation of substantial knowledge among punters, expressed in the characteristic British term of 'studying form'. I was harangued by right-wing ideologues who believed that the Lottery should have been private, or that it should never have happened at all because it discouraged initiative; and I was lectured by socialists who felt that it was corrupting the moronized poor, encouraging them to waste their money against ridiculous odds while handing the sweat of their brow to worthy causes favoured by the undeserving rich. But by far my oddest conversation about the Lottery occurred with a television interviewer famous for savaging inept or venal politicians, whom I met at a chic club-cum-knocking-shop in Soho frequented by media types. Professionally over-familiar with the indices of national decline – a literacy rate in free fall, scandal-ridden judicial and parliamentary institutions, monarchical practices preserved in the pickle jar of inanity were among those he had mentioned – he nonetheless maintained that the Lottery was the principal symptom of national collapse. 'It's scandalous,' he said, in the tones once used by Colonel Blimp, Britain's best-loved bigot, who adorned the *Evening Standard*'s pages throughout the 1930s. 'Absolutely scandalous.' I asked him whether he hadn't confused symptoms with causes. I recalled that travelling around the Depression-ridden North of England, George Orwell had said that gambling was the 'cheapest of luxuries', and, along with movies, strong tea and cut-price chocolate, the only means of averting revolution. Why begrudge people good or bad luck? 'No, no, you don't understand,' he said vehemently. 'The Lottery is a fraud – like all gambling it exists to take money from people. But it's also the way we admit to each other, finally, that nothing matters but money. You can't have a society that exists on this basis, and still retains any sense of itself.'

A fight broke out in my local newspaper store as I stood in line with my daughter for the next batch of tickets. The protagonists were a Portuguese couple, who maintained that their last batch of tickets had been incorrectly punched, thus depriving them of a small prize, and a confused young black assistant, who tried to explain that gambling was only feasible where there was a policy of sale and no return. Officiously, as if they were playing parts in a half-forgotten TV series, two policemen intervened. After the commotion was over, I looked at the newspapers around me as I waited for my own tickets. Most of them, including *The Times*, now periodically ran their own numbers games. The old pleasures of reading newspapers to pass the time or to collect ink on one's fingers were gone, to be replaced by varieties of *schadenfreude*. I only vaguely noticed what the headlines said – they were concerned with the Duchess of York's £2 million overdraft, which the Queen had now declined to guarantee, removing the Duchess' right to free use of the Royal Mail, and with the anticipated role of her American financial adviser, spotted sucking her toes on holiday in St Tropez; they would be forgotten by tomorrow – but it was apparent to me that the force of so much accumulated derision was contagious. I had lived, on and off, as long as I could remember, with the notion of genteel decline in Britain; and yet suddenly I knew what it was to inhabit a spot where all that people knew was that one could get rich, and if one was clever, or merely lucky, stay that way.

'Gambling,' noted a 1994 report of the National Gaming Board of Great Britain, 'is an activity in which the only product which changes hands is money.' This was well said, I supposed, as far as it went; but one might have added that much of British capitalism now consisted, according to this definition, of gambling. Just over a year previously, Britain's oldest bank, Barings, frequented by the Queen and members of the aristocracy who still had any money, went bust in three days, brought down by the apparently insane activities of its chief Singapore trader, who had run up debts of £800 million without telling anyone, and then decamped to the Shangri-la Tanjung Aru Hotel in Borneo with his wife. At the time, the directors of the bank, many of them Old Etonian toffs, were blamed for their oversight; and some sympathy was extended to Nick Leeson, on the grounds that he came from dull, lower-middle-class Watford, was clearly out of his depth, and had to endure the rigours of a Frankfurt jail while unsuccessfully struggling to have his case tried in Britain rather than Singapore. However, Leeson's recently published book, half convincingly, told a different story. While conceding that he committed a number of forgeries, he laid blame for his own actions on the brutalizing character of globalized capitalism itself. Bumbling and catastrophe-prone, like a character from *The Lavender Hill Mob*, suffering from compulsive-obsessive disorders – at moments of stress he ingested over two pounds of fruit pastilles, breaking the packets in two to stuff the sugar into his mouth, and he liked to display his enormous pink buttocks in mixed Singapore society – he slipped inexorably closer to disaster each day, forging Old Etonian signatures in every direction in order to catastrophically second-guess the Nikkei's movements and make good his losses. But by the time nemesis arrived, in the form of the Kobe earthquake, the need to reclaim himself as a person was uppermost; and he pleaded forgiveness (while continuing to trash his betters). 'They should have known better,' he remarked of the men who permitted him to steal so much money in order to lose it. 'The laundry on the corner, the boy who delivers newspapers – they all know that making money is never easy.'

Leeson was stewing in a Singapore jail, but his losses appeared to have a wider significance than the disappearance of one inefficient bank. Formerly in Britain, the ease with which people could be parted from their money, like the nature of risk itself, was kept carefully opaque, shrouded by the mysteries of social acceptability. In Anthony Trollope's *The Way We Live Now* the Jewish financier Augustus Melmotte seduced the City toffs of the 1870s by giving a banquet in honour of the Emperor of China, for which invitations were kept scarce, and marrying his daughter to an effete Old Etonian aristocrat, to whom he was also selling duff Mexican Railway bonds; and Trollope was impressed by his social audacity, as well as the scale of his fraud. Robert Maxwell, the immigrant publisher conman (his sons were acquitted of conspiring to defraud shareholders and pensioners), who fell or was pushed over the side of his yacht in 1991, sailing off the Canary Islands, was constructed to Melmotte dimensions, and he bought any individual or portion of Old Britain that could conceivably serve his ends, using the absurdly restrictive libel laws to inhibit exposure of his frauds; but in retrospect his overweening ventures, like his fall, were stamped with the warped grandeur of the 1980s. In the 1990s, it seemed, Britain must make do for its diversions with the idea of nonentity – minor players like Leeson and the actor Hugh Grant, for whom vestigial social embarrassment consisted primarily of being caught with their pants down, or the old Etonian Darius Guppy, whose gambling debts led him to commit insurance fraud in a Park Avenue hotel, and who, in emulation of a Hilaire Belloc cautionary tale, told everyone what he had done.

The time was said to be 'unreal', but I realized that all times in Britain seemed more or less lacking in what one might take as reality. I supposed that one could be happy to be caught out, if in the end the rules of the game stated that it didn't matter very much, and that no stigma attached itself to failure. We knew that there would be an election within a year, and we knew that the Conservatives would lose. We also knew that for all our injured bellowing about our beef, and how those wicked French, Germans, Dutch or Austrians just wouldn't eat it any more, we could not, much as our Hogarth faction of full-blown Europhobes would welcome the prospect, simply declare war on Europe and ram the stuff down everyone's throat. So instead we caught the music and lights on the old carousel while our Members of Parliament, when they were not lying about indictable offences, appeared to fend off their impending sense of anticlimax by reading the works of Joe Orton and Simon Raven, staging for our diversion the most elaborate sex pageants involving increasingly bizarre props such as oranges, black plastic bags and undersize double beds in cut-rate French 'gourmet hotels'. But waiting for the end of the Tories was now like being gagged and forcibly submerged, constrained to listen to bathwater that refused to empty; and I was intrigued when Mrs Thatcher recently appeared on television. There she was, dressed in widow's weeds and having undergone substantial dental work, come back to admonish us like a finger-wagging Dickensian aunt, or ghost of Virtue Past, for having abandoned her principles. I had business the following week in the flat Middle England of East Anglia, so I stopped on impulse in Grantham, her birthplace. In the municipal museum otherwise filled with mementoes of local boy Isaac Newton, and exhibitions of nineteenth-century earth-moving equipment, I found three dresses of hers, preserved in a glass cabinet: one blue ball gown, one severe blue executive costume, and a hound's tooth affair ('My favourite . . . the one I wore to see the President') with a matching cape of the kind Victorian policemen used to wear. Later, I stood in light rain before what had once been Alderman Roberts' corner shop, squinnying to read the modest plaque identifying his daughter's birthplace. During the 1980s, the premises had briefly harboured a pretentious French restaurant called The Premier; but now they were occupied by a busy chiropractor and the windows were filled with diagrams illustrating low back pain.

In Middle England, even in the era of globalization, one could easily find oneself with time on one's hands. I walked around in the dusk, past the town's single Chinese restaurant and its Japanese auto showrooms, until I stopped for tea in a chintz-curtained municipal arts centre whose walls were hung with watercolours depicting loud flowers and garden gates. The waitress told me that Mrs Thatcher had come twice to Grantham in recent years, in order to sell copies of her books. There were queues round the block the first time, but more recently purchasers were outnumbered by secret policemen. 'You can get bored with people, even with her,' she said. 'Anyhow, I think the locals felt that she went on a lot about Grantham without ever doing very much for it.'

While remaining sceptical, I had taken seriously the laboratory experiment performed in Britain during Mrs Thatcher's eleven years in power, because it appeared to be a sustained effort – the last one, most likely, there were only so many acts in the national drama, or indeed so many ideas knocking around – to arrest Britain's decline. 'There is no such thing as society,' she said in 1987, when the prospect of selling off every item with a public definition, thereby recreating Britain in the image of nineteenth-century Manchester liberalism, was dearest to her, 'there are only individuals and families.' I had been puzzled by this observation at the time, but now I understood its simple, unforgiving ferocity. For you couldn't have a sense of nationhood in a state of post-decline in which all institutions were held in derision – and where the only remaining guide to value was that established by the market. In that sense Mrs Thatcher's views were wholly consistent. However, as I drove back to London, along featureless roads and past trucks in the rain, I felt, too, that Mrs Thatcher had failed in her simple quest to turn everything in Britain over to the mercies of the market – she was thwarted by the dislike of excess among the British middle classes or by, what was perhaps the same thing, their attachment to hypocrisy. To Middle England, her exaltation of greed seemed ultimately exhausting; and her revivalist nationalism – on the subject of Europe, in particular – sometimes absurd. Never finding the practice of democracy congenial, she packed the old do-gooding 'liberal' Establishment committees with new men – often nonentities – of her choosing, who disguised the fact that they were objects of governmental patronage with a rebarbative utilitarian managerial newspeak.

What Mrs Thatcher really achieved, though this, too, was hidden in the best English way, was the creation of a country where most things could be subjected to the vagaries of money, and where the future, like the past, could effortlessly be reduced to the operation of financial instruments. In this respect she gave Britain a charter in which the arbitrary and the disruptive were enshrined, and where gambler's rights, once freely given, could never again be revoked. Would anyone come forward with a serious proposal for national revival after her? Reading the various modest proposals of the New Labour Party, which consisted mainly of projects to arrest the breakneck speed of the process set in motion by Mrs T., or render marginally less unpleasant its side-effects, particularily for the dispossessed, insecure professional middle classes, I doubted it. I also felt that Mrs Thatcher and her followers – full-blown Europhobes almost to a person, those who howled loudest at foreigners for not eating our beef – had exhausted the question of decline, conveniently becoming whatever it was that they and their Leader had been so determined to eradicate. All that I could be sure of was that, like everything else in Britain, Mrs Thatcher would in due course be revived, and trundled around the carousel, no doubt to the rousing strains of music composed by her court composer, Sir Andrew Lloyd Webber. As a future for her and for us, I couldn't help thinking that this left much to be desired.

I found myself complaining frequently about the ungraspability of 1990s Britain. 'The most interesting things about the decade are the ones you can't see,' a shrewd new-style mandarin at the BBC told me, and I began to follow his simple guide. What commentators called a substantial 'culture industry' existed, fortified by all the approved post-Thatcher apparatus of audience research and praised by visiting Americans, and even French. But I was struck, often, by the degree to which plays, books or films, reflecting their own status as products, didn't really manage to tell me anything special about the confusing time in which I lived. In particular, these artefacts failed to give an account of the destabilizing aspects of Mrs Thatcher. Unless one counted the latex puppets of her likeness, or the stern social-realist denunciations from a vanished Old Left perspective, it seemed that no one had much to say about her and her times, except that it all hadn't been very nice.

Just off the Brompton Road in West London I sat down with Jonathan Coe amid the dagger-like sconces and Francis Bacon-style tubular chairs of a 1980s brasserie.

Coe was the author of *What a Carve Up!*, a book I had liked because it appeared to be an exception to this rule. His story began around the time of the ejection of Mrs T. in 1990, and it concerned the efforts to survive of Michael, a writer who has had 'not a good time, on the whole' – the expression described the experience of the decade admirably – writing a couple of unsuccessful novels, finding himself dumped by his bored wife and fetching up – out of penury, but in a desire to sell out which he was only half able to acknowledge to himself – compiling a family biography of the Winshaws, a raucous, tasteless, wholly morally repellent group of upper-class characters, each of whom, whether banker, arms dealer, battery farmer or TV executive, represented the vices of the age. Blocked from completion of his labours, masturbating or watching old videos, Coe's non-protagonist came from the recognizable Middle England of almost old suburbs evoked by Orwell or Kingsley Amis; but the tone of the book was different, more remote and certainly less comforting in its depiction of middle-class defeat. Michael fell in love with his neighbour, but she died in great pain in the local hospital, after being misdiagnosed and badly treated. Angered, he took his revenge on the circumstances of his own life by re-doing the terrible Winshaws (and Britain) as farce or melodrama – by summarily dispatching each of them to the grave on the premises of their appalling country house in the manner most appropriate: breaking a neck with a pile of newsprint, skewering a voyeur's eyeballs, lopping off greedy hands with a nearby halberd.

Like his hero, Jonathan Coe grew up in Middle England, in a quiet Birmingham suburb, and he went to Cambridge. He spoke with a donnish elegance, using the sort of careful sentences, packed with various modifiers, that were once associated with the mild-mannered intellectuals who oversaw the BBC's cultural output. Coe said that he had left Mrs Thatcher out of his novel because she was herself a caricature, and couldn't be rendered as fiction – but that she was important because of what she had set in motion. He didn't believe in 'state of the nation' books, feeling uneasy with generalization and lacking the reflex of denunciation, but it had seemed important for him to describe what he thought of as the present valueless condition of Britain. Most of this feeling came to him through television or through texts, and he had tried to replicate the sense of having been got at and robbed, without quite realizing what had happened. 'We do these things to ourselves,' he said, 'then we attach responsibility for them to the shadows of people we see in the tabloids, or on TV.' I suggested that moral affrontedness was the emotion of the age, and asked him whether his book didn't in effect supply an easy, fictional form of revenge, leaving one happy experiencing what one could never, after all, perform. 'I don't know,' he said. 'Perhaps.' Later, he reiterated that he wasn't sure whether whatever had happened to Britain was reversible or not. 'Look at the sex, or the sexlessness,' he said. 'People who think, or fantasize, so much about sex suffer from the inability to perform – or perhaps when they do their sex acts turn out to be peculiar. I do think that's what you can see everywhere. It's the way British people express their sense of disconnection.'

Throughout Europe, considerations of the past and future were by mid-1995 absorbed by symptoms of the new and catching disease of Millennium fever. Over in the Vatican the ailing John Paul II was working on an Encyclical re-enjoining marital chastity and holding the line against women priests; and in Berlin the electricity authorities were hoping, more modestly, that the lights would go on at the revamped Reichstag, affirming that, after a bumpy moment around the early to mid twentieth century, German democracy was in good nick. In Britain we had Lottery money to be spent, and a suitably pompous entity called the Millennium Commission with posh premises within spitting distance of Westminster, to which, for one day every two weeks, nine Great and Gooders – 'the large-bottomed', as the mathematician G. H. Hardy called English Establishmentarians – repaired in order to examine piles of ideas submitted by the public and earnestly vetted by soberminded civil servants educated at Oxford and Cambridge.

No matter what our mental state, I reflected, or our place in the world, there were many things that we in Britain could not help doing. Perverse sex might be one of them, but Britain also bred quangos – quasi-autonomous nongovernmental organizations, in the approved post-Thatcher neo-newspeak – the way rabbits acquire extended families or Third World dictators obsolete weapons systems. The Millennium Commission had become our apotheosis of quangohood. Presiding over its deliberations were two Tories: Virginia Bottomley, a plummy-voiced ex-student Marxist moved over to the supervision of Heritage Culture (one of the most obnoxious coinings of the decade) from her catastrophic maltreatment of public medicine; and the millionaire fun-lover and gardener Michael Heseltine, with fading matinée idol looks, who was to the remaining Tory faithful what the Duke of Omnium was to his aristocratic followers in Trollope's novels. Labour was represented by an ex-chairman of the English Tourist Board that no one had heard of. Otherwise tokenism in relation to race and gender, if not class or wealth, had dominated the choice of Commissioners: Lord Glentoran, ex-bobsleigh Olympics Gold Medallist, now, less glamorously, managing director of a buildings materials firm in Belfast; Sir John Hall, developer of the Gateshead Metro-Centre shopping complex, which was the largest in Europe; the Earl of Dalkeith, heir to the Duke of Buccleuch's wide acres, one of the few remaining truly rich Scottish toffs who still voted Tory; Professor Heather Couper, astronomer, television producer and co-author of the *Halley's Comet Pop-Up Book*; Patricia Scotland, the first black female Queen's Counsel (a twofer here); and Simon Jenkins, an ex-editor of *The* (Murdoch) *Times* with an American actress wife and a penchant for agonizing in public over the rival claims of rural preservation and contemporary commerce who had also written books extolling the glories of Hampstead.

These philosopher-kings appeared to the rest of us as being reasonable, open to persuasion; between their own 'real', or day, jobs they travelled to distant provinces to ask diffidently what some of us wanted. By now, having examined so many documents and listened to so many speakers at remote village halls, they felt they were in a position to know what we might want. But they were prone to doubts about their choices, too, as some of them conceded. They must by now have been asking themselves what the term 'of the millennium' meant anyhow, and how fresh zeroes on the clock should be commemorated. Over cups of tea, or between the careful compilation of exquisitely annotated minutes, I supposed they must also sometimes ask themselves what there was to celebrate in contemporary Britain.

I spent an afternoon reading through the list of awards, and I called some of the recipients. What had the creation of a 2500-mile cycle route in Britain, the return to the

British Isles of the Scottish beaver, or the creation in London's Kew Gardens of a cryogenic 'bank' of British plant seeds got to do with the Millennium? Why was St Patrick's birthplace in Northern Ireland – the old boy died in AD 461 – eligible for a grant? What did the reutilization of salmon ladders in the Thames have to do with the year 2000? Nobody seemed to know, and nobody cared very much; one recipient of money for a millennial footbridge was honest enough to say that he didn't care where the money came from, or why, so long as it did finally arrive. Overwhelmingly greenish, such projects appeared to have come from the junk room which was the traditional repository of British middle-class pastoralism. These were dreams of long standing, which had finally come to fruition, or even older dreams, which had been abandoned, and were now dusted off once more. Nowhere could I find much idea of ambition, or risk. Asked what they wanted, British people had plumped not for the future, but for their tried method, battered over the ages, of erecting pleasant fences against uncertainty.

I wanted to go to Greenwich, site of the meridian, where the Millennium Exhibition was to be held; and on a cold day in late winter I walked past pigeon-fouled monuments of wasp-waisted generals and stoutish liberal grandees, boarding a boat just downriver from the Houses of Parliament. It was a near-freezing Sunday, raw and grey, and the river was flecked with gull feathers. We passed old embattled domes, crosses and eagles, all the melted-down cannons and hieroglyph-inscribed needles which signalled the taking home of successful plunder. Then we chugged alongside nondescript recent buildings – they ended in fake spires, or the arches of gallerias, they were faced with expensive marble and were inscribed with acronyms in gold

lettering – announcing the temporary presence, hour by
hour, of large quantities of figures switched across time
zones from screen to screen. We passed eventually under
Tower Bridge, and into miles of abandoned warehouses,
which were rapidly turned into luxury flats during the great
fast-money moment of the 1980s, and had since been
placed into liquidation. Conventional junk was piled up
here – old boats out of Whistler, picturesquely broken
cranes in the constructivist style – but against the low sky
and freezing rain their rusted charm could make no real
headway. At Greenwich, the boat turned abruptly in the
water, and I could see, half-way round the next river bend
the distant blue gasometer, situated in the midst of wasteland spoilt by gas seepage, marking the spot where the
Millennium was to be celebrated with lasers and ancient
objects, in a ritual mixing of the old and new which, its
devisers somehow hoped, would identify and preserve
some portion of the national genius for the next few
hundred years. And yet what, I wondered, would we find to
recall out of this decade – a cryogenically preserved
wagging finger belonging to Mrs Thatcher in an illuminated tank, the half-charred hoof of an incinerated Mad
Cow, a copy of the divorce papers belonging to the Prince
and Princess of Wales, a bunch of pulped sales slips from
the pre-Kobe earthquake Nikkei or, in more grandiose
style, a replica of Rodin's *Burghers of Calais* representing
the Millennium Commissioners rising from their awesome
labours to beg forgiveness for the horrors they had inad-
vertently inflicted on us?

The boat turned in the current, revealing more peel and
seagulls' feathers. Several bends further, just past Deptford
and before the sea-reach of the Thames, Joseph Conrad,
writing 'Heart of Darkness' in 1899, bobbed about in his

own small leisure craft, with its crew of impassively attentive gentlemen-navigators, and Marlow, his periphrastic narrator. Like every adopted foreigner in Britain, Conrad enjoyed the ornate junkiness of British tradition – not just the inspired hokum of maritime lore, in which a land-locked Pole could become submerged, but the endless silly disguises in which compulsively clubbable Britain decked itself – but he also understood that the British were a practical people, manufacturing things for a purpose; and for the end of the last century he wished to deliver a stern warning barely tempered by his habitual irony. He was as severe in relation to the obligations conferred by the civilizing mission as any home-grown imperialist could have wished – but, with his *mitteleuropa* sense of the fragility of things, more accurately pessimistic than contemporary Britons about the prospects of decency surviving in the new century.

'The conquest of the earth . . .,' Marlow says, 'is not a pretty thing when you look into it too much. What redeems it is the idea only. An idea at the back of it; not a sentimental pretence but an idea; and an unselfish belief in the idea – something you can set up, and bow down before, and offer a sacrifice to.' The British idea, consisting of notions like decency and freedom, as well as the sacredness of property, and what became known as 'character', had always been superfluous to national requirements; but it had survived many wars and the loss of Empire, and given much genuine happiness as well as hypocritical self-gratification to its proponents, if not always to the objects of its patronage. It had survived, essentially, by means of what Conrad called 'sentimental pretence', assisted by copious supplies of bunting, crooked knees, fake or meaningless titles and blunted halberds. What it could not survive, however, or so it now appeared, was the awesome power of money massed against it rather than directed to act on its behalf; and it appeared to be finally now expiring, far later than anyone had believed possible, appropriately enough from the consequences of the exercise of greed which had animated it in the first place.

'Where does the present go when it becomes the past, and where is the past?' Ludwig Wittgenstein once perplexedly asked himself. He might have answered: in Britain. We passed the heart of the City once again; and this time the buildings looked stripped-out in the cold, consisting of façades only, like a Potemkin village, or the absurd fake towns put up by Mussolini on the road in from the airport to satisfy the expectations of visitors like Adolf Hitler. Living in Britain as I did, I felt abruptly shut out from the realm of authenticity, surrounded by all the small, comfortable falsehoods enshrined in the national habit of resorting to the first person plural, with the remote hope that somehow, out of some reflux of remembered national solidarity, things would come all right again. But the old, public culture had disappeared long ago, pushed out to sea or wherever; and so frayed an entity as the British State now precluded celebration of any serious nature. Did anyone believe that we would still be there, putting out more flags against the wet wind, at the next Millennium?

Warsaw: Colour in Poland

Un Polonais, c'est le charme;
deux, c'est la bagarre;
trois, c'est le problème Polonais.

Voltaire

To me, Poland seemed both banal and exotic – I was never exactly welcomed, but nothing was wholly strange. I remembered sitting next to a group of Orthodox Jews, who had spent the day touring Auschwitz, and who were now confronted by a pork-only menu served by waitresses whose arms were dimpled under a cloth equivalent of the paper frills used to wrap meat in quality butchers. I also once spent fifty minutes waiting in line for an internal flight in the company of a Communist ex-shop steward and union activist from Govan, on the Scottish Clydeside. It was clear that he was extremely unhappy. He had been before to Poland, but this trip, it appeared, was less satisfactory. The shortages, far from disappearing, were getting worse, and he was upset to be still seeing drunks in the street. Of course nothing here compared to the conspicuous degradation experienced at home under Mrs Thatcher's brand of capitalism; but the symptoms were worrying enough. And there was still no toilet paper in the hotels, and no bathplug – not the best advertisement for socialism. No toilet paper!

He skidded up and down a fever chart of discontent as we moved forwards at a snail's pace while a soldier checked passports. Finally, when we were still far from the front of the queue, he began to shout first at myself, then at the uncomprehending Poles carrying string packages containing bottled pickles or legs of ham. 'Look what they've bloody done to this country!' he said. 'Look what the fucking capitalists have done with their arms race.' Then he turned to me. 'Don't you think this could have been a wonderful country under socialism?' he asked me. But his ill-feelings reached a climax when we got onto the tarmac to discover that the small plane we were to take contained a flak-jacketed Polish policeman with a machine-gun stationed in the aisle to make sure that no Pole was rash enough to use the plane in order to make a bunk for the West. This was when he started to harangue me about the awfulness of Mrs Thatcher – it was her fault, he told me with authority, as we sat down under the impassive gaze of the guard. 'Everything went wrong because of her,' he said as we finally lumbered off along the runway, taking off into a snowstorm.

I thought of him often in early 1996 while I was in Warsaw, only two months after a jowly forty-two-year-old mobile-phone-carrying Communist President had been elected on a ticket (it seemed like a Polish joke) of doing all the things required to make capitalism work – privatizing dog homes or fleabite ointment factories, talking politely to the IMF – that Communists had never been notorious for doing. I wanted to know about what academics and posh journalists had begun to call 'post-Communism'. Was it a 'transitional state' of the kind beloved by Marxist students of the Old East: nowhere leading to more nowhere? Or was it – yet another old fantasy dear to patriotic Poles and polonomaniacs surfaced here – an instance of how the country, taking a different route from the one anticipated by the West, or believed to be sensible or even rational, would nonetheless land in the right place?

The first thing I did was walk through the streets to the spire of the old Palace of Culture. This was a copy of the Lenin University Towers in Moscow, which were themselves orientalized versions of ornate, antiquarian-Gothic 1890s skyscrapers in Chicago; and it had been 'donated' by Stalin to the Polish people in recognition of their role during the Great Patriotic War. Once hated for its arrogance and anachronism, the building had been transformed – it was now burdened with satellite dishes of every dimension, and scribbled over wherever feasible with pink or green graffiti-like neon. I took the lift to the top floor, walking around in the freezing pink dusk and looking through the haze at neon and moving cars. Downstairs I examined the contents of the department store. A blurred tape of Madonna's 'Like a Virgin' was playing amid bulky mannequins displaying padded shoulders faced with velvet. There were furs, gold chains, men's coats of the kind French movie stars wore to visit Moscow in the 1950s, and heftily padded double-breasted suits with the label Vistula. Suddenly, despite the fact that there was nothing striking about these items, or the way they were displayed, I could see what Voltaire had meant by his remark that only the superfluous was truly necessary. I had felt immured by monochrome in Warsaw, as if walking around inside a 1950s movie; now the prospect of Polish colour washed over me.

Among Europeans who considered themselves to be sophisticated, Poland spelt disarray, or eccentricity, when Poles were not associated with darker and less palatable truths. The economist Maynard Keynes once described the country as 'an economic impossibility whose only industry is Jew-baiting', and, even during the Solidarity period, Western ideological tourists tended to agree. They might speak fulsomely of Polish nationalism and its relationship with Catholicism if they were conservatives, or, if they were pinkish in their sympathies (my Communist fellow-traveller was an instance of this tendency), warm to the prospect of shop-floor democracy; but they would reserve judgement in relation to the country's economic resourcefulness.

Poles were charming, brave, but unreliable – they were best in circumstances of hopeless odds. This was what they had experienced throughout their history – in their medieval battles with German knights, or their bizarre eighteenth-century experiment in limited franchise representative government (this was one of the oddest botched Utopias in European history, causing the bankruptcy of the country, from which it took two centuries to recover), when kings were elected by the nobility, and each piece of legislation could be thrown out (and was) by the exercise of an individual noble's veto. With some reason, the world believed that Poles were good at making people or things look stupid – humiliating Marxism-Leninism (and the Russian Empire) had been their greatest achievement. But Poland prosperous? Poland growing steadily at 8 per cent? The idea was novel.

I had a lot of catching up to do, and in the following days I went around dazed through the bitter February cold. Put up rapidly in the late 1940s, after its full-scale destruction at the hands of the *Wehrmacht*, and consisting of tower blocks and grey, pilastered plazas decorated with statues representing Work or Motherhood, Warsaw had always seemed one of the cities hardest to de-collectivize. But I had reckoned without the ingenuity of Poles, and, what was more important, their indifference to aesthetics. The formulaic sign-lettering which had monotonously decorated the fronts of state-owned shops was gone, to be replaced by hundreds of smaller, louder signs. Throughout the city gap-toothed sites, empty for decades, were being filled up at breakneck speed, as if to stop altering things were a sure guarantee that the magic would end. Warsaw past had been stuck in the 1940s, but now some bits of the city looked as Turin or London must have done in the early 1950s, and others had begun to resemble pieces of early 1960s Stuttgart. But whereas the recovery of Western Europe had been slow and deliberate, here the progress from rubble to consumer capitalism had been scrapped in favour of a frontal assault on planned misery. In London, a Polish friend of mine had said that I'd find the place disappointing, like a garland of lights in darkness, but I began to think he was wrong. After waiting so long, as the Poles had done, who could bear to hang around any longer?

I had been habituated to classic Stalinist hostelries – the kind of semi-correctional institutions where one waited an hour for breakfast, found, on one's way to the men's room, 220-pound prostitutes niftily changing from polyesters into spangled miniskirts, and spent enforced hours of leisure watching leather-jacketed hoods conduct intense private conversations spiced with Masonic hand movements next to thumb-printed plate-glass doors. But now the plastic potted plants were cleared away, and the bugging systems – never specially effective in Poland, to be sure – had been dismantled. Drabness was going quickly – the only remaining old-style Polish hotels provided a specialist service for travelling salesmen from Minsk or Bialystok. Whereas in the past voices would break through sleep to ask, abruptly, if you wanted Polish Woman, these days small coloured cards notified new occupants that hookers were guaranteed delivery within ten minutes. One could now pay by credit card, and the price varied according to age, sex and nationality (Poles cost more than 'Easterners', reflecting the economic re-ordering of things) as well as time spent on the job.

In the hotel where I was staying, which had begun life as the epicentre of Warsaw café life in the 1890s and, after a brief moment of post-war prestige, declined throughout the 1960s and 1970s, until it came to resemble the sort of place in which Graham Greene's drunks were washed up, and was finally shut down, there were now, instead of pot-bellied representatives of the old *nomenklatura*, sharp-suited representatives from Goldman Sachs, come to preside over the privatization of the Polish copper industry, and, in the lobby, presiding over such conversations, a large photograph of Mrs Thatcher. I recalled that the Poles had originally been encouraged to follow the British model of privatization, but that they had found it too slow, and too expensive, involving as it did the sale, one by one, of businesses by banks experienced in such matters. Instead they had given away much of Polish industry – in the past six-odd years over five thousand firms had been disposed of. They could never be re-acquired by the state – which meant that after forty years of socialism, whether anyone liked it or not, Poland was a capitalist country. Apart from the far smaller Czech Republic, no other formerly socialist country had managed its transition so adeptly.

A producer dressed in elegant cords was sitting with two starlets in the coffee shop – and when I began to explain to him that I was finding Poland unreal, he grinned and pushed a piece of paper at me. 'You want the Polish *Hamlet*?' he asked. 'Then you shall have it. The times have

changed and MTV is in fashion. Speak fast, Hamlet!' He
wrinkled his nose at the red borscht I'd ordered – it was too
cheap, reminding him of the old days. I asked what sort of
films he was making, and he shrugged. He had made a film
about a possessed girl for the French market, but he now
felt that Europe was hopeless, Marx was still around all over
Europe, and Europe was dead. The only real place for Poles
was America, where they understood capitalism. I asked
him what he thought of the new Poland, and the Communists being back, and he patted a raven-haired starlet's
wrist, jingling her bracelet. 'Anything will work here,' he
said. 'Poles are good at rejecting what's unsuitable. Didn't
we reject Marxism-Leninism? Should we care about the
new Communists? Why should we – what can they do to
us?' This, I discovered was how Poles tended to talk about
the prospect of joining Europe – they would take what they
needed of it, and disregard the rest. They were certainly not
interested in the half-progress of the Single Currency over
in Brussels – it would be at least twenty years before the
possibility of joining it might occur. Such attitudes were
very attractive to me – and they reminded me of the reck-
lessness of Old Poland. 'I do think we Poles have done
quite enough to convince everyone of our qualifications as
genuine Europeans,' the medieval historian and politician
Bronislav Geremek told me, in the accented English
adopted by Joseph Conrad, tapping his pipe rhythmically
and crossing and uncrossing corduroy-trousered legs. 'Now
I hope that Europe will come some way to adopt our way of
seeing things.'

It was snowing when I went on Sunday morning by cab
across the Vistula, and the river was iced over, circled by
large crows. To the left, I could look back at the city, which
appeared Chicagoesque in places with its new towers; when

we rounded a bend I saw an open football stadium. Wind was blowing snow around the bowl, but there were people everywhere, small stands and old trucks. This was the *Dziescieloca*, or, as it was more popularly known, the Russian market. People came here to barter, buy or sell from adjoining countries such as Belarus or Russia. Five years ago a comparable site had served a comparable purpose in Berlin for Poles; but, as the Poles became successful, they no longer needed this facility, and they had established one in Warsaw, hiring security guards to keep the mafia out. Now the stadium had become an image of Polish capitalist success. Already additional car parks and entrepôts were being created each month, and factories making jeans and shirts had grown up around it. Soon, I imagined, it would cease to be a stadium, becoming an immense heated shopping mall – if the Byelorussians hadn't created a market somewhere to the East on their own disused javelin-throwing arena.

Walking round the rim, stopping to stamp my feet, I looked at the piles of merchandise. I saw elaborate dog muzzles, left-foot bootees, prosthetic knees, mounds of angora women's hats, beady-eyed fox furs dyed blue, green, pink and yellow, piles of tinned fish, shaving cream and Cyrillic games of lotto, buzz saws, carburettors and hypodermic needles. Beside these piles, eating steaming sausages and onion, or blowing at the cold, stood elderly, grizzled men in fur hats and stout women covered with shawls. Only a few days before, the Polish press had carried the story of a bus carrying a full load of Byelorussian traders, in which a man died of a heart attack just inside the Polish border. Not wanting trouble with the police, and not feeling it was right to bury him in a strange country, his companions bundled the corpse onto the back seat, where it began to decompose, and was noticed by passers-by. One could read such stories as announcing the end of the world, in the desperation they implied; but to believers, of whom there were many in Poland, they could also seem like parables of capitalist success, or entrepreneurial solidarity. It occurred to me that not just Adam Smith, but Mrs Thatcher, too, might have found much to commend in such an instance of enterprise culture.

Were Poles happy with these new arrangements? Not entirely. Everywhere I went, among sociologists, venture capitalists or members of the old *inteligencja* now exiled from power, I encountered the same misgivings. The script went like this: formerly, Poles had been divided by ideology, and yet their Polishness had united them. Poles had even managed not to kill each other during the worst days of Martial Law, and in 1989, following honoured Polish rules of compromise, they sat round a large table, where they ushered in the first non-Communist government of the old Eastern bloc. It was they who had destroyed the *ancien régime* – everyone, including Gorbachev, had followed them. But the democrats had failed – because they were divided, or impractical, or simply because they had been too assiduous, paying politically for the seriousness with which they had introduced the reforms which led to the installation of capitalism. They had been too generous, above all, in deciding not to settle old scores, failing – unlike the more pragmatic Czechs, who hadn't offered resistance to Communism, and, as a consequence, suffered more from it – either to exclude ex-Communists from power, or to confiscate the Party's assets. And now there were new hatreds in Poland – this was a sad state of affairs.

Part of the problem was that many of the people who had sacrificed much of their lives in the struggle against

Communism now found themselves extremely ill-rewarded
– though they were too well-bred or habituated to stoicism
to complain overtly. Instead they voiced their discontent
with history by the expedient (an understandable one,
given Poland's part) of wondering whether it all could last. I
sat in the small study of a playwright whose career had
suffered as a result of his identification with Solidarity. He
had written a dialogue between two characters, *phil* and
phob, in which was heatedly debated the question of
whether Russian power would return, and with it totalitarianism. The dialogue was stacked firmly to the side of
caution, or alarm; it was as if, no matter how much he
might want to, he couldn't let go of the bad past which had
become a redeeming aspect of his old life.

It was cold the afternoon I went by bus to the National
Cemetery, and I walked quickly through the dusk. Generals
were buried here alongside Stalinist hacks and sugar-beet
magnates; neat plots marked with red and white banners
defined the presence of the dead from the various Polish
struggles, against Germans or Russians, separating the
fallen into mutually opposed factions. It was all so carefully
done and so opposed to the messiness of everyday Polish
life; and, filming here ten years ago in the face of official
disapproval, I had been astonished, and moved. But now I
couldn't find the Katyn monument, commemorating the
slaughter in 1941 of the Polish officer élite by Stalin, and,
when I was guided to the granite stone by the son of an
Anglophile ex-pilot, I told myself that it couldn't last – but
that it would all change in a different way to the one feared
or anticipated by my playwright. Polishness was special, no
doubt of that, but, beyond the circumstances of Catholicism and peripheral Europeanness, it reflected the
historically embattled condition of Poles, squeezed between

rival Empires. You could take that away, replacing it with liberal capitalism, and you would still have Poland; and yet it would be a different Poland.

One evening I met Janusz, to whom I'd been introduced as an exemplar of the new capitalism. He had worked as an economist in the food planning agency, and he had been a Solidarity militant. In 1990 an English friend representing a property company wished to buy a building, but couldn't find a surveyor. Janusz read some books over a weekend and did the job himself; later he took a correspondence course, acquiring formal qualifications, and, because he was trusted, as a Pole, he was now hired by Western businesses to value entire towns in Russia. He'd bought land outside Warsaw, and he was beginning to restore the family house; now he was experiencing such banal problems of Western bourgeois life as private school fees. He hated the Communists; but he didn't want to enter politics until he was really rich. Nonetheless, he, too, cautioned me about excess optimism. There were scandals everywhere, and the real danger in Poland was forgetfulness. Everyone wanted to forget the past and get rich, and this created a tolerance of corruption.

I said that it seemed as if Poles had somewhere acquired higher standards for capitalism than the rest of us, and he smiled. The sums were small; but I shouldn't be deluded by the scale of things. The real problem was that Communists had no conception of political pluralism. They liked money, and now they could earn it more or less legally, which they had not been able to do previously. They liked elections, as long as they were able to win them. But they had no sense, despite the invitations they had received from Western management schools or political institutes, of the inappropriateness of plunder. They had no real sense of what was appropriate – surely otherwise they would have had the good taste to exclude themselves from office.

Most of the books I had read tended to define post-Communism hazily, as a transitional psychic state resulting from the emptiness experienced as a consequence of so many collapsed barriers, or, more soberly, as a set of circumstances imposed by a messy economy, half-privatized yet possessing many of the old monopoly conditions of Communism. In Poland, however, the term was now used to mean the presence, in positions of influence, of people who had been Communists. They had never believed in the goods, or had now covered their tracks – either way they would compromise the new state. Between visits to politicians who assured me that this would or wouldn't happen, I stood in a wooden gallery of the *Sejm* – the Parliament – looking at the banks of seats I had seen so often in black and white films of the Stalinist period and trying to summon up all the lies that had been told for so many years. The décor was austere, puritanical in its greys, with uncomfortable-looking seats – I felt I was in the sort of hall where atheist funeral services took place, at which awkward commemorations of the deceased were read out to organ music. Now the Communists called themselves Social Democrats, and they wished to join both NATO and the European Union. Worse things could have happened, and had done; but I hoped that Poles would find cynicism easier to tolerate than hypocrisy.

Next day, I went looking for cynicism in an unusually neat Warsaw suburb whose streets were lined with white, freshly painted villas. There were white lilies in the lobby of *Nie!* (*No!*), along with half-surreal, mildly pornographic nudes featuring dogs or cockerels. I flipped through the latest issue, which boasted on the back page a luridly

coloured bar-by-bar guide to sex in Lodz, illustrated by a
comprehensive Michelin grading of erect penises (one to
five, instead of the knives and forks) and roses for ambi-
ence. On the inside pages articles denounced the anti-
Semitism of a Solidarity priest, or took the piss out of
Cardinal Glemp. The leader featured a picture of the editor,
a small man with the face of a defrocked Voltairean *Abbé*
and outsize bat ears; beneath his remarks (more taunts in
the direction of the defeated Lech Walesa) were ads for
porn films. Ten years ago, *Nie!* could not have been
imagined in any European country, let alone Poland, with
the possible exception of Holland; now its combination of
prurience and vituperation was quite voguish. I was
interested in seeing its editor, Jerzy Urban, because as well
as becoming a propagandist of genius (it was he, acting as
spokesman for the loathed Jarulszelski regime, during
martial law, who had described Walesa as the first author
since Homer who could neither read nor write) he had also
spent his life defending, or at least only mildly criticizing,
Communism. Also, I was intrigued by the fact that Urban
was Jewish and, unlike many of his generation, didn't hide
it, or bother to conceal his loathing of the Church; as a child
during the war he had been kept alive by Polish peasants.

He made money, and he enjoyed himself, buying new
houses and art-works, drinking too much and indulging in
British cars and tweeds. Did I think the latest Jaguar was a
good car, he asked me. Was he bored? No, not at all – there
were many things to do in the new Poland. Urban explained
that his paper wasn't 'objective' – surely an understatement,
but also the only time I heard him use a word coming from
the old days – but that it was widely believed, according to
market surveys among the Polish élite. He made a lot of
money from *Nie!* – over £2 million a year. My interpreter,

in common with most of the Poles I'd met, regarded Urban as a cynic, but I wasn't wholly sure. He seemed to belong to a small fraternity of popular journalists, including Michael Moore in Canada and Kelvin MacKenzie in Britain, whose disillusionment expressed itself by means of angry jokes directed at anything, and whose aversion to cant surpassed in intensity their weakly held ideological convictions. But it was also true that *Nie!* rarely targeted Communists, new or old; and that its best shafts were reserved for people who called themselves democrats. It was easier for Urban to announce that he had bought the Polish National Anthem, causing nervous regimental bands to enquire about the performing-rights cost, or send young and attractive female reporters to confess identical sins in confessional boxes throughout Warsaw, thus establishing by a simple Hail Mary count the indifference of the Church to crimes involving money, and its obsession with sexual behaviour.

At present, he faced the exquisite prospect of being the first journalist in Poland to be punished since the fall of Communism under the country's secrecy legislation, for having exposed, thanks to leaked documents, a member of Walesa's entourage as a police spy. He explained, smiling, that the legislation was absurd; it dated from 1918, and had never been used during the Communist period. He could be banned from editing his paper for a year, but he would appeal, and he was gratified – another smile here – to be receiving the support of so many colleagues, even those opposed to him. I asked him about post-Communism, and he said, smiling again, that not everybody had his own good fortune. There were people bewildered and left behind by capitalism; it was they who had voted for the old-new Communists. I tried to press him – was there anything new about the current situation? 'New?' he asked, laughing. 'There's nothing new in the world, unless you count money – and corruption.'

On the early-morning plane to Gdansk, half the passengers were busy examining management data supplied by the Polish outreach scheme of the Wharton Business School; the other half were reading *Nie!* An in-flight magazine explained that Polish fashion designers were at last beginning to acknowledge the fuller figure of most Polish women, coming up with darkish outfits for which enough material to cover a large sofa appeared to have been deployed. On landing I unwisely disdained an over-priced taxi, instead taking a long bus ride through desolate villages and housing developments. I checked in at the hotel, and walked a few hundred metres to the gates of the Gdansk – formerly known as the Lenin – shipyard. In front of a cluster of blue cranes the odd car drove in and out of the gates. A small souvenir stall sold over-priced Taiwanese T-shirts inscribed with the world-famous red scribble, and postcards of the Pope shaking hands with Lech Walesa. Beside a wall bearing a number of plaques commemorating casualties of the Polish struggles, including the murdered Father Popieluszko, stood three 90-foot crosses topped with anchors. They had been erected after the successful 1980 occupation of the yard in memory of the shipyard victims of the militia when riots were put down in 1970. Crows flew around me in the silence, alighting on the clean snow. The monument looked well-kept and confident; in its old-fashioned massiveness it expressed both Solidarity's origins and the pride felt by most Poles in the movement, even among those to whom militancy had been of peripheral interest. But I remembered, too, that Lech Walesa had returned here, after his defeat two months ago, to work again as an electrician; and that the new Government, having investigated the prospects of the yard with the aid of various studies, now planned to close it down.

Gdansk was surprisingly rich-looking. It bore no sign of having been destroyed entirely by the Red Army – or having harboured the most important social movement of post-war Europe. In enormous, echoing churches – one of them the pastoral base of the Solidarity priest fingered by *Nie!* for his alleged anti-Semitism – I investigated the relics of the movement: banners, monochrome photographs evoking martyrdoms, now-forgotten visiting dignitaries like Reagan and Mrs T., workers and intellectuals with hands raised high. I had lunch with Pavel Huelle, a novelist who had abruptly been put in charge of the local radio and television network, and who now wanted to leave. He didn't think that democracy was in any way menaced by the Communists, but he was fed up with their ceaseless interference. The time was no longer heroic, and he had books to write. 'I've done my job,' he kept saying. 'Let someone else deal with the bastards.'

I walked between the yards and the new boutiques at dusk. After the early surprise of seeing a workers' movement that was clerical in its inspiration, and deeply nationalist, most of my generation had finally taken Solidarity to its breast. In contemporary Europe, even if one was trying to destroy their power, as Mrs Thatcher was, it was impossible to deny the rights of independent trades unions; and this, above all, doomed the existence of the Soviet regime in the eyes of enlightened Western opinion. But I felt that we had missed an important element of Solidarity at the time, or misinterpreted it, perhaps because of all the crowds, banners and oratory; and that was the essentially private, voluntaristic nature of its inspiration, which placed the Polish movement at a distance from its

Reform-Communist Czech, or exotic-Maoist French equivalents of 1968, both of which claimed that the old liberal values of the last century had been superseded by various forms of collectivism. The revolt of Poles against Communism sprang from disgust, and it began with the inspired perception that resistance needn't be Gandhiesque in its piety, or derive from existentialist heroics, but could take the form of ordinary, persistent bloody-mindedness. Those who wanted to live free under a decaying tyranny could do so if they were ingenious, though they might not experience much in the way of bourgeois comfort. It was this that I had found so wonderful in post-martial-law Poland of the mid-1980s – the knowledge that, given porous frontiers and the spirit of mutual accommodation, large numbers of people were capable of creating, through the circulation of pamphlets, half-clandestine videos, and above all by such archaic means as the pulpit or word of mouth, their own culture of resistance.

However, in the 1990s it was possible to look at Solidarity in a different way, as the first of the nationalist movements to have arisen in the wake of Soviet Communism. Bronislav Geremek had told me that he was still proud of Solidarity, and yet, given its disintegration as a political force in the 1990s, and its reversion to the status of a trades union, he thought its importance lay not in the realm of political organization but in the values it had propagated. This was perhaps accurate – but I felt saddened by the statement. In the context of resistance, phrases such as 'political pluralism' or 'civil society' could be spoken with conviction; but they meant substantially less confronted by liberal capitalism, in which all these things, notionally, had their place, but none of them meant very much. Had the purpose of

Solidarity really been the creation of a Poland where *Nie!* was the most successful newspaper?

Going southwards by train as snow slipped by the steamed-up windows, eating kielbasa and mustard, I met a younger cousin of the Communist with whom I'd once ridden by plane. He was a vegetarian, he wore a green velvet jacket and John Lennon specs, and he taught at a university in Britain – to his chagrin, the name of his department had been changed, in Orwellian style, from Social to Management Studies. He didn't appear to enjoy fitting the workforce to the demands of contemporary capitalism, or fulfilling the new-style production norms imposed by business consultants. In Poland, where he was researching trades unions ('At least they still do have some of them,' he said), he had hoped to find some semblance of revolt; instead he was encountering demands for more management expertise of the kind he found morally repellent. For Poland he predicted mass unemployment, a possibility which the people he spoke to either refused to countenance, or – more mysteriously to him – viewed with equanimity. He was certain that Poland would end up with just a few cathedrals dedicated to capitalism in a wilderness of misery. 'The Poles are like children looking at goodies in a sweet-shop window,' he said. 'They have saucer eyes. When will they ever learn?' I was sure that he was wrong; but all I could say was that I believed in Poles. I suppose I might also have added that they did believe in capitalism, as well as looking after each other, and that if anyone was going to, they would somehow make it all work. They would certainly be helped by the fact that wages in Poland were a tenth of those enjoyed by their German neighbours. No matter what happened to the Polish application for membership to the EU, it was hard to see how the country could once again be pulled eastwards and away from Europe.

I had wanted to go to Krakow again, because it was beautiful – and it was here, most of all, that I recalled most poignantly the experience of hopelessness, faced with the social and environmental atrocities perpetrated by Soviet-bloc Communism. The old medieval and baroque city survived the war more or less intact. With its large middle class and *inteligencja*, it proved to be a source of principled Catholic and Liberal opposition; and the Communists resolved to alter the political balance of things. Bizarrely, but in keeping with the precepts of social engineering popular at the time, they did this by building Nova Huta on the doorstep of the Old City. This was a new Stalinist town, complete with what was then the largest single factory in Europe, a steelworks employing over 30,000 people, and a lignite-burning power station, which piped heat underground to the workers' flats, and which proved to be instantly obsolete, losing heat and wrecking precious statuary while it turned prime agricultural land brown for miles around.

Nova Huta was significant in Polish history because it failed comprehensively – the workers to whom flats were given rapidly turned pro-Solidarity, and it was here that the most bitter battles occurred. But the disloyalty of Poles to their Stalinist planners meant that Krakow was a very interesting city – after Gdansk, it became the centre of struggles against the Government. It was here in the mid-1980s that I met Tadeusz, formerly a lecturer in phenomenology at the Jagiellonian University. He had been sacked for holding independent views, had then written about movies and Catholicism for the weekly independent newspaper, and, with the help of a priest who got money and equipment from a generous congregation in Detroit, set up a system for making and distributing pro-Solidarity films throughout Poland. Father Jancarz, who was big and bearded, and kept photos of the Soldarity martyr Father Popieluszko beside those of the Pope in the surprisingly dainty lodgings (I remembered with pleasure his array of then-scarce Western deodorants and cologne) adjoining his concrete new church, died of a heart attack; but Tadeusz had so far prospered, finding employment in the reformed state television.

Now I drove again around Nova Huta with Tadeusz and his son, who was an architectural historian. The statue of Lenin had been removed – carted off to a municipal park somewhere in Eastern Poland, along with dozens of others – but the old centre of town had, happily, been declared an architectural monument. Boasting arcades, built radial-style along Italian Renaissance lines by a Polish architect famous for his advanced philosophical views in the inter-war period, it was now eligible for EU funds; meanwhile Poles had to learn that not everything done in the name of false humanism was entirely bad. We passed the fake campaniles of the management offices beside the factory gates. As at Gdansk, redundancies were planned, but I was told that the impact of shutting the entire plant, while it made economic sense, was considered too great – it would kill Krakow, and the entire region. We drove around the vast perimeter, where the earth, despite the importation of filters from Germany, was still a sickly brownish colour as a consequence of the twenty stacks belching smoke, as if Andrew Carnegie were still at work. Then we stopped, and walked around the edges of the new towns, where one could see that building had already begun on new suburban developments beyond the crumbling tower blocks.

We went into a number of the churches which people had built from the 1960s onwards, in the teeth of official opposition, often by pilfering materials from factories. I hadn't remembered much about these places, except that they were both ugly and impressive, transcending aesthetic considerations by the brute seriousness they represented, but I was given pause by some murals. I remembered having seen them before. The images, executed as recently as 1982, were crude and garish; the problem with them, I realized, was the way in which they represented the Jews in Christ's passion – the hangers-on around the Cross. These Jewish characters – carters, carpenters, gawkers – were given the usual hook noses of anti-Semitic caricature, but they were also placed at the edge of the canvas, outside the area where important things were going on. Beside the non-Semitic Polish Christ, and the centurions, they just didn't matter. I must have paused longer than the banal workmanship could possibly justify, because my friend's son came to fetch me. 'These aren't good paintings,' he said brusquely.

The same feeling of queasiness affected to me the next day, when I walked around the old late-medieval ghetto of Kaszimierz just below the Wawel castle in which Polish kings and heroes are buried. Reconstructed somewhat, this had served as the set for some of the scenes in Steven Spielberg's *Schindler's List*, and it now boasted several kosher restaurants and a museum inside an old synagogue. But the museum seemed pitifully inadequate; its paltry exhibits consisted of the odd candlestick, or photograph, and for revelatory qualities it was on a par with the dolls representing *kletzmer* musicians available for tourists in the Cloth Market. Once again, I was disquieted. Neither assurances from cab drivers to the effect that they had chauffeured Steven Spielberg, nor the questions from my guides, could still the feeling of aversion.

I had recently watched a long documentary film in which a Polish-American director attempted to tell what exactly had happened to the Jewish community of Bransk, a *shtetl* in Eastern Poland. A naïve young Pole of the town – a 'good Pole' to the film-maker, in the same sense that one might speak of a 'good German' – wanted to know more about Jewish history. He found out that the townspeople had colluded with the occupying soldiers, and even profited from atrocities, some of which were committed after the Germans had been defeated by the Red Army. But no one cared now. Did some Poles really, after all these years, still harbour hatred for Jews? If this film was to be believed, they probably did – even after taking their houses they remembered, often with rancour, how the Jews had been richer than themselves. Certainly, if they didn't hate Jews, they didn't care really to remember them – at the end of the film, the villagers, with the assent of the 'good Pole', who by now despaired of his compatriots, or needed, because of his political career, to get on with them, declined to incorporate Jewish history in the 500th anniversary celebration of their village. Instead they contented themselves with having *Fiddler On The Roof* played by a military band at their celebrations.

I liked my hosts very much; and I couldn't begrudge them their nationalist Catholicism. But this was a problem I had faced before with Polish friends. Not all Poles were anti-Semitic, but almost all the Poles I had met possessed a heightened sensitivity to suggestions that they might be. This was expressed by means of touchiness, as if to draw attention to such things was a way of criticizing Polish culture. But among serious historians, too, the question of

Polish anti-Semitism was not always adequately confronted, leading to evasions about the 'liberal' Renaissance, in which Jews were accepted in Krakow, or throwaway remarks to the effect that the 1930s Polish laws against Jews had not been as strict as German ones. There were half-purges of Jews, in 1956, for instance. Memorials diminished the scale of Jewish suffering. Plans to build either a nunnery or, more recently, a supermarket adjoining Auschwitz had caused much grief to Jews. Nowadays, it seemed, Poles were, on the whole, more eager to reintroduce Jewish ethnicity into the national memory than Austrians, or perhaps Czechs, too; but their efforts were often grudging. Their real feelings, I suspected, were that Jews had never wholly belonged in Poland at all, and that the ethnic cleansing practised in their country around the mid-century, while regrettable in many ways, had been of benefit to them as a national culture, ensuring as it did the existence, and therefore the survival, of a homogenous Catholic Poland.

I tried to intimate the existence of such feelings to my hosts, but I failed. Instead, I examined the sarcophagus of Marshal Pilsudski, and the various tombs of Polish Romantic poets shipped home from impassioned or dissolute exile in Paris. But I couldn't chase away my lingering suspicions, and they recurred when I returned to the hotel. Here were the new, suited *nomenklatura* – Young Presidents from all over the world assembled under the banner of the Junior Chamber International. They were visiting the new states of the post-Communist world, and they were well informed. One of them, an American, had made a point of going to every former Communist country. He told me that it was easiest to get access to the President in Moldova, though the Czech Republic and Poland were pretty good, too. 'I think you can judge the desire for democracy by the degree of access,' he said. We argued amiably about the *End Of History* view of the world implied by the inexorable progress of liberal capitalism and its institutions. But when they asked me if I would accompany them by bus to Auschwitz the next day, I was stumped for an answer. I said I'd think about it.

In the past, visits to concentration camps inevitably formed the high, or low, part of my activities in this part of the world. I was locked in the blockhouse buildings at Maidanek at dusk and released by a vodka-sodden porter from *Macbeth*. I visited Auschwitz-Birkenau with the Professor of Modern History from Oxford and a bottle of vodka bought at a garage. In the days when Poland was really cheap, I went by cab to Auschwitz from Krakow, watching the driver keep the engine running in the cold while I stamped to keep warm. I mistrusted this habit of mine, hated the rage, which was without focus. I felt that it added nothing to the store of knowledge I had accumulated through books, or by repeated viewings of *Shoah* and other cinematic records, even when the whole point was that, like Primo Levi, the authors acknowledged their own insufficiency. However, go I did each time – and I was shocked to discover that on this occasion I hadn't wanted to. I realized, without knowing why, that I had come to Poland in order not to go.

I left the Young Presidents in the bar, and took a cab to the Old Square of Krakow. It was snowing lightly, and young people in anoraks were shouting at each other across the huge space. Colour was in evidence here – and I pinched myself as a reminder that I was in Poland. Suddenly, images of the camps returned to me: railway lines, broken huts, the piles of spectacles, hair, the chewed-up ground around the half-destroyed crematorium, and the frozen pond I had encountered with what appeared to be fragments of human bone as fine as sand at the edges. I could see the ill-luck, for Poles, in such reminders of mortality, or twentieth-century atrocity, and I could understand, too, how Poles might feel that they had earned the right to eliminate the undesirable past. But I also knew that the camps were ultimately the Polish badge of Europeanness. Most Poles were aware of this, and it made them angry – as if the mark of Cain had unjustly been branded on the nation. However, being Poles, I was certain they would also find a way of accommodating this monstrous injustice.

Next morning, I stood outside in the snowy parking lot, watching the Young Presidents climb into a brand-new German bus. I waved goodbye to them.

Bosnia: in the Ruins

Who remembers the Armenians these days?

Adolf Hitler

Sarajevo in the spring of 1996 was Harry Lime without the zither music or the nylons. There were no windows in the house in which I was staying, only UNHCR plastic sheeting; and it snowed early each morning, although this was April. If I tilted the half-broken TV aerial, propping it up with a yellowing Serbo-Croat copy of *Bonjour Tristesse*, I could switch channels. Bosnian television documented the rainy non-progress of an aid conference in Brussels, punctuated by a forlorn rock performance from an underfed, punkish teenager who sang a version of the Sex Pistols song entitled 'God Save Sarajevo' against a faded background of the red and white Coke symbol bearing the city's name. On HRT – Croat television – there were passing-out parades of young soldiers dressed in forage caps and fatigues, standing under the new Croat flag with its barber-shop colouring and its *recherché* Pils-label armorial badge. But the high point of each morning was the episode of *Wheel of Fortune*. The hostess was dressed in a lively peach colour, and the MC was beefy and affable, with white teeth and lavatory-brush hair. Above the spinning wheel, a board spelt out multi-consonant words full of js, cs, ks. The prizes included a jar of red peppers pickled in brine, German salami the colour of sheep's innards, and, on a three-legged garden table, a bunch of bananas and some oranges.

The roads led in any direction through steep, cobbled streets slippery with half-melted snow. Downhill the stepped path led past more or less intact small houses built on ledges cleared from the hill, their small porches covered with ivy. Uphill I passed a half-destroyed mosque, a boarded café, burst sandbags, a number of skinny dogs and, after a series of rubbish dumps in which had been placed the entire contents of houses – old bedding, springs, fantastically twisted pieces of bicycles, wrecked fridges and cookers – the city's old Jewish cemetery. This was where the family with whom I was staying had walked each day, often through sniper fire, to get water in large pails from a standpipe. For the next kilometre or so in every direction, up the hill or down, it was like stepping backwards into the European past, in some places to what I imagined bits of Italy must have been like in 1945, in others, where the damage was most intensive, and no houses were habitable, into the awesomely cratered villages of 1919 Flanders.

I started to make notes, and I gave up. I tried to remember all the footage I had seen of the Bosnian war (at a conservative reckoning, I must have watched over fifty hours) but nothing had ever indicated to me the quality of destruction I was encountering. From some vantage points, and in sunshine, the city appeared to have suffered some large-scale accident, and the apparent randomness of destruction, leaving some of the urban fabric intact, was almost reassuring. But this was an illusion, as I discovered rapidly. Even the most apparently scattered aggressions, against individual houses or isolated or packed-together apartment buildings, consisted of an agglomeration of deliberate acts; and most of the serious destruction had been as carefully organized as a supposedly random set of effects in a chic piece of performance art.

This was the case with such major acts of vandalism as the wrecking of the marvellous oriental-arched National Library, the old pinkish Habsburg Post Office by the river, the 1970s Parliament building, and the offices of the newspaper *Oslobodenje*. 'We are capable of doing this and more,' the wrecked buildings spelt out. 'Just wait and see what we can do.' On the end wall of one apartment building I could see shell holes at each level where the gunner had carefully adjusted his sights to provide a symmetrical line of holes, floor by floor, like a line of buttons on a suit. I remembered looking at footage of 1945 Berlin taken from the vantage point of a camera installed in the nose of a bomber – minute after minute of uninhabitable ruins until it seemed there could be none left. This vandalism was careful; though on a smaller scale, in some respects it was more shocking.

I woke early each morning after amorphous bad dreams. One son of the family with whom I lived drove World Bank dignitaries around in a smart new Mitsubishi four-wheel-drive, the other had opened a shop. In the next house lived a doctor who had operated on the wounded (often by candlelight) for three years while working as a translator for foreign broadcasters. It occurred to me that I had never really seen tired people before. Along with the daily UN bread ration, they ate boiled cabbage, and they sat each evening in the close back room before an open oven heated by Propane gas. Relieved that the war was over, they were nonetheless impatient with the half-peace. There was no money for anything, even new panes of glass. The city lived entirely from aid – most of their acquaintances either made their living servicing the aid effort, or hoped to do so. Meanwhile, they dreamed of emigrating and tried, as best they could, to enjoy themselves. They were saving up for a satellite dish. I'd been warned by British officials that Bosnians were always complaining about things, but I found many of them delightful – I liked their confidence. 'We're all afraid the aid workers will go,' a decorated twenty-four-year-old captain in the Bosnian Army explained to me, sitting in a café with his girl-friend. 'The trouble is that we don't know what we'd do without them.'

Whether there were reliable signs of life in the city or not appeared day by day to depend on the weather. When it was sunny, the tiredness showed on people's faces in the trams, but when grey announced the prospect of more snow they reverted to an expression of fixed, stoic hopelessness. A branch of Benetton selling bright, politically correct T-shirts had opened next to a plaque commemorating the deaths of journalists and media workers in the war. Among props from a recent chamber production of *Hamlet*, I listened to a debate held about the future of alternative media in Bosnia. Most participants sensibly wanted to know where the money was coming from. Meanwhile in the reopened cultural centre an exhibition showed the prize-winning atrocity photographs from the American press of the past year. People paused before each image, scrutinizing the extent of the damage done to a Tel Aviv bus by a single bomb. It occurred to me that they were relieved to be finding out that their city wasn't the only place capable of harbouring violent death.

There wasn't much to do in Sarajevo. On the way back from the football ground, next to a hospital where the city's over-memorialized new Muslim cemetery was situated, I stopped to buy chocolate. Sheltering from the cold in one of the two reopened cinemas, I watched Ken Loach's *Land and Freedom*, a recreation of the fate of a volunteer battalion betrayed by Stalinists in the Spanish Civil War. In one scene the soldiers discussed for over fifteen minutes how they should proceed with land collectivization, and I smiled at the two veterans sharing the cinema with me, uncertain how to express to them my own sense of bafflement. What could this mean to them? When they next fought a war, would they know how to nationalize plum trees and stray dogs? Over grey water each cold morning, I could stand exactly where in 1914 the Serbian nationalist Gavrilo Princip had killed Archduke Ferdinand and his wife. I walked across the city to the building where foreign TV crews were housed. I had come at a special moment in the rituals of the New World Order – the moment when journalists, scenting anticlimax, packed their bags and said goodbye to their half-wrecked vans and broken camera gear. Everywhere tapes containing records of atrocities past were being dropped into cardboard boxes while Serbo-Croat-speaking assistants, facing the prospect of redundancy, flipped idly between the CNN coverage of Israeli bombing in Lebanon and images of Formula One racing from Rome.

'I'll be back soon' is what broadcast journalists said to each other, in their strange half-showbiz argot pilfered from Marlene Dietrich and Joseph Heller. They were lying, of course. I overheard a journalist using the satellite to call an abandoned mistress in Moscow who was causing trouble, warning her that he had photos in his possession, and he was prepared to send them to Russian magazines. 'They do quite good girlie mags these days,' he repeated again and again. He sat morosely for a while before a series of images of graveyards, then he called a friend to tell him he was going to Tuzla. 'I hear there's a club with Russian dancers there,' he said. Then he called his wife to ask if his silk shirt had come back from the laundry in good shape.

It cost more than £150 a night to stay at the Holiday Inn, with its close, dusted air of neglect. Among the remains of the press corps, celebrating the departure of a British colonel in the room where Mine Familiarization courses were now held, an argument broke out over whether the allies should be vigorously pursuing major war criminals or not. When a British major counselled caution in tones of bluff common sense, suggesting that it would offend the Serbs, making peace-keeping more difficult, an American wire-service correspondent who had been in Bosnia for some time began to lose his temper. He shrugged and went to fetch another drink. Later, he talked to me about Woodrow Wilson. 'Why don't Europeans understand morality in international affairs?' he asked. Still later, we were joined by an Irish official. I asked him, as I did everyone, why it had taken so long to lift the siege. 'It took a while to find the right people in 1940,' he said.

I had never seen so many varieties of four-wheel-drives, all of them brand-new and painted white, bearing logos that made them look as if they came from progressive TV channels. Everywhere there were aid bureaucrats or workers carrying smart versions of the kitbags that once belonged to Royal Navy ratings, and wearing impeccably tailored Scandinavian leisurewear. Among the garrison troops, jauntily driving around in camouflaged vans, or eating pizzas at night, I mentally awarded prizes: to the Italians, for their woollen pom-pom *bersaglieri* hats, redolent of the absurd Habsburg headgear of the past century, and to the Brits, some of whom wore shoulder flashes declaring themselves to be part of the Princess of Wales battalion (they would be obliged to change them soon, removing the HRH as a consequence of the royal divorce), for ramrod 'seen-it-all' arrogance. I wondered what they did all day – perhaps, like the French platoon I found installed outside the local pizza parlour, they caught up with avant-garde novels. But they paid little attention to the substantial 'spillage' of UN-sponsored rations occurring under their noses, though I did hear rumours of vice rings and scandals involving the sale of equipment. One evening I caught sight of a German soldier dressed in a forage cap and carrying a machine-gun, waiting in line for the 90-pfennig hamburger. He was young, and his hair was bru-tally cropped. It occurred to me that he might be feeling embarrassed by his own improbable presence in the Balkans after all these years, until I noticed that he was being cruised by two Sarajevo homosexuals.

Younger, I suppose that I might have been excited by the prospect of being under fire, extracting great pictures under extreme pressure, but, unlike most journalists, I had come to be fascinated by the idea of aftermath. In Europe, it was idle to think that things ever ended neatly, like a football game or a film. In ways that no one now cared much to address, the war had been a true European disaster, doing great damage both to the idea of international order and to its emissaries, whether statesmen or journalists.

From my own uneasily comfortable perspective in London, the war had marked the moment of the 1990s when I became aware that all of us, acting through, or being represented by, what we called Europe, would, given the choice, not honour our commitments, finding many elab-orate reasons for inaction. Although correspondents had by and large what was called 'a good war', the ultimate failure of journalism was apparent in the configuration of what were called 'Sarajevo roses'. These were the marks left by mortars on the pavement; and they were finger-deep, scattered in public places. One mortar had fallen on a bread queue on May 27, 1992, wounding 100; and another, exploding over the crowded market on February 5, 1994, had killed 69 and wounded 195. After both these incidents, UN spokesmen had intimated that the attacks weren't necessarily the work of Serbs, raising the prospect that the Bosnian Muslims had killed their own people; and the UN representative Lord Owen had appeared to acknowledge that this might be the case. Was it so unlikely that a victim people would choose to blackmail, by whatever means possible, public opinion? Some commentators thought not. But after a third attack on the market from a bomb that exploded overhead on August 28, 1995, killing 44, public opinion, now steered to the opposite conclusion, blamed the Serbs for the atrocity; and that was when the long-delayed NATO air strikes on Serbian positions finally began, leading to the negotiations at Dayton and the end of the war.

While it was in progress, the war caused much anguish among educated Europeans. In *The Troubles We've Seen*, Marcel Ophuls' film about journalists in Sarajevo, the actor Philippe Noiret remarked that the real lesson of the Bosnian war was that, whatever idealistic journalists cared to imagine, the public didn't react to atrocity. 'There were no cameras in the 1930s,' he said to Ophuls, wig in hand and dressed in eighteenth-century costume. 'And of course people later said, "Well, if there had been cameras, this wouldn't have happened." Now we know that it wouldn't have made any difference at all.' I didn't wholly agree with him – pictures or words still did make a difference. What had happened instead of this was subtler, but no less damaging. As the American psychiatrist Robert Jay Lifton noticed, war had become one spectacle among others, if admittedly a form of human behaviour that made special claims on our attention:

> We are particularily shocked by the extent of the rape – little girls, young women, old women – mixed in with killing and with arrangements for the most extreme humiliation . . . As these feelings cause us only frustration and pain, we find ourselves struggling to get rid of them. So we switch channels, or turn off our TV sets, and do what we can to call forth our psychic numbing. We feel a little better, but we cannot quite free ourselves from some of those nagging images. We are then likely to join a chorus of ostensibly well-meaning voices insisting that, though things are indeed terrible in Bosnia, it is all very complicated.

Leaving aside Lifton's psychological explanation of 'numbing', which appeared to confer some sort of dignity on those who suffered from this syndrome, I could more or less accept what he was saying. This was an entirely new development, placing carnage at the level of the many unpleasant things that people saw on their television sets, and did or didn't do anything about; and it implied that violent events, having been 'consumed' – the word was now used by psychologists in this context – could then become, among politicians as well as viewers, a pretext for doing nothing. I had been ashamed by the moral inertia of France and Britain, as they steadfastly refused to do anything for month after month. But I had never been convinced that their apathy was a consequence of geopolitical interest, or, as many commentators whose forthrightness I respected had suggested, of the memory of Munich. During the 1930s appeasement of Hitler had at least reflected a series of moral or pragmatic calculations about the scale and nature of German power, misguided though these may have been. The truth about contemporary attitudes was less glamorous – like ourselves, our statesmen had succumbed to the Great Media Age. All of us strove to acquire the illusion of participation, but we were nothing but spectators.

On some occasions European or American statesmen, having been exposed to particularly gruesome material, would see fit to congratulate themselves (and each other) for having had the courage to resist emotionalism. They were not going to be moved, because it was their job not to be – it was as if the occurrence of atrocity and its coverage, along with their own response to it, conveniently existed on a loop, going round and round with total predictability. I thought of Bosnia each time I sat at home and watched *Gladiators*, the 'real' TV spectator game of the 1990s, with its competitors from different countries and its muscular protagonists in outlandish uniforms. For all that it mattered in relation to what was going on in Bosnia, our politicians might have been furnishing commentary for a restaging of the war in a park in the middle of London or Paris, announcing their obligation as umpires to abide by the rules, not intervening until the action was over. Meanwhile they could always say, with the British Prime Minister John Major, that the carnage reflected the perpetuation of 'ancient hatreds' – a position that conveniently ignored the fact that the combatants had lived in close proximity for many centuries, without always killing each other, and that the war involved the sack of a small, recently recognized European country.

But the Bosnian war also taught me another lesson, and that concerned the place of journalists, or indeed Europeans – they were surely rated in similar terms – in the New World Order. Formerly, the occupation of journalism had seemed honourable to me, affording some possibilities of remedying the ills of the world, but now, no matter how it was discharged, it seemed to have shrunk in significance even as its technical possibilities expanded. In a different sense the same was true about the condition of being European. The Bosnian war was a contemporary version of a Shakespeare history play, full of psychopathic and literate tyrants, high Roman sentiments coming from ex-Communist dictators, victims and murderers by the thousand. It had even ended appropriately, amid piles of corpses, with the false strains of unanimity inspired by *Pax Americana*. But the European roles were those of non-participants – we supplied the breathless soliloquies at the edge of the theatrical apron, or the flatulent noises from back-stage in the safe vicinity of the arras. I couldn't estimate the consequences of the European role of self-imposed subordination, but I imagined that they would be long-term, and perhaps irretrievable, affecting both the Old Powers, France and Britain, and the idea of Europe itself. Who would ever take us seriously again?

In Ilidza, a newish village at the edge of Sarajevo, fought over for three years, and almost wholly destroyed, I watched people clearing rubbish from their wrecked houses and creating fires. One or two of them were starting to repair masonry, and they stared up as the big transport planes flew low into the airport. I hired a car with a driver for the day and went through gorges lined with explosions of yellow broom and the thick black trunks of trees that hadn't yet caught spring. Around isolated villages the woods were thickest, spooky-looking like the vertical spears of the soldiers in Bruegel's *Massacre of the Innocents*. Mostar had been destroyed, and it was now being rebuilt with EU money. In the hotel on the Croat side, which was warm and comfortable, smelling of cooking pork, I counted the pigeon-holes of fifty-four aid organizations, ranging from *Freunde* and *Agape* to *Pharmaciens sans Frontières*. I talked to a French aid worker who represented the UNHCR. She had been in Bosnia for four years, and she was lively and well-educated. Back in France I could have imagined Ariane doing PR for symphony orchestras, or supervising literary prizes, but here she appeared to be struggling with a malignant strain of black dog. There wouldn't be a Federation of any consequence, she told me – most of the EU guilt money had already been wasted. Her harshness was extended to the Bosnians, whom she described as time-wasters and professional victims. But it was in relation to Europeans, France and Britain in particular, that her sense of betrayal was most pronounced. She, too, didn't under-stand why they had done nothing for so long. At one time, it had appeared that they really were afraid – this was a persistent French fantasy, expressed by every officer with intellectual pretensions – of the creation of a Muslim state in Europe. Now, in the light of their acceptance of the Dayton agreements, she wasn't so sure.

I asked her about this. Every Bosnian journalist I had met made this point to me; but I couldn't see anti-Islamism as an explanation of apathy. Europeans weren't in a mood to crusade against anything.

'The French really like the Serbs,' she said. 'Every time they come here they tell me how well they get on with them. They respect power. They want to do business in Serbia.' Then she added: 'Anyhow, French people always think of surrender as a solution. Remember what they did in 1940. They never expected the Bosnians to fight.'

I asked her about the British, to whom this analysis didn't apply; and she sighed.

'Neither the French nor the British ever wanted to do anything,' she said. 'I suppose it was enough for them to be here. They just wanted to be considered as Great Powers.'

Restless, wanting to see more of the country, I tried to lay my hands on a four-wheel-drive in Sarajevo; but here a surprise awaited me. There were vehicles available, of course; but no Muslim driver was prepared to venture into Serb territory. Most of the broadcasters were either idle, or doing the rounds of mass-burial sites – not an inviting prospect. As a solo operator, I was offered vehicles at near-extortionate rates, and renters would pull out of the deal when I explained that in the event of my hitting a mine they would have to recoup the value of the vehicle from my heirs. But I did eventually find a reckless or merely charitable news agency, and I drove a small, back-crunching Lada away from Sarajevo one cold morning.

The roads were pitted, with more canyons containing their quota of Bruegelesque trees. Once again, the damage seemed arbitrary, and then, the more one saw, predictable. There were full buses everywhere, lumbering up inclines and wheezing down them; and I remembered so much footage of women and children herded into them at gun-point or emerging dazed, too exhausted to panic. We would surely see the bus as a symbol of this war just as we had come to see the last European one through the images of death trains. UN convoys of enormous white trucks passed me, escorted by olive-green four-wheel-drives. I began to encounter American troops, with their huge permanent-looking encampments and their splendid designer uni-forms. Whereas the rest of the NATO forces and the Russians were tattily dressed, looking like extras from a

Yugo-epic about the Second World War, the Americans appeared to have re-equipped themselves as movie futurism in the image of Schwarzenegger. I counted beach-buggy Humvees, Abrams battle tanks parked by the road-side like vast pieces of corporate sculpture, barbed-wire bundles the density of candy-floss. When I stopped at a checkpoint before passing into Bosnian Serb territory, the young bespectacled soldier saluted me briskly. 'They shouldn't give you any trouble,' he said in the accents of positive thought. 'If they do stop you, or give you trouble, just let us know.'

I was travelling with Sonja, who had a Canadian passport but whose parents were *émigré* Croats, and who was there-fore able to pass as a Serb. The countryside became wilder as we climbed, with fewer and fewer settlements, and no ruins; I could have been in parts of Scotland, or Norway. Then we came to a village slightly larger than the others, with barbed-wire encampments at the outskirts leading off into more dense woods. This was Han Piesak, headquarters of the Bosnian Serb Army, where various war criminals wanted by the International Court at The Hague were sup-posedly hidden, including the Serb commander Ratko Mladić. This was also where the remains of their arsenal (pitiful, as it turned out, implying no serious possibility of opposition to NATO forces) was stored. It was one of the Serbs' 'holy places' – a mountain which the Chetniks had successfully defended against the Croat Nazi Ustashe forces, and to which, having gone out in search of plunder or territorial aggrandizement, they had now retreated.

Tall men dressed in fatigues decorated with the red, white and blue Serb shoulder flash, sporting hunting knives sus-pended from their belts, hung around the square in large groups. There were no women to be seen. In the café testosterone levels surged over the muddy bass of patriotic Serb techno-rock. We ordered glasses of retch-making Slivovitz and talked to the clients. One by one they told us that they had won the war. It had been necessary to fight, in order to prevent the creation of a fundamentalist Muslim state in Europe. They had captured enough towns. There was an international conspiracy to brand all Serbs as criminals; but no atrocities had been committed. These were lies told by Muslims. One of the drinkers, who had just been demobbed, was happy to discover I was British. 'The British were good for us, they were very objective,' he said. All of them said they looked forward to another war. 'We will finish with the Muslims,' the ex-soldier said affably. 'You wait and see – next time we'll exterminate them.'

I asked him whether he really believed that the atrocities were propaganda. I had seen so many images of people being herded into buses, or corpses being stacked into trucks for burial. 'People are killed in wars,' he said, shrugging. 'Anyhow, the people taken away were moved for their own protection.'

He talked to some people at the bar, who laughed.

'Do you think they didn't kill our own people?' he asked.

Even in its most debased form, the practice of journalism implies the notion that people, confronted by their deeds, will converse rationally; but much about this war, like other European conflicts, had not been rationally explicable. The country was almost empty – what was the real 'territorial function' of Serb aggression? Exactly what did they find to hate so much in the people among whom they had lived for so long? No one had explained these matters to me; I suspected they fell into the category of things which either received simple, or tautologous, explanations, or were otherwise best passed over in favour of an examination of the whatness of war – the who did what and to whom questions, to which answers could certainly be given.

Dropping from hill to hill, we passed more woods. Then we came to steep gorges and meadows splashed above or below rocks. The fast-flowing river was an eerie light green, almost cobalt. This was the Drina, historically the boundary between the Serb mountain towns and the principally Muslim settlements strung out along the roads eastwards leading into the old Turkish Empire. The towns here had been the first to be sacked in 1992, by Serbian irregulars often acting with the assistance of the Yugoslav army. No complete record existed of such early 'cleansings' because they had taken place before the Western media arrived on the scene. But the fighting here had set the pattern for the rest of the war, establishing a precedent for looting Muslim villages, either killing the inhabitants or sending them to what became rural ghettoes, where they could later be cleared out once more, or, as happened at Srebrenica a year previously, taken into the hills and murdered. It was here that the Serbs learnt their lesson – that you could do what you liked, and get away with it as long as the killing took place away from prime time. I stopped the car by the river, and counted thirty-five smashed and burnt houses – even outlying shacks had been comprehensively vandalized. The village had been recently built as a showcase, probably in the 1970s, and the sides of the mosque had been ripped off, showing a bare concrete base. The dome was half-collapsed, and the minaret had been pushed over to one side by the force of the explosion. The message was simple, admitting of no equivocation: no one should live here.

I wanted to see Višegrad, the next town in the valley, because it was the setting of the Serbo-Croat novel *The*

Bridge over the Drina. Its author, Ivo Andrić, was a Croat educated in Sarajevo and jailed as a young man for being a nationalist. As a diplomat representing the inter-war Yugoslav state, Andrić wrote tracts denigrating in vehement terms the role of the Turkish occupiers; but by the time he turned to writing fiction during World War Two he supported the idea of a multi-ethnic state in Yugoslavia. Spanning almost four centuries by taking as his motif the construction of a bridge at Višegrad by a Grand Vizier of the Turkish Empire born in Bosnia, he told the story of the grudging series of expedients, some of them touching in their ingenuity, whereby townspeople, whether Muslim, Christian or Jewish, were able to live side by side. The bridge was the miracle of his book, but so, too, were many other aspects of town life, most of all the 'incomprehensible marvel' that allowed life to be wasted and spent, and even – Andrić's townspeople, Muslims or Christians, were as dour as Scots – occasionally enjoyed. But in 1914 the occupying Austrians were responsible for the physical destruction of the bridge; like a later collection of outsiders, the latter from Belgrade, they, and not the townspeople themselves, caused the killings:

> Only then began the real persecution of the Serbs and all those connected with them. That wild beast, which lives in man and does not dare show itself until the barriers of law and custom have been removed, was now set free. The signal was given: the barriers were down. As has so often happened in the history of man, permission was tacitly granted for acts of violence and plunder, if they were carried out in the name of higher interests, according to established belief, and against a limited number of men of a particular type of belief.

Višegrad was by now somewhat less grand than in the heyday of Habsburg occupation. In the main square there were a few stalls selling nothing in particular, and I bought a bottle of vinegary Montenegrin white wine. After watching an overweight Serb officer check into the run-down hotel in the company of the town prostitute, we walked to the supermarket. Apart from lurid-coloured syrups and ersatz chocolate, there wasn't much on the shelves. The woman at the till explained that the town was poor now, and they ate nothing but bread. 'It was different,' she began to say, a little wistfully, of the past. But then a boy came out of the half-empty stockroom, and told us how his father had been killed by Muslims, and was buried in the local churchyard. The woman suddenly lost the desire to talk. 'If you want to know where the mosque is, you'd better ask the police,' she said, waving us away.

Before the war around 14,000 Muslims had lived in Više-grad. A month before I went there Ed Vulliamy of the *Guardian* had discovered that many of those who were not sent by bus into exile had been kept in a makeshift concen-tration camp in the town. From there they were taken half-dead to the bridge, where they were further beaten or stabbed, and thrown over the stone rampart into the river – the killings took place in the evening, a time when most of the town would be watching. A fourteen-year-old boy helped to fish 180 bodies out of the river, many of them decapitated, some of them children of ten or twelve. He helped bury them. 'Some I knew personally, they were my neighbours,' he said. The rest floated downstream to the local hydroelectric plant, just over the border in Serb terri-tory, causing the management to complain to the Višegrad police inspector that they were killing people too quickly, and that the culverts of the dam were blocked with corpses.

As we walked around the town, I remembered the village of Rechnitz, on the remote, hilly border between Austria and Hungary, where I had been sent the previous year by an enterprising local journalist who was writing a book about Austrian attitudes to the past. There, too, people had been expelled, and their houses stolen; but the village was also notorious for having accommodated the slaughter of three hundred Jews in the final days of the war. Nothing was unusual about the way in which the Jews, who were building fortifications for some last insane stand of the Reich, were taken out into the darkness by a collection of drunk local worthies, made to dig their graves and shot; what appeared to be distinctive, however, was the reticence, year after year, of the locals, who refused to acknowledge that the incident had taken place, even though the fields around their pretty geranium-decked *platz* were ploughed up, scoured by dogs, flown over by helicopters. 'We have a right to forget,' one old woman told a visiting television crew in the accents of aggrieved righteousness. I had concluded, perhaps unfairly, that the Rechnitz story reflected prevailing Austrian attitudes; but now I saw that there was nothing un-European about the massacres in the former state of Yugoslavia except their timing – part of the European embarrassment was a consequence of the fact that in Bosnia it seemed as if the dead had indeed returned only to be killed again. But I could equally be certain that in thirty years' time there would still be people looking for the places in which those they loved had been killed and buried – and that their enquiries would be similarly met.

The bridge was silvery in the afternoon sun, and the stone was pleasant to the touch. 'Of all the things that life drives man to shape and build,' Andrić wrote, 'none, I think, is as precious as a bridge . . . They serve no arcane or evil purpose.' We stood on the middle span, where it had been widened to create a platform on which the townspeople could sit, and above which was a ceramic plaque, with arabic lettering, when I saw two policemen coming towards us. They were extremely tall, in a blue version of the fatigues worn by soldiers. One of them inspected our passports, and took notes, while the other talked on the intercom. Then they walked us back to the small car, and stood in silence, saluting punctiliously until we had driven out of the town.

I saw a lot of Serbian Bosnia in the next twenty-four hours, but through the glass of what I had already seen. Everywhere were smashed villages, guarded like compounds by UN troops, and broken bridges over torrents. At Grad I stopped and talked to a platoon of bored French troops from Marseilles squatting by the side of their off-white, dirt-streaked personnel vehicles. They wanted to know about Eric Cantona, and whether the British had forgiven him his attack on a fan. 'It's terrible,' the sergeant said, gesturing at the landscape. 'It's far worse than television, which is at least drama. Nothing prepares you for the sheer scale of the destruction.' In the Serb lands, the towns were unscathed, yet filthy, with rubbish tips where the houses bordered on the river. An American correspondent had told me the Serbs were 'cousin-fuckers', and there was an Ozark or Appalachian aspect to their empty villages. But then we came to more plateaux and woods, all of them empty; and I found that I kept thinking of the two villages, in Austria and Bosnia.

In London I owned a silkscreen print by the American artist Kitaj, taken from the cover of a Polish book of the 1960s, which bore the hazy silhouette of an image of the Second World War, a soldier aiming at the head of a mother who stood with her back to him, attempting to shield her child. The soldier seemed to be standing next to his victims, and I wasn't sure whether the images belonged together. But in Jonah David Goldhagen's book *Hitler's Willing Executioners*, which I had taken with me to Bosnia, the original was reprinted, and I could see that the photograph hadn't been doctored. Goldhagen's book received many criticisms from historians, some of whom considered his explanation of the Germanness of 'eliminationist' anti-Semitism – the killing of Jews, in simpler language – to be too sweeping, or unhistorical in its neglect of comparative examples. But I had been impressed by other qualities in his narrative, notably his ability to recreate the circumstances in which Jews had been killed, one by one, away from the camps, and the way he had established that the German perpetrators had in many instances killed in a berserk state of mind. For me the book went some way towards destroying the prevailing image of industrialized dispassionateness with which the Holocaust had been enveloped as a consequence of the proliferation of academic studies:

It is highly likely that, back in Germany, these men had walked through the woods with their own children. With what thoughts did each of these men march, gazing sidelong at the form of, say, an eight- or twelve-year-old girl who to the unideologized mind would have looked like any other girl? Did he see a little girl, and ask himself why he was about to kill this little, delicate human being who, if seen as a little girl by him, would normally have received his compassion, protection and nurturance? Or did he see a Jew, a young one, but a Jew nonetheless?

You could ask similar questions about Serbs with respect to their killing of Muslims. Lists were drawn up in each village, and the men were culled according to their importance – but, as in Višegrad, the killing was random, too. Of course there were no 'lessons' to be drawn from such scenes, although in due course such atrocities would generate their own schools of exegesis. All one could say was that the notion that such things couldn't recur was based on nothing more firm than superstition:

> We thought it would outlive all future days.
> O what fine thought we had because we thought
> That the worst rogues and rascals had died out.

I had never wanted to believe these lines of Yeats (from '1919'), implying as they did that the liberal project of humanizing the world was doomed; but now, in Bosnia, they seemed true to me.

We stopped for the night in a hotel specially designed for pilgrims in Medugorje, the Croat shrine at which a number of children were supposed to have sighted the Virgin Mary, and to which pilgrims came from all over the world. I took a garish crucifix off the wall, placing it under the bed, and I hid the bland, smiling face of the Virgin. Spinning through bad dreams, I wondered what this part of the world might have been like but for the mad dream of a Greater Homeland in which there could be neither Muslims nor Croats. Would people ever have wanted to live together? I received some sort of answer when we stopped on the road between Split and Zagreb on the edge of a village recently 'cleansed' of its Serbs and resettled by Croats.

At the King Vuonimir Inn – the monarch was a medieval Croat, famed for his consumption of sheep – Veso and

Betty, two very large and sunny-tempered Croats who had re-emigrated from Australia, held their own court among kebabs, cups of coffee, piles of chips and giant beer mugs. The waiters wore special T-shirts, and they struggled with the plates; although Betty said they were lazy they appeared to do their best. Lamb was slaughtered each morning by an impassive odd-job man dressed in blue overalls and boots and holding a large stick, and it was rotated on a motorized spit onto which a second device blew charcoal flames. Veso explained that the lamb made no money, but everyone was angry when it wasn't there.

Coachloads of German tourists, truck drivers, businessmen in BMWs wearing shades came and went. The local judge and the mayor were eating lamb beside me. At the door, waiting for Veso, were two small Indonesian soldiers dressed in immaculate uniforms holding glasses of Coke – their job (sanctioned by the occupying forces, Veso assured me, who encouraged community work) was to shift the restaurant's rubbish. Veso, who had worked in Zagreb as a bouncer in a night-club as well as a policeman, and who had at one time advised President Tudjman about foreign affairs, had been able to acquire the restaurant at a knockdown price because it had formerly belonged to Serbs. He had borrowed lots of money from friends, but he had already bought a huge silver Mercedes. 'I love it,' Veso said. 'This is my country and I love to be here. Only I never see Betty because I get up so early. We never even spend time in bed together.'

The lamb was, as he had promised, astonishing. Veso scraped his chair backwards, and went off to supervise the Indonesians clearing rubbish. I asked him the same question as I had the woman in the store at Višegrad. Wouldn't it have been better if the Serbs hadn't been kicked out?

'They're pigs,' he said. 'They don't know how to behave. You should have seen the mess when I got here. We're better rid of them. Anyhow, if they hadn't gone I wouldn't have my restaurant, would I?'

Dublin and Belfast: Imaginary Irelands

I hate Ireland.

Elizabeth Bowen (1972)

I once spent a long summer in a suburban Cambridge house in the company of a friend's father, an IRA veteran who told me that he had been excommunicated by the Catholic Church as a young man during the 1920 Civil War. He and his friends had tied the Bishop of Tralee to a stake at low tide, and left him there, on the mistaken assumption that the waters would rise far enough to drown him – finding him alive when they returned, they cut the Bishop loose. My friend's father was old and ill, and he would brood over the past, or the unattractive Republican-coloured peas, accompanied by rubber wood pigeon, that we retrieved from the freezer every day. But I also remember what happened when he asked me whether I liked Irish poetry. To please him, and because it was true, I said yes, I liked William Butler Yeats, indeed I knew a lot of his poetry by heart.

'A phoney!' he said, banging the table so that his peas shuddered on the plate. I asked him why he believed this to be the case – what was phoney about Yeats, whose work I had been persuaded to regard as the epitome of artistic integrity? 'A bloody Englishman pretending to be an Irishman,' he said.

Thereafter I felt ill-qualified to deal with what I was assured was the reality of Ireland, in particular as it came to me through the favoured Irish medium, that of words. Not that I disliked anything about the place when I went there, even in times of violence; but I did experience the sense of being shut out from something rich or important, and I was mildly resentful. The writer Elizabeth Bowen, like Yeats an Anglo-Irish Protestant, described the relationship between English and Irish as 'a mixture of showing-off and suspicion, nearly as bad as sex'. This was apt, if one added the pantechnicon guilt adopted by some English in relation to the colonial past; but it was also evident to me how Irish friends living temporarily (or even settled) in England sometimes found things difficult. They might reveal how much they disliked aspects of the Republican tradition, but I could never be sure that such attitudes weren't adopted for English consumption – and I noticed that they weren't happy disavowing the violence of the Irish past, its repressive Church, or the crushing politicization of every Irish institution. In parallel with the vocal, ultimately exhausting Anglophobia a tradition of false friendship had grown up, where much was left unsaid – but this meant that much had been lost to people living in the British Isles by the lopping-off of Ireland and its half-conscious reduction in status to a place where one sometimes went on holidays, and where people, for inexplicable, half-forgotten reasons, tended to kill each other.

However, in the 1990s I began to notice how much I enjoyed going to Ireland. It wasn't just a question of the freshly built roads and bridges, earnestly marked out with yellow and blue flags, or the priestly misdeeds paraded on Gay Byrne's national institution *The Late, Late Show*. Mysteriously, and without undue fuss, it was suddenly more than all right to be Irish – and I wasn't surprised that this happened precisely at the moment when one could say the opposite about the condition of being English. Meanwhile something had changed about the geography of Ireland. In the past the island had been a green blob fastened to what people persisted in calling the 'mainland' of the British Isles. Now Irishness could appear to be attached to a variety of other places, depending on who you were talking to – to America, of course, with its sixty million Irish and its money, to the rest of the world (Irish speakers gestured hazily in the direction of the country's tradition of internationalism, consisting of sending nuns or priests to the poor of the world, and its neutralist support of organizations like the UN as a consequence of its own experience of colonialism), but, above all, to Europe. Here it seemed to me that prodigious self-reinvention had taken place. Once upon a time there had been an Old Ireland, which was a colony of Britain but which was also romantic and violent. Then came a Less Old country, a boring place to live, because it was poor and dominated by the Catholic Church, in European terms almost as isolated as Salazar's Portugal or Hoxha's Albania, sending its young to rebuild dull cities on the bigger island. Finally, and in a matter of only a few years, to the astonishment of many Irish and the bafflement of the British, few of whom realized what was going on, Ireland had Europeanized itself. The ninety-year-old Lord Longford, a proponent of Irishness as well as a campaigner on behalf of lost causes, acknowledged the change when I met him amid the green sofas and carpets of the faded ascendancy Irish Club in London's Eaton Square. 'It is a better place,' he said, smiling. 'People don't think the changes are real or lasting, but I do.'

Unlike the British, the Irish had seen their opportunities in Europe and taken them – indeed, they had used the new relationship to prise themselves away from Britain. Their success ran on engagingly parallel tracks to the story of British failure in a way that George Bernard Shaw would have instantly grasped and found amusing – a major pre-occupation of leader-writers in the excellently written *Irish Times* was how to stop the country being held back by the old-fashionedness of English nationalism. But the success of Ireland also suggested that Europe, far from merely shoring up the dull *status quo*, could imply change and subversion, and that one could find oneself suddenly modern by being European, strange as these ideas might seem in either Brussels or London. What did the New Ireland mean? What did it imply to suddenly find oneself European, no longer patronized or rendered insignificant by peripheral status? In the short term, it spelt frenzied activity and hectic self-examination – an attractive combination. 'Consciousness has developed faster than our ability to legislate,' explained an elegant woman reporter I met. She was on her way to examine one of the dark places remaining in Irish life – yet another scandal involving the suppression of paedophile acts, though she assured me that this time the Catholic Church wasn't involved.

In Dublin, where I spent some time in the summer of 1996, I could sit comfortably in the bar of the Shelbourne Hotel and eat Irish stew, drink Powers or Guinness and watch from the vantage point of a comfortable tartan-covered chair as the city's politicians, professors of litera-ture and cineastes mingled with old gentry, horseflesh-pressers and beef *nouveaux riches*. They were enthusiastic, but they seemed nervous, too, and I began to recognize the ironic recitation of success as the primary characteristic of contemporary Ireland. It wouldn't do to be boasting, but wasn't the economy growing as fast as eight per cent – twice the rate of the nearest EU rival? Didn't Ireland now provide Olympic swimmers, good football and rugby teams, but also the current Nobel Prize-winner for literature? But there were also people who viewed these developments with less than whole-hearted affection, decrying the disappearance in Ireland of the traditional attitude of 'begrudgery'. For Seamus Deane, who had just written a book about growing up in 1950s Derry in a Catholic working-class family, the reinvention of Ireland remained grounds for irony or mild complaint. Deane described himself as a Republican; but he now resented the watering-down of Irishness. 'I suppose we have to get used to many consequences of success, including the commodification of literature,' he said. 'But being favoured is a most un-Irish experience.'

Deane's book *Reading in the Dark* (winner of the 1996 *Guardian* Fiction Prize) recounted the wrongful betrayal of an uncle as an informer, and the family cover-up, involving the spiriting away to America of the real culprit. Nothing was correctly remembered in the world in which he grew up – but nothing was forgotten. Sharp-faced and bespectacled, wearing faded black Levi's and a smart if worn tweed jacket, Deane, who now worked the Irish scene in America, told me that he had met his first Protestant at the age of seventeen. Like most of his generation, he was still uneasy with partition but (another switch in attitude, made easier by the new porousness of Europe) he appeared to have become reconciled to its existence. 'I still am a Republican,' he said. 'For all the recent diminishment of the ideal, I cannot abandon the ideal. And I would hope that some time – we have had to abandon any notion of a time-scale – it will come about. I still think it will.'

Ireland was a somewhat simpler place for the next generation. With Irish music and films to help them along, having the run of Europe as well as Britain, and an Ireland more congenial than the one their parents had inhabited, it was easier for them to put off the Republican future. For the *Irish Times* columnist Fintan O'Toole, who had written a funny book about the grotesque Irish beef scandals which had come with EU subsidy, the success of Ireland could be expressed, other than by the practice of traditional political skills of swag-carrying and clientelism, in the Irish abandonment of what had for a long time, beneath the thumb of the Church and its supporters among conservative Irish politicians, been considered to be Irishness. In the past the Irish constitution (unlike the British one, it was written down, containing clauses encouraging the preservation of the family, and it required a referendum to change anything) had impeded the modernization of the country, but the existence of European law over and above local provisions had changed all that. European legislation helped Irish judges in their struggles with English courts – suddenly, reform became fashionable. It was significant that the Irish élite, stumbling over each other to abolish the last vestiges of clericalism, should after the referendum on abortion have adopted a law regarding the age of consent for homosexuals that was more liberal than the British one. 'This is really the end of the Counter-Reformation,' O'Toole explained, smiling. 'The Protestants should put up a monument. They are the only people who don't understand what has happened.'

It was in the older and larger nations of Europe that frustration was to be encountered. In Dublin, I found the same kind of buzz as in Helsinki, another poor and peripheral city prised apart from an Empire, now stuffed with EU money and good feelings. Litter-strewn only recently, looking like water-logged cardboard, the old Georgian centre had recently become spiffy – 'de-paddyized' was an expression I heard – no longer an attractive English-looking provincial city dumped negligently on the edge of a green island, but a European capital. One morning I left the beautiful trees of St Stephen's Green, walked down Grafton Street past the Dáil and around Trinity College. Then I crossed the Liffey, walking up O'Connell Street past the pillared GPO, still pock-marked from the 1916 Rising, into the Municipal Gallery of Modern Art, situated in a tatty Georgian house on Parnell Square. Here I sat and looked at the fifteen-odd paintings from the 1920s, most of them by John Lavery, which had been reassembled and exhibited as they were when they served as the inspiration for William Butler Yeats's 1937 poem 'The Municipal Gallery Revisited'.

The room was empty, smelling of floor polish and potatoes, and it contained a snug assemblage of faces not dissimilar to those I had recently left in the Shelbourne. There was a moody-looking picture of Yeats himself from his London days, when he roomed near Euston Station; of his friend John Synge, his Anglo-Irish patroness Augusta Gregory, and her son, who was killed flying over France in 1916 and whom Yeats depicted as a gentleman-Nietzschean hero.

> The years to come seemed waste of breath,
> A waste of breath the years behind
> In balance with this life, this death.

Next came Anglophobic Irish politicians in states of elaborate, frock-coated self-importance. But amid such Establishmentarian stolidity my eye was caught by the presence of Roger Casement, being tried for collaboration with Germany, soon to be executed; by a lurid picture of Michael Collins laid out beneath an Irish tricolour; and by a religiose rendering of the blessing of the Irish colours by a figure described by Yeats as 'an Abbott or Archbishop with an upraised hand'. Yeats had ostensibly wished to write about the 'glory' of having known such friends, but he still included a characteristic dig at the country of which he was the prime adornment:

> 'This is not', I say,
> 'The dead Ireland of my youth, but an Ireland
> The poets have imagined, terrible and gay.'

Later, after a short bus ride past the tarted-up Guinness distillery, I stood in the gravelled yard of Kilmainham Prison. This was where, after a week of fighting, in May 1916, Pearse, Connolly and the other fifteen were shot in the consummation of blood sacrifice, eliciting the hostility towards the British of the stolidly loyal Dublin middle class. It was quiet and warm, under the usual low grey sky, and no one else was there. I thought of what had happened here primarily as a sign of late-imperial-era stupidity. But I recalled a recent altercation between the Irish novelist Colm Toíbín and a literary critic, Declan Kiberd. After Kiberd had depicted the Uprising, somewhat blithely perhaps, as a form of street theatre, lethal for its participants but redounding to the fame of Ireland as a generator of post-colonial consciousness, Toíbín had taken him to task. His view was that violence had served to legitimize generations of violence, and that such sentimentalism, from which he had suffered at school, was anyhow distinctly *passé*.

Neither of these positions was exactly new, but the difference was that Irish people could hold both of them at once. 'I'm a post-nationalist: I'm through with flags and anthems,' a friend explained; but I noticed that he had done so while explaining how wonderful it was to be Irish. Yes, the whole history of Republican violence should be viewed as pretty much what the British would call a load of rubbish (an Irish Western was the usual expression – that explained the idiocy of sacrifice in movie shorthand), but it had anyhow come to serve its purpose, increasing the sense of nationhood and periodically furnishing plots for movies. It was, within whatever frame you chose to place it, either deeply serious, or silly, or both – but in the new Irishness all of these separate attitudes somehow must have their place. In the Old Ireland, I remembered, there was such a thing as an 'Irish fact' – something that might or might not be true, but anyhow should be.

On the way back I called at the memorial for the Irish Great War dead designed by the British architect Lutyens, which had been allowed to decay, and had only recently been refurbished. Standing amid neat flower beds I admired the un-Irish sense of tidiness represented by the gesture while feeling that it had come somewhat late. Recent 'revisionist' historical writing had seemed to conclude that Ireland might under different circumstances have stayed within the Empire or Commonwealth; but the presumption that there was nothing inevitable about the creation of nations could nowadays, especially if one adopted the Irish perspective, be twisted to any conclusion. I wondered whether Scottish and Welsh nationalists shouldn't somehow feel cheated by the British failure to

arrange similar bloodshed in Cardiff or Glasgow. Wouldn't
they be better off – the thought wasn't cynically inspired –
if they, too, had revolted against the British, ultimately
finding themselves represented as separate countries over
such questions as beef bans or film quotas? Wouldn't they
have thereby acquired what Scots nationalists didn't have –
a poetics of blood and nation? Riding back to the centre I
remembered that it was the neutralist De Valera, father of
the Irish nation, who offered his condolences to the
German Ambassador in Dublin on receiving news of
Hitler's suicide, explaining helpfully that he wasn't going to
add to German humiliation in the hour of defeat. Was Irish
nationalism *really* so very wonderful anyhow? How was it
that the same people who abhorred expressions of 'big
nation' English or German nationhood – the Falklands war
had seemed particularly repugnant to them – found themselves so captivated by it? Perhaps they felt it was harmless
because the country was so small – or perhaps the theatric-
ality of Irish violence did make it attractive to those (North
Americans were most susceptible in this respect) who
weren't forced to experience it at close quarters. I didn't
have the answer to this contemporary riddle.

Temple Bar, the area of the city by the Liffey recently
Bohemianized and filled with new-old pubs that were
prototypes of the world-wide craze for Irish décor, also
contained a new Irish Film Centre, built in part with EU
regional development money. Back in London, I had once
endured the lugubrious experience of British indifference
to or miscomprehension of Ireland by watching every film
made in Britain about Ireland; and I now gave myself the
parallel experience of looking at old Irish films. The earliest
Irish films were made by Fenian Americans keen to redress
the unfairness of history. Out of focus and filled with black

and white figures, when they weren't rehashing the plot of *Romeo and Juliet* – in Irish versions, the woman was always Catholic, but in the English equivalent, Juliet was Protestant – these films recited the 1798 Rebellion, the Potato Famine or the Great Martyrdom of 1916. By the 1930s, however, the grip of American studios, influenced by Hollywood Anglophilia, prevailed, and a cutesy ruralism came into fashion. After that, sadly, came a long period in which, with the exception of Carol Reed's *Odd Man Out*, nothing in particular was filmed in Ireland, except for celebrations of peat cutting or Church orphanages – until, in the 1980s, things were suddenly altered, and the doors flung wide open.

During the 1890s Irish nationalism, like its Czech or Polish equivalents, was kept alive by the rediscovery of the Gaelic language, and the development of an élite, ostensibly native literature. British officials, asked to comment on the rising tide of nationalism, would affirm in their reports that it was only literature. Something similar had happened during the 1980s with the invention of an Irish cinema capable of attracting audiences throughout the world. The first film of the New Irish cinema was *Angel*, by Neil Jordan, and it described the flight through ruined fairgrounds and lonely back roads of a no-hoper reluctantly entangled with the violence of the IRA. The story wasn't original, but I remembered being convinced that something was going on – Jordan was a real poet, but, much more important, an Irish poet. Then came a trickle of productions, some good and some bad, all of them possessing the same quality of poetic localism and yet making Ireland available to anyone. By the end of the 1980s, the trickle had become a small flood – *Eat The Peach*, a story of would-be entrepreneurs building a Wall of Death; *My Left Foot*, the biopic of the

paraplegic writer Christy Brown; *The Commitments*, Roddy
Doyle's chronicle of a band; *In The Name Of The Father*, a
rendering, much criticized in Britain but a hit in America,
of the trial and imprisonment of the Guildford Four; *The
Crying Game*, Jordan's most successful if not best film, a
unique, un-Irish foray (sex had not yet come to Irish films,
save through the theme of unwanted pregnancy) not just
into the ambiguities of terrorism, but of transvestism, too.

Some aspects of these films – their small, always under-
financed scope, the little-man heroes, whether band leaders,
con men or reluctant killers – recalled Italian neo-realism,
or, if one allowed for the different practice of irony, Czech
comedies; others – the winsomeness of small domestic disasters, and the placing of green Dublin buses – reminded
me of the self-consciously small English films of the 1960s.
But there was something different, too, and something truly
Irish about them apparent in the concern for morals and
sensibility as well as for stoutly constructed episodes. They
were combined with Irish pubs as evidence of what Deane
had called 'commodification', and yet I felt that this didn't
entirely do them justice. Irish films were likeable because
their makers had real reasons for creating them outside
the nexus of quotas and money which the European film
industry had become. Perhaps this was the link with the
literature of a hundred years ago – they were articles of
belief as well as items of consumption.

In the Dáil, waiting for the Minister of Culture, I sat
beneath a full-dress military portrait of Cathal Brugha, first
Chief of Staff of the IRA, with a group of grizzled farmers
in blue serge or grey-brown Donegal tweeds, with large,
shiny black shoes reheeled in metal. Then I walked through
a modest corridor, on the doors of which were inscribed the
names of each Irish cabinet minister. Michael D., as he was

called – the Higgins was by now redundant, everyone knew who he was – was a small man with an aureole of white hair surrounding a baby pink dome, and darting, impulsive hands with beautiful fingernails. His suit was a luminous green-blue colour and I wanted to ask him where he got it. There were many questions, indeed, that I wanted to ask him but he talked so much that I couldn't get a word in.

Journalists loved Michael D. because he would call them next morning after drinking with them and enquire how he had behaved. 'Was I goodish or baddish?' he asked one of them. 'Just ish,' the reporter replied. He had been a lecturer in sociology at Galway University, who dabbled in foreign affairs on behalf of the Labour Party, going during the 1980s to such hell-holes as Nicaragua, El Salvador and Gaza. It seemed that he was appointed the first Irish Minister of Culture in 1993 because he wrote poetry, and because his wife was an actress. Michael D. explained to me that there was a tradition of being kind to creative types in Ireland (they didn't have to pay taxes on what they earned directly from their work) and that, once in place, he set about using the device to transform the Irish scene. In his eagerness to tell me everything he was doing he spoke faster and faster. People knew about Section 35 – this was the system of tax breaks encouraging investors to gamble on Irish films. However, they were less familiar with the Gaelic television initiative, and the doubling of the works budget to allow the comprehensive modernization of everything, from cathedrals to heritage sites to waterways. Michael D. was a European in what I had come to see as the Irish style – pragmatic and successfully opportunistic. He didn't agree with the French sense of cultural exclusiveness ('They *will* be élitist, won't they?') but he felt that this was how Europe would be created, through culture. Meanwhile, the Irish hour had come – alone, Ireland and its history were capable of touching Europe, America, the Third World. And Michael D. didn't feel art should be consumed; instead it should be made to benefit – I scribbled the phrase – 'a tapestry of citizenship'. Did I realize that there would be as many Irish films made in the last decade of the twentieth century as there had been in all the previous decades put together? I did – but by now, eager to stem the flow of magniloquent exposition, I asked him feebly what was the purpose of all this. 'The purpose?' he asked, looking smaller and pinker. 'The purpose?' He scratched his head. It was important that until the mid-nineteenth century most Irish people did not speak English. 'I love Latin American literature,' he said. 'Don't you think that Irish writing is more like Latin American fiction than English fiction? Couldn't we have a tradition of Irish film that surpassed anything in its possibilities? And don't you think we're just beginning?'

Driving across Ireland along empty roads fringed with isolated small towns, farms, cows or EU development signs, I looked back at the encounter with astonishment. In Britain one could never have found anyone in a position of authority whose views were to such a degree at odds with the prevailing mean utilitarianism according to which every expression of the national culture must find its place within the market-place. But Michael D.'s views were not just generous-spirited – they made good sense, too. The Anglo-Irishman Burke had once declared tartly that for him to love his country, it must become more lovely; and this was something that Ireland had taken to heart. Culture these days could be made to sell other things as well as itself. It helped if your national expression of self didn't come packaged in the obligation to make rotten beef or nuclear testing acceptable to the world. I supposed that it could be argued that words or images, by being sold in this fashion, changed their nature (this was the neo-Marxist view held by those who taught media studies), and yet there was no way round this dilemma, as Michael D. had rapidly discovered, but to make a good shot at selling the stuff, and hope that it came out well.

There were two kinds of pub in Galway: those that were filled with American executives being schmoozed by their Irish counterparts, and those harbouring very loud electronic fiddle music. Over Guinness at lunch I found one of Michael D.'s poems, 'A Race Night Reflection in the University City of Galway 1970', in which the Minister-to-be, slumped over the bar, grumbled at the philistinism of his fellow-drinkers:

> Estate agents, insurance brokers and bankers,
> This is your week . . .

It took me time to find a hotel room, and by the time I did I was distressed to find that it was over a kitchen, and wasn't cheap. Ill-tempered, I drove out of the city again, towards Sligo. After a sharp turn and a few kinks in a small road, I found a stream. Beyond it was Thur Ballylee, the half-derelict Norman tower where the middle-aged Yeats, wishing to be a gentleman and find a remote place in which to heed the messages implied by his new wife's visions, settled in 1917.

A bus filled with Dutch tourists disgorged its load into a small restaurant adjoining a well-stocked bookshop. I listened impatiently to the audio-visual presentation, though I was intrigued to see how the very scholarly text played up Yeats's Anglo-Irishness, even stressing his hostility, as a senator, to the Catholic nature of the new state, evident in his reluctance to accept the prohibition of divorce. Then I climbed the stairs, past the dreadfully uncomfortable rooms where Mrs Yeats had her visions, and Yeats read the (Protestant) Bible to his son, until, passing a nest of what appeared to be small owls, I reached the roof. There, overlooking low hills dotted with yellow over which very low clouds passed rapidly, sheltering intermittently from the rain, I looked again at my old copy of Yeats.

They were the greatest poems, certainly – no one, I felt, had evoked more powerfully the character of twentieth-century violence, in particular the way it had entered the fabric of thought itself:

> Now days are dragon-ridden, the nightmare
> Rides upon sleep: a drunken soldiery
> Can leave the mother, murdered at her door,
> To crawl in her own blood, and go scot-free;
> The night can sweat with terror as before.

But now it was Yeats's cunning that I noticed, too, and the invention in his work of an Ireland acceptable to his countrymen. The violence was general, not purely Irish, miles away from the merely local phenomenon of soldiers from each side coming down the lane, or the odd corpse in a nearby village. All of us, by the time he was finished, not just Irishmen fighting what to Yeats seemed an absurd war (he was against it; his views about Ireland and John Bull shifted by the day, like his famous stream in which the obdurate stone sat, depending on what he felt he could say, or wished to, as well as what he believed), somehow became guilty participants as well as high-minded observers.

Still, the poetry worked on me – it was still there as I went to what, for most British people, had come to seem the

current home of Irish violence. On the train going to Belfast
I could see patches of sea, or old-fashioned fairgrounds, but
it was the grey crust of the houses I noticed, and the way
more and more of them were made of red brick the closer
one came to the North. Only five years ago, I'd had to get
out of the train, to be driven by bus across the border; but
now the crossing passed without incident. I flipped through
the latest volume of Ireland's new Nobel laureate as we
passed Armagh villages. Freedom was now achieved not
by isolation in draughty Norman towers, but transatlantic
flight:

> Up and away. The buzz from duty free.
> Black velvet. Bourbon. Love letters on high.

During the 1970s, Seamus Heaney encountered on this
very train, 'as if he were some *film noir* border guard', a
grim petitioner:

> So he enters and sits down
> Opposite and goes for me head on.
> 'When, for fuck's sake, are you going to write
> Something for us?' 'If I do write something,
> Whatever it is, I'll be writing for myself.'
> And that was that. Or words to that effect.

Like Yeats, Heaney was good at what the British in mistaken
derogation – I supposed it was a last vestige of the national
puritanism – called 'having it both ways'. But I couldn't
agree that the cultivation of gesture was either useless or
dangerous; *au contraire*, as Samuel Beckett once said when
asked if he was English, it was an admirable quality in poets.
It was useful among politicians, too. And it was this quality

which had enabled Heaney in his Nobel Prize acceptance speech to wriggle through the contradictory burdens of the Irish past, calling for the old border I had just passed to become like 'the net on a tennis court . . . allowing for agile give and take, for encounter and contending'. I couldn't see what was wrong with this formulation except that, like Yeats's and indeed Heaney's poems, it consisted of words used for their magical properties of ambiguity or imaginative solace.

The train arrived on time in a dour and grey Belfast station festooned with recognizably British advertisements, and I walked into a place which I knew I admired, but where I had never for a moment, even when no acts of violence were taking place, felt comfortable. Words and effects, as I discovered, were also important in Belfast, and in copious supply – they were how people, used to the idea of the worst, got their own back or fended off the prospect of still more awful acts. I stayed in a large red-brick house, with a beautiful poplar in the garden which whistled softly all night, and beyond which one could see the edge of the city and blue hills. I was the guest of a friend who had sung folk songs, published books and made films, a Protestant who lived in a very proper Protestant street, but who wasn't a Unionist. Elections were taking place for a body supposed to unite all parties in the quest for a new mechanism of representative government, but Davey sighed when I suggested I should watch some parade or other. 'At least the coarseness has gone,' is all he would say. When I asked why it shouldn't all start again, Davey shrugged. 'It's never safe to anticipate anything here,' he said, halting the car at some lights, to our side of which the hirsute image of Gerry Adams looked at us, a wooden tongue behind a mouth concealed by generous if unattractive facial hair. 'On the other hand, it seems so absurd, doesn't it? Can't you see people coming to Belfast in twenty years' time, and asking: "What was it all about, going on for all that time?" '

In Belfast I encountered the familiar British-Irish tangle twisted to different shape. Unlike the former English administrative city Dublin, Belfast had been built as an industrial and shipping centre, but reconstruction in the past three years had comprehensively remade the city in the idiom of post-industrial Britishness. 'We have had yet another invasion to experience,' Davey told me, and I could see what he meant – chrome and brick frontages, and, on the cream and red sides of buses, un-Protestant Calvin Klein waifs selling underwear. I met friends of his – people he approved of, which was difficult, for his standards were exacting – who wanted to talk about poetry. I had never thought there were so many people in what we used to call the British Isles who cared so passionately about poetry. As much as the formal results of the election – they were incomprehensible, enabling everyone to claim success and superseded by the wholly predictable squabbling that began next day – such private acts of definition mattered to them. Most of the Protestants I met were too polite to admit that they did feel threatened by the prospect of British lack of interest – it was the question of how they were presented, in films or literature, that counted. They would have been happier if Seamus Heaney had not been Catholic, and had stayed in the North. Awkwardly – everything they said carried the stamp of difficulty – they resented the successful self-advertisement of the South in relation to their own perceived sensibility of intransigence. But they were also proud of who they were and how they had come through.

One afternoon I slipped away from the poets, and walked through the centre of the city. On previous visits, it had been raining, and British Army rifles pointed at me through the drizzle. Now the sky was blue, the red-brick surveillance towers looked like junk-shopping-mall ornamentation; it was apparent to me how grand the city was. I stopped at the domed, Raj-and-Athens City Hall, from which emerged contingents of party workers, coming from the electoral count, some of them wearing the tell-tale baggy jackets that allowed for shoulder holsters. There was a statue of Queen Victoria, dedicated to her 'dear people', some Great Ulstermen, members of the Junkers-like imperial class of soldier-administrators – and, nearby, a memorial to the people of Belfast who drowned on the *Titanic*, their names listed not in alphabetical order, but in the approved style of the day according to precedence.

There were three types of toilet on the *Titanic*: marble for first class, ceramic for second, and iron for steerage. Although the bulkheads separating different sections of the ship hadn't saved the *Titanic*, it was nonetheless easy to lock the doors leading to the lower part of the ship, with its steerage passengers. In 1912 the most advanced technology in the world sailed out of Belfast to be dumped on the bottom of the Atlantic. The *Titanic* supplied the world first with a number of gargantuan insurance claims, then with a series of metaphors – warnings about the hubris of technology, etc. – and finally with the commodification of catastrophe: paintings, kitsch objects, relics and films, even periodic efforts to recover bits of the wreck. The German poet Hans Magnus Enzensberger wrote *The Sinking of the Titanic* in 1970s Havana, where socialism had just gone down, and discovered that his completed manuscript, bound in oilcloth, was lost at sea by the Cuban postal service:

> Afterwards, of course, everybody had seen it coming
> Except we who perished. Afterwards
> premonitions were rife, and rumours, and scenarios.
> All of a sudden dog races were mentioned, dog races
> held on C-deck . . .

No one anticipated the collapse of Empire; and then, once it happened, no one could find a way of reversing it – in the end the Scots-Irish Protestants defended themselves by getting what they could from the wreckage. In my host's dining-room hung a photograph from the early 1900s of the Harland and Wolff workers – Protestants to a man, Orangemen – striding purposefully out of the dock gates. The men who built the *Titanic* had much they wished to defend – and their descendants created a one-party state no less obnoxiously repressive, though in a different way, than the Catholic regime of the South. Even during the decline of Belfast's old industries, and the collapse of Empire itself, they continued, against the evidence presented by the world, to believe in their own superiority. All the rain in Ireland, let alone the efforts of other Irishmen, abetted recently by the British Government, hadn't been able to rid them of this firmly held conviction.

It was sunny the morning I went back to Dublin, and this time the train was filled with well-preserved middle-aged specimens of the Belfast Protestant middle classes – sternly dressed, serious men and women in tweed or tartan reading British newspapers of a conservative orientation, pursing their lips at the latest accounts of the non-progress of the Royal divorce and drinking cups of tea. I had with me Churchill's famous Parliamentary speech from 1922:

> Great Empires have been overturned. The whole map of
> Europe has been changed . . . The mode of thought of men,
> the whole outlook of parties, all have encountered violent
> and tremendous changes in the deluge of the world, but as
> the deluge subsides and the waters fall, we see the dreary
> steeples of Fermanagh and Tyrone emerging once again.
> The integrity of their quarrel is one of the few institutions
> that have been unaltered in the cataclysm that has swept the
> world . . .

More Great Empires had been overturned; but I wondered
whether the integrity of this quarrel wasn't finally
threatened. Perhaps at the very least one could say of the
pulling-together of Europe that, although it might not actually stop them, it did deglamorize such conflicts – they
became, in the approved euphemism, 'regional' disputes.
They were less important now even if it was also apparent
that they could never be resolved. Also – though this was
something the Unionists could not be expected to understand – a borderless Europe in which minority rights were
guaranteed, while it might diminish British influence, also
removed once and for all the possibility of an Irish government choosing after British abandonment to remove the
rights of Protestants, sending them 'home' to the place
many of them had left almost four hundred years ago. In
this respect these British Irish could think of themselves as
more fortunate than the many ethnic Russians marooned in
such outposts of the ex-Soviet Empire as Latvia or Kazakhstan – though I didn't imagine they would enjoy such
analogies.

At Dublin I changed trains, taking the soup-green DART
along the coast to the small seaside town of Howth, where
Yeats as a very old man had another of his visions of imma-

nent beauty when he remembered the great love of his
youth:

> Maud Gonne at Howth Station waiting a train,
> Pallas Athene in that straight back and arrogant head.

Nowadays, Howth boasted a new marina and shops selling
golfing equipment. I walked up the hill past neat villas
sporting Mediterranean palms, and went down from the
peak to a small cream-coloured house with a glassed-in
porch overlooking the sea. This was where the politician,
professor, writer, polemicist and wit Conor Cruise O'Brien
lived. Some years ago I had produced a programme in
which he forthrightly attacked John Paul II. He commended
the Pope for having restored to him the faith of his child-
hood – not in the Catholic Church, which he abhorred, but
in the Enlightenment, Voltaire and Rousseau. At that time,
it was impossible to find a restaurant serving even com-
munion wine on a holiday Monday, and we drove around
Dublin haplessly looking for what he called, to the bemusement of waiters, in his elegant Irish-French, *appelation
controllée*. The Cruiser's pink-rimmed blue eyes, the lizard-
like precision of his gestures and his slow, perfectly enunciated sentences came to fascinate me; I got in the habit of
going to see him in search of enlightenment. Now I wanted
to know why it was that he had enraged Dublin opinion by
standing at the age of seventy-nine or thereabouts in the
Forum elections as a Unionist.

Long ago, in a book written at the beginning of the last
and most durable cycle of the Troubles, he had identified
the existence of an impermeable and very old frontier area,
psychologically separating the inhabitants of Ireland and
placing under threat 'the affection, the peace, the mutual

concern and the courtesy' of Irish life. The only rational conclusion to be drawn from this was that partition should continue until those whom it protected – *all* of them – wished to see it cease. The Cruiser was one of the first to say so forthrightly, incurring much hostility. Now he believed that it was the Unionists who had changed – they had been forced to by the British, who had removed their privileged state, abolishing discrimination – and that it was the Republicans, for their part, who made no concessions, still relying on violence as a means to unity; and that they were now supported by the Irish Government and a British Establishment grown tired of post-imperial duties and self-absorbed. Nonetheless Irish people should wish to protect the rights of all of those who lived on the island – this was why he had stood for election in a poll the results of which he acknowledged would be at best that nothing would happen. I realized that it was this stubbornness, coming with the quota of inspiration I took for granted in Irish intelligence, that made me like him so much.

We walked to the top of the hill above his house. Spry, wearing a natty tweed jacket, looking the part of a slightly Americanized Irish sage, he waved his walking stick at the sea. There were no solutions of an easy kind in Ireland, least of all those enshrined in equivocal language. Poems were written by poets – history was something entirely different, and it was important not to be taken in by the superficial evidence of change represented by the Irish *dolce vita*. The Europeanization of Ireland, he believed, was yet another siren melody devised to drown out deep notes.

'In Ireland, we should try to hobble through the millennium to the early decades of the twenty-first century,' he said.

I remarked that his view didn't seem so different from the Nobel laureate's tennis-court view of the future.

'Too optimistic,' he said, and then, waving his stick at me as he said goodbye, smiling mischievously: 'Well, you weren't expecting anything jollier, were you?'

I walked back towards Howth through more evidence of the Irish *dolce vita* until I saw, standing next to a largish palm tree in a front garden, a medium-sized grey horse. I drew nearer, wondering whether the horse was tethered or not. In Britain, a few months before, a well-oiled Cabinet official at a Christmas party had expressed British policy as being one of vigorously doing nothing. 'You have to place trust in time,' he said. 'Anyhow, there is nothing else one can do.' At the time this seemed a typically British view of things, but I now saw that it wasn't far from the Irish position, although the latter found more vigorous expression. For while one could do nothing *for* or on behalf of Ireland, everything did, finally, change in its own way – and meanwhile everything could be reinvented. I watched as the horse pawed at the ground, shaking its head – it wasn't tethered, and it neighed loudly in my direction. I took the train from Howth feeling, as I had done most of my time in Ireland, that there were many ways of being right about things. Nonetheless, so much ambiguity finally ended, if not by making things clearer, at least by rendering them easier to endure – and it was a pleasure to argue about everything. As I stood among the crowd going to the dog races, I was sure that I could have been happy being Irish. Perhaps – the illusion lasted a full minute – I still could be.

Berlin: Good Dreams after Bad

Is it possible for anyone in Germany,
nowadays, to raise his right hand,
for whatever the reason, and not be flooded
by the memory of a dream to end all dreams?

How German is it Walter Abish (1982)

When members of the Du Pont family first arrived in America, they disembarked by an empty Indian village which contained a large table spread with food. Imagining that the hand of Providence lay behind this occurrence the antecedents of chemicals billionaires ate what proved to be the first Thanksgiving feast enjoyed by white men. The same sort of thing happened to me on my first night in Berlin. I walked out of the brand-new, over-chromed hotel where I was staying into a large, empty quarter rendered in post-modern corporate vernacular. I went round two enormous 1940s-style vacuum-cleaner-shaped office towers, and through a blank plaza where outsize adolescents were wrestling with a fountain of which the centrepiece was a rotating marble ball. Then I crossed a bridge decorated with stone art deco bears, going under lime trees, through illuminated greenish streets echoing with the noise of the Euro '96 football championship, broadcast from England, until I heard voices. I walked into a vast, well-lit room, filled with well-dressed, faintly Bohemian-looking, middle-aged people (the men sported Boss black linen suits, moustaches and imperfectly controlled waistlines in the style of Günter Grass, the women, also a little over-weight, wore frizzed hair above silk floral dresses of the kind considered fashionable in the early eighties), at the end of which stood a rock group wearing new jeans and cowboy hats.

Speeches were being delivered by well-groomed white-haired men, and I gathered that one of them was the Presi-dent of the Federal Republic. I could understand the drift, which was that art, far from being a province of the market, or a minor leisure activity of the middle classes, was indeed a Serious Thing. Someone gave me a beer and a joint, and someone else – a professor's wife – asked me to dance. As we rotated politely to Rolling Stones or Sex Pistols covers, I strove to reorientate myself. This, I had learnt by now from a Swiss conceptual artist specializing in calligraphy, was the Kunst Akademie, a repository of avant-garde aesthetic theory and practice; but by now – after inhaling – it wasn't the art chat that interested me. Instead, I counted silver nose-rings and tattoos through a haze of narcotized good fellowship. These were people I might have known, or been taught by, at university. They had survived intact through years when, in Britain or America, they would have been persecuted by budget cuts and management obligations, or immured within the horrifying mandates of correctness. Although they, too, were beginning to complain, they were sleek, happy with themselves.

However, as I was to discover throughout my time in Berlin, German generosity still went with worry. I couldn't avoid the cringe-making apologies about the Mad Cows (this was at the height of our ill-starred 'war' against Europeans) but once hypochondria had received its due, I found them wanting reassurance. Craving to be metropolitan, they still (inexplicably to me) felt provincial. In between swopping destinations for their impending, and very generous summer holidays, they appeared anxious about the oddest things – such as whether people in Berlin dressed formally enough for public occasions. They were envious of the British record in the contemporary avant-garde, which they attributed, perversely, to the punishing environment installed by Mrs Thatcher. They worried lest the new capital, by assuming the functions of government, also acquired the boredom of Bonn. They were above all perplexed in relation to the matter of banality. Would the new end-of-the-century architecture measure up to the past? Would it ensure, finally (this was the question behind every German question), the definitive location of Germany within the European fold?

My dancing partner thought the idea of rebuilding Berlin was too bourgeois. A razor-cut middle-aged culture bureaucrat dressed in black jeans and T-shirt suggested that in Germany wealth was uncongenial to the exercise of creativity. 'There are too many competitions, too many grants,' he said gruffly. 'Too much tolerance of "everything goes" means that you have a banal orthodoxy of taste. Non-shockability is the cause of a crisis in subsidized art.' While they argued among themselves about the softness of Germany, I asked why Germany shouldn't once again become the centre of European culture. 'Politicians . . .' groaned the bureaucrat. 'The only good thing about their coming here is that there will be S and M clubs again. Don't you think that politicians and black leather go together?' Later, we talked about transsexuality. I think someone explained about the work of Magnus Hirschfeld, the sex guru of inter-war Berlin, whose books were suppressed by the Nazis. I should go to San Francisco, not Berlin, if I was interested in these problems, he said. Alas, compared to America, Berlin had become quiet.

For the moment, I couldn't agree with him. From the first time I went there as a schoolboy, I had loved Berlin; no other city, with the exception of New York, gave me the same sense of freedom and possibility. But I had another mission on this occasion. After many visits, I found that I hadn't been to Berlin since the Wall came down, and I wanted to know how the city had adapted to the end of the role it had occupied in Cold War theatre. But there was another reason for my being here, and it had to do with the pattern of my discoveries while writing this book. Throughout Europe, the excessive presence of the past had first perplexed, then haunted me. I wished to see whether the future, lost to Europe for so many decades, could once again be found in Berlin.

Three times during the century – at the moment of Wilhelmine Empire, during the Weimar Republic, and once again, beginning with Hitler's squalid 1936 Olympic Games – Berlin had depicted itself to the rest of Europe as its future. Of all European illusions, Berlin's was the grandest and most fateful – it was the place where everything seemed periodically about to go right, and failed to do so. And yet, even in its worst times, during the awful post-war period of poverty or the long dead years when the city became a stage-set on which the tiresome rituals of the Cold War were endlessly re-enacted, its promise had never quite died. I had sensed its fitful, half-extinguished life while filming ten years ago amid both the gimcrack, puritan severity of the GDR and the self-conscious shop-window Berlin of Western capitalism. If ever the Wall did come down, I remembered thinking, as I crossed back and forth through Checkpoint Charlie, it would be here that signs of new life would appear. But walking around the city amid cranes and dust, I did at last feel that something was happening.

On a Sunday, I went past allotments and public housing through deep greenness to the *Siegessäule* with its magic, burnished Teutonic angel. The old Berlin woods were blasted by artillery in 1945, and cut down during the terrible winter of 1947 or the airlift a year later; now they grew higher, year by year, so that they appeared to smother the city. There were tour buses at the Brandenburg Gate, and Russians selling straw hats. I inspected the Reichstag, recently wrapped in curtains by Christo, now shrouded with functional plastic by Sir Norman Foster. Heading past the fenced-off, unkempt mound of sand on top of what had once been Hitler's bunker, I found myself in the former centre of the city. There, counting cranes and more cranes, I climbed the outside stairway of the Potsdamer Platz Infobox. I could see bloated coloured gas pipes and growths of metal and concrete. A small portion of the Wall had been left intact, and it seemed comforting in its familiarity beside these alien structures. Inside the ugly chrome Infobox, a ponderous exhibition complete with confusing models described the imminent transformation of Berlin in relation to a reworked Europe stretching from the Altantic to the Urals. Magnetic trains, new autobahns, clean air, fresh water and gas pipes were promised – but it was the new centre of the city, here advertised by a series of architectural exhibits, that most interested me.

Under the beneficent astrological signs of Sony, Mercedes-Benz and Hyatt, what the exhibition described as 'the new heart of Europe' was laid bare. This turned out to be nineteen distinct projects incorporating 340,000 square metres of floor space, out of which had been carved offices, convenience apartments, shops, restaurants, a multiplex cinema. In the midst of such largess stood the dilapidated Kaisersaal ballroom, formerly part of the GDR's Esplanade Hotel, now by means of a remarkable feat of German engineering lifted eight feet by hydraulic jacks, placed on a compressed air float and trundled 100 metres to its new home. No one could have accused the Senate of being remiss in supplying information, but I sensed a spirit of bemusement or even frustration among those around me. 'Is that all that's left of the Wall?' a large man wearing shorts, a Bayern München shirt and a white baseball cap asked. 'I don't know what it's for,' an old lady said. I could see what she meant. It was clear what these buildings would look like, and what functions they would ultimately accommodate. What they would ultimately mean for Berlin, however, or for the post-millennium Germany of which it would become the capital, was somewhat less evident.

I went out on the platform again, and looked at the astonishing green; but I was still less certain when I returned. Maquettes, like architect's drawings, have by now acquired their own debased idiom; but I felt the offerings of Renzo Piano, Richard Rodgers and José Rafael Moneo had been unexceptionably tailored to contemporary international idiom. Only the wedge-shaped pastiche of 1920s modernism from the Berlin architect Hans Kolhoff – at one time he submitted two sets of designs, one set of skyscrapers, one arrangement of GDR-style blockhouses, both at odds with the competition rules – offered much of the spirit of architectural innovation from the city's awesomely chequered past. However, I also felt that the problem ran deeper than the difficulties posed by coherence and originality. Many people had wished to make a statement out of the new Berlin, that was clear; and yet it struck me that what they really wanted to say – and what emerged from these plans – was less easy to define. Relief no doubt had entered their minds, and something just short of contentment – but these were not the emotions customarily associated with great architecture. They had certainly not been uppermost in the minds of those who had thrown this city together.

Among tasteful 'virtual' depictions of Boss-suited Berliners walking their hounds, samples of cladding were on display whose wintry Prussian hue of dark clay or grey appeared to have come straight from the neo-Expressionist designer palette of Baselitz and Kiefer. They were tasteful, and might have been considered to be appropriate; but they, too, appeared not entirely adequate to the occasion. In the summer of 1939, on one of the innumerable occasions when he examined Albert Speer's plans, Hitler suggested a modification to the design of his great hall, capable of housing 100,000 people. He wanted the German eagle on top of the 290-metre dome, but it should be holding a globe in its claws, not, as previously agreed, the swastika. 'Have the eagle perched on top of the globe,' he told the amenable Speer. I began to appreciate the special problems posed by Berlin. Given the shadow cast by Adolf Hitler and Albert Speer, no one had given excessive thought to redesigning the city – but then no one could have been expected to anticipate the bizarre twist of history whereby Berlin had suddenly been turned into the capital of the most powerful European country.

In 1985 the Federal President Richard von Weizsäcker told Germans that they had to live with the sins of their fathers:

All of us, whether guilty or not, whether old or young, must accept the past. We are all affected by its consequences and liable for it. The young and old generations must help each other understand why it is vital to keep alive the memories. It is not a question of coming to terms with the past. That is not possible. It cannot subsequently be modified or made not to have happened . . .

Whether they could in reality be heeded or not, such stern obligations meant that history and culture, never unimportant, remained big business in Germany, and the availability of so much money after the Wall came down in 1989 coincided with an explosion of conceptual self-definition. A fresh compound extension was created to accommodate the new spirit – *Vergangenheitsbewältigung*, meaning 'coming to terms with the past'. However, although they were conducted with exemplary fairness by a representative range of experts and local worthies, the results of the various competitions were nonetheless also criticized. One of the most expensive, and perhaps most difficult to fulfil, was for a Holocaust Memorial located on the site of Hitler's driver's bunker. It was postponed at Helmut Kohl's insistence when it was clear that the 108,000 sq foot tombstone on which the names of everyone who died were to be engraved would cause a 'scandal' – and require elaborate security arrangements. But the most cogent onslaught on the new architecture came from Daniel Libeskind, a Polish-American architect who specialized in designs where the inner structure of the building, and thus its relation to the environment, were explicit.

I met the architect's wife Nina, and together with a student taking photographs we went around his half-finished building commemorating Berlin's twentieth-century Jewish culture. How could one commemorate loss or atrocity? Ramps and tunnels conveyed the visitor from the old baroque section of the museum. On each floor passageways crossed over six internal voids – spaces within the building that were unheated, covered with skylights – made out of raw concrete. Traversing the voids a visitor was to be reminded of the fracture in history which had destroyed the Berlin Jews. The building was in the shape of a star of David which had been pulled to pieces, and its exterior was made out of a greyish zinc that would turn blue when exposed to rain and snow. The last void, which commemorated the Holocaust itself, stood apart from the museum. It was a large, dark funnel, and I felt trapped standing within it. Then I noticed an ugly line of metal stairs leading from the pebbled yard to the skylight. 'Oh, that's for the fire regulations,' Nina Libeskind explained. 'Daniel hates it. But what can we do? This is Berlin, and fire regulations are taken very seriously.'

Until recently wasteland, the area around the museum was now filled with nondescript, hastily thrown-together buildings. Libeskind believed that the architects and bureaucrat-planners had sold out the distinctively German twentieth-century innovations of the Bauhaus school in the name of a pseudo-rationality dictated by the demands of mass consumerism. The giveaway aspects of this non- or anti-style (much evident in the maquettes at Potsdamer Platz) were box-like structures with punched-out holes for windows, and, to conceal imaginative poverty, the excessive use of cladding. This gave to these old-new buildings a pervasive air of emptiness and fake seriousness, whereby architects sought to erase or parody the history of the city, instead of exercising their responsibility, which was to accept its existence, whether they liked it or not. Calls for 'solidity' from interested architects, Libeskind helpfully explained, echoed the frightening precedent of the Third Reich and the GDR, in which people 'believed . . . that cities were made not of citizens but brick walls'.

Libeskind was born in Poland, and his foreignness (and Jewishness) gave him the right to make assertions at which many of his German contemporaries might perhaps have balked. His essay, provocatively entitled *The Banality of Order*, was a half-facetious echo of Hannah Arendt's description of Eichmann, Hitler's perfect bureaucrat, as the embodiment of banality and evil. The tone of his assertions reminded me of Walter Abish's novel *How German Is It*, which described the efforts of an architect to build a new town – named Brumholdstein, after a philosopher with a dubious past, resembling Heidegger – on terrain where the past of mass graves couldn't, no matter how hard anyone tried, wholly be fitted in to the well-meaning present. Other novelists had dealt copiously and earnestly with the matter of German guilt, but Abish, like Libeskind, was adept at describing the rueful, half-anaesthetized emotions that follow acceptance of guilt, only partially displacing it, and finding their way into every contemporary aesthetic or ideological question:

Past Riches

Sooner or later, every German, young or old, male or female, will come across some description in a book, or newspaper, or magazine of those grim events in the concentration camps, and not necessarily the remote ones in Poland, but camps in the heart of Germany, and neighbouring Austria, camps a short drive from Munich or Weimar or Berlin . . . But how reliable is this evidence, these articles by former inmates or by writers who specialize in the sensational, in the outrageous? Is it simply in order to make a splash? It's one way of getting into print? And then of course there are the films and the photographs. What is one to make of them?

Despite all the money spent on memory it was becoming clear that 'coming to terms' with the past, no matter how much Germans might wish to do so, just wasn't possible. Perhaps, as James Fenton had understood in his poem 'A German Requiem', there were occurrences that required oblivion:

> It is what you have forgotten, what you must forget.
> What you must go on forgetting all your life.

Nonetheless, I couldn't wholly reproach the new builders for having chosen compromise. Correctness was a very German invention, as important to post-war identity as German engineering; and it implied the wish, learning from the past, to seem relatively modest, or if that wasn't possible if one were building on such a scale, at the very least – a New Berlin word – pluralistic.

It was hot the next day in the reconstructed Prussian hall of the Historical Museum, where an exhibition depicting the relationship between Fascism and art was being opened, and members of *le tout*-Berlin fanned themselves impatiently, wiping their steel-rimmed glasses or patting down their linen. Suddenly, there was a small rush of excitement on the part of the camera crews, and I saw the Chancellor standing in front of a salvaged GDR statue of Lenin, with a rocket to one side of him, and two elegant early BMW models, one in maroon, the other in black, separating him from the crowd. The applause was earnest, and appreciative; and he paused briefly in recognition, though without the suggestion of a smile. Forewarned by the caricatures of British newspapers, I had expected him to be large, if not fat; but I wasn't prepared for the dimensions of the anonymous-looking blue-grey cloth which had gone to make his toga-like lounge suit.

Kohl made a long speech about how the past was a warning for the future, and how the European Union would forestall chaos, obviate disaster or keep doused the flames of nationalism. While he was speaking I wandered around images of the European style of the 1930s: the more or less identical blank domes or pillars proposed by Mussolini, Hitler, Franco and Stalin. 'In a world in which the menace of the future weighs heavily, it has seemed for some time that civilization has begun to lose faith in itself,' the French Commissioner of the 1937 Paris Exposition declared. 'And now here is the answer . . .' The last time I had been in this building, it was to film a guided tour of Utopia ('forty years of lying' is how a dissident described it) given to teenage pupils by a GDR teacher. At that time there were few exhibits relating to German history from the Hitler period, and those of the museum placed the responsibility for his existence squarely at the door of monopoly capitalism. The GDR was commemorated by a series of exhibits devoted to the technology of Wall-building. So much concrete, the inscriptions neatly affirmed, was there to protect freedom from the ravages of capitalism. These were breath-taking lies; and yet the teacher, who was an intelligent man, appeared to believe them. But now it was very different. While Kohl stood in the cobbled courtyard, raising a glass of fizzy white wine, more black linen suits meandered about the gallery devoted to German totalitarianism, lingering before a newsreel neatly recording Adolf Hitler's visit to the earlier exhibition. They seemed unimpressed; I assumed they felt that they knew enough about German horrors.

'I am a camera with its shutter open, quite passive, recording, not thinking,' declared Christopher Isherwood's Berlin narrator. When he wrote these words, Isherwood was, as he later admitted with the perspective of many years spent in Santa Monica, pondering prospective encounters with rough German boys, but, like the good, over-educated, partly repressed Englishman he still was, he was alert to the imminence of catastrophe around him. Camera-style I walked down the rest of Unter den Linden to Karl Lieb-knechtstrasse, crossing the horrible concrete of Alexander-platz to the hideous needle of the GDR's TV tower. In the old days the ascent was laborious and claustrophobic, like being immured in a Pharaoh's tomb and slowly hoisted skywards; but now, courtesy of new German engineering, the hike took rather less than forty seconds. In awe, weak-kneed from the sight of so much power stamped on a city-scape, I scanned the skyline, from the wastes of the Stalinist Karl Marx Allee (with 'brutal, undistinguished façades', as the guide helpfully informed me) to Speer's equally bar-barous, though more picturesque Olympic stadium.

Albert Speer's last sight of Berlin before he was incarcer-ated for twenty years in Spandau Prison was from the window of an American DC-3 passenger plane, and, according to his biographer Gitta Sereny, he was still elated by the sight of his famous East-West axis, and the half-blasted remnants of Hitler's Chancellery. I could now see the cranes encroaching on the rubble. The cunning knit-ting-together of so many separate growths of concrete was clear to me; and yet suddenly I felt the pangs of nostalgia – for dreadful high-rises, or Arno Breker statuary, for any remnant of outrage so long as it was capable of jogging, if only for a few more years, the memory of catastrophe.

Each day, early or late at night, I walked through more building sites. Some of them had been turned into parks in which young artists exhibited salvaged rusted metal, others were squats awaiting their transformation. Criss-crossing from East to West and back again I noticed degrees of dust, as well as social or architectural distinctions. I coughed unstoppably in the East because of the building sites. Meanwhile, amid the graffiti, which were everywhere, uninspired by comparison with their New York originals, I noticed sallowness on the U-bahn stations, or different-shaped guts. In the West fat was worn proudly underneath Kohl suits, or football-style shirts covered with logos; in the East it sagged listlessly within salmon or grey polyesters. Immured, kept poor, filled with starch or propaganda, these Easterners now looked more German than their Western counterparts. I wasn't surprised by the many articles telling me how much they resented their status as poor, long-separated cousins become objects of concern or charity.

Due to long separation, the city felt half-complete; but for the visitor there was also the bizarre effect of time shifting: it was as if towns separated only by green patches existed side by side in different decades. In London the post-war policy of public housing meant that rich and poor lived close to each other, while in Paris they were rigorously kept separate by the designs of planners. In Berlin, now, everything was being energetically pulled together with a noise of cracking joints. So much chaos was temporary – but it was attractive, too. I walked hour after hour through the city, through the Tiergarten with its Barbie-doll hookers waiting for cars, under the tatty neon of the Kurfürsten-damm or the railway arches of Friedrichstrasse full of

Chinese Quick stand-ups, in the planners' wastes of Karl
Marx Allee or the junky, half-renovated, patched-up
Bohemian territory of Prenzlauer Berg. I took the U-bahn
and the S-bahn east and west, watching families of Turkish
immigrants, young professorial-looking couples pushing
bicycles, drunk shaven-headed squatters with torn jeans
and grossly sculptured cockatoo hairdos, people in soiled,
ragged garments dancing erratically to tunes in their own
head.

One day I went by S-bahn to the remote stop of
Mahlsdorf, beyond the city limits of the old East Berlin. I
walked along a boring road past the bus station and over
a nondescript crossroads festooned with second-hand car
dealerships. A few hundred yards further on, I turned right
past a scrapyard, ringing the bell of what appeared to be
the shabby gatehouse of an old estate. Here I entered the
informal museum of Charlotte von Mahlsdorf, the most
famous transsexual of the GDR. Born into a Junkers family,
with a lesbian aunt who approved of cross-dressing, she
had murdered her Nazi father in 1944 during an air raid –
the circumstances weren't clear, but it seemed he was
beating up her mother – managing to escape before the trial
could take place. She survived by working as a gardener, or
odd-job person, eventually buying this house, in which,
year by year, she placed samples of Wilhelmine Berlin furniture in forgotten styles like *Neue Renaissance* or *Neu
Gothik*, of a bulk and horsehair austerity that would not
have disgraced the rooms of Fräulein Schröder, Isherwood's landlady. But there was a twist to the story, as she
explained to me in slow English, gesturing gracefully at bar
stools and chamber-pots. This was the unfortunate decision
by the Berlin Senate not to subsidize the museum, despite
its acknowledged place as a cultural centre. In her late sev-

enties, therefore, she was going to Sweden, with her companion. There she planned to open another museum. As I left, she waved at me, a genteel, robust, distinctly English-looking figure in a faded floral dress – I felt I had been present at a scene out of a coloured magazine print entitled 'The Last Day'.

I sat each evening at one of the benches informally placed in front of the golden dome of the partly restored synagogue in Oranienburgstrasse. I marvelled here, not just at the fact that I could eat kosher food at one in the morning (my fellow-eaters were dressed in black linen and wearing steel-rimmed, lozenge-shaped glasses) but that it was possible to entertain the 24-hour presence of a police guard and his Rottweiler. Completed in 1866, the greatest synagogue in Europe was sacked during the *Kristallnacht*, and blasted to pieces by the British in 1943. Rebuilding had begun under the GDR, and the project had benefited from the way in which Communists reconstituted the past so literally. After the Wall came down the decision was made to leave it opened up at the back, with a glass wall, so that, while standing inside, one could retain the illusion of seeing into the destruction, or through it. I went back many times, standing before the great lamp, which was exhibited as it had been found, half-broken. In New York I had once made a film about Roman Vishniac, a Russian Jew who spent the 1930s making a clandestine photographic record of the ghettoes and *shtetls* of Eastern Europe before they were destroyed. Vishniac told me that he took his non-Jewish girlfriend (later his wife) to a Chinese restaurant around the corner from the synagogue, in which Jews were permitted to eat with Aryans. 'Never in the history of humankind did so many Jewish intellectuals eat so much Chinese food,' he explained. After 1945 he never went back to Berlin, which he had loved, and he never photographed human beings again; instead he recorded plant life, or machine parts. Roman Vishniac was dead now, but I wondered what he would have made of kosher food eaten in a Berlin without Jews.

Each morning a driver came to collect me in a different model of black Mercedes. I admired the brand-new models, which felt like the American cars that Germans had never got round to building, and now could afford; but I also had a soft spot for the blocky 'Turkish' range of the 1970s beloved by cab drivers and now to be found, with their fifth owner and third engine, throughout Poland and Croatia. The discreetly chromed, front-lounge-seated 1955 'Adenauer' was new to me – a self-consciously boring limousine for those forbidden to flaunt wealth or express power. But I was charmed most of all by a 1937 police model with doors that opened the wrong way, an outsize metal steering wheel and a ventilation system supplied by an elegantly hinged front window. Going at speed from green suburb to green suburb, to Charlottenburg along the old autobahn used as a motor-cycle track in the 1930s, past the *Funkturm*, from which the first television pictures were transmitted, and the Wannsee lake, where, in a bourgeois villa, the Holocaust was organized, I experienced German modernity in all its seductiveness. New York and Los Angeles had once boasted more ambitious road systems; but the Berlin autobahns had been under-used because of the Cold War, and they seemed brand-new. These cars were at least ten years in advance of their counterparts. They made me wonder not what would have happened had the Germans won the wars they inflicted on Europe – a fantasy often explored in popular fiction – but what Europe would have been like if these wars, by some sudden access of liberal-humanitarian instincts on the part of the Hohenzollerns, had never happened.

Much would still exist the loss of which was, beyond doubt, irreparable and beyond calculation, and whose going destroyed European optimism and self-confidence. Otherwise, it struck me that what had happened recently would simply have occurred earlier, and with less pain. There would be a predominantly Jewish European Holly-wood making happy, brassy movies with lavish musical numbers, and some kind of half-formal, consultative hegemony, maybe (who knows) even located in Brussels. Perhaps – one had to assume that the camouflage of power wasn't wholly a consequence of guilt – there would be a British-style German monarchy replete with scandal as well as mahogany fascia on British cars built by BMW.

'Don't mention the war' is how Basil Fawlty, faced with the prospect of German visitors, instructed the long-suffering staff of Fawlty Towers. Nowadays the real European problem wasn't the war, which received due commemor-ation each night on TV, or the prowess of German football teams, but the sheer size and unstoppability of Germany itself. I recalled an exchange published recently in *The Times* between Karl Lamers, Christian Democrat spokesman for Foreign Affairs in the Bundestag, and Lord Rees-Mogg, formerly editor of the paper. At first reading the Europhile Lamers appeared to make the usual good German show of jollying along recalcitrant Brits, but I was struck by this discordant paragraph:

> The gap between existing reality and perceived reality, between the supranational facts and the national conscious-ness, is for the British the central problem of European integration. Here then is a paradox. Both the Euro-optimists

and the Euro-sceptics can be considered realists. One group
– the Euro-optimists – take as their starting point the objective, external reality. The others – the Euro-sceptics – deal
with the inner, subjective reality of the consciousness of the
British people. It is, if you like, the forces of Logic pitted
against the forces of Psycho-Logik.

This was as near as I had heard a German come to saying
that the British, given the extent of German power, had no
choice but to accept it. In response Lord Rees-Mogg did
mention the war – more than that, he scoured many centuries of history, going from Charlemagne via Bismarck to
Hitler ('The *Wehrmacht* in 1940 cleared the forest in which
the European Union has historically been able to grow . . .')
in order to show how the rest of Europe did what Germans
wanted. But this wasn't good enough for Herr Lamers, and
he wrote a letter chiding Lord Rees-Mogg for ignoring
'objective, external reality'. The implication, politely stated,
was that it was all very well for Britain to fuss around
the edges of the German table, standing on its threadbare
dignity, but it would make no difference whatsoever.

Each morning, driving to Potsdam, I took a different
route through the suburbs to the west of the city. The old
American barracks at Zehlendorf still possessed some sort
of grandeur, like their abandoned counterparts in East
Anglia; but it was in the ex-British sector, amid the neat
front lawns of Hampsteadstrasse, near Spandau Prison in
Charlottenburg, that I fully experienced the scale of diminishment implied by the end of the Cold War. As Noel
Annan, once a young officer in the army of occupation, had
written when visiting Berlin in 1990, the British had indeed
become specks of history. These were unpleasant thoughts
to many people, but they did mean that there was no point

in striking moral attitudes in relation to German advantages. What we should all do now is what the British ought to have done fifty years ago – organize Europe and ourselves around the raw facts of German power. However, as many Germans had begun to realize, the British were unlikely to do this. They were capable of acting against their interests. They had done so once in 1940, and they might do so again.

When they were not entirely indifferent to British attitudes, most Germans appeared to be impressed and exasperated by such stubborn disregard of what they considered to be the facts. Many years ago, as a young journalist working for the BBC, I witnessed an outburst of Helmut Schmidt on this subject. This was just before the 1975 British referendum on the subject of Europe. Schmidt was plainly enraged by the behaviour of a country he still respected. It took so long for the British to make their minds up about anything, and when they did, it was usually too late. However, as Schmidt understood, British democracy was in part to blame for their erratic behaviour. But why had the British, in Annan's phrase, so heedlessly 'thrown into the gutter the leadership of a European Community that was hers for the asking'? Why did they feel so hostile towards the idea of Europe? Germans of Schmidt's generation who unaffectedly admired the British role in defeating their country had been prepared to assume that such indifference to self-interest must be motivated by logic of one sort or another; but they were having second thoughts now.

Although I had never envied the Germans their wealth, I was beginning to change my mind. However, there was one remaining feature of German life which gave me pause, and this was what political scientists called its excessive, often caricatured 'normalcy'. 'We don't want to be ourselves – we

don't need to be so long as the rest of you make it possible
for us not to be' was the German position on Europe. This
was thrust at the rest of us as a noble, clear-sighted gesture
– the idea that the awful German past was over was on a par
with the abandonment of sin as a guiding force in human
affairs by enlightened Victorian clerics in favour of rational,
attenuated greed. But for obvious reasons no one in Britain
could ever quite believe that German good behaviour was
permanent.

I talked about these things sitting in the Café Einstein on
Unter den Linden with a German friend. Jens was educated
in Afrikaaner South Africa, where his father started a business, at Dachau (his high school was within spitting
distance of the camp gates) and at Balliol College, Oxford.
He was convinced that what he called 'the empty hole' of
German identity was itself a consequence of guilt. There
was no danger of reversion to historical type – however,
with time the characteristics of post-guilt lost themselves in
the wider question of what it was to be German. You could
never, whatever the odd, pathetic skinhead believed, be
German in the old way – and any 'new' Germanness would
have to take account of this.

I wanted to know whether being German wasn't now
taken up with denial. 'I wouldn't call it denial any longer,'
he said. 'It's handy for us not to be "too German".' The
concern with propriety was a creed that had to be observed.
For there were certain things that Germans couldn't,
mustn't ever appear to be doing. To avoid the suspicion of
even contemplating such types of behaviour, they must be
seen continually to be looking the other way. So Germans
had to be Europeans, not Germans – they could be secure
in their not-Germanness.

Jens shrugged when I raised the question of boringness.

'You get used to it,' he said. 'Anyhow, Germans are so rich – what they really think about are cars and houses. If they want the excitement of societies where it is permitted to hate one another, they can always go on holiday to Britain or France.'

This was all well and good, it allowed for reconciliation of a kind; and yet it bothered me that in the German mind the question of Europe, like that of Germany itself, appeared to have been irrevocably resolved. I wondered whether there was really no room for doubt or scepticism. Were the rest of us supposed to share these German views until the end of time simply to make a recurrence of the old 'German problem' unfeasible? At a conference held at the East Berlin Old Rathaus, within spitting distance of tasteless statues of Marx and Engels, I wasn't reassured by the theological tone of the proceedings. I noted that 69 per cent of Germans were opposed to the extinction of their currency, although a timetable for monetary union had been drawn up, extending even to the designs of the notes – they were to be near-abstract, with architectural designs rather than real buildings or local flora, in case, being used far from their originals, they provoked a sense of alienation among the users. The only speakers opposed to the project talked in terms of means rather than ends – they felt a small delay might be convenient. To the question of how Germans should be persuaded that giving up their currency was a good idea, a government spokesman replied that the media would be relied on for help. With 'positive' coverage the figures would move in the right direction. Meanwhile, for the recalcitrant or merely poor, the possibility of a 'variable geometry' or 'varying speed' Europe was mooted until, mysteriously and in the fullness of time – the soft tones of progressive Anglicanism entered their discourse at this moment – all economies would 'converge', coming to resemble the German one.

Bad British beef and worse British behaviour were meanwhile monotonously cited by each speaker as a reason for 'moving forwards'. Fiddling with embarrassingly helpful tomes recounting German success while I waited for elusive end-of-sentence verbs, I wondered what would cause such convictions to be abandoned. It was a question I asked a tall, grey-haired director of the European Monetary Institute as we stood in front of a building site, facing a young *autonome* with a shaven head and an enormous tattoo on her half-exposed left breast, but he didn't answer. Instead, he talked about cranes. Didn't I think cranes were firm evidence of economic activity? I had been perplexed by his presentation, which was full of what a Frenchman described as '*quincaillerie*' – elaborate plumbing, the installation of which was described step by step with the assistance of compound nouns. Perhaps the real problem with the German arrangements, I suggested, was that they precluded second thoughts. The prospect of being lumbered with something that no one wanted couldn't entirely be ruled out – and unlike the GDR, one couldn't pull down 'Europe' in a few months. The new German Europe was being constructed along what once had been called technocratic lines – plans had been drawn up not in a flexible or generous spirit of democratic conviction, but according to models of fiscal rectitude supplied by bankers. Europeans would think of this end-of-the-century creation as a German one; they would blame Germans if it went wrong.

The director replied – it was by way of reproach, but said more in a spirit of sorrow – that the Germans had already given up their currency at Maastricht. 'What is Europe other than markets and money?' he asked me. Later he asked me what sort of Europe I would have wanted. When I said: 'The Europe of Willy Brandt,' meaning more democracy, an openness towards the East, real rather than sham democratic practices, he was silent. They had tried to insert such provisions, he said, shaking his head; but the British and French had vetoed them. Still, he must have felt it was worth trying again because he came back to me an hour later bowing towards me in the old-fashioned German way I associated with characters out of Thomas Mann: 'My town is important to me for some things,' he said, 'my region for others, my country for others – and Europe for still more.'

At the Staatsoper performance of *Fidelio* that night the chorus of prisoners were dressed in red Zek costumes, and, for the closing numbers in which they listened to a Ceauşescu-lookalike Don Fernando, in EU blue. There were large flats onstage in the shape of the barracks that Daniel Libeskind hated so much, and they moved Escher-style from horizontal to vertical, changing colour from light blue to black. I looked around at the GDR plush, which, I imagined, had housed many repellent propagandist opera productions, and, not for the first time in Berlin, I was moved as well as excited. It was so much better than the recent past, unimaginably so.

Later I went to the old GDR Mitte quarter with its all-night bars filled with the young, the adventurous or the merely curious. I had arranged to meet a young German film-maker who lived in London, and she told me why she kept coming back to Berlin. 'You want to see how it's going to end,' she explained. 'Month by month it's entirely different – it's as if the future is being continually altered.' Banners stood over the old Volksbühne, home of official GDR culture, and we stopped to drink in a bar filled with stills from the now-defunct Socialist cinema. I could see why Germans had such confidence in their power to shape and transform; but the British story gave me pause. For in every Empire, commercial or otherwise, there was a price to be paid. To the Germans, it seemed that their European arrangements were non- or anti-imperial (and I was by now convinced of the genuineness of such emotion), devoid of hegemony and even of a pecking order, resting as they did on the 'pooling' of power, or the collective exercise of authority, moral or administrative; but to me such notions seemed illusory, while the real stay remained concealed for the moment among tons of scaffolding and misleadingly obscured by the winking logos of industrial supremacy.

Cranes did indeed imply economic success, but in the New Europe we wouldn't live off cranes alone. There would be bad times and with them would come British Europhobes bellowing about roses stricken by greenfly, or xenophobic French or Italian politicians clamouring to exclude the dark-skinned victims of eco-catastrophe. 'All the world is in trouble,' said the British Foreign Secretary Ernest Bevin in 1945, 'and I have to deal with all the troubles at once.' Someone would have to face up to these matters in the best liberal-imperial way, and it would now fall to the Germans, urged on by the peculiar context of privilege which was a consequence of their apocalyptic past, to do so. I felt that I would rather live in a Europe where there were so many good Germans, but that in my heart of hearts I, too, like everyone else, would come to resent their monopolistic professions of virtue as well as their great wealth. I had found a future in Berlin, but it wasn't the one I had been looking for – nor one I could specially welcome. Still, it was there – and that was something.

St Petersburg: Night Outside

It's night outside.
The deceit of the rich is all around.
It's après moi le déluge.
And then what? The citizens will be hoarse,
and there'll be a crowd in the cloakroom.

Osip Mandelstam (1933)

Somewhere alongside a frozen ditch beside the old fortress of St Peter and Paul, below a truckful of police-force synthetic winter hats, I came across the doll costumes. They were meticulously executed in perfect equivalents of the sturdy dark blue or khaki of the originals, and they came attached to a piece of cardboard with a faded photograph showing what your Barbie doll would look like if it were properly dressed. I fingered the Red Army one, admiring how the minuscule star had been sewn onto the forage cap – it was the one worn by the woman soldiers who directed the traffic around Berlin in 1945 – then I turned to the more elegant Navy uniform, with the striped vest and the cadet's hat bearing an inscription in minuscule embroidered Cyrillic script that I couldn't read. The wind was bitter, the river was edged with ice; and I hesitated. It wasn't the price – 35,000 roubles, or £5 – that gave me pause, but the ridiculous sense (I was sure that it wasn't shared by the vendor, who was cold, too, despite his own outsize surplus hat, jumping up and down) that something was wrong here, something had occurred which, I was told by every piece of mental circuitry I possessed, should not have. I walked around more piles of hats, but by the time I returned the man had gone.

The dolls set me thinking about other visits made to Russia, in what had been known as the Soviet period. I remembered in particular a tour of the furniture store of the old Gostelradio in Moscow. It was a hangar that turned out to contain nothing but a range of red plastic stars, sofas, armchairs, brass spittoons and aspidistras, through which I had walked in the cold for an hour until I found the perfect specimen. The next day, badly hung over, I had been taken on a special visit to the greenish corpse of Lenin, suspended in marble the colour of diseased liver. Then I found myself sitting in the only bug-free room at the American Embassy, discussing whether it could be proved that SS-20 rockets existed or not in the company of a mild-mannered strategic expert and an irascible Professor of History from Edinburgh. Although I was more than familiar with the literature of fellow-travellers in the West, I had never quite understood the claims of Communism to represent the future, and I found it more convenient to see in such emblems a past of sorts, now pretty much defunct. But even then, in the early eighties, sliding inebriated around the freezing Moscow boulevards amid the hulks of collectivism, it was hard to concede that anyone had ever really believed in all this. I began to wonder when or how they had lost their beliefs. Often, following what had happened to the Soviet Union from the comfort of the West, I wondered about the implications of the death of the twentieth century's last god.

Now, in late 1995, I was sitting in a cramped, dark room on the walls of which were pinned a map of the city studded with seventy-odd red pins, and several rows of Polaroids from which gazed faces surprised by flashlight. These were adult versions of some of the 102 babies, fifty-one of each sex, who were born on July 19, 1961 in St Petersburg, a day when Brezhnev was in the Kremlin, when the weather was warm and sunny, windy with the odd shower – and when *Pravda* reassured its readers (somewhat misleadingly, as it turned out) that the final ends of Communism would be achieved within twenty years, and that in the meantime the maize crop was good, and sugar-beet yields up on last year.

'A human being steps into the river of life,' the director (also born on that day) liked to say. 'Whether for happiness or suffering, the cosmic act has been performed.' But for Viktor, who drove me around the city from person to person, recording the implications of such cosmic acts had become more complicated than he had anticipated. What did he want to say about these people who shared his birthday? Among them were a masseuse, a man who imported frozen chicken legs, ticket vendors, ex-physicists, two petty criminals, a tour guide, a Casanova and quite a few drunks. Two of them (one an alcoholic married to a drug addict) were about to give birth to their own children. Viktor was wondering what significance could be attached to whatever it was they held in common. They were cut loose from the ordered premises of the fictitious future once offered them – but the meaning of this disconnection at present eluded him. We drove around town, over canal bridges and through deserted squares. Passing a statue of Lenin, Viktor explained that it was still standing because its sculptor had been highly thought of, and was now very ill. 'When he dies it will be melted down,' he said. We stopped for a traffic cop, and Viktor took out the certificate of a medal he had received for his last film, an exquisite Gogolesque study of two ageing drunken brothers and their sister, living crazily out of time with their animals and their garbled memories in the middle of nowhere. When he got back in his old black Volga limousine, after paying the 5000-rouble fine (less than £1) for going through a red light, he was angry.

We drove along wide, deserted avenues, stopping just short of the monstrous bright blue and white baroque hulk of the Smolny monastery. Then we walked across dirty snow to a large courtyard, from the roof of which sheets of rusted metal and planks of wood were randomly being thrown. A small man with black hair dressed in a dirty apron came running out, and he hugged Viktor, crying on his shoulder. This was Igor, who was placed in the next bed to Viktor and who, after being abandoned by his mother, had lived in this hospital for the mentally ill for the past thirty-three years, washing pots and pans and cleaning the ward for a monthly wage (his girl-friend, who worked in the laundry, got a little more) consisting of enough to buy the two Barbie outfits I had just seen.

We walked quickly from ward to ward. In some of them, where the drugged inmates sat watching tumbling acrobats on television, there were still posters of Leningrad, tacked up in the Soviet era and discoloured. Igor shared his ward, which was close and smelling of cats, with three old men, one of whom was lying on the metal cot turned to the wall, snoring. His own corner of the room was decorated with coloured photographs taken from magazines: flowers, animals, bright prairie green and yellow fur. Igor held his razor, sobbing as he hugged us in turn. Afterwards, under falling bits of roof, standing among kittens scampering in every direction, Viktor didn't appear wholly discouraged. 'He has a terrible life,' he said. 'But it isn't sad.'

Soon afterwards, I had to leave, and months passed; someone broke Viktor's jaw, causing delays. What I saw of the film was a catalogue of horrendous misfortunes, and I could understand why Viktor wasn't happy. Who would watch such misery? But next time I came, Yeltsin had just won the elections, and he was less glum. The city was green, and it was light for most of the night. I stayed in a former Communist Party guest house with a rocket-proof door, in which long corridors led to suites with gold or red net curtains, and cramped 1950s bathrooms featuring hybrid hip baths and showers as difficult to extricate oneself from as they were hazardous to enter. I watched with interest as one or other of the handsome, slightly faded women who ran the nameless hotel bent over to weigh pieces of pork in their rooms filled with potted plants, or scribbled voluminous rouble quantities in huge ledgers while following the progress of the Russian acrobats in Atlanta, or the latest bulletins regarding President Yeltsin's deteriorating health. Each morning, blinking at the salt cellars, rubbing my ears because of the amplified Madonna, I chewed haplessly at pink gristle. I ventured out through the shuttered metal door. To one side of the Stalin-era block in which the hotel was situated was a factory that appeared to be abandoned, but if I walked in the other direction I passed courtyards in which bonfires were lit, and abandoned shops before which stood vague, white-haired women smoking cigarettes and holding string bags. A large, discoloured building to which a grain hopper was attached still bore a frieze depicting Lenin's head in profile accompanied by drooping ears of wheat. Each year, according to Viktor, the building had to be emptied of rats with the help of a gas similar in properties to Zyklon B. The rats rushed out of the building and ran across the road, drowning themselves in the river. I stood before this spot each morning, watching dogs the size of small ponies pull their ageing owners across the road, wondering how these animals could be fitted into the crowded life of a communal apartment. A cortège, or indeed a moving automotive cemetery passed me by. The trucks were in dun colours of muddy blue or brown, and they wheezed past, broken-backed, with bald tyres and shattered windows. Each time the traffic stopped, they stalled, backfiring as they were started again.

This time I got to know Viktor better. He was stocky, with a smooth beard, a soft voice, beautiful brown eyes and an absorbed, distant manner. Rare among Russians, he was a vegetarian, and he wore natty German suits; when stuck for words, he would bang the table. 'I feel like a baby' is how he described his struggles with English. Viktor's great-grandfather was an emissary of the Tsar, and the day he was born his father crashed a motor-cycle while celebrating, killing Viktor's uncle. His parents separated and he grew up in Kazakhstan, and in a space shared by ten families in St Petersburg. But now Viktor had been given his own apartment, and he was prosperous enough by Russian standards to have to worry about his safety. We ate mildly hallucinogenic mushrooms and sour cream and drank Bordeaux in a small sitting-room lined with bookshelves containing the collected works of Dostoevsky, Turgenev and Pushkin, which he consulted frequently. Viktor loved the Russian nineteenth century, and there was nothing whatsoever I could see that identified him with the recent Soviet past. 'I was lucky,' he said whenever I asked him about the progress of his life. 'But I also believed in my luck.'

The process of completing films usually involved the methodical junking of material, but Viktor was even now adding material as he pulled what had been edited to pieces. One afternoon we drove over to the old studios of Lendoc, where he had trained as a cameraman. Filled with marble, gilt and long-forgotten prizes displayed on shelves, the lobby was like a Bronx cinema. Upstairs a solitary old lady in a white coat oversaw the archive: hundreds and hundreds of film cans meticulously inscribed in Cyrillic script. At one point six hundred people had worked here, making more than a film a week, and yet all the films were made to formula – the same voice was used each time, the same shots, even (people were shipped to official demonstrations, having been selected for their looks by factory managers) the same extras. After a ceremony in which new-born babies were inducted into the Soviet world, receiving a special book from a Party official, we watched as Fidel Castro addressed a 1961 crowd outside the Winter Palace at his habitual length. 'Goodbye, Fidel,' said the commentary. 'Be happy, and see you next time.'

Later, we were sitting in a restaurant listening to an austere young woman playing the harp when four men wearing bulky suits came in with a tall blonde clad in a leather miniskirt. They were joined by a man with the craggy, silvered looks favoured ten years ago by the producers of American soaps like *Dynasty*. Viktor raised an eyebrow, as he did on such occasions, and the other guests talked desultorily in English about sons of friends who had become entangled with the mafia, and killed. It appeared that members of the old *nomenklatura*, whose privileges had been removed, were most susceptible to recruitment. Someone said it was starting to be hard to distinguish between the criminal and the merely rich, and that this could be considered a sign of progress. 'They're a new breed,' the studio head said. 'They never existed before.

Soviet Man meets Barbie.' It was no good asking Russians whether things were better, but I did want to know what, if anything, was beginning. I couldn't begin to comprehend the impact of so much destruction. 'For the first time almost in a hundred years, no one knows anything about the future,' Viktor told me. 'They have forgotten all of the past. This means that Russians live in a state of permanently being between things. It gives so much freedom, but so much fear, too.'

Next day was the three-hundredth anniversary of the Russian fleet, and people were already milling around the Winter Palace when I arrived, crowding towards the bridge over the Neva that led to the two flaming rust-red torches on Vassilievsky Island. There were ships from the US and Britain, but the Russian ones were bigger, with more rocket tubes and flags, and more ratings assembled on deck. I watched as small planes performed acrobatics and parachutists jumped from larger ones. A fly-past of World War Two aircraft took place, followed by noisy star turns executed by more recent if equally obsolete additions to the arsenal. The crowd was enormous, genial, dressed in bright colours, swaying with happiness; many of the sailors were drunk already. They congratulated each other on the anniversary. One sailor told the reporter beside whom I was standing that it didn't really matter that no one in the Navy had been paid for six months – the Russian ships were best.

Suddenly I found myself in the midst of one of the scenes beloved of the Magnum photographers of the 1950s from Paris, for whom, after the Leica or high-speed film, mass society was the great invention of the century, and who, shepherded assiduously from steel mill to collective farm, naturally considered it had found its greatest expression in the Soviet Union. But this particular crowd, more and more drunk as the afternoon wore on, were cheering Yeltsin, and the ships, as I reminded myself, impressive as they might seem, were about as useful as the *Temeraire*. The only reason strategists could give for examining the capability of the Russian Navy these days was to find out whether its rusting submarines would leak more radioactive waste into Arctic waters, thus furnishing scenarios for thrillers on the proceeds of which they could retire from Whitehall or Langley to the South of France.

After sampling the American band, who were red-faced from playing Glenn Miller and Sousa, I went through deserted back streets. I came to a spot on Nevsky Prospect over the road from the famous domed bookstore and in front of the Kazan Cathedral, formerly containing an exhibition describing the progress of atheism, but since the fall of Communism dedicated once more to the triumph of religion. The crowd had swollen now as people walked back through the dusk to the Metro. They were by now astonishingly drunk – I had never seen so many transcendentally inebriated people. But they also appeared to be happy – conscripts threw their frisbee-like hats in our direction, or jammed them on their girl-friends' heads, whistling and waving at each other. Viktor said that such displays of emotion in public would have been unthinkable even three years ago.

People told me that St Petersburg was a museum, and that the city had fallen behind Moscow, which had become the New Babylon; but I found the past closer here than in the rest of Europe, not least because it appeared to be unfinished. One morning I walked by the river through more derelict factories to the old Smolny Institute, a nondescript institutional building set amid tatty municipal flower beds. This had been a girls' school for the daughters of the St Petersburg rich until in 1917 it became the headquarters of the Soviet of Workers' and Soldiers' Deputies. Lenin had taken up residence in the Institute, and a shrine had been created out of the austere bedroom occupied by him and his wife Nadezdha Krupskaya. Now the city fathers had reoccupied the building – a polite guard told me that nothing of Lenin could be seen.

Meanwhile, there were new shrines to be seen. Going down the Fontanka Canal, through the weedy forecourt of the crumbling Shermetyev Palace, I came to a large inner courtyard filled with overgrown trees where nice-looking women who might have been schoolteachers sunned themselves. It was here, coming one night to see the poetess Anna Akhmatova in 1946 amid the ruins, that the philosopher Isaiah Berlin, at that time working for the British Embassy, encountered the tipsy voice of Randolph Churchill as the latter stumbled in the dark, having lost his way. 'Isaiah,' Randolph shouted, as if he were in Tom Quad in Oxford, 'Isaiah!' Foreigners didn't visit poetesses in those early Cold War days, particularly if they came accompanied by the son of a notorious imperialist; and as punishment poor Akhmatova was shortly afterwards denounced by Andrei Zhdanov, ex-boss of the Leningrad Party and Stalin's 'overseer of ideology', in the style of literary criticism latterly adopted by fundamentalist Muslims. Her poetry was, Zhdanov declared, 'pathetically limited', and she was 'a crazed woman . . . neither nun nor whore, or rather both nun and whore, whose lust is mixed with prayer'.

Upstairs was a rather posher version of the communal apartments I had seen with Viktor, smelling of polish and drains. There were no books in the room which Akhmatova had occupied – most of her library she was periodically obliged to sell – only a small drawing by Modigliani, with whom she was once in love, and an exquisite ceramic statuette of herself. The room was packed with visitors quietly reading her poems to each other:

> We thought: we are paupers, we have nothing.
> But as we started to lose one thing after another
> So that every day became a memorial day –
> We began composing songs
> About God's great munificence
> And about our former wealth.

In this poky room overlooking trees some smallest portion of the discomfort she endured for most of her life was apparent to me; but I remembered, too, how in the old St Petersburg catastrophe was a pretext for elaborate opera or ballet stage sets, and cabaret spectacle organized by the young. Art was important here – as the city successively experienced revolution, Utopia, famine, repression and marginalization, it became the way those who clung to the idea of St Petersburg kept memory alive.

Akhmatova lost one ex-husband poet to a firing squad. Her second husband, who was an art critic, died in a camp. Her scholar son spent eighteen years in detention. Her own behaviour was scrutinized for signs of deviance while she scraped together a living as a translator. Most of her friends, including Osip Mandelstam, who died in 1938 in a transit camp in Eastern Siberia, were victims of state terror. Her greatest poem described the moment when, queuing outside the prison, she was recognized, and asked to commemorate those who waited 'where they never, never opened the doors to me'. This was a burden she was glad to accept (humility was a virtue of hers, not modesty), with the thought that if perhaps a bronze memorial was raised to herself it should be here – but that the bronze should, like her own poetry, be allowed to weep. And yet Akhmatova, ultimately, was the victor. By means of what she was able to publish in the rare moments when she was in favour as well as through the knowledge of her suppressed verse, circulated after it had been learnt by heart, she, and not Lenin, created the twentieth-century identity of her own city. But she could also be mischievous when asked to rehash the apocalypse for visitors. 'Leningrad is in the end extremely well-suited to catastrophe,' she told a would-be biographer, sounding like Lady Bracknell. 'That cold river with heavy storm clouds over it, those menacing sunsets, that operatic, frightening moon . . . It's all frightening. I cannot imagine how catastrophes look in Moscow; they don't have that sort of thing there.'

Catastrophes still occurred in St Petersburg, like the recent murder in a mafia war of a British businessman enjoying his tea, and it had become necessary to pass through metal detectors when entering the poshest hotels. Sitting in the bar, drinking vodka and listening to Chopin, looking out of the window at a stretch of pavement from which the hotel staff had tastefully excluded vagrants, I came across a piece in *Le Monde* by the French futurologist Jacques Attali. The world had become confusing since the collapse of Communism – no one knew where they stood. Did we still have 'classes' in the West? What was the new shape of things? Well, the poor were still with us, but Attali was able to announce a new social phenomenon: the 'over-class'. These were the new rich of our time – and they were quite different from the old rich. 'Liberal or Marxist theories do not apply to them,' Attali helpfully explained. 'They are neither enterpreneur-creators of wealth . . . nor capitalist-exploiters of the working class ... they are the possessors of nomadic wealth, monetary or intellectual in character, and they use such wealth on their own behalf.' I liked the idea of nomadic wealth; but I felt, too, that we had been here before. The Second World – the name was invented in the 1950s by a French intellectual to distinguish Communism both from capitalism and from the bits of the world at that time presumed to be 'developing' – had fallen. Its disappearance had put many new and impoverished workers on the market. Nowadays, Russia was starting merely to look like the rest of us, only more so. It was certainly what sociologists called 'porous', and many of its richer citizens could have been called nomads. But I imagined that some of their strivings for acceptability chronicled each day in the St Petersburg English-language paper – sending their children to Eton, or declining to go to such hotels as the Negresco in Nice, on the grounds that they were full of Arabs richer than themselves – would have made Attali wince.

There was an astonishing similarity between the old pre-upheaval Russia and the present condition of the world. Sixteen people lived in the average 1904 St Petersburg apartment, and the death rate from cholera was the highest in the world. 'One cannot help but note the premature decrepitude of the factory women,' a doctor reported in 1913. 'A woman worker of fifty sees and hears poorly, her head trembles ... She looks about seventy. It is obvious that only dire need keeps her at the factory, forcing her to work beyond her strength. While in the West, elderly workers have pensions, our women workers can expect nothing better than to live out their days as lavatory attendants.' This was definitely the sort of world favoured by nomadic capitalism. Once 'stability' was assured – it was much prized in the Tsar's time, too – the nomads would be back. Some of them were already sitting here beside me in the bar, preparing to meet the hookers dressed in what appeared to be Gianni Versace, who manned the Nevsky Prospect shops by day and flocked around the bars by night.

At the Russian museum I sat in front of I. Repin's gigantic, perplexing study of the Imperial State Council in St Petersburg, meeting in 1905. This had taken over two years to complete and contained eighty-one figures dressed in gold braid and assembled in various postures of stiff-jointedness. Seated at the back and to one side, so that he didn't appear to be the centre of the canvas, wearing a blue sash to distinguish him from ancient retainers, the Tsar was raising a piece of paper to chest height. Exactly what was being discussed, or why, was hardly important – but the grouping conveyed the illusion that there still remained time before the paper fell to the baize, or the order was given and not obeyed. Repin was a constitutional liberal, and I wondered whether he had ever consciously experienced the pessimism revealed in this canvas. Probably not, I concluded – instead he must have longed for the advent of photographic techniques, making the taking of such pains redundant.

In the company of Nadezdha, a nice, brown-haired curator, I walked through a hidden door just beside the icons. Here six women sat looking at huge books in the postures I was familiar with from my hotel, while a young man with long hair and steel glasses looked earnestly at an old piece of canvas. We went up some flights of stairs, and through room after room of stacked canvases, until I lost count. I glimpsed Tsars laid out on the floor for reframing, giant families requiring larger and larger quantities of French or English nannies. I lingered over a wonderful Condé Nastish portrait of an artist's wife with a pet wolfhound. Then we reached the locked rooms containing the pictures painted between 1900 and 1914, and my companion began to pull canvases from the racks – Cubist-looking street scenes from St Petersburg, or interiors from estates, peasants in shawls or simple red jugs or crosses against white or black.

Nadezdha greeted the paintings one by one with affection. 'This is my favourite,' she said, or: 'This was thought to be painted by someone, but I got the attribution changed.' There were paintings by Kliun, Popova, Larionov, Gontcharova, Malevich. Nadezdha bent over each painting. I noticed that she was happiest when her favourite painters had stayed in Russia – defections to Paris she viewed with sorrow, and her regret that those exiled had died in poverty was tinged with the sense of just deserts. I had seen some of this art in the West, but never so much of it in one place, and I had never experienced it so intimately as I did now. For many years it had lain unseen, locked up, as a consequence of official disapproval; but now the museum lacked space or money to show it. St Petersburg greys, Moscow yellows, countryside oranges, duck whites, vivid greens, purples and magentas stood out from the sallow green walls, startling me. In 1895 Friedrich Engels, referring to the Wall of China still isolating Russia from the West, pointed to the 'most incredible and bizarre forms of ideas' – he thought they arose from the existence side by side of so many phenomena belonging to different civilizations. Between when he wrote this and 1914, Russia was opened up. Russian artists took the side of the Revolution. They created great revolutionary art, but they were betrayed. Thereafter Russian art was once again kept apart. I asked Nadezdha what would now happen to the collection of Soviet art. Would it be destroyed, or sold? She frowned as she explained that it would all be kept. But the canvases were very big – most of them had to be rolled up, and they were locked away.

Waiting for Viktor, I realized that I had never encountered a place where the activity of hanging around seemed so natural or inevitable. Built for a purpose, abandoned before becoming useless, utterly destroyed and totally rebuilt, finally neglected, St Petersburg lived through reflections. On hydrofoils or canals, I tried to read Russian poetry in translation, but I had no sense of the original from these earnest, laboured efforts on the part of Anglo-American poets; and I ended up looking at the water instead.

I wondered what was being produced now in the way of art. Was it possible any more for a metropolis suddenly to become a centre of world art? Was it likely that St Petersburg, outside the network of hype which the international art market had become, could once more attain such a position? Just off Nevsky Prospect, near the video and computer software stores, was a large building handed over to the city artists. The courtyard sounded and looked promising – heavy metal, Malevich graffiti – but much of what it contained was, to my regret, much what one could find in the West only some years behind – campy videos set to opera, or lurid if less than competent protest art. A would-be gallery owner explained to me that life wasn't easy here. In one year he had made only £1000 in sales. Then a man had come to him guaranteeing him £30,000 if he allowed the gallery to be used for the occasional transaction of his choosing. While he was hesitating over whether to accept this tempting offer, the man was shot dead in the street.

At the back of the Hermitage, I went into a posh apartment building, the first with a lift that I had encountered, though it was broken. I climbed six storeys, entering an apartment decorated like a loft in New York, with high-tech lamps and garish brocades, and a large window that overlooked a small park. Beyond it were the light-bulb domes of the Church of the Resurrection. This was where Sergei Bugaev, aka 'Afrika', the city's most successful artist, lived. He was small and energetic, dressed in the style of a Western art entrepreneur. While we watched television – there was an item about Chechenya, in which the reporter got into a hot tub with the troops, that made him click his tongue in disapproval – he introduced me to his beautiful girl-friend. 'She's fifteen,' he said. 'I met her when she was fourteen. I like to live dangerously.'

Ten years ago Bugaev had dressed up in drag, and won a St Petersburg beauty contest. After the collapse of Communism, declaring himself to be suffering from disorientation, he checked into a Crimean mental asylum, and documented his own treatment for twenty-eight days, with photographs of the other inmates, the doctors, the drugs or appliances used to pacify the patients. Next he started a beautifully produced constructivist-style magazine, and began to collect images of Soviet civilization at a time when people were throwing them away – he even saved a twelve-foot-high statue of Stalin. Bugaev's studio was visited by Westerners. 'The world has de-realized,' the French psychiatrist Jacques Derrida exclaimed, confronted by Bugaev's statue of Stalin. 'Reality has no way of supporting itself any more.'

Bugaev sought out the old ladies, now impoverished and in retirement, who had once sewed the gold inscriptions on Soviet banners. Reluctant though they were to create pornographic images, they nonetheless made Donald Duck and Lenin replicas in embroidered velvet – and these sold quite well. But Bugaev told me he was fed up with art. Nowadays the awfulness of the Russian media was more interesting to him, and the ineptitude of politicians – public life in Russia, he believed, had become like the child's game in which a blind hunter pursued a rabbit, but killed every animal in sight except that rabbit. 'But one can perhaps accomplish something in relation to politics,' he said. 'As an artist, all one can do is beg.' Bugaev was packing to go to the Crimea on holiday as he talked. I asked him whether he believed, as most of the people I had met appeared to, that all Soviet painting was awful, or whether some of it was better than the rest. 'Socialist Realism was OK,' he said. 'It's like the Soviet world – important because it was there. No one can ever get rid of it. It's part of the way we look at the world.'

Viktor was more optimistic when I telephoned him from the street; he thought he had an ending for his film now. But he was hard at work, so I took a cab to Moscow Square, where the last statue of Lenin still stood, its sculptor by now sicker than on my previous visit, and in intensive care. I walked around the enormous lump of bronze. It did seem somewhat better than some of the others, perhaps because Lenin had been given a longish nineteenth-century jacket, the cut of which (from some aspects only, admittedly) gave him the air of a poet. Walking around the image, I remembered its ubiquity – the horrible baby Lenins with curls, the ardent adolescents, the stern early-adult figures wearing caps, the mature, wholly bald representative of the proletariat perched on an armoured car, the statesman in his dotage sitting *al fresco* on a park bench, kibitzing with his successor Stalin. The images shared the 'meaningless expression' noticed by the poet Joseph Brodsky. They inspired severe disorientation or even terror. No one, no matter how aesthetically impaired they might be, could ever feel wholly contented in the vicinity of an image of Lenin.

I watched Viktor's film later that evening. He had assembled all these bits of lives around the story of the alcoholic and the drug addict. They were told that it wouldn't be prudent for them to have a child, but, after disregarding the doctor's advice, they now sat waiting for the event with their huge dog. They wondered whether the future should be induced or not. The labour pains (filmed by Viktor with compassion but what must be called a lack of discretion) were prodigious, and the baby, when it finally arrived, was small, and made no noise. 'Is it alive?' the woman asked. But the tiny thing did somehow live, to the astonishment of the doctors; and one could next see the mother hovering over her, unable to change a nappy, but crying tears of drunken happiness, while the enormous dog looked on, thumping the floor vigorously with its tail and whimpering. 'I want my husband to be like Dostoevsky, and I want my daughter to grow up healthy,' the woman told Viktor. All this should have been depressing, but somehow it wasn't – I did believe that at least one of her wishes might come true.

My old Volga cab broke down in the vicinity of the smashed-up freeway with its wheezing trucks, and it was late by the time I got back to the metal door with its impassive keeper. I got in and out of the hip bath, and found I couldn't sleep. Sick of poetry in translation, I turned to the remaining book I'd taken from London. *Soviet Communism: A New Civilization?* was published in the midst of the Depression, and written by Beatrice and Sidney Webb, Fabians, fellow-travellers, founders of the London School of Economics, later Lord and Lady Passfield, gurus or ageing consciences of Britain's 1945 Labour Government. They went to the Soviet Union in the hope of finding out whether Utopia could be achieved without coercion. After due accumulation of statistics, many hilariously supervised interviews and disgusting meals, they concluded that yes, it would be possible, though much urging towards virtue – the idea of propaganda was not antipathetic to these diligent educationalists – was no doubt required. On page 1135 of the second volume, they unveiled their conclusions:

> Science, whether in the discovery of truth about the universe or the dismissal of untruth, is not, by itself, enough for the salvation of mankind. If scientific knowledge is to be brought to the service of humanity, there must be added a purpose in man's effort involving a conception of right or wrong . . . The feature in this new morality [of Soviet Communism] which stands out in sharpest contrast with the morality of capitalist societies is the recognition of a universal individual indebtedness. No human being reaches manhood without having first incurred a considerable debt . . . That debt he is held bound to repay by actual personal service by hand or by brain.

I was still wide awake. A 'new morality'? It was easy to make fun of the Webbs, as Malcolm Muggeridge, their nephew by marriage, had done, imagining them sitting in a stationary train applauding the scenery as it failed to go by; and I saw no reason to deprive myself of honest entertainment. But it was getting light now, and I could hear copious gurglings or muted explosions as guests negotiated the plumbing appliances of the hotel, banging their lavatory seats, or struggling either to remove or put in place the ill-fitting plugs. I resolved to come to St Petersburg for the end of the century. If I wasn't too drunk, I would try to remember to drink a toast to the teetotal Webbs.

How to be a European

'England', 'La France', 'Das Reich', their words
Are like the names of extinct birds.

W. H. Auden (1940)

I'm a European. I want to die in Europe.

Ludwig Wittgenstein (1950)

Only months previously, in the summer of 1944, allied bombers had destroyed the never picturesque port of Le Havre, taking with it the spare and ugly Protestant *temple*. This is why my parents were married in the village church-yard of Le Hanouard, deep in the Pays de Caux. My mother had been to Britain in the 1930s as a girl; and my father was introduced to her by one of his fellow-officers, who had kept her address. I have a photograph of the occasion, which shows threadbare French attempts to keep up with the impressive chic of British Army brass. I admire my mother's and grandmother's floral dresses, and I like to look at the roguish expression of my French grandfather, decorated veteran, failed cotton-broker, football-club manager, black-market dealer, keeper of a POW camp, *coureur* – the word is untranslatable. And I see my tall father, for the first time in his own life truly leaving Britain and his mother.

I find in the group photograph – it must be one of so

many taken that year – the attempts of Europeans to make the best of things and be happy after catastrophe. These are lucky Europeans, of course. For them the condition of liberation is real, and so, too, though they wouldn't put it that way, being pragmatic people exhausted by war, is the idea of Europe itself.

But I also tell myself that this is a private fiction of mine. These are French and British people in the photograph, and that's how they will stay. My father will return home with his French wife, and I will be born. The frontiers will go up, and something known as the Cold War will come to dominate most of my life. I will try to write about the strange hybrid quality of a 'Europe' that, outside the realm of geography or regulation, only half exists. I'll call myself 'half-French', or 'Anglo-French', aware that this is a less than satisfactory form of self-definition and wishing periodically that Europeanness could be made to mean something outside the passport queue.

It also occurs to me that autobiography European-style is a tendentious activity. Am I French or British? Does it matter? A little – to me it matters, anyhow. I suppose it ensures a double loyalty, or even a triple one: first British, or French, then European. But I sense that the third must remain problematical. What does it mean to be European? Does it mean anything at all?

There are the near-infinite Europes of memory, and these comprise our private imaginations, and there is the not-so-new 'Europe' which is neither public in the old sense, raising armies or confidently dispensing laws, nor wholly certain of what it is there to do. Somewhere between them lie the old nation-states of Europe, which are starting to look distinctly tatty, threatened in some instances by newer, less effective versions of themselves under the guise of such mysterious imperatives as regionalism or – the most confusing entity of all – federalism. These Europes coexist in each consciousness, but they have no real connection to each other. To be a European at this moment is to slide or jump uneasily from one Europe to another – they are like computer programs, which though they can be run together cannot merge.

In the old days national 'character' was exalted, often as a means of driving young men to get themselves killed. Now we have the cultivation of identity, and it suits us to presume that nations, like individuals, are capable of destroying and recomposing themselves. In the new historical orthodoxy, nations are both necessary and contingent. We need something like them, and yet they needn't exist. These days the poetry of nations attracts psychopathic poets *manqués* like Radovan Karadzić. The most cogent and humane authority on the subject of nationalism, Ernest Gellner, conceded that, over time, national cultures might come so much to resemble each other that 'inter-linguistic differences' might give way to phonetic ones. But he could still see no reason why what he called 'independence-worthy cultures' (i.e. those which had attained something like autonomy) should wish to disappear or be ruled by a third party; and he could anticipate, as a revenge against sameness, the flourishing of 'secondary cultural pluralism' – i.e. national characteristics that were revived in a conscious act of homage to the ancient gods of solidarity. But for him, the question was complicated by the ridiculousness of nationalism – the detestable elevation of the third-rate, whether in political rhetoric or folk dancing, in the name of national-ethnic solidarity. He once said that national prophets weren't worth reading – you knew pretty much what they were going to say. Presumably, he would have come to feel the same about national characteristics preserved against the logic of time, after their apparent usefulness was diminished.

I have always been perplexed by British nationalism. The question of identity first arose for me amid the ivy and fake-Tudor of my preparatory English school. There, to the astonishment of the masters, while my peers were interested in rock stars or serial killers, or even Tory politicians, I collected stamps of French Resistance heroes, filling page after page with their stern likenesses like a Young Pioneer commemorating Marx and Lenin. I also began to compile a biography of Charles de Gaulle. I was concerned not with the stout, monarchic figure of presidential iconography, but with the man as underdog, standing alone in 1940, or facing down the *colons* and their allies in the French Army to preserve democracy. Without knowing it, I suppose I already wanted to see something in France that was no longer there.

De Gaulle now enjoys the attentions of left-wing French exegetes like Régis Debray who opposed him in the 1960s; but he is valued as an artefact from France's glorious past, or a mysteriously honest, upright man, not as a figure in whom anything important to France's present or future resides. De Gaulle's world view, consisting of a powerful France pitted against Anglo-Saxondom by an alliance with Russia, belonged in the junk shop by the 1960s, and he achieved nothing by leaving the French chair empty at meetings in 1966, thus snubbing 'Europe', or punishing Britain with exclusion – he did return to the chair, and Britain was admitted, after his own end as a consequence of the 1968 upheavals. And the same will surely be the case in relation to Margaret Thatcher, whose vision of Albion Reborn was extinct by the time it was supposed to come to fruition, and yet whom it is possible, still, to admire as a *personnage* while acknowledging the doomed nature of her enterprises.

My own feelings about Margaraet Thatcher defy paraphrase – by themselves, her anachronistic sense of national confidence and campy evocations of British destiny leave me overwhelmed by contradictory emotions. But the tone is different whenever Europe is concerned. Here there are long menus to be sat through, punctuated by outbreaks of perfidy:

> He seemed to have a positive aversion to principle, even a conviction that a man of principle was doomed to be a figure of fun. He saw politics as an eighteenth-century general saw war: as a vast and elaborate set of parade-ground manoeuvres by armies that would never actually engage in conflict but instead declare victory, surrender or compromise as their apparent strength dictated in order to collaborate on the real business of sharing the spoils.

This isn't F. R. Leavis' judgement on the moral worth of Count Mosca, the spider-like genius of Stendhal's novel of political intrigue, *The Charterhouse of Parma* – it is Mrs T. describing the after-dinner intrigues of Giulio Andreotti, Prime Minister of Italy, since placed on trial for his mafia connections. Like the BBC comedy figure she sometimes resembled, Mrs Thatcher often felt bested by Europeans. 'As always with the Italians, it was difficult to distinguish confusion from guile,' she ruefully observed in relation to a successful Italian manoeuvre. And yet for all its perceived absurdity, her quality of stubbornness, as well as her stiff-necked insularity, did enjoy cult status in the rest of Europe, particularly in France. This was because, unlike de Gaulle, whose excessive sense of dignity precluded low farce, she always put on a good show, but, more importantly, because she seemed a collector's item – interesting in what Europeans have come to think of as a 'very English' way.

Still, there is another, more flattering side to Mrs Thatcher's kind of loyalty. In the post-war period the notion of supranationality was much in vogue as a means of ensuring that the nationalism which had wrecked the world could be kept at bay – this was the *raison d'être* of 'Europe' and it is given a good airing in official histories of the EU. But the real history of supranationality was far from glorious. Here is Albert Speer's account of his meetings with Jean Bichelonne, the young Sorbonne professor who was Minister of Production in Pétain's collaborationist government in 1943:

'He was a passionate nationalist but very sympathetic, as I was, to pan-European ideas. When Bichelonne and I played with the idea of a European Economic Union, we thought of it as Utopian, But . . . it wasn't all that Utopian, was it?'

It sounds as if with this youngish, like-minded Frenchman Speer found some lightness of spirit.

'We agreed that in the future we would avoid the mistakes of the First World War generation . . . Europe had to be economically integrated; for this, I told him, I would happily oppose Hitler's plan of carving up France . . . which I considered wholly unnecessary.'

Appeasement was practised by sensible, well-educated politicians enjoying the support of the electorate, who believed in the virtues of compromise. It has become a tradition of the New Europe – nothing would get done if European politicians didn't attend to the requirements of their partners. However, the Albert-meets-Jean cosiness is sometimes demeaning as well as exhausting. No one who has spent even the smallest portion of his or her life in the vicinity of Brussels can fail to long for the sort of archaically reliable character type represented by Mrs Thatcher.

Was the creation of 'Europe' an adequate answer to the horrors of the mid-century? Historians now tend to think that its importance in creating stability or 'containing' Communism was overestimated beside such devices as the American Bomb. Nowadays, the principal historiographical dispute in relation to 'Europe' lies athwart the issue of whether the yellow stars were placed on the blue background to ensure the death of nations, and nationalist politicians, or their survival. One side, known as 'functionalists', alleges that from the beginning the Community was designed to replace the nation-state. The other insists no, that was never the intention, expressed though it may have been in numerous hand-outs. For the heretics, appropriately led by a British historian, Alan Milward, the real purpose of 'Europe' has been to shore up existing nationality by strengthening the nation-state. The paradox is that, in the 1950s, and later, this could only be achieved by the abrogation of some of their old functions in what was known, euphemistically, as the 'pooling' of sovereignty. This is perhaps good history, but the role of propaganda is important, too. Although the Community did originally shore up European nations, its politicians swiftly became adept when it came to the expression of ambiguity. They presented measures leading to the restriction of national power as if these would lead to its enhancement. It was President Mitterrand who became the master of such strategies – his speeches, less than comprehensible as they usually were, invariably expressed the idea that France would be strengthened the more she gave away.

Are the states of Europe now really 'stronger' than they were around the mid-Fifties? Does nationality have a future? To a person, dressed in their anonymous lounge suits, or workmanlike *costumes*, the young civil servants clustered around the departure gates at Strasbourg or Brussels answer: no. Among such people the idea of nationalism has died. Old entities like France or Britain are no longer taken seriously – unless, of course, they are considered as the recipients of cohesion grants, or become the objects of half-nostalgic, half-derisive subsidized films. (A double standard operates here, between 'small' national cultures, which receive patronizing attention, and the larger, old ones, about which only the most critical perspectives are allowed unless, like Germany, they are very rich or have cut themselves off from the idea of nationhood.) So much derision has undermined the prospects of nation-states. De Gaulle's project of national regeneration was taken wholly seriously, but Mrs Thatcher's efforts were not. Outside Germany, and in a different way Britain, nationality in Europe is now viewed as what politicians have to talk about in order to get elected.

Among *stagiaires*, many of whom sound like earnest Communists of the 1930s, *Volk* loyalty is desperately, terminally unchic. The only way in which a present-day nationalist can be taken seriously in Brussels is by evoking *Heimat* – turning the fires of unity into the artificial grate of sentimentalist localism, complete with armorial crest, brewery, local multinational and soccer team. This would be experienced as a momentous development if it were fully understood; but it is hidden by the sheer time taken in the European laboratory. For 'Europe' changes at the speed of a surly glacier, or an Andy Warhol movie of near-Biblical pretensions. The softness of Europe, its habit of changing conceptual shape while remaining substantially the same, gives the illusion of permanent arrangements that are also permanently transitional. We Europeans are rich, we are the lucky ones; there is no obligation to decide who we want to be. We can experience, simultaneously, any number of views about 'Europe', and then none of them. Later, we may have to make up our minds, but not now.

At my school debating society I spoke little, despising what I thought of as its introverted Englishness, and the way it sustained the notion, far from inaccurate at the time, that those who attended the school would shortly come into possession of the country itself. But I did once defend the internationalism of the day. I found a copy of the book from which I cribbed my speech: *Struggle For The World*, by the Labour MP Desmond Donnelly. This was a lyrical polemic about trading blocs and democracy in the manic-depressive style encouraged during the 1960s. Maybe World Federalism was going to be a losing wicket, and yet I recall my failure as conspicuous. I'm not even sure that my efforts could be considered a good try.

I was in France when Britain's application for membership of the EEC was finally accepted. Did any of my friends wish to make a career out of covering Brussels? They did not. Did they discuss the idea of Europe in an inspired or entertaining fashion? Did they discuss it at all? They did not – nor did the French people I knew. In 1970s France political answers were still thought likely to come from Marxism, just as later in Britain they would appear to be forthcoming as a consequence of newly freed markets. But no one really believed that anything would change – the existing arrangements in Europe, stamped on the landscape by means of reinforced concrete and barbed wire, made any reconsideration of the nature of our continent impracticable.

In 1975 I went to work in America. Seduced by what appeared to be the novelty of eighteenth-century language and the momentous provisions of the First Amendment, as well as the food, architecture, climate and just about everything else, I did think briefly of becoming American. But it was not the constitutional arrangements of America that fascinated me so much as its underlying, abstract purpose – the pursuit by any legal or moral means, given the loosest definition of what, properly, constituted civilization, of the idea of happiness. No European state could conceive of the purpose of democracy in this fashion; indeed, I felt that it would be hard as a European, given the blood spilt over ideology, to contemplate living by such simple abstractions. This was partly why they were so attractive to me.

Americans were among the earliest boosters of European federalism during the late 1940s, but from the perspective of convenience or impatience – Europeanists like Dean Acheson and George Ball felt it would be easier to handle all those Europeans if they got together, dumping all the separate habits which had got them into so much trouble. For some Europeans, America did come to stand in the imagination of the early proponents of European unity as a great, good place which, given time and luck, it should be possible to emulate. Liberal, decentralized, anxiously upholding minority rights, the post-war Anglo-American creation of the Federal Republic of Germany appeared to contain all that was best about the New World. Why should it not ultimately be possible to recreate the whole of the 'free' side of the continent in this image?

Only one of the founders of 'Europe', Jean Monnet, did have an extensive experience of America. Born in Cognac, to a wealthy brandy-producing family, unusually for a Frenchman an autodidact, Monnet learnt about getting things done when he arranged for the British and French governments to acquire and jointly ship grain and *matériel* during the Great War. Although he worked on Wall Street for a while, Monnet was too wayward to adapt to investment banking; and he fell foul, in different but wholly predictable ways, of both the enthusiasm-proof snobbish British élite, and the carefully self-graded, repressed mandarinate of France. He felt most at ease with Americans.

Monnet was a representative European of this century, but perhaps not quite in the way imagined by his admirers. He fell in love in 1929 (at the age of forty-one) with Silvia Bondini, nineteen years younger than himself, and married to one of his employees. Unable to secure an annulment of his own marriage in Italy or France, disdainful of Reno on aesthetic grounds, the so-European Monnet arranged to become a citizen in Stalin's Soviet Union. He was divorced in Moscow, and he remarried the same week. He and his new wife then travelled by train to Shanghai. As he explained to a friend, the marriage 'took months and cost a fortune'. Monnet's efforts on behalf of Europe were similarily ingenious, consisting of one complicated bureaucratic improvisation after another. His style of action, as a shrewd biographer explains, was 'closer to the outlook of the citizen than that of the servant of a state'. Breezy, full of *savoir-faire* and therefore naturally at ease with the generation of technocrat-gentlemen who ran Truman's and Eisenhower's America, Monnet came unstuck when appointed President of 'Europe's first government', the Coal and Steel Community. His hands were tied by the 'real' national governments over whom he was supposed to hold sway. He quickly became an unhappy man.

Perhaps it is wrong to expect a fixer of genius to have any amply developed rationale for his actions, let alone the 'vision' with which politicians are supposed to be endowed. Monnet did formulate many of the themes by now trotted out by Brussels savants – the importance of the Franco-German relationship, institutions as a basis of cohesion, 'moral force' as a factor bringing together nations, the 'pooling of sovereignty', etc. – but one can find next to nothing in his memoirs about the kind of Europe in which he wished to live. By comparison with Jefferson's, his formulations seem thin:

> 18 August.
> Liberty is civilization.
> Civilization consists of rules and institutions . . .
> 1. It's a privilege to be born a man.
> 2. It's a privilege to be born in our civilization.
> 3. Do we intend to limit such privileges to the national boundaries and the laws which currently protect us?
> 4. Or do we wish to try to extend such privileges to others?

Monnet believed that the construction of institutional Europe, with its cross-committees of experts and governmental officials, would by itself lead to the creation of a 'real' Europe of the imagination. 'Via money,' he declared in 1957, 'Europe could become political within five years.' It didn't occur to Monnet and his colleagues that politics couldn't be conjured into existence over the heads of the peoples of Europe. No real political culture was in any case feasible in 1950s Europe – for different reasons, the nation-states and their American protectors forbade any such ideas. Meanwhile there were the aloof British, perhaps the only people capable of imposing democracy in Europe. But they didn't want the experiment to succeed.

What Mrs Thatcher referred to as 'the un-British combination of high-flown rhetoric and pork-barrel politics' therefore comes from the earliest years of the post-war period. So does the rhetoric of bureaucratic action, equivalent to the contemporary cult of gestures in post-war existentialism. To retain the illusion of significance, 'Europe' was obliged to assert that it could matter, and would do, if only anyone would take the idea seriously enough. Was anyone listening? This has remained the formula to this day, and it accounts for the frustration of sceptics. One can ask, legitimately by now: 'Well, but what is it that you want? Tell us what you really want.' But the answer comes back: 'Well, it depends what *you* want.' The special (and infuriating) aspect of the EU lies in its odd combination of empty impermeability and gassiness, like the solid void that was dreamed of before modern physics. Nothing will get rid of 'Europe', and yet it can claim never actually to do very much apart from issuing orders to clean up the odd dirty beach. Governments do, it is true, blame the EU for actions which are unpopular, but 'Brussels' has become adept at avoiding responsibility for much of what is done in its name.

The Union still inhabits a conditional realm. There are so many things that would have been done had it been possible. They would be done now, but they probably won't. Perhaps they will be, but it would be surprising if they were. Meanwhile at Brussels the court ritual continues. On a bad day no place can seem so unserious, so draining in its inertia, so frustrating in the weight of its archaic and meaningless ritual. Does it matter that a spy satellite can traverse

Belgium in the wink of an eye? Or that billions of foreign-exchange currency changes hands in London each day, causing the idea of money itself to have become, like that of frontiers, abstract? Or that there are 200 million Chinese under the age of twenty-one, who have no special regard for the rights of Belgian *cheminots*? It does matter, certainly, but in Brussels what is called globalization doesn't rate as highly as index-linked pensions, euro-denominated, *bien entendu*, and the prospect of another banquet. The world is being pulled in two directions, by the new world market, and by fundamentalisms of one kind or another. Humanely, but in a muddled way, the EU strives both to accommodate these forces and to minimize their importance for Europe. So far these efforts have been in vain.

What is the EU really like? How does it look to the rest of the world way beyond its own changing and artificial frontiers? It appears ridiculous – the pretensions of late twentieth-century power hitched to the mores of a late eighteenth-century German court. The only fiction to have captured such hopelessness is Alasdair Gray's bizarre Scottish masterpiece *Lanark*. The novel describes a Glasgow full of lethal, half-destroyed slums populated by addicts, ruled from a great distance by the anonymous, bland (and English) Lord Monboddo, but it evokes, surreally, the anti-spirit of Brussels:

Hour 10. World Health Debate. Chairman, Lord Monboddo.
Opening speech: 'Kindness, Kin and Capacity.'
Hanseatic delegate and sociopathist Moo Dackin
explains why healthy norms must be preserved by destroying other healthy norms.
Speeches. Motions. Voting.

Hour 15. Lunch, social and informal.
Hour 17. The Subcommittees report. Voting.
Hour 21. Press Conference.
Hour 22. Dinner Speeches. Opening Speech: 'Then, Today, and Tomorrow.'

Such procedures, say the defenders of 'Brussels', exist because we will them there. Are they harmless? Probably not. Are they important? More than those who call them boring – there are many of them – care to admit. But will they last? Translated into its own terms, which are anyhow inadequate, that would seem to depend on the EU neither becoming a real federal government nor becoming so conspicuously useless as to offend the vestigial puritanism of its paymasters. The balancing act requires a mixture of skills, among them the capability of not changing or doing very much while giving the impression of purposiveness. The EU appears to be good at this.

I have 1980s images from what was then called the Eastern bloc, or the Other Europe. They consist of small, beautifully kept apartments in tower blocks that looked unkempt from the outside, or meetings at which small groups of people wearing worn denims discussed in draughty rooms the application of Adam Smith's ideas to twentieth-century collectivism. We must all be allowed dreams, and mine concerned the application of what the people I met, jumping centuries back to the Scottish Enlightenment, called 'civil society'. Where previous generations had hoped that the marriage of Central Europe and Marxism would somehow provide a new society, I hoped more modestly for a restoration in the atomized, consumerist West, through the example of dissident culture, of such notions as pluralism and free association. If this sounds abstract and implausible now, it didn't at the time. There was a real difference between the way *we* lived and the way *they* lived. No great perceived moral advantage lay in arranging ballet lessons for one's daughter in the West, or familiarizing oneself with the works of long-dead philosophers; indeed, such activities appeared increasingly quixotic and marginal. But they did matter for a time in Central Europe.

Only a romantic would have imagined that the transformation of the West would happen overnight, after the abrupt ending of Communism in a matter of months, and I never shared the pervasive expressions of gloom according to which 1989 was compared, with the lugubrious wisdom of hindsight, to 1848. But I was alarmed first by the slowness with which Western European politicians responded to 'destabilization', and later by the way in which, when they did react, it was by unpacking their yellowing Baedekers, setting out again on the road from which they had been unhealthily diverted by the crush of events. For that was, essentially, the purpose of the 1992 Maastricht Treaty. As previously, the rhetoric consisted of evocations of the European future, but these belonged already to the European past. Few efforts were made to speedily incorporate the countries of the old Eastern bloc within a genuinely new Europe. Instead, coloured by such macabre episodes as the long public death of François Mitterrand, or the failure of the post-Communism experiment of market capitalism in Russia, the politics of 1990s Europe took place in an atmosphere of dread, or anti-climax.

'The age of Europe has dawned,' remarked Jacques Poos, the Luxembourg Foreign Minister, before setting out to broker peace in ex-Yugoslavia. Britain and France have been blamed for the catastrophe of European policy; but it was the newly named Union which failed to establish a European context in which these two 'former Great Powers' might have been effective. From the beginning, the EU expressed itself in relation to the fighting war not in the language of power politics, which the aggressors might have understood, but by acting as though the war was caused by some quirk or twist of Balkan temperament. Crises were habitually solved by the expedient of 'banging heads together'; but unfortunately this proved to be impossible in Yugoslavia. 'They all look so rich and old,' said Wittgenstein of the European group portraits of 1930s bourgeois statesmen. It was the grotesque overestimation of European capability that led to the discrediting of the principle of internationalism in Yugoslavia, and to the notion among Americans, not wholly inaccurate, that European statesmen had never ceased to be appeasers.

There never was, until the end of the war, which came about as a consequence of American impatience, a European position. Rather than defending those who had been attacked, the European aid measures, coupled with ineffectual negotiations, rewarded those who had perpetrated aggression and sponsored or carried out ethnic purges. Prolongation of the war caused many needless deaths, and yet its effect on the idea of Europe itself was less certain. For the EU was never supposed to exercise decisions on behalf of the real Europe. No enlightened European expected it to do so and, when it failed, no one was specially outraged. When the war ended, the European Union put its money and its four-wheel-drive vehicles to the test – but that, too, was what everyone in Europe had come to expect.

Meanwhile representatives of member states could concentrate on the prospect of creating a Single Currency by the year 2000. This offered many fruitful possibilities. It was the culmination of fifty-odd years of proto-federalist exchanges, reflecting the adroit stewardship of the idea of Union on the part of its two most assiduous and powerful sponsors, and the European 'political class' were disposed to treat the matter as a *fait accompli*. However, times had changed, and there was by now less unanimity among better-informed populations. In 1921, after witnessing the failure of American public opinion to support Woodrow Wilson's peace initiatives, to which, as a young man, he had been ardently committed, Walter Lippmann wrote a long essay reflecting on the problem of knowledge and consent in democracies. He wondered why it was that opinion in democracies was so fickle, and he concluded that part of the problem was the laziness and lack of expertise of the electorate, or the triviality of what we would now call the 'tabloid' media; but he also felt that the affairs of modern government had become too complex for the citizen. 'The amount of attention available,' he wrote, 'is far too small for any scheme in which it was assumed that all the citizens of the nation would, after devoting themselves to the publications of all the intelligence ... become alert, informed and eager on the multitude of real questions that never do fit very well into any broad principle.' If he were Italian, no doubt Lippmann would have flirted with Mussolini's Fascism; as it was, starchily but in good faith, he prescribed a system of 'bureaux' where impartial people like himself could sift through the evidence, judiciously guiding the uninformed to the proper conclusion. But Lippmann's approach to such problems, though it had been adopted everywhere in the West, was by now largely obsolete. People were affected by television news, and they were better educated than in the early days of post-war Europe – and something as complicated as the Single Currency couldn't easily be summarized by experts. It wasn't evident that the idea was catching on. What was so attractive about living in a country of which the economic policy would be determined in perpetuity by a group of bankers? And why get rid of the old notes with their nice designs? If the Single Currency was accepted – and this seemed probable – it would be a consequence of the absence of excessive hostility on the part of Europeans. This wasn't the best foundation on which to build the New Europe. In Berlin, I heard an official say that it wasn't the currency that had led to more unemployment – the efforts of nation-states to fulfil the criteria were to blame This was like listening to an architect who felt that the building he had designed would fall down, and was blaming the builders while the foundations were being laid. I wondered how such ideas would sound in ten years' time. Those who had lost their jobs – many of them were from Europe's disregarded ethnic minorities – would not find them convincing.

As a reporter, I had abandoned the notion of 'impartiality', tending to believe that just as the reader could be influenced by whatever was described, what journalists called 'reality' was in turn capable of making its own claims on the observer. But I found that reporting Europe posed its own special problems. Nothing much was there at the centre, and the edges, far from falling into the pattern admired (and often invented) by analysts, went in different ways. But I found that my own uncertainties were an advantage – they enabled me to see how widely these were shared. Only those who disliked the idea of Europe knew what they thought.

I asked the most naïve questions – all I wanted to know was what it meant to be a European. The task was easiest in Britain, where it was a matter of how you chose to express hostility, discreetly or not. For Teresa Gorman MP, arguing with her local council over her right to renovate the small Tudor house, half pebbledash, pokey and filled with new or old half-timbering and puce-coloured velvet chairs, there was no room for equivocation. 'I'm an outer,' she told me. 'They' – she used the word indiscriminately, about Brussels, or 'the French', whom she specially disliked – 'want us not to stand up for ourselves. They want us broken up into little pieces, as if we were Belgium.'

Strident as she was, dressed in bright green, Mrs Gorman believed in a Britain acting independently of Europe – which hadn't been seen since the mid-seventeenth century, or perhaps even earlier. Elsewhere among people calling themselves sceptics I was struck by the ingenuity with which the past could be elaborately enlisted in the cause of hostility to the European idea. For John Charmley, author of several 'revisionist' books about Churchill – not a designation he entirely accepted, to be fair – this meant shifting the blame from Chamberlain (an 'appeaser' whose reputation he now wished to rescue, as a defender of Empire) to the object of his researches, on the grounds that it was Churchill's over-reliance on America that had destroyed British power, wrecking the Empire, and later causing our surrender to Europe.

Charmley I had met on the grey, windswept campus of the University of East Anglia, but the *Daily Telegraph* editor Charles Moore was snugly accommodated in an office examining the day's proofs. 'I would say I'm a Euro-sceptic,' Moore said, evoking the new spirit of happiness that would envelop the country once the grey clouds caused by the proximity of the European Union had dispersed. Moore believed in keeping the balance of power (non-existent by now), telling the Europeans (politely, of course –

he was courteousness incarnate) how we had done things in our way for so many centuries. His father had worked in Brussels; he had been educated at Eton, and he was a Catholic convert. I found myself admiring the nattiness of his Bertie Wooster suit, and the high precision of his diction. He seemed free of doubt, and equable in his convictions. His office was furnished with a nineteenth-century desk and chairs, but no spirit of self-parody was implied in these arrangements. Recalling that the Canary Wharf complex was located in a building developed by a now-bankrupt company based in Toronto, and that the proprietor of his newspaper was a Canadian, I began to think that Britain might ultimately come to believe its cherished offshore myth, and one day soon resolve to leave Europe behind. This would be a pity, not because Britain would necessarily cease to exist, but because, in our delusions and surliness, we British (with the Danes and now the Swedes) had come to represent some glimmer of subversiveness in Europe. And Europe required British nagging and disgruntlement, just as Europe needed the kind of institutional robustness which Moore and his likes jealously wished to keep for themselves.

In Britain I sensed the prevalence of delusion, but in France I was up against what psychiatrists had come to call denial. For while France was certainly the country that had done least well out of its European relationship in the past ten years, it was also a place where robust criticism, of the kind taken for granted in Britain, simply wouldn't do. Newspapers failed to print critiques of 'Europe' because it was thought that no such views should exist, given the unanimity of 'official' opinion. I didn't believe, as many conservative British commentators appeared to, that French attitudes to Europe arose from the débâcle of 1940, which had given the country a taste for collaboration. Instead, they were the consequence of the peculiar French aversion to empiricism. Long ago, the French administrative class had decided that Europe was theirs; although this notion was by now clearly an absurd one, as quaintly removed from reality as the practice of having nobles sniff the Roi Soleil's stool each morning, they wouldn't now change their minds. 'Europe' was the French totem in a civil religion that had taken the place of republicanism. As an idea, its function was to protect France from many things – from the Germans, from the Americans, from the awful prospect of reality itself. The fact that the French relationship with Europe was more like a bad marriage, with France the wronged partner, was accepted by few French people whose views were considered important.

The most positive interpretation of 'Europe' was to be found in small, or poor countries – the former because their power was enhanced, the latter because they received so much money – so it wasn't surprising to find Finns and Irish the most enthusiastic participants, eager to wrest themselves free of their once-powerful neighbours, and hardly capable of believing that they had found an organization willing to pay them to do so. Among EU officials the idea of a Europe with the psychology of small countries was periodically floated, but it seemed of limited applicability – it required the larger countries to re-evaluate their notions of scale, or importance, which they wouldn't do. The problems of big and small, as well as rich and poor, would surely become more acute if the Union ever extended membership to the fifteen-odd countries wishing to join.

It was in Germany, of course, that the European idea was given its fullest, most coherent expression, and yet the problem here was that Germany required 'Europe' for its own special reasons, rooted in a reading of German history; but these were only partly (or even fitfully) compatible with the interests of other European nations. According to the new German theory, we were all supposed to come to resemble each other in a late version of the European Enlightenment, but all the reprised choruses from Beethoven couldn't convince me this would be so:

> The French dominated the western world, politically, culturally, militarily. The humiliated and defeated Germans, particularly the traditional, religious, economically backward East Prussians, bullied by French officials imported by Frederick the Great, responded, like the bent twig of the poet Schiller's theory, by lashing back and refusing to accept their alleged inferiority. They discovered in themselves qualities far superior to those of their tormentors. They contrasted their own deep, inner life of the spirit, their own profound humility, their selfless pursuit of true values – simple, noble, sublime – with the rich, worldly, successful, superficial, smooth, heartless, morally empty French.

This was the philosopher Isaiah Berlin, speaking of the impact of eighteenth-century Enlightenment France on the rest of Europe, though he might have been alluding to Teresa Gorman. I could see the twig beating away when the features of German dominance became evident. The intensity of such emotions could be anticipated already in the rising support, year by year, for the National Front and its leader Jean-Marie Le Pen. We were not seeing the death throes of ethnic nationalism in Europe – of that I could be sure.

In October 1996 I attended the first conference of Sir James Goldsmith's Referendum Party at Brighton. Inflated bananas held up by students of the 'Great Britain in Europe' movement decorated the promenade. I stood with a solitary, bearded member of the UK Independence Party. 'It's the flag of a foreign power,' he remarked, pointing at an EU button on a bystander's lapel. 'I'd be ashamed to wear it.' His view was that Europe never could be democratic, and that we should leave even if the implication was that we would become another Iceland. Inside the hall I noticed blazers and tweed suits of the kind poets wore in the 1930s – but also the accumulation of heady emotion. These people might not agree on what they wished to do about Europe, but it was clear that they hated it. In speech after speech the loudest applause was secured by jokes about Italians, Germans or French. It was this rather than the lame or perfunctory evocations of Englishness or Britishness that gave the gathering its distinctive character.

I did speak briefly to Sir James, and it was the cut of his Savile Row suit that I first noticed. Something was wrong about the combination of so much herringbone and his staring eyes – I was reminded of my Anglophile French grandfather's absurd shooting outfits. Sir James was half-French, too, and despite his grandee manner, I felt his Englishness was contrived. He wasn't convincing speaking about 'these islands' – I could see myself sounding equally ridiculous if I expressed such sentiments. But I also wondered why he was doing all this. Did he, like myself, periodically feel the need to belong? Was that in part why he didn't like 'Europe' – because it mirrored his own complex lack of authenticity? 'You're asking if I'm bonkers?' Sir James said to me. 'I'll say so. I must be bonkers spending all this money. No one would do this who didn't really believe in what he was doing.' Was Sir James telling the truth? I couldn't see why not – but I was both saddened and angered by the gathering. Elsewhere in Europe – in France or Austria – such views would have come with a style of political extremism that was recognizably antipathetic. But I found that I didn't at all dislike these people, and that made it worse.

I got a lift back from Brighton with the writer Ian Buruma, whom I'd met that day. Half-Dutch, Ian was perhaps more of a stranger in British society, and therefore more attracted to what it offered in the way of exoticism. But he had been as upset as myself by this gathering – it seemed both a celebration of separateness and a sadly defensive affair, as starved of real ideas as it was filled with fear of the unknown. As we drove through the crowded roads of Southern England, I felt that I wouldn't be able to live in a Britain that had successfully cut itself off from Europe. I told Buruma what I felt. 'If you're born here, it's so easy to feel you have a place in Britain,' he said. 'The result of that is that everything else can be made to seem strange – you want to keep your club, your village, your habits. The prospect of a world where these are diminished by other things isn't welcome in the least. That's the strength and attractiveness of Britain – and its weakness, too.'

With its monotonous, paranoid attacks on the Brussels cancer or the venality of 'professional politicians', there was nothing new about Sir James's peroration, and the poorly delivered, fustian style reminded me of Oswald Mosley. Sir James, to his credit, didn't appear to dislike foreigners; but some of his followers' efforts made me recall another outburst. This was Treasury Chief Secretary Michael Portillo's informal address to students at Southampton University in 1994 in which he suggested that foreigners cheated at their exams. 'If any of you have got an A level it is because you worked at it,' he said. 'Go to any other country, and when you have got an A level you have bought it.' Portillo did, it is true, apologize for these remarks, and he said that they had not been made for public consumption. However, they were part of a Europhobe binge – they slipped out in the midst of what had become the usual rant about Brussels, Britain etc.

Portillo was half-Spanish – self-ingratiation alone might be the explanation, but I doubted it. Five or even ten years ago, no politician would have spoken in this way; but Sir James and his supporters showed me that such views were likely to become commonplace. They would say that the existence of such views meant that Britain should now distance itself from Europe, in case they became more pronounced. I preferred to draw the opposite conclusion. It wouldn't do any longer to assume that people, lied to or given half-truths about the nature of the New Europe, would simply go along with them. The clubby atmosphere in which co-operation between élites was discussed was by now dead. But it would also require more than mounds of confusing information to convince people that the whole game was worth the candle. Europe must be more than geography – it had to mean something, too. A real Europe worthy of the name would be a place where all its peoples, not just its prosperous élites, wished to live. I could see this happening only if Europeans took into account the opposition to their project, and responded to it.

There would have to be less of many things – subsidies, grandiose language, indexed pensions at the very least. But above all Europeans would have to lose their illusions. They would have to accept the consequences of democracy in Europe – in particular the notion that, to be acceptable, whether it was called a Federation or not, Europe would be a place where relatively little happened at the centre. Should the Parliament, for instance, really be offering itself as a place capable of legislation on every matter? Wouldn't it be better for the moment if MEPs turned their attentions to the workings of the EU – and were allowed to do something about them? The same principle would have to be applied to European law – it would only be accepted in the long run if its scope was also limited. If it was not, arguments for disobeying its judgments would become more powerful – and not just in Britain.

'No man can struggle with advantage against the age and spirit of his country,' wrote the French sociologist de Tocqueville. In Britain, I found that I resented the anti-Europeanism of the foreign- or expatriate-owned press even as I sometimes found it hard not to be influenced by the sentiments.

I wrote questions down as I wrote this book, or took to splitting myself in two: *phile* and *phobe*. I began to wonder (it was an emotion with which many of those I interviewed were familiar) whether I wasn't bored with the whole question of Europe. Why was it proving so difficult to organize something which, by the standards of European history, appeared relatively uncomplicated? These days nothing occurs to us with any flash of the kind with which eternity was once supposed to be apparent; but I did find my way through this wood. I began to think that if the structures of Europe were unsatisfactory or inadequate, this was perhaps less important than I had anticipated; and that it might ultimately be possible for institutions whose power was limited to coexist with a stronger sense of Europeanness. Here I could see the rapid Europeanization of sport or food as a precedent. And I found it easy to believe that very soon younger people, even in Britain, might come to interpret the question of sovereignty less literally than their fathers or grandfathers had done.

Meanwhile I could imagine a set of half-Europes incompletely defining wherever it was that we all of us lived. They might be concerned with money, or justice, with communications, or merely with the shifting loyalties implied by habit or geography. I could see why they would be considered weak by the traditional standards of the nation-state, or lacking in coherence in the light of French bureaucratic procedure, or even extravagant (this would be the British view) in their procedural rituals. But they would at least fulfil the current European ambitions – both to be left alone, as states, regions, cities, villages, families, and to be part of something more substantial when the occasion arose.

So plural a Europe nonetheless left open the question of whether it could share anything at all, or whether it wouldn't, despite all the effort, amount to nothing. I could see the point of such observations – but I didn't trust them. Europe had in the past come unstuck in the pursuit of big ideas, and I felt it was likely to happen again. But this still left unanswered the question of what it meant to be a European. Why was it so important to me? What was it that made me wish to accept the idea of Europe?

Here I was helped by a small piece of my past. White and orange-tiled, like something on the fringes of Brentwood, my uncle's house was a family museum, filled with photographs of the horses my grandfather did or didn't back, the fishes my uncles caught, and the yellowing remnants of my grandmother's compendious library of classics. As usual in my family, in between the three-fish *rillette*, prawn *vol-au-vents*, the Château Le Pez, conversation drifted between the educational accomplishments of distant cousins and the claims of culture, French-style. For some reason we started talking about the sixteenth-century writer Montaigne, who had lived nearby, and the more my uncle suggested that the castle he had lived in wasn't interesting, and in a poor wine-growing region, the more I wished to go there.

It was extremely hot outside. I took the Bordeaux six-lane Rocade through more *faux*-Californian suburbs, stopping at wine shops, where I bought Médoc and St Emilion in plastic tubs, or in hangar-like malls where I tried to avoid acquiring bottles of haricots and salsify or children's diving gear. Then I drove around the white soil of famous vineyards. I was upset, to begin with, at the seeming ordinariness of so many regularly planted vines by the side of Dallas-like fake chateaux, or pylons, but I was half-reassured – this was not a good or original European thought – by the combination of age and aggressive modernity evident in the landscape.

After poorer, bushier vineyards announced by signs in scrolled Gothic (the monks, infallibly a sign of mediocre wine, had been removed, their presence only vestigially present in fake-parchment labels) I took smaller and smaller roads. Abruptly, passing outsize, musty-smelling green trees, I came to an ugly nineteenth-century wine baron pile, and by its side a small, rough, circular stone building topped by a conical roof the shape of a New York water tower.

The top room was tiled, with windows in each direction over a valley and poor vines. Inscriptions from the Latin had been carved on its beams, and, to begin with, I noticed nothing but the heat and the putty colour of the walls. While the painfully slow guide told me that Montaigne's library had consisted of a thousand volumes, many of which were lost now, I began to imagine these books flying back, Disney-style, to reconstitute themselves, fitting densely into a number of low shelves where they could be consulted far more rapidly than we could now find things in so much excess of information, or access them electronically via the Internet. Suddenly I understood how the idea of a European experience could have passed through this room, and how in its turn it might have formed more European experiences, century by century. Often, in Europe, I had been concerned with the public face of architectural plans or legal prospectuses, whereas what I had before me, in the empty room, was the private, autobiographical Europe.

Michel de Montaigne was a lawyer and a soldier as well as Mayor of Bordeaux. He wasn't particularily nice or loyal – and he sold out those whom he admired, failing to protest when Protestants were massacred throughout France in 1572 on St Bartholomew's Eve, although he was sympathetic to their cause, fleeing the plague when he was Mayor, and declining to return when he was pressed to do so by the citizens whose interests he had undertaken to represent. He was proud of his rather ordinary erotic exploits, despite his small, unreliable member, which he called '*monsieur ma partie*'; but in middle age, suffering from kidney stones and colic, alienated from his wife, he became something of a voyeur, attending Jewish circumcision rituals in a spirit of anthropological prurience or simply peering behind the masks that women still wore in public. Quite the French man of letters, one might say – except that Montaigne taught himself powers of observation and analysis that to this day never fail to startle. And he learnt by travelling (he forgot his stomach pains on horseback), or talking, that nothing was the same as anything else, or, equally important, that illumination came in the oddest quarters. This wasn't just a question of noting that the Pope wore soft white leather bootees on which were embroidered white crosses and carried two identical red velvet hats with him when he went to Mass, that German linen or fish was superior to the French version, or that Italian lamb was disgusting – it also led him to such discoveries (momentous even two centuries later) that women really did experience pleasure during sexual intercourse, or that Brazilian savages enjoyed a wiser and more profitable relation to their unrapacious rulers than did contemporary Frenchmen.

Montaigne discovered that the idea of coherent rules applied to human beings was absurd:

> Not only does the accidental wind blow me about according to its inclination, I also fidget, troubling myself by my own instability; and whoever looks at himself carefully will barely ever find himself twice in the same state of mind. I give to my being one appearance, then another, depending on what side I have slept. If I speak of myself in different styles, it is because I look at myself differently. Every contrary feature is apparent in me in some form or another. Sheepish and bold; chaste and pleasure-loving; gossipy and taciturn; plodding and light to touch; ingenious and befuddled . . . liar and truth-teller, clever and ignorant, generous and mean, and prodigal, all of this . . .

Such views earned Montaigne reprobation among the thought police of his day, who doubted his soundness, or, as the British would say, his 'bottom'; and he was even now, despite respectability, sometimes sniffed at as a 'cultural relativist' – the *Front National* municipal government took his subversiveness seriously enough to decline to acquire a copy of a biography of him for the Municipal Library of Orange. But Montaigne was also one of the first people in modern times to re-acquire the notion that truth wasn't arrived at easily, or held to for long, and the implication of his ideas was that all institutions had best either remain imperfect, barely heeded, or should somehow be made to reflect, in a spirit of extensive bet-hedging, the endless, unknowable contradictions of each human being. This was his legacy to Europe.

Present for some time in eighteenth-century Britain, and afterwards lost to Europe as a consequence of various forms of bigotry, these ideas had latterly enjoyed a surprising return to fashion. They were present in the concept of 'civil society', according to which the informal arrangements – family ones, work groupings, personal tastes, religious obsessions, obscure leisure activities – took precedence over formal governmental structures, not merely surpassing them in importance, but often influencing them, too. I began to wonder whether such a spirit of scepticism – the conviction that so many ways of knowing things or arranging life existed, and that those who claimed the right to impose any one of them, whether churches, political sects or authoritarian individuals, were bound, one way or another, to be proved inadequate – was the real European invention of modern times, mysteriously surpassing in its durability the endless attempts to redraw maps or reformulate, in a variety of building materials, the paradoxes of representative democracy.

Scepticism, I felt, was right for the end of an often bad century, and it was right for Europe, where there was no escaping the weight of experience. My only regret was that the word, which described the only attitude an intelligent person could take to the real European future, had been wrenched from its true meaning and set to propagandist work. Still, as any European must know by now, nothing, least of all the fate of individual words, was certain. I had faith that one day the quality of scepticism would be reclaimed and enshrined in Brussels. I resolved to keep faith in the quality of doubt. I would continue to believe that Europe existed, not for the arrogant superstructure currently implied in its official existence, but for the tradition of uncertainty itself. That was how I would be a European.

Notes and acknowledgements

The author gratefully acknowledges the following works:

Page 1 'I sat . . .' Erich Kästner, *Fabian*, Atrium Verlag, Zurich, 1969.

Page 6 'So there you are . . .' Robert Musil, *The Man Without Qualities*, tr. Sophie Wilkins, Picador.

Page 10 'No-one . . .' *op. cit.*

Page 22 'Resolved to bring instead . . .' *Les Institutions Européennes*, Editions Le Monde, Paris, 1994.

Page 27 'It's immense . . .' Albert Cohen, *Belle De Seigneur*, p. 58, Gallimard, Paris, 1970.

Page 39 'Europe will take place . . .' Jean Baudrillard, *Libération*, Sept. 4, 1995.

Page 44 '*Brüsel*' From Benoît Peeters and François Schuiter, *Brüsel*, Casterman, Brussels, 1992.

Page 48 'The cold statistician . . .' John Maynard Keynes, *The Economic Consequences of the Peace*, Macmillan, 1919.

Page 49 'The *Royaume* . . .' Richard Cobb, *Promenades*, Oxford University Press, 1980.

Page 61 'I dreamed . . .' quoted in *In These Great Times, a Karl Kraus Reader*, ed. Harry Zohn, Carcanet Press, Manchester, 1984.

Page 80 'Orthodoxy . . .' George Orwell, *1984*, Penguin Books, 1950.

Page 82 'For most people . . .' Don DeLillo, *White Noise*, Picador.

Page 83 'Re cynicism . . .' George Orwell, *The Lost Writings*, Arbor House, N.Y., 1985.

Page 85 'Nothing . . .' Saul Bellow, *It All Adds Up*, Secker & Warburg.

Page 91 'The Vatican . . .' Pier Paolo Pasolini, *Scritti Corsari*, Milano, quoted in Paul Ginsborg, *A History of Contemporary Italy*, Penguin, 1990.

Page 99 Asa Briggs, *The History of Broadcasting in the United Kingdom*, Vol. v, Oxford University Press, 1995.

Page 105 'Rich . . .' Jean-Paul Sartre, *La Nausée* (1938), Gallimard Folio, Paris, 1993. Author's translation.

Page 111 'To tell the truth . . .' Albert Camus, *Le Témoin de la Liberté*, Nov. 1948, *Essais*, Editions de la Pléiade, Gallimard, Paris, 1965.

Page 116 'A revolutionary . . .' Jean-Paul Sartre, *Actuel* 28, Feb., 1973.

Page 120 'The two young men . . .' Ford Madox Ford, *Parade's End*, Everyman's Library, 1992.

Page 122 *L'ENA, Miroir de l'État*, Jean-Michel Gaillard, Editions Complexe, Paris, 1995.

Page 130 'The French have long held . . .' Theodore Zeldin, *An Intimate History of Humanity*, Sinclair-Stevenson, 1994.

Page 139 'I've known . . .' Jean-Paul Sartre, *La Nausée* (1938), Gallimard Folio, Paris, 1993. Author's translation.

Page 142 'It's no go . . .' Louis MacNeice, 'Bagpipe Music', *Collected Poems*, Faber and Faber, 1966.

Page 199 'We are particularily shocked . . .' Robert Jay Lifton, Introduction to *Sarajevo: A War Journal*, Zlatko Disdarević, p. xvii, Fromm International, N.Y., 1993.

Page 207 'Only then did . . .' Ivo Andrić, *The Bridge over the Drina*, The Harvill Press, 1995.

Page 211 'It's highly likely . . .' Jonah David Goldhagen, *Hitler's Willing Executioners*, Little, Brown, 1996.

Page 212 'We thought it would . . .' W. B. Yeats, 'Nineteen Hundred and Nineteen', *Collected Poems*, Everyman's Library, 1992, A. P. Watt Ltd on behalf of Michael Yeats.

Page 215 'I hate Ireland . . .' Elizabeth Bowen, quoted in R. F. Foster, *Paddy and Mr Punch*, Viking, 1995.

Page 216 'a mixture . . .' Elizabeth Bowen, *The House in Paris*, Penguin, 1976.

Page 221 'The years to come . . .' W. B. Yeats, 'An Irish Airman Foresees His Death', *op. cit.*, A. P. Watt Ltd on behalf of Michael Yeats.

Page 222 'This is not . . .' W. B. Yeats, 'The Municipal Gallery Revisited', *op. cit.*, A. P. Watt Ltd on behalf of Michael Yeats.

Page 229 'Estate agents . . .' Michael D. Higgins, reprinted in *The Irish Review*, 1994.

Page 230 'Now days are . . .' W. B. Yeats, 'Nineteen Hundred and Nineteen', *op. cit.*, A. P. Watt Ltd on behalf of Michael Yeats.

Page 231 'Up and away . . .' Seamus Heaney, 'The Flight Path', *The Spirit Level*, Faber and Faber, 1996.

Page 232 'The net on a tennis court . . .' Seamus Heaney, *Nobel Prize Lecture*, Faber and Faber, 1996.

Page 235 'Afterwards, of course . . .' Hans Magnus Enzensberger, *The Sinking of the Titanic*, Paladin Books, 1989.

Page 235 'Great Empires . . .' from *The Field Day Anthology of Irish Writing*, ed. Seamus Deane, Vol. III, Field Day Publications, Derry, 1991.

Page 237 'Maud Gonne . . .' W. B. Yeats, 'Beautiful Lofty Things', *op. cit.*, A. P. Watt Ltd on behalf of Michael Yeats.

Page 240 'Is it possible . . .' Walter Abish, *How German is it*, Carcanet Press, 1981.

Page 247 'All of us' Speech of Richard von Weizsäcker, quoted in *The Germans*, Gordon A. Craig, Penguin, 1991.

Page 249 'Past Riches . . .' Walter Abish, *op. cit.*

Page 250 'It is what . . .' James Fenton, 'A German Requiem', *The Memory of War*, Salamander Press, 1982.

Page 257 'The gap between . . .' *The Times*, Apr. 27, 1996.

Page 259 'Thrown into . . .' Noel Annan, *Changing Enemies*, HarperCollins, 1995.

Page 265 'It's night outside . . .' Osip Mandelstam, *The Moscow Notebooks*, tr. Richard and Elizabeth McKane, Bloodaxe Books, 1991.

Page 275 'We thought . . .' Anna Akhmatova, quoted in Alexander Volkov, *St Petersburg*.

Page 284 'Science, whether in the discovery . . .' Beatrice and

Sidney Webb, *Soviet Communism: A New Civilization*, Longmans, 1935.

Page 286 'England, La France,' unpublished notebooks W. H. Auden. 'I'm a European,' quoted in Ray Monk, *Ludwig Wittgenstein*, Vintage, 1991.

Page 288 'secondary cultural pluralism . . .' Ernest Gellner, *Nations and Nationalism*, Blackwell, 1983.

Page 290 'He seemed . . .' Margaret Thatcher, *The Downing Street Years*, HarperCollins, 1993.

Page 291 'He was a passionate . . .' quoted in Gitta Sereny, *Albert Speer: His Struggle With Truth*, Macmillan, 1996.

Page 292 'good history . . .' Alan S. Milward, *The European Rescue of the Nation State*, Routledge, 1992.

Page 296 'closer to the outlook . . .' François Duchêne, *Jean Monnet: The First Statesmen of Interdependence*, W. W. Norton, N.Y., 1994. The divorce story is told on pp. 55–56.

Page 297 '18 August 1966 . . .' Jean Monnet, *Mémoires*, Fayard, Paris, 1976. Author's translation.

Page 297 'Via money . . .' Duchêne, *op. cit.*

Page 299 'Hour 10 . . .' Alasdair Gray, *Lanark*, Panther Books, 1982.

Page 300 'civil society' Ernest Gellner, *Conditions of Liberty*, Chapter 2 in particular, Hamish Hamilton, 1994.

Page 303 'The amount of attention . . .' Walter Lippmann, *Public Opinion*, The Free Press, N.Y., 1967.

Page 308 'The French dominated . . .' Isaiah Berlin, *The Crooked Timber of Humanity*, John Murray, 1990.

Page 316 'Not only does . . .' Michel de Montaigne, *Essais II*, Gallimard Folio, Paris, 1965. Author's translation. The biographical details are taken from Jean Lacouture, *Montaigne à Cheval*, Editions du Seuil, Paris, 1993.